TEMPTING FATE

BOOK TWO
THE IMMORTAL DESCENDANTS

APRIL WHITE

ENTERTAINMENT

The Immortal Descendants Series

Marking Time
Tempting Fate
Changing Nature
Waging War
Cheating Death

Tempting Fate. Copyright 2014 by April White
All rights reserved. Published by Corazon Entertainment
Palos Verdes Peninsula, CA

Edited by Angela Houle
Cover Design by Penny Reid
Cover images by Shutterstock

ISBN 978-0-9885368-0-7
Library of Congress Control Number: 2014908488

First American edition, June 2014

"May your coming year be filled with magic and dreams and good madness. I hope you read some fine books and kiss someone who thinks you're wonderful, and don't forget to make some art – write or draw or build or sing or live as only you can. And I hope, somewhere in the next year, you surprise yourself." – Neil Gaiman

THE IMMORTAL DESCENDANTS

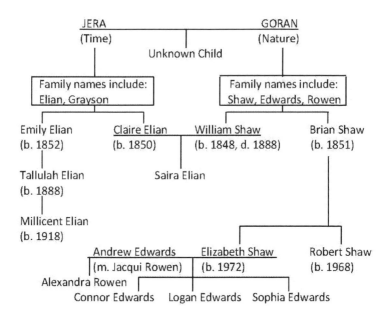

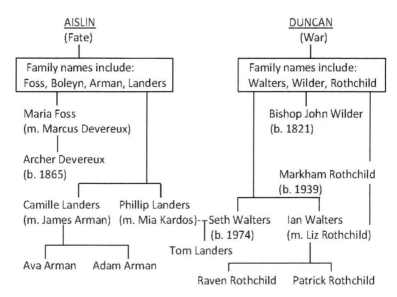

 RUN!

I ran. It's what I did. To escape. To hide. And for the pure rush of freedom.

But this time they were tracking me.

Still a couple hundred feet back, but closing in. From the footfalls I counted at least five bipeds and maybe a Wolf, but it was the Monger with them made my skin crawl. Mongers had hunted me before I even knew such a thing existed, and I could feel them in my guts like the onset of food poisoning. I picked up speed and played the options out in my mind.

The sun was still high and glinted off the upper windows of St. Brigid's school. I could head back to the safety of the building, but that might put us all at risk. Besides, after three months here, I knew these woods like an old friend. Good trees with thick branches were obvious climbers, but I'd get treed if they looked up. I could cut down the pack if I scaled the old stone wall to my right, but not stop them altogether. The barn just past the woods was good, but I'd be trapped. Unless I was the one doing the trapping.

So, my best bet was camouflage.

I saw the low branch an instant before it would have brained me. I ducked it and kept my path a straight line so they wouldn't veer off course, then counted to thirty and waited for the first

1

contestant in a little game I called *What's The Worst That Could Happen?*

Thunk. I winced at the yell behind me as the branch took someone out - one of the normal humans that ran with this pack. Assuming there was such a thing as normal in my world since I discovered I was a Clocker, descended from Time.

But that meant one down, four to go. And the Wolf, which I sensed circling, trying to outflank me. Not good. I swerved left across some soft ground. Leaves hid a three-foot-deep hole I'd dug out here a few weeks ago. Who would hit it? Who would be contestant number two?

Crash! A yell, and another one went down. Not the Monger though. I could still feel him coming. The Descendants of War were relentless hunters, which was why Mongers had proclaimed themselves enforcers of Descendant law. I'd broken one of those laws when I was born, but thanks to my Clocker mom's trip forward in time, no one found out about me for seventeen years. Until a nasty piece-of-work Monger named Seth Walters, or Slick, as I un-affectionately called him, found and hunted me right into the arms of an Immortal Descendant family I didn't know existed. For all I knew Slick was still stalking me, and the twisty-gut sense *this* Monger invoked pushed me faster now.

The fallen trunk of a massive Scots pine tree loomed ahead. Climbable, but the bark would be rough and full of splinters. I dug deep, hit the highest branch I could reach without hands, and pushed off. I arched up and sliced the narrow gap between branches in a hands-and-head-first dive. Then I tucked. I hit the ground shoulder first, but the bed of needles that littered the forest floor took a painful impact down to uncomfortable. I'd survive the bruise.

I crouched, caught my breath, and prepared for the final round – all or nothing. To my left the big pine trunk hid a small ditch with a void under the trunk. An animal escape hatch. Perfect.

I flattened down to a belly crawl and pulled my body into the cramped den, pretending those weren't spiders that skittered away in the darkness. I counted on camouflage to hide me and forward momentum to carry my pursuers far away.

Pounding feet split the silence and I froze. They padded over the tree without hesitation and continued on. The Wolf. No question. Then a second set went past. That was the Monger, his feet pounding the ground angrily. Then the Seer. I knew them the way prey knows its predators. I could feel them in the blood that chilled in my veins. The Seer surprised me though. He stopped on the fallen tree, searched, then called. "Hey! Guys!"

Crap. Game over.

The Monger shouted something in the distance. The Seer yelled back, "Over here!"

Approaching footfalls and then the Monger scrambled over the top of the tree trunk spewing very inventive curses with each bite of the bark. He paused at the top of the trunk. The Seer spoke.

"She's still here."

The Seer didn't know that. He couldn't. Unless he'd Seen it.

"She's long gone."

"No, you should have Seen her too. You're not using your senses."

"You're just mad I was faster than you."

"I can beat you any day."

Oh good. Just what I wanted. A dogfight over my head. Speaking of, where had the Wolf gone?

"That's it. I'm out." The prickling in my gut diminished as the Monger trudged away.

"What crawled up his butt?" The Wolf had doubled back.

"Nice. You kiss your mother with that mouth?"

"No, I kiss yours."

Punk. I had to fight the giggles.

"Ass."

"Nah, I leave the ass-kissing to you, too."

"Listen, mutt. I know she's close."

I felt the edge of a ward rise up, like instinct throwing an icy, invisible shield around me, but I firmly pushed it down. The Seer

3

was too close and knew wards. He might feel the temperature fluctuate.

"Wait, I think … she's definitely here. I'm getting a read on … that's weird … on what she sees?"

Damn! I shut my eyes and slammed a ward up so fast it was almost audible.

"Hang on … it's gone." The Seer sounded bewildered. I was so sure they'd find me, I braced myself for impact.

"I didn't know you could do that … see out of someone else's eyes. That's not cool."

"I'm not even sure that's what happened. But whatever it was, it's gone now. I'm getting radio silence from the Sight."

"Dude, sun's going down, I'm hungry, and we're not even supposed to be here."

"*She's* not either. I'll wait."

"I'm out." The Wolf called out to me, "I'll catch you later, Clocker." Footsteps moved away.

I felt my ward slip down with the Wolf's departure, and the Seer must have sensed it too because all of a sudden his face was inches from mine.

"Gotcha."

I didn't jump. I lunged. Right at him.

"What the hell, Saira?" My giant idiot Seer friend, Adam Arman, stumbled backward in surprise and landed squarely on his butt.

I pinned him. Face to face. "Lesson of the day: if you get cornered, throw 'em off balance and take the upper hand." I got up and pulled him smoothly to his feet. He dusted pine needles from his jeans and we started walking back toward school.

"That was a pretty fancy move. Reminded me of a Wolverine Shifter I used to know."

"Did he smell as bad as actual Wolverines do?"

Adam grinned. "We called him Stinky Winky, if that's any indication."

I laughed. "Sounds vaguely nasty."

"There was nothing vague about his nastiness."

4

"Hey, did Connor stay human the whole time, or did he run as a Wolf?"

"He stayed human, but did you just segue from 'nasty' to know-it-all science geek, Connor Edwards? Somehow, I don't think he'd appreciate it."

"You're a troublemaker, and I segued from 'Shifter.' I swear I sensed a Wolf during our run, but then again Connor could have caught me in about a minute if he was in his animal form." Despite the fact that Connor was only fourteen, he was smarter than almost anyone I knew, and fit right in with the pack of guys I was teaching to free-run.

Adam shook his head with a grimace. "Yeah, but that's what you Americans don't get about us Englishmen. It wouldn't be sporting to run a girl down."

"Except the girl in question can run, climb, and tumble circles around all of you."

"I'll show you a tumble." I was pretty certain Adam had a mild form of Tourette's. There were very few other explanations for the garbage that came out of his mouth.

"You just can't help yourself, can you?"

"Why hold back? We're a foregone conclusion, Clocker."

I snorted. "Sorry, I don't date outside my species."

Adam stopped and looked at me strangely. "Because I'm a Seer?"

I stared at him. "What? No! It was a joke, Adam. Since when can't you take a joke?"

"Since in the world outside St. Brigid's, Mongers are hunting mixed-bloods and breaking up inter-Family hook-ups. We both know I'm a rule-breaker, and so are you. It just surprised me, that's all."

"I can't believe you, of all people, would think I'd care what Family you're from."

"I hope not." Adam's voice sounded strange. I couldn't read the expression on his face. It made me nervous. And suddenly there was a whole bundle of nerves seething in my guts. I took a step backward and then recognized the feeling.

5

I callcd out to the silent woods around us. "Hey, Tom! Are you still out there?" Tom Landers was Adam and Ava's cousin, and the half-Seer/half-Monger who had helped Slick run me down in California.

"He went back before Connor."

I shook my head. "They're messing with us then, because I've been sensing a Wolf, and I'm getting a read on a Monger too." I moved closer and leaned up to whisper in Adam's ear. "Let's ambush them."

Adam turned toward me, close enough that I could smell the toothpaste on his breath. He was close enough to kiss me. And he didn't move away. It caused a stomach flip that had nothing to do with a Monger.

"What are you doing?" I was still whispering.

He stepped back awkwardly. "Nothing."

The thing was, Adam Arman was never awkward.

"You have a girlfriend." A stunning Shifter named Alexandra Rowen who had already left St. Brigid's school and lived in London.

"She's afraid to be with me."

I couldn't argue that, but Alex was a Gazelle Shifter. She was wired to be afraid, and Adam hadn't been kidding about the ban on inter-Family hook-ups. Alex had broken up with Adam last year so the Mongers didn't go after him, but they had decided to try again and keep it under the Monger's radar.

"I have a boyfriend."

"Really? I don't see you hanging out together. And you're always with us anyway."

"What are you saying, Adam?"

He stared at me, and I couldn't read a damn thing that crossed his face. "Nothing, Saira. I'm saying nothing."

I didn't want this. Neither did he, no matter what his words hinted. So I bolted and called out over my shoulder, "Last one to dinner's a Stinky Winky."

Adam swore under his breath and took off after me, but I had gotten the jump and was out of sight a minute later.

6

What. The. Hell. I shut off my over-active brain and focused on running as fast as I could, with nothing but the next five steps in front of me. That kind of running has no room for thinking. Because my head wasn't a safe place to be.

When my lungs burned I leapt up a boulder and stopped at the top to catch my breath. St. Brigid's School was far away, and everything about this day was out of bounds. I'd broken rules to go free-running, made the guys complicit by teaching them, and then there was that thing with Adam, who, with his twin sister, Ava, had been one of my first friends at the school for Immortal Descendants. What the hell was he thinking? Friends. That's all. Just friends. And my pounding heart was just from running and not from what Adam may or may not have been about to do.

I screwed my eyes shut to change the channel on my mental picture. Adam's face inches from mine – click. Next image – Archer. My Archer. Dark hair, usually tousled, blue eyes, usually looking at me … *for* me. The man who loved me a thousand times more than I knew how to love. Click. Tom. Tom? Why did Tom Landers just intrude on my brain? We were barely friends, more like allies. Tom was the darker, sharper, gypsy version of his cousin Adam. They were best friends, but Tom and I had an odd truce. He had been the Seer kid Slick coerced to find me, and Tom didn't believe what I knew – that he wasn't just a Seer. He was also part Monger, and we both pretended I couldn't feel him and every other Monger like an oncoming flu.

Which is what I was feeling at that moment. Time to go. I jumped down, ready to run again, and a truck slammed into me. Everything went black. Maybe not a truck exactly, but someone strong and fast with a spectacular tackle. A dark hood went over my head, and I was prodded to my feet while a sneering voice with a heavy eastern European accent growled in my ear.

"Move." He sounded like a cartoon bad guy as he shoved me forward, and I dubbed him Boris.

I stumbled deeper into the woods, and Boris pinned my hands behind me. I pushed past the panic and blindness as I tried to use my 'other' senses to get an advantage. I was a Clocker who could travel through time using spirals painted on walls. But I was also part Shifter. It was an illegal mix. Hell, every mix was illegal in the world of Immortal Descendants, where the original Immortals – Time, Fate, Nature, War and Death – lived forever, and their Family lines had skills beyond ordinary mortals. The Descendants were human though, and we could die.

Boris was something else, something not Shifter, but definitely animal. "This is for my brother." He yanked my arms up and suddenly I knew Boris; the surviving Romanian Werewolf brought to St. Brigid's School by the Monger teacher, Ms. Rothchild. They had come to hunt for Archer. Problem was, Archer had killed Boris' brother.

Killed, as in dead. And now Boris had me.

I'd just become contestant number three in *What's The Worst That Could Happen?*

 MONGER

I recognized the smell of the gardener's shed as Boris shoved me through the door. We were at the edge of the forest, far from St. Brigid's. Far from help. But we were not alone. Two Mongers were there. I couldn't see them, but they stood out over the compost and manure, burning my gut like poison. Boris planted me into a chair and bound my hands in a long piece of rope. As I expected, he wrapped it too tight and I could feel the blood start to throb in my fingertips.

"Tighter." That surprised me. The voice belonged to Raven, Slick's Monger niece and my former roommate. Raven, affectionately known to her enemies as The Crow, was proof that beauty is only skin deep, but ugly is to the bone.

"Uncle Seth give you a job, Raven?" I kept my tone deliberately light and conversational. I couldn't believe I'd just been bagged by such a small-time school bully.

"Shut up."

The hood was ripped off my head, and my vision adjusted instantly despite the low light. Raven stood in one corner, her arms crossed in front of her with an ugly sneer on her face. I knew it was a stupid thing to do since my hands were literally tied, but I couldn't help it – I laughed. Mostly at her wardrobe, but also at her whole bad-guy attitude. She'd dressed for the role of kidnapper in stylish black with tall, expensive black leather boots and a black scarf artfully draped around her neck. I couldn't see more than a bit of Boris, the Were, since he had positioned himself just out of sight behind my shoulder, but I knew him from his scent. Which was fetid and smelled like unwashed socks under a pile of wet towels in the corner of a teenaged boy's room. The third member of the party was another dismal surprise, because I half-expected their uncle, Seth Walters, the Monger enforcer who had it in for me because he suspected my mixed blood. But it was Raven's punk brother, Patrick the Spawn, who scowled at me from the other corner. Fascinating and definitely disappointing. Not a bigwig bad guy in sight, which made me feel pretty stupid for getting caught at all. When had the school bullies decided to get so bold? And why were they trying out their fledgling criminal tricks on me?

"Where is the Sucker?" Ah yes. There it was. The motive. Not to mention the ridiculous nickname for Vampires, the Descendants of Death. Everyone seemed to conveniently forget that all Vampires had started off as Descendants of another Family before they got infected with the porphyria-like virus that put their cell-death on permanent hold. No, people spat the name "Sucker" like it was a great big glob of green snot. Not that Clocker, Seer, Shifter, or Monger were much better nicknames, but at least those names didn't evoke images of leeches and mosquitoes.

To the rest of the Immortal Descendants, *my* Vampire, Archer Devereux, had been all but invisible since his presence became known after he helped me get my mom back from the clutches of Jack the Ripper. My mom had explained the edict against Death's Descendants to me over Christmas break. It went all the way back to the original Immortals, when Time and Nature (Jera and Goran) fell in love and had a kid, despite Fate's insistence it was a bad idea (Aislin, the Immortal Seer). That kid was apparently another Immortal, and in a fit of power-possessiveness, Death (Aeron), with War (Duncan) whispering encouragement in his ear, had the kid killed. In the end, the mixed-blood moratorium became Descendant law – I guess the original Immortals didn't want to have to share power with someone new – and Death's punishment for killing the innocent child was the so-called Death Edict, which allowed the destruction of all Death's Descendants. The fact of the matter was that Descendants had always had a license to kill Vampires, but the Mongers put a bounty on it and made it their mission.

"I don't know what you're talking about." My voice stayed calm and conversational, and Raven's eyes flashed murderously.

"You know exactly who I'm talking about. The Sucker who got in the way of my uncle doing his job?" She meant the job of hunting mixed-bloods. Hunting me. Raven's voice grated like nails on a chalkboard. "The one worth ten new pair of Jimmy Choos when I bring him in?"

"Really? A life for a pair of shoes. Yeah … no. Even if I knew, it wouldn't happen."

"You know where the Sucker is, and you're going to tell us."

"Or what? You'll tell your charming uncle?"

"There's always your mother."

I stared at her, then laughed. "You'll tell my mother?"

"No, we'll arrest her."

I scoffed. "Okay, playtime's over. Untie me and everyone will go their separate ways. You won't brag about bagging me because then you'll get busted for it, and I won't report you because I'll never admit you beat me in anything. And you don't have crap on my mother, so quit with the empty threats."

"She broke Descendant law when she whelped a mixed-blood."

My blood ran cold, but my voice stayed calm. "Prove it."

The Spawn actually smiled. "Okay."

He flicked open a knife and took a step toward me. "Get me a jar or something to put her blood in." He was talking to Raven, and she actually glanced around the gardening shed for something.

Seriously, had the guy never paid attention in Shaw's class?

"You'd contaminate any sample you get. It'll be no good for testing."

He scoffed. "They can do DNA testing on a piece of bloody rag."

"Doesn't matter. Won't hold up."

11

Boris finally spoke, and it was like he had a mouthful of gravel. "Give me the knife. I'll cut her just for fun."

This was the first thing anyone said that actually scared me. I looked at the Spawn. "You going to take a chance with Were bloodlust?"

"Crap." Clearly he hadn't thought of that.

"Untie me, Rothchild. You know the trouble you guys will get in if someone finds us, and my friends are expecting me back. Cut the rope, and this whole thing will go away like a bad dream."

Boris stepped up behind me. "Enough! Tell us where the Sucker is." He yanked my arms up nearly over my head. I felt a POP, and white hot fire shot through my shoulder as it dislocated from its socket.

I screamed.

This wasn't happening. Their little Monger game had turned into something nasty and unpredictable, and I had the horrible, sinking feeling that the Were was calling the shots now.

"What did you do to her!?" Raven's shriek had a panicked edge to it, and the only thing that gave me comfort through the nausea and pain was the thought that she was freaking. Out. Badly.

Except for the part where freaked out people do stupid things. Because apparently, Spawn and his knife were freaking out too. "She'll tell on us Raven! Should I kill her?"

I gritted my teeth through the sheer ball of fiery agony that used to be my shoulder. A jackhammer to the head would have been preferable torture. "Don't be a moron, Rothchild. Untie me."

Then I heard something outside the shack, and my guts told me it was another Monger. Could the day get any worse?

But Boris heard it too with his Were ears. "We're not alone."

The Spawn swung his knife around toward the door just when it crashed inward and knocked him on his butt, leaving the knife stuck in the rough wood. Adam stood in the opening, grinning like the over-confident idiot he was, and then Boris launched at him. They went flying back outside, and the sounds of fierce and dangerous growling in the woods nearly wilted whatever courage I had left. But then Spawn made a go for his knife. I stuck my feet out, he went down, and I got a kick in for good measure.

Spawn and Raven bolted, and the horrendous sounds of fighting carried themselves further away. And then Tom was inside the shack with a worried look and a very big stick. "Saira! Are you okay?"

I shook my head. The sweat was starting to bead with the effort to keep from screaming. "Cut the rope."

Tom was behind me in an instant and was working at it. The pain in my shoulder was so intense now that my wrists and hands seemed almost like a tickle in comparison. "It's too tight, I can't."

"There's a knife in the door."

Tom wrenched the blade from the wood and used it to carefully slice through the rope. When my wrists were finally free, gravity pulled my arm down, and with no more strength to give a proper scream I could only manage a gasp. "Raven and Patrick …" I must have scared Tom because he got all busy and bossy with me – usually my job.

"Don't worry about them. We have to get you to Shaw."

"My shoulder's dislocated." All I had left was a teary whimper.

"I can see that. Come on, I'll help you walk."

"It's a Were out there with Adam. We have to help him."

Tom hesitated just a moment, then shook his head decisively. "He has Connor with him. In Wolf form. They'll be fine."

A sob caught in my throat as Tom eased me to my feet and threw my good arm over his shoulder. He wasn't big or tall, but he had the strength of a distance runner, and I set my teeth and sucked it up like the tough girl I pretended to be.

I couldn't hear the guys in the woods anymore, and I hoped with all my heart that they were fine and had scared the rabid Were away.

Tom told me in a low voice that Adam was shocked when he made it back to school before me. He tried to pull his new trick of

13

seeing like he was in my head, but it was too dark, he said. So then Tom tried. He told me, in the same quiet voice, how easy Mongers were to See in his visions, and because I was with Mongers he was able to zero in on me in that shack. Connor came out in his Wolf form, and between his nose and Tom's sight they were able to find me pretty quickly.

"But something's different now, Saira. The visions with Mongers. They're getting … stronger."

"The visions or the Mongers?"

Tom sounded worried. "Both."

"Have you told anyone else?"

He shook his head gravely. "I can't … my dad … being a powerful Seer is everything to him. I can't let anything Monger taint him."

Personally, I thought Phillip Landers was a jerk, but he was Tom's problem, not mine. And the fact that Tom was even thinking about that told me he knew about the Monger that was mixed in with his Seer blood, even if he didn't want to admit it. "Tell someone."

He sighed. "I just did."

In a weird way his Monger-directed sight made sense. But only a select few people who had been under the London Bridge the night the Mongers almost got me knew that Tom's biological father was Seth Walters. He had assaulted Tom's mother eighteen years ago, but no one on the Immortal Descendants Council, which was our governing body, had ever pursued criminal charges against him because it would have officially outed Tom's mixed-blood status.

I think I was only about half-conscious on the trek back to school, and nearly cried out again when we slipped in through the broken Solarium window. We had been cocky enough to believe no one knew about our unsanctioned free-running classes, but obviously the Mongers were on to us. So at this point, we were busted no matter what, and I very clearly needed Mr. Shaw's help.

The Bear was still in his office when we stumbled inside. He'd been working with my dad's old microscope, and I think we

14

actually managed to surprise him. He took one look at my face and was across the room with the speed I've only heard about with bears in the wild. He eased me down into a chair and started prodding my shoulder with firm, gentle fingers. I whimpered quietly and concentrated on the many colors of red, orange, gold and brown in his unruly hair.

"Tom, I need you to hold Saira's other arm and shoulder down." His voice made me jump, I'd been concentrating so hard on not vomiting or passing out. "Get behind her and pin her to the chair if you need to, but I need her held steady."

Tom kneeled down and wrapped his arms around my waist from behind the chair. He spoke softly into my ear as he basically pinned me in place. "Sorry."

"It's okay. Thanks."

Mr. Shaw picked up my arm and rotated it slightly. My shoulder screamed in agony, and tears sprang to my eyes. "Look at me, Saira." His voice was calm and matter-of-fact, and I had no choice. I met his eyes, and he locked our gazes together. "You're going to want to scream, but you'll pass out instead."

There was a massive pop as he jerked my arm, and my world exploded into bright white fiery light. And then I was out.

SHAW

I snapped back to consciousness when Adam's voice intruded on my blissful blackout. "I don't know if it was a bite or just a scratch. But the bastard was a Were."

"Who's hurt?" I struggled to sit up, but my shoulder was bound up in ace bandages and had a big ice pack attached to it. Adam looked rough, Tom looked worried, but it was Connor the Wolf who raised his hand with a weak smile. Mr. Shaw, a Shifter who turned into a Bear on occasion, was examining Connor's other arm carefully and finally sat back with a grim expression.

"It's a bite, I think."

"Crap."

"Quite."

"Is a Were bite infectious?" My limited education about Immortal Descendants hadn't extended to Weres. I just knew them as Romanian badassery for some particularly mean Mongers.

I could see from their looks of surprise that Connor, Adam, and Tom didn't know the answer to that question, but Mr. Shaw assumed his teacher voice as he cleaned the wound on Connor's arm.

"Weres are not Shifters like Connor and I are. They're the product of a different neuregulin one-type promoter combination interacting with an outside contaminant."

Adam glared at Mr. Shaw. He was clearly worried about Connor. "In English, please?"

The Bear was equally worried and didn't take offense at Adam's tone. "Okay, simple terms? Think of Weres as mutts - a crude combo of the MAO-A gene Mongers have, with a lysaavirus mutation, otherwise known as a form of rabies."

A rabid Monger. Awesome.

"They're mixed?" Tom's voice broke on the question.

Mr. Shaw shook his head. "Not mixed. It's a true genetic anomaly that's promoted by a different neuregulin one promoter than all of us have, but it gets activated by the lyssavirus contaminant in Were saliva. It's much like the way Vampires are infected by the porphyria-like contaminant in blood-to-blood contact. Except Vampires have to be Descendants first, with our neuregulin 1 promoter, to modify the porphyria into something that won't kill them. Were's can't be."

"What does that mean for me?" Connor sounded strong and brave, but I was suddenly reminded he was only fourteen years old and way too young to be getting into fights with full-grown Weres. Or full-grown anythings for that matter.

"It used to mean a massive, sometimes debilitating fever as a Descendant's immune response went into overtime to fight off the Were contaminant."

"Debilitating?" Connor's voice was starting to betray his concern, and Mr. Shaw didn't pull punches.

"Loss of consciousness, sometimes coma, often taking weeks from which to recover."

"So a Descendant can't become a Were?" Trust Adam to get right to the heart of the issue.

"No. We don't have the right genetic anomaly, and neuregulin one, type six is a dominant gene promoter, so the contaminant makes us sick, but doesn't make us change."

"You said it *used* to mean fever." I'd watched Connor grit his teeth in discomfort at Mr. Shaw's final alcohol swab, and I wanted something positive to take his mind off the pain.

Mr. Shaw looked up at me. "I've been working on a kind of genetic chemo for exactly this."

"You have?" I knew Mr. Shaw was a medical doctor, and the best science teacher I'd ever seen, but I'd never really connected the dots to realize he was a researcher too.

He got up and unlocked a cabinet on the wall. Inside was a kind of mini-bar full of glass jars with handwritten labels. Mr. Shaw selected one and brought it back to his work table. He put a cotton pad in a petri dish and poured the contents of the bottle over the pad. "Because Connor's wound is still open, this will work much the same way as a poultice does, drawing out the contaminant and killing it onsite."

He picked up the pad with tweezers and placed it over the wound on Connor's arm. Connor winced slightly. Mr. Shaw nodded. "It bites a little, I know. That's the chemo-type reaction burning the contaminant out."

"Like a chemical burn?"

"More or less. Except not chemical. It's more like an immune-system takeover. It's an amped-up version of the green antibacterial ointment I make." Mr. Shaw's green medicine was legendary at school for cuts, scrapes, bites, and rashes, and I'd been trying to copy it for months in botany class. We watched as he wrapped the pad into place with a long piece of gauze bandage. "It'll leave you vulnerable to other infections for a few days, young Master Edwards, so I suggest you take yourself off to bed and stay there as much as possible."

Connor seemed surprised he was done, and he got up to go before Mr. Shaw could change his mind and do more uncomfortable stuff to him. "Thank you, Uncle Bob."

Mr. Shaw's detached, professional demeanor slipped, and he looked at Connor with genuine concern. "Get some rest, young man."

"Yes, sir." Connor slipped out of the room and closed the door behind him.

The softness in Mr. Shaw's expression hardened the instant he turned back to the rest of us. "A dislocated shoulder, a Were bite, and off school grounds if the state of your clothing is any indication. Explain."

The three of us looked at each other with the guilt and confusion of conspirators with no time to get their story straight. Tom opened his mouth, but then shut it at a look from Adam. I knew none of us stood a chance against the sheer power of our teacher's determination to get the truth, and ultimately, we were way past "in trouble" anyway. So I spilled.

To their credit, Adam and Tom looked relieved, so I got a little more confident as the story went on. No one was surprised that the Mongers wanted to know where Archer was. Even Mr. Shaw had asked me about Archer's daytime lair more than once. But they were all surprised at the threat to my mother, and I could see Mr. Shaw's spine stiffen and his eyes narrow dangerously.

The guys both weighed in on my rescue and the fight in the woods with the Were. Connor may be only fourteen, but his Shifter Wolf had proved a formidable opponent to the mangy Werewolf. So after getting his teeth on Connor in the tussle, Boris disappeared into the woods.

Mr. Shaw finally sat back, sighed, and rubbed his eyes. "You've made rather a mess for me, you realize." He looked at me, but included Tom in his gaze. "You are only safe so long as you are under the protection of the staff of this school."

"Not all the staff." It was clear I meant the Rothbitch, Ms. Rothchild, who was Raven and the Spawn's mother, and the oldest daughter of the head Monger, Markham Rothchild. Mr. Shaw's expression hardened.

"She can't stand against Miss Simpson, and she knows it."

"Meanwhile, her kid pulls a knife and threatens to bleed other students."

"Students who are off grounds, putting themselves directly in harm's way. No, I don't think I'll be making that public." Mr. Shaw sounded grim, and Adam was incensed.

"So that's it? Raven and Patrick get away with kidnapping Saira, torturing her, and threatening her mother?"

"It's likely. As you will get away with your off-campus free running classes *if* you agree to certain provisions."

19

It was so much more generous than I'd hoped, and I could tell Adam and Tom felt the same. We waited silently for him to continue.

"I've been wanting to teach an outdoor survival course for quite a while, and now seems like an excellent time for you three in particular to learn some skills."

That was a condition? That felt more like a reward to me, and I saw Adam's eyes light up with as much excitement as I felt. We nodded quickly.

"When you do your free-running classes you will check in and out with me. And you'll provide me with a list of class participants."

Adam spoke up. "What if the other guys don't want to be listed?"

"Then they won't be participating."

I cut Adam off before he could protest. "No problem. Anything else?"

"I need to know how to find Devereux."

My heart clenched in my chest. I trusted the Bear more than just about anyone in the world, but I couldn't give up Archer's daytime resting place. I'd promised him. Both Adam and Tom watched me warily. "I'm not going to tell you that."

I could have cut the tension rolling around the room with a knife, but instead of backing down, I dug in and looked each of them straight in the eyes. Tom and Adam looked away first. Good, I was still Alpha on this, but Mr. Shaw held my gaze steadily. Bear Shifters don't back down from anyone.

Finally, Mr. Shaw gave the slightest nod as if to say 'later.' I could live with that.

"Right. Off with you all. We'll give young Edwards and Miss Elian time to heal, and then we'll drag you both into the woods with us for a Descendants-only outdoor survival course."

I pulled myself to my feet with my good arm, and Adam and Tom were already at the door when Adam turned back. "Thank you, Mr. Shaw." The words clearly surprised the Bear. He and

Adam had a tenuous relationship at best, since it was Mr. Shaw's niece, Alex, that Adam was dating.

"You may still be able to catch the tail end of dinner if you hurry."

I wrapped my good arm around him in a side hug. "Thanks for fixing my shoulder."

His voice was gruff. "You're welcome."

The other guys raced off to charm some leftovers from the cooks, but I wasn't hungry. I just wanted to crawl in a hole, nurse my aching shoulder, and sleep. I debated going to the room I shared with Adam's twin Ava, but I knew she wouldn't let me rest until she had confirmation of every single thing she'd Seen happen today. Or I could have gone to my mom's rooms for comfort, or to the Clocker Tower for solitude.

Solitude was my default choice, since I'd been mostly alone my whole life. Even here, at boarding school, I often felt alone in the crowd of Descendant kids with their lifetime of knowing who they were. Except that for the first time in my life I actually had people: my free-running class, affectionately known as my 'pack of guys,' my mom, who taught history here now, Mr. Shaw, who was probably in love with her, and Ava and Olivia, the only two girls who didn't seem to hate me on sight. And I had Archer.

The first time I met Archer was about four months ago. He had already been a Vampire for 125 years and had loved me for all of them, which sounded impossible except that I'm a Clocker who can travel through time – not a normal skill for a seventeen-year-old free-running tagger, but it was useful when I needed to rescue my mom from Jack the Ripper and the nutjob Bishop Wilder, who almost killed her. I met Archer's human self then, in 1888, when he was a Theology student working for Wilder at King's College. He was the second son of a Lord, and had some Seer skills he inherited from the mother who died in childbirth. It was Archer who first told me about the Descendants and what I was. We didn't find out that Wilder was a Monger and a Vampire until just before he killed my dad, a Shifter Lion, and bit Archer, turning him into a Vampire, too.

The fact that I'd fallen in love with Archer-the-human in 1888 messed me up when I came back to the present where Archer-the-Vampire had spent his very long life loving me. It took a little emotional bandaging before I was really able to see the student I'd known in the guy he'd become, not just 'before' and 'after,' and we'd spent the past three months learning each other. Talking, laughing, free-running in the woods, cuddling, kissing, and more talking.

And tonight, with all that had happened, he was the only person I wanted.

I slipped down to his hidden part of the cellar under the kitchens, even more vigilant about watchers and spies than usual. I wanted comfort, and I wanted to be held. It wasn't something I did often, maybe once or twice a week. And I'm not even sure it was enough for me, but it's what I did. It wasn't by design or agreement, but he was a hunted Vampire, so he didn't come to me. He waited for me to come to him.

The sun had long since set, and I half-expected to see him at the chess table, a new game ready for me, or by the electric fire with a book he'd marked with quotes I might like. I didn't want to think how often he waited like that when I chose a night of hanging out with Ava or solitude with my paints instead of going to his cellar.

I didn't want to leave him waiting tonight.

So, I pushed open the door and slipped inside Archer's lair. I smelled his scent, warm and spicy, lingering in the cold cellar, with only a dim table lamp to light the empty space.

He was out. Hunting maybe. Or to London. I might have cried if I'd had the energy, but the pity-party tanks were dry.

The ice-pack had melted a wet stain on my hoodie, so I pulled off the sling, unwrapped the bandage, and dropped everything on a chair. I draped the hoodie over the back of it and snagged my favorite silk t-shirt from Archer's wardrobe to replace my wet one. Then I took off my boots, the best I could manage one-handed, curled up on his bed, and pulled an expensive fake fur blanket over me to combat the shivers.

It wasn't his arms, but it was his, and I drifted off to sleep.

ARCHER

This time I expected the plunge and closed my mouth. The man 'olding my 'ead underwater was wicked strong, and I knew 'twas pointless to fight.

"Stop! You'll kill him!" The fear in 'er voice wasn't helpin' my situation, even as 'e hauled me up from the cistern. The bastard loved power, and makin' a Lady beg for a thief's life 'ad to top the list of good times for the man. It didn't matter that she knew naught 'bout me. 'E did.

It meant I was good as dead.

"What is his life worth to you, my Lady?" One eye was blurry and 'urt like 'ell, but I had enough vision to see 'er flinch from the fist in 'is voice. 'Er skin was transparent, and I knew it was all she could do not to shake with the effort of standin'. But she was strong. And a fighter.

"It is a life. That is enough. Remove your hands from him at once!"

"Tell me what you See, my Lady. Tell me how this will end, and I'll end it."

She glared at 'im like a fishmonger's wife. I was proud of 'er for it.

"I'm sure I don't know what you mean, sir."

The bastard sighed. "I can do this all night, my Lady." And like that, my 'ead went into the cistern again. Things got dark 'round the edges as my brain starved of air. When the bastard's 'ands finally dragged me up, I couldn't 'ardly take a breath.

Somewhere, from very far away, 'er whisper drifted across the room and into my brain.

"Fated for one, born to another
The child must seek to claim the Mother
The Stream will split and branches will fight

Death will divide, and lovers unite
The child of opposites will be the one
To heal the Dream that War's undone."

The bastard went completely still. The iron grip 'oldin' me was 'abit more'n anythin' else since 'e was like a moth to a flame wi' her.

"It is not the prophecy I seek, it's the answer."

She glared at 'im, fierce. "You asked for the end. I gave it to you. Now release him."

I could practice that tone if I ever got out o' this. The edge of it was razor sharp and would cut most mortals. Sadly, the bastard was inhuman and unimpressed. And 'twas me goin' t' pay.

Just then 'e yanked me from the cistern and 'auled me over to the guard who 'ad brought the Lady to this place. 'E was big and ugly and looked like somethin' bloodthirsty gnawed at 'im. "Watch the thief." The bastard shoved me to my knees and turned on the Lady.

"Do you know what I have in my possession, my Lady?" 'E stalked across the stone floor and pulled a wooden seat up off of a stone bench. A shite hidin' place. I'd 'ave found it in my first sweep. 'E lifted out a small chest and opened it, removin' a rolled up scroll which 'e untied and 'eld up for her to see. I couldn't make out the words, but the Lady could, and she trembled.

"You'll notice the traitor's signature at the bottom. Yes, that is, in fact, blood in which he signed. His own, of course, which will no doubt impress the queen."

The Lady was outraged. A bit o' spirit that made me grin. "These are nothing but lies!"

"I'm not one to let the truth get in the way of my plans. And we both know that your life is forfeit the moment your sister receives this letter."

"Do what you will to me, sir. My fate has been foretold."

The bastard stared at the Lady as 'e rolled up the parchment and closed it back up into the bench. "It is not your fate that interests me. It is mine." Then 'e stalked across the room and 'auled me to my feet. 'E dragged me to the darkest corner of the room. The evil-lookin' guard at the door grinned like 'e knew what for, and the Lady couldn't move for starin'.

The bastard 'eld my 'ead over the stinkin' privy and forced me to my knees. The maw of filth and 'orror winked evilly at me and in a moment of *madness, I pushed back. 'Twas a mistake to fight 'cause the next instant the bastard shoved me deep into the stew.*

'Twere no time to hold my breath, and vomit filled my mouth. But to release the sour retch was to let the filth in. Madness threatened with the choice. The bastard 'auled me up again, and I spewed vomit and filth from my mouth.

"Tell me something then; who is the one in the prophecy? Who is this child?" The bastard's casual tone was at odds with 'is punishing 'ands.

The Lady looked faint, and 'er whisper had all the substance of a ghost. "I know not."

The iron grip on me let go, and I dropped to the floor. The bastard slid a sword from the guard's scabbard. I struggled to my feet, cursin' me shakin' legs. The Lady clutched the table behind her for support as the fear in her eyes screamed at me. The bastard moved like an animal and 'is eyes glinted with the steel of the blade 'e raised under my chin. Its point pierced the skin at my throat, and I knew I was a second away from being run through. 'E licked 'is lips.

And I spit in 'is face.

Shock lit up Bishop Wilder's eyes, and 'e slid the tip of 'is sword down from my neck to the base of 'is ribs, leavin' a slashed tunic and a thin red line to mark the passage.

"Shall we continue, Lady Elizabeth? I believe your lad, Ringo, can take more." The sudden grin on the bishop's face made my knees give way. The bishop pulled 'is sword back to grab for me 'fore I could hit the floor. Then 'e turned my 'ead and pressed me down toward the privy.

Bishop Wilder's voice in my ear chilled me to my stones. "Rest assured, young Ringo. I will have the name of the child, and then I will make your lady bleed."

"Ringo!"

I sat bolt upright and gasped at the fire in my shoulder. I jumped again at the body next to mine.

It was Archer, curled up around me. His eyes were locked on my face.

"That was Wilder with him! What's he doing with Ringo?" I struggled as the image faded from my mind and finally loosened its stranglehold on my breath.

Archer's voice was deep and soothing. "You were dreaming."

"You Saw it too, and I don't get dreams from you." My words were clipped and angry. I didn't like not knowing.

He sat up. "But you get my visions?"

I nodded. "Well, you *are* a Seer. And when you were sick, before ..." *Before you became a Vampire.* I didn't say it, but he saw it on my face. He'd had a long time to get over being turned, but my brain was still laced with guilt, since it was my journey back in time that caused it. "I saw your vision of where Wilder kept my mom in the Bedlam cellar. Where he bled her."

Archer's proper British accent was at odds with his bed-tousled hair. "But even if it was a vision, I can't see what's already happened. Only the future."

"So maybe it hasn't happened yet."

He stared at me. "The clothes ... the sword. And Ringo? That wasn't 1888. And who was the girl?"

"I don't know. A noblewoman, I guess. Some sort of Seer."

Archer frowned. "It wasn't real. Visions don't generally come to Seers in first person. At least not ones about other people. Dreams do that."

"I guess you're right." Ava and Adam could See through each other's eyes in visions, but I thought that was a twin thing. The last time I saw Ringo was three months ago. He was sixteen, and the year was 1888. I missed my friend with the suddenness of a punch to the gut, and Archer was the only person in the world who could understand it, because I knew he did too.

On impulse, I kissed Archer's cheek.

He touched the corner of my mouth. "God, you're beautiful." This, coming from the handsomest guy I'd ever met, with his dark blue eyes, strong jaw, and nearly black hair that made me feel practically monochromatic. My hair and skin were vaguely honey gold, and the lack of sun in England wasn't doing

27

me any favors. I had a jaw that I'd probably like when I was old and wrinkled, but for now it just added to all the angles I sported instead of curves.

I wanted to melt into his touch. Wanted to lie back down and let myself surrender to the whisper of his fingers on my face. But I was suddenly aware that I'd broken my own rules about falling asleep in Archer's hideaway and looked around at the clock. "What time is it? I should go."

He touched my arm. "Saira, we need to talk."

I flinched. I didn't want to talk, not about us. But I couldn't slip around, slide under, or dodge this like any other obstacle in a free-runner's way. So I waited.

Archer ran his hands through his hair. "Do you know where I was tonight?"

"Hunting?" I winced at the mental image.

"Yes, I was hunting. But not for sustenance. I've been hunting for Wilder's genealogy."

The book in question was one Archer had been compiling back in 1888 for his boss, Bishop Wilder. The genealogy contained the family bloodlines of all the Immortal Descendants going back hundreds of years, and my least favorite Monger, Seth Walters, had stolen it from a church at King's College a few months ago. Archer figured it could be used to track mixed-bloods. Like me.

I opened my mouth to respond, but he wasn't done. "I've been doing it for nearly three months, ever since you came back, but you wouldn't know that because I only go when I'm sure you won't visit me here. Or after you're gone."

I could feel the tightness begin in my chest as Archer continued quietly. "I didn't wait tonight. I didn't think you'd come."

I couldn't speak. The words got lost in the nest of guilt that rats had been building in my guts. Archer searched my eyes, then looked away sadly and climbed off the bed. The movement jarred my shoulder, and I bit my lip against the pain so he wouldn't see.

He pulled a jacket off the back of a chair and noticed my discarded sling and ice-pack. He finally met my eyes again. "What's this?"

Crap.

"I hurt my shoulder free-running with the guys."

Not technically a lie, but definitely not the whole truth. And he knew it instantly. His eyes narrowed, and I wished I could take the words back.

So then facts tumbled from me in a rush, like telling it fast would make up for trying to hide it.

Archer watched me wordlessly as I told him about Boris and the Mongers, about their threat against my mom, and the fact they were hunting him. And I told him how the guys had rescued me, and that Mr. Shaw treated our wounds and knew the whole story. His expression didn't change once, and the look in his eyes was unreadable.

He picked up the sling and came over to where I sat on his bed.

"I didn't tell you right away because I knew ..." What did I know? He was worried about me, tried to protect me, got angry at himself for having to sleep during the day. "I knew you'd feel bad that you weren't there to stop them. I was fine though. Adam and Tom were there. Even Connor fought a full-grown Were and came out of it with just a small bite."

Archer's expression was like ice, and guilt twisted in my stomach, making me defensive and mad. He reached for my shoulder and tried to help me with the sling, but I flinched away. "I can do it."

His gaze locked on mine. "So Adam can help you, but I can't?"

I stiffened. "What's wrong with Adam? He's my friend."

Archer's voice somehow combined anger and seduction. "You and I were friends, Saira. And I knew from the moment I saw you that I could never love anyone else." I think my heart stopped beating when he narrowed his eyes. "But you put your friends first. And I wait here, wondering if this is the night you'll

29

come, if this night you'll choose me. I can't live like that, and I won't stand by while your *friend* looks at you as he does."

My heart pounded. He took a step back and I felt the absence of him like sudden shiver. "I've been hoarding moments with you, and I've hidden here too long." I opened my mouth to protest, but the words died in my throat when Archer took my face in his hands with painful tenderness. "You are the woman of my dreams, but a dream isn't enough. I want more."

Ever since my mother began Clocking out when I was twelve, I vowed no one else would have that power over me. That leaving power. I thought I'd protected myself, thought I'd held him just far enough away that I could love him without risking the pain.

My voice cracked with unspilled tears. "What are you doing?"

"I'm the reason you were attacked tonight. I'm going to London. I'll find the book, and you'll be safe."

"You can't leave me behind."

"I have to."

His eyes locked with mine one final time, and then he left.

SCHOOLED

I woke early, before dawn. The joint in my shoulder throbbed, and I debated leaving the sling off just to punish myself with the pain. But I needed my shoulder to heal quickly, and there was no room for self-pity when I was so busy pretending not to care. I dragged my very sore, incredibly whipped carcass out of bed and awkwardly slung my arm. I wished I hadn't been so proud about letting Archer help me. I wished a lot of things.

Ava cracked open an eyelid when she saw me. "Sorry about your shoulder."

"Did Adam tell you?"

"Hmm mm. Saw it. Not soon enough to warn you though."

"I'm okay." I rifled through my dresser drawers and pulled out an Ugly Kid hoodie I got off a cute, skinny guy in Venice Beach who wanted to trade for one I'd painted with my tag. I pulled it on carefully over a clean tank. I still usually dressed like a tagger – t-shirts, skinny jeans and boots – but my association with Archer's wardrobe had given me access to cashmere sweaters that frequently took up lodging in my own closet. He was generous like that. I had to be careful what I admired because things had a way of just showing up in my room.

I winced, not just at the pain in my shoulder.

"You're not okay."

I looked sharply at Ava and tried to ignore the hollow feeling in my chest. It was a survival technique I'd learned the first time my mom moved us when I was a kid.

"I will be." Ava watched me yank on clean jeans and slip my feet into combat boots. I left them untied; laces were too much to ask of any friend.

I made my voice as casual as possible, as if I'd just remembered to mention it. "Archer left."

I looked up to find her still watching me silently. Even first thing in the morning Adam's twin took the blond surfer looks of her brother and refined them into an ethereal fairy, with smooth, silvery hair and pale, milk and honey coloring. "I'm going back to sleep for an hour. After you get your coffee, go find Miss Simpson in the library."

I guessed we were done. "See you in class later."

She caught my eye as she climbed back under the fluffy white duvet. "He didn't leave *you*, by the way. He just left."

I tried to pretend I hadn't heard her as I shut the door firmly. I waited until I was out of earshot before I muttered, "Same thing."

With a steaming mug of coffee in hand and a stern warning from the school cook, Mrs. Taylor, to get some sleep before the bags under my eyes turned into suitcases, I made my way through the dim corridors to the library. It was one of the few places at St. Brigid's where I could shut off the noise in my brain and just become one with the books. The rows of shelves stood like sentinels in the pre-dawn gray light invading through tall, mullioned windows. An electric light drew me to the private office at the back of the library, and I smiled a little in anticipation of an early morning talk with the headmistress of St. Brigid's School, Miss Simpson.

She already had her tea poured and was sitting in an armchair with an open folder on her lap. Miss Simpson always looked very prim and proper, yet she gave off a vibe of warmth and gentle strength that made me wish she'd been my grandmother instead of Millicent Elian. Not that Millicent actually was my ancestor at all, more like a much-removed cousin or something, but that didn't stop her from trying to hand out edicts like Halloween candy.

"Good morning, Saira. How is your shoulder feeling?" I must have looked surprised. "I've had a note from Mr. Shaw. He explained everything, so unless you have something to add, we don't need to revisit your adventures of yesterday."

As proper English ladies went, Miss Simpson had a very down-to-earth way of keeping it real. I flexed my shoulder experimentally and winced. "It'll take a couple of days to heal, I think, but I'm fine. The main thing I'm concerned about is Boris."

Her eyebrows went up in a question, and I quickly clarified. "The Were. Ms. Rothchild brought two of them here, and I thought the surviving one had gone back to Romania. Considering they came to hunt for Archer, it makes me nervous that one's still hanging around."

"I agree it's of concern, though Mr. Devereux's departure from St. Brigid's alleviates some of the immediate risk to his well-being. I'll be speaking to Ms. Rothchild about it this morning."

She knew Archer was gone, but wasn't asking about my feelings. That was seriously good intuition.

"If you talk to Rothchild about the Were, how do you keep her kids out of it?"

Miss Simpson looked at me levelly. "I have no intention of keeping *Ms.* Rothchild's children out of it."

A million different responses skipped through my mind, but in the end I settled on a simple fact that I rarely gave anyone credit for: she knew what she was doing. I took a sip of my coffee. "Is there anything you need from me?"

She studied me over the rim of her teacup. "I imagine you won't be teaching your running class until your shoulder heals properly?"

"I wasn't planning to run until I can do it without too much pain, but I'd still like to work with the guys on some skills."

"Can those skills be taught in the building?"

I thought about the jumping and climbing I usually used trees and walls for. "Can we use the kitchen garden walls?"

"If you confine your work to daylight hours, you may use the grounds and whatever deserted areas of the school you need, so

33

long as you repair anything you break." I smiled at that. Most people would say 'don't break anything.' Miss Simpson took a sip of tea. "At least until we've determined the whereabouts of … Boris."

"Okay. Thanks." I considered telling her where I'd be taking the guys, like out windows and to the roof, but figured it was easier to ask forgiveness than permission.

"Now, your mother needs a teaching assistant for her fourth period history class. Would you be interested in the position? It's worth an extra history credit."

"Sure. I have fourth period free right now anyway. But why didn't she ask me herself?"

"She was concerned it might be awkward for you to work for her."

I scoffed. "I'm her daughter. I'm used to doing whatever she tells me."

Miss Simpson's smile was amused. "As I understand it, that hasn't been the case in a long time."

She had me there, and she read my silence perfectly.

"I think you'll enjoy your mother's teaching style, and who knows? If you pay attention, you may even learn something useful."

I didn't see Adam until just before fourth period when I was on my way to my mom's big history class. He was walking with some of his guys, but sent them on ahead so he could talk to me.

"How are you?" I'm not sure I would have believed the look of concern in his eyes if the almost-but-not-quite kiss hadn't happened the night before. And he was the only one who actually asked about the whole me, not just the part that was injured.

"Mad more than anything else."

"I'm sorry." There was more than 'that sucks' in that 'sorry.' It was like he was felt responsible for my getting nabbed, and I could feel my spine stiffen like a pissed-off cat.

"Don't." It came out harsher than I intended, and Adam flinched. "Don't do the must-protect-the-girl caveman thing. I can't stand it. It's not your fault I got jumped. I'm the one always talking about 'listen to your gut, know what's around you, use all your senses.' I'm teaching the class on it, damn it! And *I'm* the one who got complacent and stopped looking over my shoulder." I ignored the protest that was forming on his face and put the final nail in it. "Being friends with you guys has made me soft. I stopped watching my own back, and that can't happen."

His voice sounded hurt, and I hated the guilt that gnawed at me. "Other people can watch your back too, you know."

"I can't count on that though. I have to be able to do it myself."

Adam looked at me a long time, and I could see shutters dropping over the hurt on his face and wiping it blank. "Right. You never know when you might need to escape a Victorian nuthouse or something."

"Or something." I whipped out my driest delivery and then stuck out my tongue at him as I turned to head into my mom's classroom. Adam's bark of laughter followed me in and made me grin. We're good, I thought. Good enough, anyway.

My mom was already at her desk, but only about half the seats were taken yet. She looked happy to see me, and I realized she must have heard about my run in with the Were from Mr. Shaw. "Hi, Mom. Sorry I didn't come by this morning."

"Bob said you'll heal well. How do you feel?"

It was so weird to hear my mom talking about the Bear. He was such a huge presence, his first name just didn't seem big enough.

"It hurt, but Mr. Shaw's a good doctor."

"I stopped by your room last night."

Crap. Of course she did. I had never spent a whole night out of my room and was usually in bed by midnight. I told myself it was because I didn't want anyone looking for me and finding him, but I knew that wasn't the only reason.

"I fell asleep in Archer's room. He's gone to London, by the way, so I was alone."

35

Her gaze lingered on me a long moment, and she might have been about to say something else, but the bell rang. So she stood and addressed her class instead. "Okay, guys. As you can see, we have a new teacher's assistant. For those of you who don't know Saira, she's in sixth form, and she lived in America until this year, so her English history's a little more of the 'we kicked you and your tea-taxing butts out' variety than ours." The class was full of fourth and fifth formers, and I only recognized a couple of kids from the halls.

"So, the British monarchy in the sixteenth century. We've discussed Henry VIII and his six wives, and we left off last week with the rocky reign of his oldest daughter, Queen Mary I. Within a year of Mary Tudor's ascension to the throne, she had her cousin, Lady Jane Grey's head forcibly removed, and the persecution of Protestants was in full swing. She also had advisors who wanted her sister, Lady Elizabeth, the Protestant daughter of Henry and Anne Boleyn, tried for treason and taken out of the picture entirely."

An alarm bell went clanging in my head. The queen's sister. The Lady Elizabeth. In an age of swords and wearing a dress that would win a Renaissance Fair fashion show. Could the young Seer woman in Archer's vision have been Elizabeth Tudor, future queen of England?

HISTORY

My mother's lecture had suddenly become very, very interesting.

"So, those are some of the background players. Now let's look at the star of today's class. Lady Elizabeth Tudor was twenty-one years old in 1554. Technically, she was a princess, but there were issues of legitimacy so no one called her that. The Wyatt Rebellion, led by Sir Thomas Wyatt, had just failed, but it had put Elizabeth directly in the gun sights of her sister. Wyatt named Lady Elizabeth in his confession, and advisors convinced Queen Mary she needed to try her sister for treason. Step number one? Put her in the Tower."

Seriously? The Tower of London in 1554? Could that be where Wilder held Ringo to get Elizabeth to talk? Notwithstanding the temporal issues of Ringo being from 1888, the rest of the details kind of fit. *If* Wilder could time-travel. And *if* Ringo somehow did too. There were so many *ifs* it made my head hurt, but something about the whole idea went 'thunk' in my brain.

And then there was the fact I had grown up fascinated by old castles, prisons and fortresses, and the Tower of London was top on the list of places I wanted to explore. But it's a major tourist attraction, so un-accompanied, self-guided tours were somewhat frowned upon. Call me crazy, but it never occurred to me to explore it in a different time … like the 16th century.

My mom had continued her lecture. "The thing about being a prisoner was that 'accidents' happened to them all the time. And

Elizabeth's biggest fear was that some quiet, deadly accident would make life much easier for everyone who had conspired to put her there in the first place."

"Lady Elizabeth was fiercely intelligent. She'd been educated by private tutors as if she'd been a boy, which, at that time, was saying a lot for her education. She spoke several languages fluently, and had been literally fighting a political game for her life since her mother was beheaded when she was three years old."

"Because divorce was too messy?" A kid in the back gave the perfect dry delivery that had the class laughing. My mom continued gamely.

"Lady Elizabeth was pulled in for questioning by the queen's council more than once, but despite being young and terrified, she maintained her innocence of anything to do with Wyatt's Rebellion. In fact, the council was hoping to break her by having Wyatt denounce her before his execution, but that backfired. Wyatt apparently refused to speak against Elizabeth, and in fact, he fell to his knees and declared her innocent of everything."

"So was she released after that?" One of the girls at the front of the class was practically leaning across her desk in anticipation of the story. Mom smiled at her and continued.

"Actually, I think Wyatt's declaration fueled something a little desperate in one of the queen's bishops, Bishop Gardiner. There's a story that an order for Elizabeth's immediate execution was drawn up and sent to the Tower. Sir John Brydges was the Lieutenant of the Tower, in charge of executions." My mom paused for dramatic effect, but believe me, I was already hanging on her every word.

"So the order for execution went to him, and he was told to make it happen immediately with no fanfare and no warning. Sir John, though a staunch Catholic with no love for Elizabeth or the Protestant supporters who championed her, apparently had much more common sense than the queen's bishop hoped. When he saw that the order for execution wasn't signed by Queen Mary herself, he realized that if there was any backlash at all about Elizabeth's execution, it was going to fall squarely on his shoulders. It's unclear exactly what happened, but diary entries from Sir John's wife have shown historians how very close the Lady Elizabeth came to losing her life that night in the Tower."

Mom handed me a stack of papers to pass out to the class "So, here are the written accounts we have from that time. Look through them, do your own research, and then write down what you think happened the night England almost lost its greatest queen."

When class let out I stayed behind to help her straighten up.

"That was really good stuff, Mom."

"It is good, isn't it? I loved hearing about the Tudors when I was young. They all had very big personalities, and at least Henry and Elizabeth had intelligence to match."

"When was Elizabeth in the Tower?"

"She was there from March 18th, 1554 until May of that same year."

Okay, so at least I had concrete dates to check out. But that year sounded familiar for something else, I just couldn't remember what. I tucked the knowledge away to discuss with Archer, whenever I finally saw him again, then kissed my mom on the cheek and packed up my school bag. "Do you need anything else before those papers get turned in?"

"Just you. My door's open anytime you want to talk about things ... with you, friends, your relationship with Archer."

I knew that she wanted to be there for me. I just wasn't ready to admit out loud that I didn't know if I still had a relationship to talk about.

I spent a couple evenings alone in the Clocker Tower, avoiding my friends, sketching tags and stencils, and trying very hard not to draw Archer's face. I missed him. I almost went down to his cellar to visit him a couple of times before it slammed home in my brain that he was gone. I even picked up the phone to call Bishop Cleary, the current bishop at King's College. The genealogy had been in his archives until Seth Walters stole it, and Bishop Cleary was as interested in getting it out of Monger hands as we were. He was also someone both Archer and I considered a friend. But I hung up before I finished dialing the phone. Pride is a ridiculous thing.

A couple of weeks after the whole Jack the Ripper/Bedlam cellar incident, I went back to Bedlam. I didn't tell anyone I was going, and I traveled through the painting in the Clocker Tower. The collapse had been shored up, the wing sealed off, and the cellar seemed completely devoid of everything I remembered. I found a discarded chess game, and in a weird fit of nostalgia, I set the board up on a makeshift table near the tunnel door. The set was missing some pieces, so I scavenged some broken bits of plaster to be the white pawns, and used a modern one pound coin as a black bishop. I knew I was taking a risk leaving that coin behind, but I couldn't think of anything else that would mark my presence more than something from the future. Before I left the cellar I moved a white pawn two spaces forward.

I'd gone back twice more since then, and both times black pieces had been moved. I wasn't sure who I was playing chess with, but I knew who I hoped it was.

On my third night of self-imposed solitude I couldn't stand my own mental whininess anymore. I pocketed a Maglite and the little knife that the Elian Manor housekeeper, Sanda, had given me, and clenched my teeth against the nausea that came with Clocking. As I began tracing the spirals in the Clocker Tower painting, I set the image of the Bedlam basement firmly in my mind. My mom couldn't focus her travel unless she wore the clock necklace that had been in our family for generations, but my skill seemed to be stronger than hers, even though I was only half Clocker. The other half of my blood came from my Shifter father, and that mix was a very sore subject for most of the Immortal Descendant world.

I didn't know what they were so afraid of. All I could figure was that they – the Council of the Immortal Descendants and anyone else who decided the rules – were afraid. Afraid that a mix of skills would make something they couldn't predict.

Which sort of made me determined to be unpredictable.

40

But it's also why I'd been more or less confined to St. Brigid's. The list of people who knew my heritage was small, but it included at least one Monger. And if Raven's threats about my mother were any indication, it was suspected by more.

I gasped with the effort of hanging onto the contents of my stomach when I landed on my knees in the Bedlam basement. The air still carried the lingering scent of mortar dust from the cave-in, but the debris had been swept away, and the only remnants of the night my father had died were the vivid images imprinted in my brain.

My Maglite's beam lit up the chessboard. The black bishop had slid backwards three spaces, which put the white queen directly in the line of fire. I debated moving her, but that left her open to attack within two moves from at least three other pieces. So my hand went to a pawn.

Then I heard the faintest scuff of a footstep, and my hand went for my knife instead.

"You leave her vulnerable." The voice was quiet and came from the blackest corner of the room. My knife hand jerked, and a sudden flush of heat crept up my neck.

I managed to find my voice where it had fallen somewhere behind my spine. "She's been vulnerable since her knight fell." I wasn't talking about chess.

Archer stepped into the light of my upright Maglite. The skin of his face was drawn tightly over his bones, and his eye sockets looked like something just this side of sinkholes. I stood to face him and covered my sudden bout of nerves with a mental shake, then I searched his face. I hadn't put away the knife yet, but my grip on it slackened.

"You haven't fed enough." It was very strange to sound like my mother, but even weirder that I was concerned about a Vampire's eating habits.

"Why are you wearing a sling on your arm?"

I blew out a frustrated sigh. If I told him the real story his protectiveness would come out in full-force. "I landed wrong on a flip." His eyes narrowed. Damn! I'd forgotten, yet again, that he

41

could see the colors of a lie around me, so I changed the subject. "Have you seen Ringo?" I wanted to make sure he was still firmly lodged in this time so I could discount the vision and call it a dream.

Archer studied me a long moment. "Only in visions."

That surprised me. "Why? What do you see?"

"I see him with Charlie. They're in his flat together."

"Is that weird that you have visions of Ringo?"

"He cared for me in Epping Wood. It is perhaps not so strange." Guilt slammed into me. It should have been me taking care of Archer after he was bitten by Wilder and began the painful transformation into a Vampire. No matter how logical it had been at the time, the fact was, I left him behind to be cared for by the Missus and Ringo. Archer gave my expression an odd look, then shook his head. "I won't see him in person until I can get the bloodlust under control."

"How's it going? The control?" I still hadn't put the knife away. Archer noticed.

Archer's eyes traveled to my face. He stayed away from me, just at the edge of the pool of light. "Too slowly."

It seemed like there was a whole novel unwritten in those two words, but I folded up the little knife and put it away. I faced a brand new Vampire unarmed. On purpose. The only difference between brave and stupid is reflex speed. And trust.

Suddenly, Archer was in front of me, and his eyes swept over my face like he was memorizing the details. He leaned closer until I could smell the faintest scent of spice and something musky and warm. His gaze drank me in, and the air disappeared from my lungs, but breathing was overrated when he was so close to me. My heart re-started with a resounding THUMP, and a sudden flush of heat rose off my skin like my body was calling to him.

"It kills me. The wanting…" The growl in his throat was raw with emotion, and when he stepped back from me I shivered from everything undone and unsaid.

But then Archer resumed his place at the edge of the circle of light.

"Why are you here, Saira?"

"I missed you."

He looked at me a long time. "Why?"

"You're in London."

"I wouldn't leave you."

I sucked in a breath against the pain, and my expression hardened. "You did though. You think you're a danger to me. And ... other reasons."

Archer looked completely shocked for about a second, and then he took another step away from me. Into the shadows.

"Good bye, Saira."

The room went very cold.

I leaned down to move my queen. Though she was now out of reach of the bishop, it was the black knight who could take her down. I spun away from the chessboard and stumbled to the spiral before the tears could blur my vision.

 FOUND

The next few days I pushed my shoulder harder than I probably should have, mostly to keep my brain on mute, but except for some residual muscle ache, I had decent use of it again. If Ava said anything to Adam about Archer's departure, I didn't hear it, and I definitely didn't pick that scab open with anyone. Self-pity was bad enough; anyone else's would have been intolerable.

Connor was laying low in his room recovering. I stopped by his room every day to bring his science homework, and he seemed to be healing really well. He said he was just more tired than normal, and we were all waiting for him to be pronounced fit enough to do Mr. Shaw's outdoor survival class.

Just when the boredom of inactivity threatened to send me into a coma, Adam and Tom tracked me down in the library. "Hey, Elian. When are you going to be good to run again?"

"I know you're not talking about skill since I can kick your ass even with one shoulder trussed up like a turkey."

Adam barked in laughter. "You are maybe the only person I know more naturally arrogant than me. It's why I love you, Elian." He pushed on my good arm in a friendly way, but it didn't negate the odd twinge his words caused. Not the arrogance part, I didn't care what anyone thought of my attitude. It's part of what kept me safe in crappy neighborhoods near Venice Beach. But the casual way he dropped 'love' into it. I shoved that thought somewhere down around my ankles and considered his words about running. I knew Connor was still out; Mr. Shaw had him on bed rest all week. And the other guys didn't really have as much natural skill as Adam and Tom did, so they weren't quite as fun to train.

"Okay, meet me on the third floor in the west wing in fifteen."

"But that wing's locked."

I grinned at Tom. "Use your imagination."

Adam slapped Tom on the back with a grin that matched mine. "Let's go."

The guys took off running, and I figured even if I babied my shoulder I could still give them a five minute head start.

On my way up I ran into Olivia on the main staircase. She was carrying a pile of books and had a graphic novel perched on top. I eyed the stack with a smile.

"How's he doing?"

Olivia grimaced. "Bored. Getting peevish."

"He'll feel better when he can get up and go running with us."

She rolled her eyes. "Are you kidding, free-running with you and the boys is all Connor can talk about. You'd think he was in a cage having to stay in bed."

I shrugged. "I'd feel that way too if I were him." I eyed her tiny frame. Olivia was probably really strong for her size because she barely had any body weight to lift. She wasn't an Immortal Descendant like about half of us at St. Brigid's were, but she was descended from something almost as old. With Pict blood in her, she came from the same family as the Missus and Sanda – tiny, capable, and very long-lived. "Have you ever wanted to come with us?"

"I'm not a runner."

"Bet you're a climber though."

She gave me one of those lingering looks that I'd learned meant she was deciding how much to tell me. "Maybe."

I laughed. "Come on. Drop those with Connor, and let's go show some guys how we do it."

She didn't even hesitate. "Two minutes." She sped off down the hall toward the boys' rooms in the west wing, and in the time it took me to re-tie my boots, she was back with a mischievous smile. "I told Connor what I was doing. I've never seen him look so mad. It was brilliant!"

I told her about my challenge to Adam and Tom. She suggested exactly what I'd been thinking to keep some of the pressure off my shoulder, and we made our way up to the south tower. We didn't need to break into the actual tower since the window at the end of the hall was unlocked. Once that was open and we were through, it was just a matter of picking our way across roof tiles to the fire escape at the end of the west wing. Olivia dropped down first to make sure the window was unlatched, and by the time I landed on the balcony she had shimmied it open and was climbing through.

We closed the window behind us for good measure and scanned the deserted hallway. There was no sign that the guys had been there yet.

Olivia tried one of the doors to the empty rooms. "Locked."

"Know how to get in?" She shook her head, and I grinned mischievously. "Wanna learn?"

"Definitely!"

I found a print on the wall with cardboard backing and did my key trick. The cardboard was a little thicker than others I'd used before, and the key got hung up while I was sliding it under the door, but Olivia's nimble little fingers pulled it out the rest of the way. We turned the key in the lock, and it opened perfectly.

"Fantastic! Is this how you got your own room last term?"

I nodded. "And how I got out of Millicent's prison. It's why she sent me here."

"Isn't awful though, is it?"

"Nope. First time in my life I've had friends."

I guess I assumed people kind of knew that about me, but the look of sadness that crossed Olivia's face made me think I'd done too good a job of being tough and mysterious. I gave her a genuine smile. "Kind of puts my pathetic people skills into perspective, huh?"

"Actually, it goes a long way to explaining your game-free nature."

"You lost me."

"You don't play the game. You either like people or you don't. Who they are and how connected they might be doesn't seem to matter to you."

I scoffed. "Sounds like something Archer said to me once, a long time ago. Except he basically called me an innocent little girl." My heart twisted a little at the thought of him, but if Olivia noticed, she said nothing.

"If 'innocent' means 'real,' I'd take it."

There was a muffled "Ooof!" from outside on the fire escape. Adam was out there trying to haul himself up over the ledge. Olivia and I watched in fascination as Adam collapsed to catch his breath for a moment, then leaned over the railing to help haul Tom up. Both of them were sweaty and exhausted, despite the chill in the March air.

Olivia and I busted up laughing at the same moment. Adam couldn't believe what he was seeing.

I opened the window for them, and he and Tom dragged themselves through.

"You guys have the key," he accused me.

I held up the room key we'd just liberated. "We do now. But we came in through the window, same as you."

"Not possible." Tom was in rough shape, still trying to gasp enough air into his lungs to use all his voice.

"Yes, possible. We took the roof."

Tom paled. I'd never actually seen someone lose all the color in their face at once. And with Tom's gypsy coloring, that was saying something. "Are you about to puke? Because dude, if you're going to puke, find a toilet." My tolerance for puke is higher than most because it's such a nasty side effect of Clocking, but I'm all about not getting it on my shoes if it can be helped.

Adam glanced at his cousin. "He's not going to puke. He just hates heights."

Olivia looked at him with wide eyes. "Really, I love them! I feel like I can see the whole world from the top of a tree, or a house, or a, I don't know, bridge?"

I didn't think it was possible for Tom to lose any more color, but he did, and he gulped. "You've been on *top* of a bridge?"

"You know the walkways that connect the two towers of Tower Bridge?"

Tom seemed to visibly relax. "Yeah, they're covered and enclosed. I've been up there."

Olivia grinned evilly. "I've been on top."

Tom was done. He got up and walked away on shaky legs. I had to restrain myself from either laughing or going after him – he wouldn't have appreciated either one. Meanwhile, Adam was looking at Olivia with frank disbelief.

"You did not!"

"My uncle was one of the builders who worked on the restoration in the eighties. He knows all the secrets of that bridge, and he took me there last year after I built an obstacle course in the top of an old oak on his property."

A quiet gagging sound came from the direction Tom had gone.

Adam seemed to look at Olivia with new eyes. "How old are you?"

She narrowed her gaze dangerously. I'd been on the receiving end of one of her tirades, and I kind of wanted to see Adam get hit in the eyes with one, just because he deserved it on principle. "Why?"

"Because you're the size of a twelve-year-old with the balls of a twenty-year-old bloke."

Uh oh. Wait for it …

Her eyes flashed and she … burst out laughing?

Oh, come on.

But her laughter seemed to help Tom get over himself, and he rejoined us with much more human-colored skin tone.

I pointed to him. "You and I are going to need to work on your acrophobia. You …" I pointed to Adam, "just need to learn to see the problem from all sides before you make your first move."

"Hey, we made it, didn't we?"

"How many sides does a box have?"

The look he shot me was somewhere between confusion and annoyance. I knew Adam hated it when I turned on my teacher voice, but without fail, he provoked it every time we ran. "I don't know, four?"

"Six. There's a top and a bottom too. Sometimes the best way to get somewhere is working from the top down."

Adam's eyes danced teasingly. "So, if I think about the problem as if I were seducing it, you know, working top to bottom, I'll have better luck?"

"That requires you to know what you're doing, and I'd never assume something like that."

Olivia and Tom busted up, but Adam smirked. "You're right. You should never assume. Always find these things out first hand, that's what I say."

"Well, your hand would know all about that, now wouldn't it?"

Olivia interrupted what was about to become a little nasty, based on the size of the breath Adam took to launch his attack. "Guys, if we want to do some more vertical stuff, I know a place."

Tom instantly backed away. "Okay, seriously? I'm out. Saira, I'll take height lessons later, after major fortification of food, sleep and maybe a little testicular growth. Any chance you can unlock the hall door with the key you magically procured?"

I laughed and led him down the hall. "Come on. I'll teach you the locked-door thing as a reward for a day of heights." We walked down the hall toward the locked main door, and Tom sighed dramatically. "Oh joy, I can't wait."

I showed Tom how to get out of the hall and locked the door behind him, then came back to find Olivia and Adam laughing about something Connor had been moaning about as he convalesced.

"Okay, tell me about vertical places," I prodded Olivia.

"You guys have been to the attics, right?"

Adam and I looked at each other blankly. The attics? Olivia stared at us both. "Are you kidding? The attics in this place are huge! All the big manor houses were built with a lot of little box rooms for luggage and holiday storage."

We must have still looked blank because Olivia's eyes were going back and forth between us with growing astonishment. "You really haven't explored the attics? Wow, you guys don't know what you're missing. There are things that have been up there so long people forgot they forgot about it."

"I know they keep old furniture in the cellar." Even as I said it, I bit my tongue. Hard. I don't think either of them even thought twice about why I'd know something like that, but I couldn't believe how close I'd come to giving a clue about Archer's hideaway.

"Yeah, but these things are *personal*. Like clothes, hats, shoes, books, jewelry … it feels like you can figure out a person's whole life by what they've left behind in the attics."

"Even here? I mean, this is a school, not a manor house."

"Yes, but it was built in the 1500s. That's a whole lot of students who have come through and left things behind."

A light bulb in my brain lit up my eyes. "*That's* what else happened in 1554!" I pictured the date above the school entrance in my mind. "St. Brigid's opened."

"Yeah? So?" Adam and Olivia looked confused.

I shrugged. "Just something my mom was teaching in her history class. It's no big deal."

Olivia grinned at us. "So, do you want to go?"

"Yeah, of course. But what's the vertical part of it?"

"Oh, the doors are always locked. So the only way into the west attic is from the top of the south tower."

"I'm in!"

"Me too." Adam swept his arm out like a gallant knight. "Lead the way, small person."

I rolled my eyes and braced for fireworks again, but Olivia just giggled. Seriously? Was Adam really that charming? He obviously didn't get slapped nearly enough for the trouble he stirred up.

"Let's go climbing."

THE ATTICS

Olivia's route took us up the outside of the tower, which was totally climbable with big, fitted stones and weather-worn mortar for handholds. Then down to an attic fire escape ledge just behind the tower. The window was unlatched, and Olivia's practiced fingers slipped the catchment pane up.

Once we were all inside, Olivia closed the window behind us, then shrugged at the question on my face. "It's England. It rains."

The room we entered was smallish, and the light was dim from the fading daylight coming in through dirty windows. "Are we going to have to leave the same way we came in?" Adam said what I'd been thinking. It's not generally a good idea to go climbing around the outsides of tall buildings in the dark.

Olivia nodded. "I found a laundry chute, but I haven't had the guts to try it."

"Right. Then we're out of here in fifteen, otherwise we get caught in the dark." I pulled my mini Maglite out of my back pocket and flicked it on. The warm yellow glow was comforting in all the gray light of the room.

"The good rooms are this way." Olivia led us down the silent hall and across to an unlocked door. "The relics in here look kind of Victorian."

There were big wardrobes lining the walls, and I opened one to reveal some fairly musty-smelling day dresses. I wrinkled my nose. "Lots of wool in here. Smells like a wet dog."

Olivia was already pawing through the clothes packed away in the wardrobes. She pulled out something pale and held it up under her chin. The dress was fairly simple, but had really pretty embroidery all around the bodice that looked like flowering vines. "What do you think?"

"It's gorgeous. You would have fit right in wearing that."

Adam shot me a look over Olivia's head. I forgot that she wasn't officially clued in on my time traveling abilities, because even though she probably was a Pixie in real life, and her family had been working for my ancestors forever, it wasn't something we'd ever talked about. So, I took a deep breath and a calculated shot.

"These would have been really good to know about when I went back to 1888." I held up a man's frock coat. There was a plain white shirt hung beneath it, and because I'm 5'10" tall, it looked like it would fit me. Olivia regarded it critically for a long moment, but said nothing. It was Adam who looked a little shocked.

"You went back dressed as a man?"

"Well, yeah. Women couldn't go anywhere alone then. And besides, I'm too tall for their dresses." The image of the stunning midnight blue brocade gown that Archer had made for me flashed through my brain, and it was one of those memories wrapped up in guilt and tied with a pain bow. I firmly shoved it away and watched Olivia for her reaction.

"I think it's too early. Like, a lot too early. I think this jacket would have worked better for 1888." She held up a dark grey wool jacket that looked much less formal than the one I was holding. "The other one might have gotten you arrested for stealing wardrobe from a rich old man."

I laughed out loud. "So you knew?"

"That you're a Clocker?" She looked at Adam. "And you're a Seer? And Connor's a Shifter. Yes, I knew."

"When? I mean, when I first got here you talked about 'weird nicknames' that certain kids had for each other, and I just figured … you know."

Olivia hung the man's coat back in the wardrobe and continued searching the dresses for things her size. "I've always

53

known about blood magic. I just didn't know exactly who was what until I asked my mum at Christmas."

"Blood magic?" Adam's look was drawn with a skeptic pen. "The Descendants don't do magic."

"I didn't say you did." Olivia fixed Adam with one of her famous glares, and I grinned. Finally.

"Then what's blood magic?" Adam didn't seem affected by the glare.

"Inherited traits that science hasn't fully explained yet."

Adam was about to protest but I cut him off. "I like it. Do Pixies have it too?"

"A little. Ours is more in tune with nature I guess."

Adam looked back, and forth between us with growing astonishment. "You're not just saying 'Pixie' because she's small, are you?"

The glare was back and Olivia turned its full force on the Seer. "My family is descended from the Picts. We've always been small and smart and very capable, not to mention fierce and dangerous when we're crossed."

"And apparently bipolar." Adam glared back at Olivia just as fiercely, and I thought flames were going to shoot out of her eyes. Until she smiled.

"Maybe a little of that too."

I tried very hard not to roll my eyes. I hate it when words fail me and eye-rolling is the last option, so I took a deep breath instead. "Guys, as fearsome and entertaining as you both are, we're running out of daylight."

"What? Shopping for vintage clothes isn't your thing?"

"Not even a little bit." Okay, I lied. I was definitely more than a little bit drawn to the beautiful fabrics and gorgeous colors of the clothes, but for a girl who lives in combat boots and runs with a pack of guys, I had an image to uphold. I think I'd do damage if I ever showed up in a dress around them. "Are there any books or art or anything else not-clothes?"

"I saw some stuff covered in sheets a couple rooms down."

We shut the wardrobe doors and slunk down the hall. I tried a door at random. The handle turned and I peeked inside. More wardrobes. I pulled it shut and followed Olivia and Adam into a room near the end of the hall. At first I thought it was empty, but then I realized there were sheets draped over something against one wall. I lifted a sheet and shone my Maglite down on a stack of paintings propped on the floor, their ornate frames gleaming dully in the yellow light. The first couple were just random landscapes painted by a mediocre artist with no sense of scale. The last painting was the biggest and best of the lot. In fact, it was so much better than the ones in front of it that I must have gasped, because Adam came over and crouched next to me to look.

"That's St. Brigid's." He was close, and I could smell the clean combo of sweat and soap that came off his skin. It was unsettling.

"It's Doran's work."

"Who's Doran?"

"Some long lost cousin or something. He randomly drops in and hands out nuggets of wisdom like the frickin' candyman."

"Drops in? Like present tense?"

"Yeah."

Adam studied the painting more closely. "This was painted a long time ago."

Olivia joined us, crouching down in front of the St. Brigid's painting. "How do you know?"

"Well, first of all, there's no tree." Adam pointed to a spot on the canvas I knew well. It was a blank spot where the very tall tree I'd climbed to get in the second story of St. Brigid's my first night at school should have been. It was the kind of very tall tree that took several hundred years to grow.

Olivia shrugged. "So maybe he went back a couple hundred years to paint it."

I shook my head. "Not just a couple hundred. This is a Renaissance style painting, same as the one he did of the Immortals that hangs at Elian Manor."

55

"How do you know it's Doran's?" Adam sounded skeptical. I stood to lift it out of its stack.

"Help me. It's heavy." The ornate frame was massive, carved wood, and painted with gold leaf and Adam had to hold it by himself so I could push the painting out. I showed them the signature on the edge of the stretched canvas, just where Doran had signed the Immortals. "See? Doran."

"And you've met him." Adam's tone was disbelieving.

"Yup."

We propped the painting back up against the wall, and Adam looked at me. Oddly. "The Renaissance was, like, five hundred years ago."

"More or less."

"Is this guy from then, or does he just randomly pop around in history, painting landscapes whenever the mood strikes?"

I rubbed my eyes tiredly. "I don't know. I barely know him. Like I said, he's dropped in on me a couple of times and randomly dispensed little wisdom tidbits about being a Clocker. I'm usually mad at him for not telling me enough, and I'm lucky to get in two or three questions before he Clocks out again."

"Sounds like a charmer."

"You have no idea."

I studied the painting more closely. Something was odd about the stones in one of the towers, but I couldn't see it until I shined the Maglite directly on it. And then I knew. "Crap."

"What?" Adam tried to see what I was staring at.

"Part of a spiral. See here, where the bricks make a pattern?" I pointed to it, careful not to touch the canvas. I was afraid the painting was a portal, just like the London Bridge painting in the Clocker Tower.

"It's not complete. It doesn't look like the one in your tower."

He was right, it was the outside edge of one spiral, like the other four were around the corner of the tower. "But it is the Clocker Tower, isn't it?" I touched the painted spiral tentatively, waiting for the tingle that I got when I hit a live portal. I held my

56

breath and pushed my finger around the first turn. Nothing. I traced all the lines of the spiral with growing confidence. Still nothing. "Whew. It isn't live."

"So why's it there?" Adam studied my face.

I cringed. "I don't suppose there were any Renaissance clothes in those wardrobes, were there?"

Adam looked sternly at me. "Just because there's a spiral doesn't mean you have to go."

I sighed. "Try telling that to Doran."

"Guys, we should probably head out before it gets dark." Olivia was looking out the window at the graying light. She was right, and I was actually relieved. I didn't really want to think about why there was a spiral painted in a five hundred-year-old landscape of the school, and I had the horrible feeling I was going to find out. Adam helped me to my feet, and we covered the stack of paintings with the sheet again and closed the door behind us.

I was glad it hadn't rained in the time we were exploring the attics, because stones and roof tiles get slick when they're wet. But all three of us were competent climbers, and even with my injured shoulder we made it back down to the second floor in less than ten minutes. Olivia took off to check on Connor before dinner, and I ditched Adam to go to the kitchen garden and help Mrs. Taylor. I'd gotten pretty good at pretending Adam didn't put me on edge, but I didn't like noticing things like the scent of his skin. And it was getting harder to ignore the longer Archer was gone.

I was in the walled garden picking mint and thyme for dinner when my mom slipped inside and closed the door behind her. I smiled at her expression of total exhaustion.

"Hiding out?"

She pushed her hair back from her face and sighed. "I have immense respect for teachers who know what they're doing. I feel like I'm just winging it most of the time, and a pack of wild twelve-year-olds will see my weakness and tear me to shreds."

I laughed. "They love listening to you, and you're just fishing for compliments."

She smiled. "You're a very good daughter when you're not stealing my art supplies. What's Mrs. Taylor making in the kitchen tonight?"

"I think she's doing shepherd's pie and minty peas."

"Mmm. Here, let me help." Working next to her in the garden reminded me of times when things weren't so complicated, when the only thing that could suck was her disappearing, and then moving us every couple of years. Maybe we had stopped changing residences now that my Clocker heritage was out in the open, but our relationship was still finding its footing, and navigating the mother/daughter thing was far from simple.

"Mom, when you had to go, you know, *back* all those times, why'd you leave me?"

She closed her eyes like she'd been waiting for the question. And dreading it.

"I shouldn't have. No matter how responsible and capable you were when you were twelve, I never should have left like I did."

"I understand why you had to go, I guess I just wonder why I was alone."

She stared at me. "Saira, you weren't alone when you were twelve. Our neighbor, Mrs. Shack, she took you in."

Now it was my turn to stare. "No, she didn't. She came by and dropped food off for me, but I was on my own."

A choked sound came from my mom and her face was pale. "Saira ..."

"You didn't know? How could you not know that, Mom?"

"You never said ..." She took a breath to calm herself. There were tears in her eyes. "I never asked, did I?"

I shook my head, and she wrapped her arms around me. Something broke loose in my chest. Knowing that she hadn't intended to leave me alone mattered somehow. I took a deep breath, and realized I could do this.

"I want to go to London to find Archer."

"No." She pulled back to look at me, and my eyes narrowed at her abrupt answer.

"I'm almost eighteen. I'm not really asking your permission."

She sighed, and I could feel her try to soften the edges "Sometimes a little space isn't a terrible thing."

"Sure. When it's not messed up by a fight."

"I think your relationship is complicated by many things, Saira. Time apart can sometimes bring perspective. And with everything going on in Family politics, I don't want you to leave St. Brigid's. You're safe here."

Except from Weres and little Monger bullies. I hadn't lost my bitterness, because that incident had exposed more than just my own weakness. There was a fault line in my relationship with Archer that got put into perspective too, and time apart was the last thing it needed. I'd been doing way too much of that already. My silence stretched to fill the space, and she put her arms around me, apparently deciding I'd given in.

"I wish I could dump the full contents of my experience into your head so you didn't have to learn your own lessons."

I crushed some mint leaves between my fingers, letting the minty smell ground me. My mom was lost in her own thoughts though, and couldn't read the turmoil in my heart.

"But that wouldn't work either. You should never have to feel my pain of losing the love of my life."

"But if I had your experiences, I'd have actually known my father."

Her voice had the weight of the world behind it. "And then he'd be your lost love too."

LONDON

About a month before the thing with the Were in the woods, Archer had shown me something he found on a brick wall just inside his part of the school cellar. Behind a bookcase was a piece of plaster that must have covered the entire wall at one time. Most of it was gone now, but the piece Archer found had part of a Clocker spiral carved into it.

It was the first spiral we'd found that was actually part of the building, but because most of it was missing it couldn't be used as a portal. He told me I could repair it, but I hadn't been anxious to then. The spiral was inside his lair. If someone besides me ever Clocked into his space while he was in it, he'd be totally vulnerable.

Since Archer had gone, the instinct to finish that spiral burned in me. It was something to connect me to him. A way I could find him from anywhere.

I had decided to finish the old plaster spiral in white chalk, which would show up well on the exposed brick. The familiar tingling began almost as soon as the first spiral laid down. I took extra care with the five spiral design, giving special attention to symmetry and adding just a little flair. I wanted it to be beautiful, and I also wanted Archer to notice it.

It had been tough to feel completely confident in my own strength standing next to a man like him. A man, not a boy. Not even a twenty-three year old man like he looked, but one who had lived almost a hundred and fifty years. I was putting my time travel skill in plain sight for him to see I wasn't just a kid who needed his protection.

But I also knew that finishing the spiral in Archer's lair was a sign of ultimate trust. He had given me total access to him, even when it meant making himself vulnerable.

The buzzing started, and I pictured the cellar of the War Museum that used to be Bedlam, but I made sure to use specific details from modern times so I didn't accidentally send myself backwards again, a charming thought that was lost in the pulling and stretching feeling that consumed my body as I Clocked.

I had a moment of panic when I landed because the room was much brighter than either the War Museum or the Bedlam cellar had ever been. But then I realized there were electric work lights strung across the ceiling, and they were blazing. So at least I hadn't gone back to Victorian times.

A noise startled me, and I spun around to face whatever was coming. Bishop Cleary's expression was equally shocked at the sight of me, and then his face split into a smile and he rushed forward to sweep me into a big hug. "It's so good to see you, Saira."

I grinned into his soft sweater. I had felt immediately comfortable with the jeans-wearing, silver-maned bishop, and his was the hug of a favorite uncle. He held me at arm's length and studied me. "You look fit and strong. Archer said you've been training the young men in Parkour?"

I grimaced slightly, and Bishop Cleary smiled. "A source of discord between you? It's not as discordant as it may seem, Saira. For all of his Victorian upbringing he's coming round to the realities of loving a modern young woman of remarkable strength and courage … with only a little kicking and screaming."

I kissed him on the cheek. "Thank you."

He beamed and gave me another squeeze before leading me toward the small records storage room in the back of the cellar. "Come and see what we've been up to."

The storage room had been transformed into an office, with a big work table at one end and files stacked on every available

61

surface. "I've managed to secure permission from the War Museum to work here, so at least I'm not getting attacked by my guilty conscience every time we use the tunnel."

"What have you told them you're doing?"

"A version of the truth. The genealogy was stolen while in my care, and the history of its commissioning might give us a clue to its importance. The hunt for the book itself has taken your friend to every building Seth Walters is associated with, but so far, there's been nothing. And since I'm staying out of the breaking and entering business, I've spearheaded the effort to locate Bishop Wilder in history."

"Found anything?"

A deep, quiet voice spoke from behind me. "Finding nothing is perhaps more telling."

I spun to face Archer as he stood in the open doorway. All my reserve and cool went straight out the window at the sight of his face, with a gentle mouth and slightly wary eyes. My brain pretty much lost control of my body as I flung myself at him and jumped into his arms. It was a good thing his reflexes were so quick, because I would have taken anyone else out. But Archer held me tightly as I locked my legs around him and kissed him with the force of my whole body.

"Ahem, right, well, I'll leave you to it then." Bishop Cleary sounded like he was smiling through all his embarrassed Britishness as he slipped past us and out of the room.

Archer made a low growling sound deep in his chest when we finally came up for air. "You are killing me."

I smiled against his mouth. "You've said that before."

He pulled back and looked in my eyes. "When did I say that?"

Too late to take back, and frankly, I was sick of trying to keep stories and facts straight. "I've gone back to see you."

There was no expression on his face. "Indeed."

I took a deep breath. In for a penny, in for a pound. "I missed you, and … I wasn't confident enough to come here first."

The strong muscles of his jaw relaxed and his eyes softened. "You? Lacking confidence? I find that hard to believe." He smiled at my wince. "I know you went back. I remember."

That's right. The memory thing. When I went back and changed something, it was like the memory for it got unlocked. "Not to mention the fact that you can read my honesty."

"You're a deep, lovely blue with not a bit of green in sight."

"Really? Not even the blue-green of omission?"

He smiled. "Why, are you planning to withhold something from me?"

I raised an eyebrow. I tried for slightly seductive, but I'm pretty sure I just sounded like I had a cold. "Not anymore."

His eyes widened perceptibly, and I burst out laughing. "I think you're safe from me, Archer. I won't compromise your honor without your permission, I promise."

There was a purr in his voice. "I'm not certain I intend to let you keep that promise."

I gasped at the multitude of meanings behind his words.

Archer finally set me down gently so my feet were back on the floor. "I missed you."

I took a deep breath. No withholding. "I thought if I could hold a piece of myself back it wouldn't hurt so much if you left." His arms tightened around me at my words. "But instead I just drove you away."

"You didn't drive me away, Saira. And you're here now."

Maybe it was just the tip of the iceberg, but it was a start. And being back in Archer's arms made all the noise in my head drop down to a whisper. I melted into him for a long time before I finally spoke again.

"Tell me about what you've been doing. You haven't found anything?"

He kept my hand in his and led me over to the table. A map of London and outlying areas was stuck with several pins. "These are the buildings owned by Rothchild or controlled by Walters. I've managed to bypass security in all but four of them. So far, I've found nothing of the book."

Then he showed me a notebook full of names. "Cleary's been digging through every publication from every university, hospital, tax assessor, voting registrar, church, or chapel in England from the years 1888 to 1900. And though Bishop Wilder is frequently mentioned until November 9th, 1888 in several publications across quite a few disciplines, there is absolutely no further mention of him from that date forward."

I looked at the notebook for a long time. "How far back do the records go?"

Archer eyed me carefully. "You believe the Lady Elizabeth and Ringo were a true vision?"

"I think the Lady Elizabeth might be Elizabeth Tudor, before she became queen."

An eyebrow raised. "That's hundreds of years before Bishop Wilder was born."

I walked out into the main cellar of the War Museum, near the spot where the old Bedlam wing had collapsed. Bishop Cleary was sorting through boxes out there, and I waved him over as I found the remains of the original spiral portal. I ran my hand lightly over the grooves. "Mr. Shaw believes Wilder drained my mother's blood so he could Clock. And I think he Clocked back to 1554."

Bishop Cleary made a noise of amazement in his throat and stepped forward to touch the spiral. I turned to face Archer. "Wilder had a paper signed by 'the traitor' that he threatened to show the Lady Elizabeth's sister, 'the queen.' Think about it, Queen Mary had Elizabeth imprisoned in the Tower of London after the Wyatt Rebellion, and she was there when Thomas Wyatt was beheaded for treason on April 11th, 1554. What if he's the traitor and Wilder has somehow forced a confession from him?"

Archer was silent a long time, his gaze faraway until he finally spoke. "Would you believe I've never been to the Tower of London?"

"If that room is in the Tower, we could almost prove it was March or early April of 1554. Elizabeth Tudor was a prisoner there for only two months, and everything else fits."

Archer winced. "Sadly, the Tower doesn't keep nighttime hours, and it is, after all, meant to be a fortress. Not so easy to break into."

"I might be able to help." Bishop Cleary spoke behind us, I'd almost forgotten he was there. "An old friend of mine works with historical documents at the Tower. I can make a call."

I grinned. "That would be awesome."

He laughed and headed toward the document room.

When we were alone again I grabbed another quick kiss from Archer. I had tried so hard to pretend I hadn't missed him the past week, and I clearly sucked at self-delusion. He held my face in his hands. "I'm glad you're here."

"Everyone wonders where you are." Archer's expression darkened and I quickly continued. "Not all bad though. Mr. Shaw is hoping you'll give him some blood. He's trying to isolate the porphyria mutation to see if it really does draw the promoted Descendant gene into itself."

A smirk. Archer and Mr. Shaw had the interesting relationship of alpha males who respect each other's skills. "Tell him I'll come in when I'm back at St. Brigid's."

"You *are* coming back?" I tried to sound casual, but knew I'd failed miserably by the stricken look on Archer's face.

"Of course I am. How could you even imagine I wouldn't?"

"I didn't want to assume."

He pulled me into his body and held me tightly. "Assume."

I tried not to show how relieved I was, but I'm pretty sure the way my knees gave way was a big clue.

"Okay." My voice came out in a whisper, and Archer kissed me again, very gently.

Bishop Cleary cleared his throat noisily as he came back into the main room. "So, I talked to Professor Singh's secretary. He's up at the Tower tonight for a gala. Some very stuffy historians apparently cut loose once a year, and I managed to charm Indira into putting your names at the gate." He winked. "I owe her dinner as a thank you."

65

I kissed the bishop on one cheek. "You're awesome. And I'll be your excuse for a date any time."

He opened his mouth to protest and then shut it again with a laugh. "Lying's a sin, so I'm just going to say hurry up. The event started an hour ago." He looked me up and down. "I don't suppose you have a cocktail dress up your sleeve, do you?"

Archer smiled and grabbed my hand. "I'm sure we'll figure something out."

My Vampire knew clothes. And places to shop that stayed open for his hours. But then again money wasn't an issue, and he insisted I had to have the gorgeous black, long-sleeved dress that clasped behind the neck and was otherwise completely backless. I was a little nervous about how far the cut-out dipped until I felt Archer's hand on the bare skin of my low back. Somehow everything was right when he was touching me. Heels weren't an option if I wanted to explore the Tower, but the salesgirl pulled out a pair of gladiator sandals that totally worked with the dress. Although, the way I felt in it, even fuzzy bunny slippers would have been perfect. I wrapped my hair up into a low twist, and added some eyeliner and mascara. The person who looked back at me from the mirror was glamorous and intriguing instead of my usual uncomplicated and casual. For once I actually felt old enough to be Archer's date.

"You are exquisite." Archer's eyes drank me in.

"You're not so bad yourself." I couldn't manage a casual tone. I was too giddy.

Archer, of course, looked effortlessly handsome in a cashmere sport coat, black sweater, and slacks, which he had with him at the bishop's. Of course he did.

A taxi dropped us in front of the Tower of London and I looked up in awe. The whole complex was lit with low floods that slashed light up the stone walls, and the unmistakable sounds of a party carried on the night air.

As promised, our first names had been left at the front gate, but Bishop Cleary had given us both his last name just in case anyone was looking for a Devereux or an Elian. Archer's hand was at my low back as we were escorted in to the White Tower, and I felt like his skin was fused to mine. Regardless of our purpose there, we were walking into a party, and it seemed like a date. Our first one, actually. In public, where people could see us together. A real couple. I liked the feeling.

The room was full of men in suits and women in short dresses. Most of them were probably in their thirties, but there were a couple of younger people and some much older ones too. Archer asked someone where we could find Professor Singh from the maps department, and we were directed to a very distinguished-looking, white-haired man. Archer hesitated just a fraction of a second.

"What's wrong?" I whispered in Archer's ear when Professor Singh noticed us.

The color seemed to drain from the older man's face when he saw Archer. "Devereux? Is that you?"

Archer's hand tensed at my back and I could feel his indecision. But then the professor spoke again, as if to himself. "No, it couldn't be. Don't be ridiculous."

I was about to say something, but Archer held out his hand with a smile. "You must have known my grandfather, Archer Devereux. I'm told I look very like him when he was young."

The relief on Professor Singh's face when he shook Archer's hand was palpable. His expression seemed to say 'thank God I'm not crazy,' and I felt my heart re-start in my chest. I held my hand out with a big smile. "Hi, Professor Singh. I'm Saira. Bishop Cleary called Indira so we could meet you tonight." My voice seemed to snap the professor out of his daze, but his eyes never left Archer. I tried again. "I hope it's not too big an intrusion if we ask you some questions about Elizabeth Tudor's time in the Tower."

He finally seemed to realize I was the one speaking. "I'm so sorry." Then his eyes went back to Archer. "I knew your grandfather during the war. We worked at Bletchley Park together

67

and became great friends. I always wondered what happened to him."

Archer smiled, and I felt his hand relax at my back. "Well, he found the love of his life, and I suppose the rest is history." Archer wasn't looking at me directly, but I knew, and then couldn't wipe my smile off. Archer's fingers caressed the small of my back as he continued. "My grandfather has spoken very fondly of you, and he was honored to have been your friend."

"Ah, right. Capital, capital. It was very mutual. Well, my dear, I'd be delighted to answer any questions you may have. In fact, if you like, I can show you some documents pertaining to Elizabeth's time here as a prisoner."

Archer seemed amused at Professor Singh's enthusiasm for his subject as we walked to his office within the Tower complex. He pointed to a spot that used to be called the Queen's Garden, and showed us the piece of foundation from the nearby Royal Residence, which had already fallen into disrepair by the end of Elizabeth's reign. Most historians believed Elizabeth Tudor had been imprisoned by her sister, Queen Mary I, in the Bell Tower, but he was one of the few who thought that was 'poppycock.' I bit my lip to hold back that laughter, and Archer tickled my side to tease me with it. A quick jab to Archer's ribs to get myself back under control, and Professor Singh was in full swing on his theory.

"Queen Mary had never denounced Elizabeth's relationship to her – they were half-sisters and daughters of Henry VIII - despite imprisoning her for conspiracy to commit treason. Elizabeth was a king's daughter, and would have been afforded every privilege of one, except freedom, of course. The idea that she was held in a tower with only one upper and one lower room is ludicrous. Records show she had at least four of her ladies with her, and there wouldn't have been enough room in the Bell Tower cells for that many people."

"Can we visit the Bell Tower?"

The Professor shook his head. "The last time it was open to the public was several years ago. The only access in is through the

68

Queen's House, which is what the Lord Lieutenant's private lodgings are called. At the time of Elizabeth's imprisonment, however, there was no 'Queen's House.' The Royal Residence, now demolished, housed the queen's *apartments*, which Henry VIII had renovated for Elizabeth's mother, Anne Boleyn. The confusion over the names is likely the reason for the modern confusion over where the Lady Elizabeth was held prisoner."

In his office, Professor Singh gave us a copy of a map of the Tower from the late 1500s which showed the demolished buildings. He also let us see the blueprint of the Bell Tower rooms, and laughed at my question about toilet facilities for prisoners. He explained that each of the prison rooms in the Tower complex would have had a privy or garderobe, depending on whether they were on the ground or upper floors.

The professor had a replica of the Armada Portrait of Queen Elizabeth hanging above his desk. It was painted after she'd been queen for a long time, and I'd seen one of the original versions in the National Portrait Gallery of London during Christmas break.

"My mom told me the story of how Elizabeth got the six-strand black pearls that she's wearing in that portrait, but not what happened to them. Do they still exist?"

Professor Singh looked up at the portrait lovingly. "It's yet another mystery of Elizabeth's reign. Presumably they were broken up and sold by Cromwell in 1649, but we've found no record of them, and they're not in the current queen's jewel collection. Do you see the crown on the table behind her?"

The version in the National Portrait Gallery was cut down on the sides and didn't have the same detail as his print did, so I studied the jeweled crown carefully.

"I've seen the crown jewels, but that isn't one of them."

Professor Singh nodded. "Again, Cromwell. Historians and jewelers recently recreated the Tudor Crown. I saw it on display at Hampton Court."

"The pearls are prettier."

He smiled. "Mary Stuart, also known as Mary, Queen of Scots, was a great collector of jewels. It was something she had in common with her cousin, Queen Elizabeth. However, Mary Stuart never actually agreed to sell them to Elizabeth. Jealousy, perhaps, or competitiveness. But the agents from Scotland were more interested in buying England's goodwill than humoring their own monarch. And so Elizabeth got the black pearls and eventually, Mary, Queen of Scots got the scaffold."

When we finally left the professor's office my head felt crammed full of Elizabethan Tower trivia, and I think I surprised him with my quick hug. "You're an excellent teacher."

His eyes were bright and he smiled at me. "Well, you're a lovely student, Saira. I'd be very happy if my interns were half as interested as you obviously are."

Archer clasped Professor Singh's hand warmly in both of his. "It was a pleasure seeing you tonight, and your help has been invaluable."

Professor Singh searched Archer's eyes as we said goodbye, and I heard him mutter to himself. "Remarkable, really. So much like my old friend."

Archer held my hand as we walked away, and from his grip I could tell he'd been affected by our time with the old man.

"You knew him when he was young?" I kept my voice quiet.

"Ravindra Singh is one of the best men I ever worked with." I felt his breath catch just before he squared his shoulders and led me around a corner. He kissed me quickly and looked into my eyes. I waited for him to say something about being immortal, about watching people he loved get old and die, about how much it sucked that I would get old someday too, but he just smiled. "Let's go explore."

It was after-hours and unsanctioned, and it was awesome. We dodged Yeoman Warders, the guys who had been guarding the Tower of London since the beginning of the Tudor dynasty, and took ourselves on a secret tour of the oldest parts of the complex.

The Yeoman Warders seemed to concentrate their guarding efforts on the Jewel House and the White Tower, where a sort of mini-museum had been set up with Tower artifacts. We concentrated on everything not those. We also kept our distance from the Queen's House, since the current Lord Lieutenant still lived there.

The battlements were fair game though, and we played stealth tag across them between towers. The wall was high enough to run unseen for the most part, though the Bell Tower was a dead-end so we avoided it. Salt Tower was easy to get to, but Beauchamp Tower took a little effort. The easiest climb was near the barracks, which was dangerous because it's where the on-duty Yeoman Warders lived, but the shadows there were great. Staircases were too easy, and therefore usually shunned, but without my boots I didn't have a choice.

We were able to stay out of the wide-open spaces near the White Tower, and we concentrated a lot of our search on the ground floor and cellar chambers, looking for something with a privy or a cistern that matched Archer's vision of Ringo's torture. But with every new discovery, finding the room took a back seat to just exploring. My favorite thing was the graffiti. It was everywhere, mostly done by Tudor-era prisoners. Robert Dudley's work was intricate and gorgeous, and I could imagine him chipping away at that wall every day for the year he was in the Beauchamp Tower cell.

We found prison cells and storage rooms, underground passages connecting towers, and small staircases that led nowhere. I wished the Royal Residence hadn't been torn down. The few pieces of foundation that were left told us very little about the layout of the place, and we could only guess where the queen's apartments had been. Most of the upper floors had evidence of garderobes, which were seats with a hole in them for the waste to fall in the moat outside the Tower. If I thought the Thames stank in 1888, I couldn't imagine what it must have smelled like with all that raw sewage flowing in.

Nothing we found was exactly what we remembered from Archer's vision, but the architecture seemed close enough to guess it was the Tower. And the blueprints from the Bell Tower showed a room tantalizingly similar to the shape of the room we remembered.

We had explored as much as we could without breaking into locked doors, and I was starting to get cold. Archer saw me shiver and wrapped his soft jacket around my shoulders. The way out was through the gate at the Bloody Tower, and because the place was closed for the night, Archer boosted me over the fence at the entrance so I wouldn't tear my dress. When we were finally snuggled into the back seat of a taxi on our way back to the War Museum, I leaned my head into Archer's chest and sighed. "This is the best night I've ever had."

I could hear the smile in his voice. "So, dungeons and secret passages in a sexy dress is your thing?"

"My combats are the only thing that could have made it better."

He laughed and pulled me close. "The next dress you wear will go with combat boots then."

I gazed up at his smiling face with a blissed-out look on mine. "Thanks."

He kissed me softly on the lips, then pulled me back in to snuggle against his chest.

Playing With Fire

Ava was waiting for me when I swung by our room the next morning for a change of clothes.

"Mr. Shaw came looking for you last night."

Oh, crap. Of course he did.

"He's more worried than mad though, so don't sabotage this. Science is going to be fun today."

"And you know this because you talked to him?"

Ava rolled her eyes. "Why would I go to the bother of a conversation with someone in such a bad mood?"

"Awesome."

I hung up my new black dress and caught the look in Ava's eye. I didn't say anything, just dug out black jeans and laced my combat boots over the top. A white wife-beater tank with a black v-neck sweater and my long hair tied back in a messy bun, and I was almost ready to face Shaw. Almost. I grabbed Archer's black leather sport bike coat and threw that on over the top, kind of like armor. Yeah, it was going to be one of those days.

Ava looked meaningfully at the dress, then jumped off the bed and left the room with me. "So, I'm guessing you spent the night in London?"

Not much got by the next-in-line to head the Seer Family. I nodded, swerving to avoid a group of girls coming out of the bathroom. "My mom tried to tell me not to go."

"So of course you went."

"Of course." I smirked. I'd only known Ava for a few months, but she already got me better than almost anyone, except my mom, and maybe Archer.

"I told you Archer didn't leave you."

That was just semantics, but I didn't want to get into a debate with Ava. "We made up. And had kind of a spectacular date." I tried to kill the smile that threatened to give me away. Couldn't do it.

"Good. You guys deserve to have fun. And just so you know, it was really hard for him to be away." I couldn't tell if that was just friendship talking, or if her Seer sense had kicked in, but I was grateful. Ava grabbed my hand and stopped me before we headed down the big stone staircase to the classroom level of St. Brigid's.

"I Saw the book last night."

"What book?" My heart started pounding, and I knew what she was going to say before she said it.

"The genealogy. It's in a warehouse, somewhere in London I think. Raven's uncle was reading it." She closed her eyes and tried to give me something else, but her voice came out in a regretful sigh. "That's all I know." As much as I wanted to pump her for more information, I knew it was pointless. They Saw what they Saw, and that was it.

"Hey Elian, are we running before survival class?" Connor was walking with Olivia, and despite the interruption, I was glad to see him looking back to normal.

"Depends how much I get yelled at by Shaw."

"You mean, he yells, we run?"

"Exactly."

"Sorry to say, but here's hoping you get torn a new one."

Olivia punched Connor in the arm playfully. "Just for that, you can sit on your own at lunch."

"Oh, come on, Liv. You know I'm just kidding."

I sneered at him, "If we do run, you'll need four legs to keep up with me today, Edwards. Oh that's right, you've been holding back because you're English, and it's not sporting to run down a girl. Well, this girl's been kicking your butt."

Connor's eyes narrowed a little as Olivia laughed and dragged him away. *Good, he'd need that edge if he was going to beat me at tree-running.*

Some of the tension seeped out from under my armor just before we rounded the corner toward Mr. Shaw's classroom.

Until I saw the Bear.

Mr. Shaw was guarding the door, making kids sidestep furtively past him into the classroom. He looked growly and unkempt, like a mosquito had tormented him all night, or maybe a Clocker had worried her mother when she spent all night in London with her boyfriend. I plastered on a smile and approached with caution.

"Good morning, Mr. Shaw."

His voice rumbled in his throat. "Miss Elian. You've graced us with your presence." It wasn't a question, more like an accusation.

I bristled. When had I ever missed one of his classes? Sometimes they were the only thing worth sticking around for. His eyes glinted, and I could see he was spoiling for a fight, so I took a breath and brightened up the smile. "No place I'd rather be than in a classroom with you."

My tone had been completely respectful, so he could only hiss cartoon steam from his ears as he closed the door behind us and took his place at the head of the class.

"We've entered the astrological sign of Aries, who, apart from being the god of war in Greek mythology, is also symbolized by fire."

A girl next to me whispered under her breath, "Astrology? Is he kidding?"

I shook my head. I already knew where he was going with this and excitement had started somewhere around my toes. "Fire," I whispered back.

"Fire," Mr. Shaw echoed, "is the substance of life. It exists in only the most extraordinary circumstances in nature, and yet

75

without it, humans would be little more than primates." He looked directly at me, a smirk tugging at the corners of his mouth. "I'm sorry to disappoint you, Miss Elian, but you will not be in a classroom with me today."

A sick feeling swept through me. Was I seriously about to get kicked out of class?

"Because we will be working outside as we attempt various ways, physical and chemical, to create fire."

The relief I felt must have showed on my face because it seemed to put Mr. Shaw in a better mood. "To the gardens. There are tables set up under the shade structure, and you'll be working in pairs, so partner up."

Chairs were pushed back and we headed for the door. I had just caught Ava's eye for the 'you, me, partner' nod when Mr. Shaw passed me. "Miss Elian, you're with me."

Startled, I mouthed an apologetic 'sorry' to Ava. She shrugged, unconcerned, and turned toward Carmen, whose room was next door to ours in the girls' wing. She'd probably seen it in one of her visions anyway.

"Walk with me, Miss Elian." Again, there was no question mark in Mr. Shaw's voice, and no option to do otherwise. I fell into step with him as we made our way out of the building.

"Your mother was very concerned last night." He spoke in low tones meant only for my ears. The rest of the class had already gone ahead. "She came to me in tears when she couldn't find you at three a.m."

"She knew where--." I felt like I wanted a brick wall at my back and Wolverine claws for hands, and this was going to go badly unless I shifted things. I took a deep breath and tried again. "I didn't mean to make her cry, and I'm sorry for that. I was with Archer and Bishop Cleary doing research, and I should have checked in with her when I got back so she didn't worry. It wasn't considerate and it won't happen again."

There. An apology with no promise to reform the offending behavior. It was the best I could do and all I had in me. Mr. Shaw studied my face for a moment.

"You know the chalkboard outside my office? Why don't you just make a mark or something whenever you go, then another when you get back so you two don't fight about it, and I can tell her where you are if she asks."

I had to admit, the Bear could surprise me. "You realize that asking a tagger to make a mark is like giving an alcoholic a drink." He smirked, and I could feel the armor slip off another notch.

He straightened the collar of my coat with a smile, then narrowed his eyes dangerously. "You stayed in the present?"

I nodded. This time. No one but Archer knew I'd gone back since I brought my mom home.

I could see about ten things the Bear didn't say flit across his face, but to his credit, he changed the subject. "Let's go play with fire, shall we?"

The corner of the field where tables had been set up was clear of almost any kind of foliage or flammable substance, and remarkably, for a March day in England, it was sunny and calm. Perfect fire-starting weather.

"Okay, many of you are familiar with the primitive ways of making fire. It's a skill every hiker, traveler, or adventurer should have in their repertoire, and with the right materials, it only takes determination and a little muscle."

Mr. Shaw passed out a notched board, a couple of sticks, a bow, and lots of straw tinder to the various groups. Then he demonstrated all the friction methods of fire-starting I'd ever read about or seen Bear Grylls do on TV. The bow drill method had always seemed like it was the most efficient, but Mr. Shaw got fire from all three. Then he set different teams to the task of different friction methods and made it a contest. Ava and Carmen got the bow drill, and he gave me the most primitive way to start a fire: a stick, a knife, and a piece of wood. I'd paid attention when he made his hand drill, especially to the fact that a small piece of dry leaf or bark next to the notch is the best way to carry a tiny spark to the nest of tinder. I was feeling pretty good about being the second one done with a decent-sized flame to show for it, and I could tell it made the Bear happy that I'd managed it on my own.

"Okay, those are the primitive means to fire-making. Another method, requiring slightly more modern tools, involves rubbing the contact points of a battery over steel wool that's been spread out flat. The sparks on the steel wool can be used to ignite whatever tinder you have available, and it takes much less time to accomplish."

He ran through a couple other options, like lenses, flint and steel, or even a coke can and chocolate, and then finally looked around at all of us with a grin.

"Of course, chemistry can also produce fire. Who can tell me the ways phosphorus is used?"

A couple of hands went in the air.

"Matches."

"That's right. Anyone else?"

"Isn't there phosphorus in fertilizer?"

"Absolutely. Without phosphorus in the soil, nothing would grow."

"They use phosphorus in bomb-making."

Mr. Shaw smiled. "Yes, it's used in incendiary devices, as evidenced by match heads, and by the use of fertilizer in homemade bomb-making. White phosphorus, the stuff in flash bombs, is among the most unstable explosives ever discovered. Do you know, a German scientist made the first white phosphorus in the 1600s from urine?"

Several groans of disgust came from the class. I loved this stuff.

"He was trying to isolate gold from urine, thinking it caused the yellow color. But the super-concentration and evaporation left him not with gold, but with white phosphorus. In fact, a fairly simple method of achieving the same result uses urine concentrate, charcoal dust, and cinnamon powder." More groans, but a lot of smiles too. Mr. Shaw definitely knew how to play to the class.

"One would need a distillation system of closed containers and glass tubing, with the urine mix on one side, and a container of water on the other. When the urine mix is boiled, the steam drips into the water and causes a waxy substance to form on the bottom. That's white phosphorus. Expose the bottle to light and it will glow in the dark for several hours. Expose the substance to air and … BOOM!"

His voice was so loud and unexpected, we all jumped, then burst out laughing.

I raised my hand. "What about gunpowder? They made fireworks with it in ancient China, right?"

He nodded and deadpanned. "I wonder how many British laws I'm breaking by teaching you how to make chemical incendiary devices?" The class laughed. "The ingredients are simple: saltpeter, sulphur and coal. The tricky part is getting the right kinds of ingredients, plus the right mixture for the maximum explosive effect. So, who can tell me where to find saltpeter?"

"At the chemist's!"

A guy named Niko in the back raised his hand. "It's in fertilizer."

"Right, Niko. Potassium nitrate, or saltpeter, is a major component of fertilizer. One of the primary natural sources of it is in caves in the form of bat guano."

"It's poop!"

Mr. Shaw deadpanned, "The most explosive things usually are." When the laughter died down again, he continued. "Have you ever seen the white crust on the dirt of a leach field? That's also saltpeter. Pretty much any evaporated human or animal waste …" The class groaned and made appropriate puking noises. "… is a source of potassium nitrate."

While the class got itself under control again, I spoke directly to Mr. Shaw. "So, charcoal comes from burned wood, right?"

He nodded. "The harder the wood, the more ash though, so soft wood is better."

"Okay, what about sulphur? Where does that come from?"

The class had settled and was listening to our conversation, so Mr. Shaw included them in his answer. "Sulphur is a naturally occurring mineral, most often found around geothermal sites."

"Like the hot springs at Bath."

"Exactly. Any geothermal spring that smells like rotten eggs has sulphur in or around it."

"So what's the ratio?"

Mr. Shaw looked at me through narrowed eyes. "Planning to make gunpowder any time soon?"

"Nope. Just fascinated."

He grinned. "Me too. The ratio is approximately six parts charcoal to two parts each saltpeter and sulphur. I think there's slightly more saltpeter than sulphur in the mix, but there's usually some slippage due to the quality of the materials."

In the distance we could hear the end-of-class bell, and my classmates actually groaned.

"We'll be studying other primitive chemical combinations in the coming weeks. Thanks, everyone."

He got a round of applause from the group and looked around blinking in surprise. Ava was right, it had been a great class.

"Thanks, Mr. Shaw. That was awesome." Ava and I helped him clean up the fire-starting supplies and then we walked back to school together.

"There will be a small group of Descendants tonight. Meet in the Solarium after dinner and dress warmly."

SURVIVAL

The Bear surprised me. Ava and I thought we'd figured out who would be in the solarium for the survival class, even including the two Descendant kids I didn't know, but he pulled out a wildcard. Two wildcards actually. Alexandra Rowan, Adam's girlfriend, stood off to one side of the room, and Mr. Shaw was in a different corner talking to my mother.

Tom came up to Ava and me when we entered the room. "Does Adam know Alex is here?"

"I don't know. *I* didn't know, so maybe not." Ava sounded worried.

I suddenly didn't want Adam to be blindsided if he wasn't prepared to see her, so I darted back out of the solarium and down the hall until I ran into him walking with Connor.

"Alex is here," I blurted. I couldn't have been less subtle if I'd written it in neon paint. Adam stopped in his tracks, and I could feel Connor's eyes doing the tennis match back-and-forth between us.

"I'll see you in there, Arman." I didn't think it was a question, but Adam seemed to have to think about it before he nodded at Connor.

"Yeah. I'll be there in a minute."

Connor left quickly, and I waited until his Wolf ears were out of range. "You didn't know she'd be here?" I took a step closer so he could hear my near-whisper.

He shook his head. "I haven't talked to her in a couple of weeks."

That shocked me. Despite the fact she had left St. Brigid's already, I thought they'd been in touch more than that since they got back together at Christmas. "Why not?"

His eyes searched mine for a second before he looked away. "It's not as easy as…"

My tone got sharp. I couldn't help it. "As what, Adam? As flirting with me?"

He sighed. "Yeah. I know I almost pushed it too far that day in the woods, but I'm so sick of all the secrets. It doesn't feel like a real relationship when it's hidden all the time. Messing with you is safe because you're here, you bite back, and you're not interested. I can totally be myself without worrying I'll say the wrong thing."

I didn't expect relief to hit me as hard as it did. "You're an idiot."

He looked startled. "Why?"

"Because saying the wrong thing is your specialty, and if you think Alex expects anything different, you don't give her enough credit. You guys chose each other, remember?"

"But she left me once. What if she does it again?"

God, did I really sound as pathetic as he did now with all my internal whining about being left? I must have winced because Adam did too.

"That was lame, wasn't it?"

"Yeah. I might have to revoke your man-card for that one."

"You're right. I'm definitely an idiot."

I gave him a hug. "Yeah, but you're her idiot, so she has to deal with your raging insecurities, not me." He cringed, and I laughed. "My own are crippling enough."

Adam still seemed rooted to the spot. "I'll be damned if I'm missing this class just because you can't figure out how to talk to your girlfriend." I blew him a kiss and sprinted back down the hall.

I suddenly felt so much lighter, and when I re-entered the solarium my eyes found Alex's. Her flawless coffee-colored skin, long black hair, and almond-shaped eyes were a striking combination with the regal way she held herself. Everything about her screamed 'dancer.' I went over to her.

"Hi. Welcome back."

"It's really strange to be here. Uncle Bob had me hang out in his office all afternoon; I think he's worried Ms. Rothchild will give me up to the Mongers."

"Yeah, it seems pretty risky to bring you in, especially with Monger-Spawn getting all feisty about their Vamp-hunting." I looked at Mr. Shaw. "I didn't think he was okay with you and Adam."

Mr. Shaw's voice made me jump. "Alexandra is the best snare-maker I've ever taught. She surpassed my own skill when she was about Connor's age, and she also happens to be a very good teacher." He dropped the volume of his voice to speak directly to us. "And, as you say, with feisty Monger pups on the prowl, trap-making skills could come in handy."

I hid the smile, but Connor was proud of his half-sister. "You didn't expect a Gazelle-Shifter to be an expert trapper did you?"

"I think it's awesome."

She leaned forward and whispered to me when Mr. Shaw walked away. "He's not cool with me and Adam yet, but I'm working on it."

Adam had just walked into the solarium, and his eyes went from Alex to me to Mr. Shaw.

I grimaced at the look of panic on his face. "Good luck with that."

Mr. Shaw's voice cut through all the conversation in the room. "If any of you have brought anything other than the clothes on your backs, leave it here."

A young Shifter kid I didn't know very well named Owen spoke up. "What about a knife?"

"I have one for each of you if you don't have your own. It's the most useful tool you'll ever carry and one you should consider keeping with you at all times."

Owen murmured happily to himself. "Brilliant."

It had never been very smart to carry a knife as a teenage tagger in Los Angeles, where being armed could get a person shot. But since Sanda had given me her little inlaid pocket knife, it had gone with me everywhere I went.

He handed out small folding blades, but I declined and showed him Sanda's. He nodded, then reminded me about the mini Maglite I always carry, so I left it on the table in front of me. I didn't mention the orange marker that lived in my inside pocket, because what could I do with it, draw myself a shelter? When Mr. Shaw was done he addressed the group. "Good. Can someone tell me what the basic elements of survival are?"

"Fire."

"Water."

"Shelter."

"Food."

Mr. Shaw nodded after each thing was called out, then he paused a moment. "There's one more element which can be critical to your survival, according to your circumstance."

I thought about the fact that he'd risked Mongers and his own issues with Adam to bring Alex back to St. Brigid's. Snares and traps weren't just for food.

I called out. "Defense."

"Why? There aren't any big predators in England. They hunted bears and wolves to extinction a long time ago." That was Owen again.

I saw Connor shudder slightly.

"Owen, your people are Thorins, right?" Mr. Shaw didn't elaborate when Owen nodded, but I saw Connor's eyes narrow slightly, and Alex slide almost imperceptibly away. The Thorins must be something that didn't mix well with the Wolf and Gazelle of the Edwards family. "Then you'll be familiar with the biggest and most dangerous predators. They're in evidence all around us."

"Humans." I said it matter-of-factly. I'd been the prey of humans recently, and I hadn't enjoyed the experience.

84

"Humans," he agreed. "It may seem an odd thing to learn as part of a wilderness survival course, but make no mistake, these skills can be applied equally to the city and the wilds."

Mr. Shaw ran through a couple of basic safety rules, and then we headed out of the solarium. It would be dark in about an hour, so I figured we'd use the light to find and set up a camp, then maybe get into the more theoretical lessons around a campfire.

I slipped in next to my mom as we headed toward the woods.

"I'm sorry I worried you."

"Bob told me about your system."

"Is that okay?"

She sighed, but gave me a smile. "I'll take what I can get, Saira. I just want to know you're safe."

I winced. "Between you, Mr. Shaw, and Archer, I feel like I'm constantly in danger of being leashed."

My mom laughed out loud, startling me and a couple people nearby. I stared at her. "What's so funny?"

"I was about your age when I met your father. My sister and I had gone to Epping Wood to stay with the Missus, and she'd sent us into the forest to gather plants."

Okay, change of subject. But my mom so rarely talked about her past that I rolled with it. "For her poultices?" I could tell by her face I'd surprised her, but then again she'd been unconscious when the Missus had set me to mixing up a poultice for the Vampire bite that had turned Archer.

"Exactly. The Missus taught me to find most of the things she used, and I was quite arrogant about my knowledge. At least until I reached for water hemlock instead of yarrow."

"Mom! Even I know the difference between those."

"I hadn't heard him until he came up behind me and grabbed my arm to keep me from picking the hemlock. Emily screamed, of course. She was like that. But precisely because he'd scared me I got furious. I didn't even see how young and handsome he was until he started laughing."

I smirked. "Which, of course made you madder."

"Of course it did. I stalked off to the cottage and slammed the door hard enough to get yelled at by the Missus. I fumed that whole night, but the next day I managed to find an excuse to go to the woods alone just so I could look for him. He was waiting for me where we'd met the day before, and he had a whole bouquet of yarrow flowers waiting. He apologized for startling me, and I apologized for yelling at him. From that moment on we were best friends. We prowled the woods together, gathering plants for his research and talking about everything under the sun. Falling in love snuck up on us, because of course we knew about the moratorium and it wouldn't have occurred to either of us to go against our families on purpose."

She was so much stronger now than she'd been right after he died, I almost wanted to change the subject so she didn't get sad again. But I never got to know my dad, and the only thing I had were her memories of him.

"Because he had saved my life when we first met, I think he always felt like my safety was his responsibility. We broke rules to marry, and then when I was pregnant with you his protectiveness of me was so fierce it landed him in Bedlam, and us forever on the run." She stopped walking and looked me in the eyes. "So I understand leashes. Especially the ones attached by the people who love us."

Wow. Okay. Way to throw down the guilt, Mom. Subtle, yet very effective.

I smiled at her. "So, I shouldn't do the exact opposite of whatever you guys say to do, just because you say it?"

Her eyes sparkled. "It would be helpful."

I looked over at Alex and Adam, walking together, but separated by several feet. "Do you think they have a chance?"

She thought about it for a minute. "Do you?"

"I think if you love someone enough you can figure out a way to be together."

My mom wrapped her arm around my shoulder and gave me a quick hug. "Me too."

86

Mr. Shaw led us to a clearing in the woods I hadn't been to before, and the light was fading quickly by the time everyone was together. There were ten of us, including the Bear, my mom and Alex, and the only two people I didn't really know were the Shifter kid, Owen, and a Seer named Kelsey.

"Saira, Ava, Adam and Tom go with Alexandra to set up camp defenses, and the rest of you will work with Ms. Elian and myself on fire-starting and getting the camp together."

We broke into our groups, but Adam and Alex stood on opposite sides of our huddle. I had never seen Adam so awkward, and for her part, Alex looked brittle. She was holding herself more stiffly than I thought it was possible for a dancer to do. I could feel my own tension building as we left the camp clearing, and it was starting to piss me off. I'd looked forward to this class all week, and those two, with everything they weren't saying to each other, were messing it up. As soon as we'd moved out of earshot of the camp I stopped them.

"Okay, guys. I know it's weird to be thrown together in such a public way, especially by Mr. Shaw. But it's weirder that you are so uncomfortable around each other. So deal, please, because your giant pink elephant in the room is getting in the way of me learning some very cool stuff."

"Oh, I think it would be fun to ride the pink elephant. You should keep being ridiculous with each other until I've had my chance." Ava's voice was airy and light, and I could have hugged her when the stares of shock at my outburst melted into laughter.

Magically, the laughter made the weirdness go away. Adam moved up behind Alex and wrapped his arms around her. She leaned back into his arms with easy grace, and I could tell they were comfortable that way in their private life. I caught his eye and mouthed, "idiot" to him. He blew a kiss to me that was more of a 'kiss my booty' than anything else, and finally, all was properly right in our world.

"Well, since we've stopped here anyway, let's see what will work for perimeter defense." Alex stepped forward out of Adam's embrace and was instantly all easy confidence. It was such a shift

87

from the petrified Gazelle I first met that I finally got how well she and Adam fit together. "We'll need sticks, rocks, and anything else you can find that might be turned into a trap. You've got ten minutes to scavenge, but take a partner and watch each other's backs."

Ava and I set off in the opposite direction from Adam and Tom. The full moon made the woods feel like a black and white photo with the contrast set on high. The blacks were really black, and everything else was bathed in silvery light.

I took off my hoodie and tied the sleeves together. "We can use this to carry whatever we find." I found a couple of y-shaped sticks that would make great slingshots if I could figure out what to use for the stretchy business, then filled my sweatshirt with quarter-sized rocks to use as ammo.

"We're going to need lots of leafy branches." Ava spoke with that certainty that came with her visions.

"Pit traps or hiding spots?"

"Both?" I guessed visions could be like that: just random images unless you knew what you were looking at. "And something else … something pointy."

I hoped Adam and Tom were having similar visions so they'd know what she meant.

"I think we need long sticks." Ava's whisper was tentative, but it definitely made sense to gather as much as we could. We could sort out the useful stuff later.

"How come you didn't see that Alex would be here?" I kept my voice as low as I could, figuring Alex probably had super Gazelle hearing, considering she shifted into an animal that was dinner for predators.

Ava shrugged. "I didn't look."

That surprised me. "You can direct your sight?"

"Sometimes, but that's just because I'm the heir. But if I use Aislin's cuff I can focus on something specific."

"What's Aislin's cuff?" I'd never really asked too much about Seers before, and I'd discovered that very few Descendants were in the habit of volunteering information about their skills. "Unless it's, like, Seer Family stuff that you can't talk about."

Ava hesitated for about a fraction of a second, but she was always so open about everything else I heard it in her voice instantly. "No, it's okay. I think I should tell you." She took a deep breath, like she was revealing some ancient Chinese secret. "Aislin was in love with a Persian prince, like eight hundred years ago—"

"I'm sorry, did you say eight *hundred?*"

Ava nodded. "I've heard that Aislin is the only one of the Immortals who still hangs out with humans."

"Eight hundred years ago isn't *still* hanging out." I felt like I was pointing out the obvious, but Ava shrugged it off.

"She's still around somewhere. I'm just talking about the cuff."

"Right. Sorry." I was trying very hard not to sound like I didn't believe her, mostly because I'd recently learned that impossible things were sometimes true.

"Anyway, the prince had the cuff made for Aislin as a gift before he died."

"He knew he was going to die?"

"She did."

Of course she did. Aislin was the Immortal, Fate. She knew pretty much everything. "Sorry, go on."

"Anyway, his best silversmith wove intricate patterns about fate and destiny into the design, and the inside is smooth so it acts like a mirror to reflect the visions we have. But my favorite thing about it is the poison compartment."

"It had a poison compartment?"

"Well, it's not really for poison, but Adam and I have always called it that because it seemed like a great place for captured princesses to keep deadly poisons to paralyze their enemies and escape with their lives."

She said that so matter-of-factly that I almost burst out laughing. I could just imagine the games Adam and Ava played when they were little rugrat twins running around their parents' perfect mansion. At least I assumed it was perfect, and a mansion, since I'd seen their mother and didn't think she'd live anywhere else.

I struggled to keep a straight face because Ava had one and I wasn't going to laugh if she didn't. "So what did the poison compartment hold?"

Ava shrugged. "Who knows? Maybe just poison. But if you look at the concave mirror inside the cuff just right, it can direct a vision to a specific person, place, or event."

"Just like my mom's clock necklace."

Ava's eyebrows raised questioningly, so I explained that the necklace, passed down through generations of Elians, could direct the wearer's Clocking to a specific time and place. It's how my mom got us forward in time from 1871, the year I was supposed to have been born.

There was a sharp whistle, like a bird call, that I knew couldn't have been made by a bird since all but the owls were asleep. "I think we better go."

We gathered all the sticks and rocks we'd found into my sweatshirt, and I slung it over my stronger shoulder. The other one didn't hurt anymore, but it had gotten weaker during the time I kept it immobile. As we headed back toward the others I continued our conversation in a low voice.

"Does the cuff still exist?"

"Oh, yes. It gets handed down to each Head of the Family. My mother has it right now, and I'll inherit it when she steps down. It's one of the reasons Tom's dad wants to be Head so badly. He wants the cuff."

Well, that was interesting. It wasn't just power over the huge Seer clan that lit Mr. Landers up, it was the perks too.

We rejoined the others where we'd left Alex. Adam and Tom were already whittling the ends of long straight sticks to sharp points. "You guys got the 'pointy things' vision too?"

Adam looked at Ava oddly, then shook his head. "Alex said we were going to make one of those barriers like they used to use against ancient cavalries. With sharp sticks pointing out like a deadly fence."

"We'll need to dig some pits too, but this dirt is pretty hard-packed, so I'm afraid it'll take too long to get deep enough to make a proper pit-trap." Alex was stripping long fibrous grass to use as twine to connect the sticks.

"Alex is right. It took me all afternoon to dig the pit that Max landed in the last time we went running."

Tom looked up in surprise. "You dug that? I thought he was just phenomenally unlucky and stepped in a fox hole or something."

"The ground was really soft there, which gave me the idea, but I had a shovel and it still took hours."

Adam looked at me through narrowed eyes. "How long ago did you dig that pit?"

I shrugged. "I don't know. A couple of weeks?"

"You're scary."

"Prepared."

"Prepared to do damage. It's the same thing."

I shot him a dagger glare, and he wisely refrained from commenting further.

I had just discarded a stick that was too short for the guys' pointed fence, but I picked it up again and broke it in half, so each side had enough of a point to do some damage. "What if we don't dig traps, we dig trips."

"Trips? What are you talking about?" Adam didn't sound derisive, just confused. I appreciated the difference.

Alex was studying the short, pointed sticks in my hands. "You're thinking about shallow holes filled with one or two sticks each?"

I nodded. "Covered with enough leaves to hide the points. Kind of like a low-tech minefield I guess."

Adam was looking back and forth between me and Alex. "You're both exceptionally frightening, and I'm very glad we're on the same team."

Alex and I traded glances, then laughed. She got busy assigning tasks, which we all jumped into with both feet. The guys were digging trip holes while Alex and I whittled sharp points on short sticks. Ava positioned the long sticks around the edges of the minefield to discourage people from skirting the sides, and finally Tom spoke the question no one had asked yet. "Against whom are we defending ourselves?"

Alex sat back from having just buried three spikes in a shallow depression. She wiped the hair from her face with the back of her hand and looked up at Tom. "No one." He nodded and turned back to the hole he was digging. "Yet."

Adam regarded her steadily. "But you expect there will be someone?"

She nodded. "Yeah, I do."

"Who?" Tom winced, like he expected the answer but didn't want to hear it. Alex looked steadily at him.

"You spent time with them, Tom. You know what they're like."

She meant Mongers. Of the enforcer variety.

"You think they'd come here? To St. Brigid's?"

Alex shrugged. "Uncle Bob does. Or at least he doesn't want to leave it to chance. Anyway, these are useful skills for you guys to have." She raised an eyebrow and looked at me. "You never know when you'll have to fend off a pack of wild boys."

Ava's cheery voice piped up. "Or pink elephants." Which, of course, cracked everyone up and diffused the tension so we could focus on the tasks at hand.

Alex made a very cool rabbit snare with the grass she'd woven into a kind of rope. She held it up at rabbit head height with little notched sticks and looped it to a tree. The sticks reminded me of my own slingshot sticks, and I pulled them out. "What can I use as a band to turn these into slingshots?"

Alex regarded the stick in my hand for a long moment, then finally smiled. "Underwear elastic."

I laughed. "Perfect."

Adam smirked. "Somehow I don't see you girls volunteering your skivvies in the name of weaponry."

"Why not? We do it all the time." Alex delivered the line so casually it took Adam a full ten seconds to finally get it while the laughter erupted all around him. I really liked his girlfriend.

I unbuttoned the top two buttons of my jeans and pulled out my knife.

"Whoa, hey! What are you doing?" Adam looked a little freaked out as I tugged the top of my pink and leopard bikini and got ready to separate the elastic from the fabric. It was kind of a bummer because the panties were cute.

"Making a slingshot."

I'd shocked him. Which would have been funny if he didn't try to grab my knife away from me and almost made me cut myself. "What the hell, Arman?"

He sounded like he was strangling on his words. "Don't. Cut. Those."

I stared at Adam, then looked at Alex in confusion. She rolled her eyes and shook her head as if to say 'who the hell knows?' So I matched his tone. "Why. Not?"

"Because if you destroy them he won't be able to imagine you wearing them anymore." The smooth tones of a cultured male voice seemed to melt out of the woods and I spun toward the voice.

"Archer!"

FIGHT OR FLIGHT

I ran toward him as he emerged from behind the trees. Something Adam had said about secret relationships not feeling real had landed hard with me, and I suddenly wanted everyone to know Archer was mine.

Archer's eyes flicked to the knife still open in my hand, and I practically skidded to a halt, embarrassment flaming my face. "Oh. Sorry." I folded Sanda's knife and quickly buttoned my jeans before stepping into his warm embrace.

He nuzzled my hair near my ear and spoke so only I could hear him. "Your friend would like to kill me." The matter-of-fact tone of his voice didn't require me to do anything about it, but I was sick of all the pink elephants. I turned to Adam and struggled to keep my voice calm and even.

"You all know Archer, right?" There was tense silence from my friends. Well, except for Ava. I don't think she ever got tense.

Ava's voice was warm and generous when she greeted Archer. "It's nice to see you again." She moved forward to kiss him on the cheek, and I loved her for it.

Archer gave her one of the melty smiles that turned my insides to mush on a semi-regular basis. "It's very nice to see you too, Ava." He gave Alex the same smile but with the wattage turned down slightly to adjust for the fact that she'd gone rigid at his appearance. "I'm impressed with your defenses, Alexandra. They're very well planned."

The wary expression on her face didn't relax as she nodded acknowledgement. I was proud of Adam for moving protectively closer to her, misplaced though it was, and I tried to ease the tension. "Archer won't hurt you, Alex. He's not like that."

Adam's voice was laced with nails. "He's a Sucker, Saira, and Suckers kill."

I whirled on Adam, ready to unleash the full weight of my temper, but Archer's low voice stopped me. There was an edge to it that sounded dangerous, but also completely controlled. "I am deadly, Arman. I need blood to survive. But I am a man, not a monster. I do not kill for pleasure, and I can certainly control my need to eat as easily as you can, or perhaps more so, since I don't enjoy my food. Becoming a Vampire did not remove all reason or humanity in me."

It could have been my imagination, but the dangerous edge in his voice seemed to soften slightly. "So, although I struggle with my own insecurities about your friendship with Saira, I will not harm you or anyone you love. And perhaps, if I'm lucky, I might find my own brand of friendship among those of you who can stomach the thought of associating with a Sucker." He included Tom, Ava and Alex in his gaze, and I let my fists unclench.

Adam blinked, clearly unsettled by Archer's speech. But Alex was the one who moved first. She stepped forward, a little like she was offering a slab of steak to a lion, and put out her hand. "We weren't formally introduced before. I'm Alexandra Rowan, Shifter."

He took her hand in his and smiled carefully at her. "I'm glad to meet you properly, Alex. I'm Archer Devereux, Seer, and now something far less socially acceptable."

Then Adam stepped forward and I tensed again, not sure what he was up to. He put his hand out to shake. "Adam Arman, Seer, and fellow over-protective ass."

Archer laughed and clapped Adam's hand in one of those manly handshakes that crush bones. "It's good to see you again, Arman."

Tom stepped forward to shake Archer's hand and clasp him on the shoulder with the other. "Sucker." He barely held back a grin.

Archer returned the shoulder clasp and the suppressed grin. "Half-Sight."

Tom's eyes narrowed, and then he smiled. "Welcome back."

"Thank you."

"Where've you been?"

"London."

"Taking on the town, huh?"

Archer grimaced. "Sleeping in an altar and spending my nights in a cellar. Hardly a party."

"He's been looking for Wilder."

Tom shook his head. "Okay, sleeping in an altar I want to hear about, but I don't get why Wilder matters. I thought he was dead."

"Archer had a vision of him, and I saw it."

Adam's eyes widened. "You…saw it?"

I nodded and looked at Alex. "Have you ever seen anything that Adam was Seeing, just because you guys were next to each other?"

Adam looked shocked, but Alex glanced over at him, then bit her lip before nodding. Her voice was almost a whisper. "I saw Ms. Rothchild and her brother-in-law coming after us to take Adam away from me."

Adam looked at her, horrified. "You saw that? But it couldn't have been a vision. It didn't happen!"

Her eyes filled with tears, and I could tell it mortified her. "Because I left, Adam. I ran away before it could."

He stared at her, then looked helplessly at his sister. "It doesn't work like that though. We can't change the future."

I shook my head. "You're confusing past and future. We can *always* change what hasn't happened yet. It's called free choice."

"But—" He sounded lost, like his foundation had just been rattled by an earthquake of existential proportions. I knew him well enough to know he was sick to his stomach because it was his vision that had sent his girlfriend away last year. And his fault they broke up.

Shaw's sudden whistle pierced the night, and every one of us flinched. Ava's eyes went glassy in a way I knew meant she was Seeing something, and then Adam shuddered. They shared a look of twin communication, and just as Adam opened his mouth, Tom's voice cut in, answering the unspoken question. "But you're back together now. And they're coming."

BATTLE LINES

There was a look of relief in the Bear's eyes when he spotted us.

"Kelsey Saw Mongers—"

Adam interrupted him. "We know. The Rothbitch, Walters, the Were, and a couple others. We Saw them too." Tom and Ava nodded silently, and Mr. Shaw's eyes darkened perceptibly.

"I'll go talk to them."

"There wouldn't be so many if they were here to talk." Archer spoke quietly, and Mr. Shaw's head whipped around at the sound.

"Right. Devereux, they'll be after you, then?"

Archer stiffened. "No one knows I'm back."

Mr. Shaw studied him for a long moment, then finally nodded. "Then I'm glad you are." He looked at Adam and Alex. "I suspect you two are their excuse for coming. Though the resumption of your relationship was quiet, it's been noticed."

Alex's voice was a whisper. "I'm sorry, Uncle Bob."

Even though his expression was stormy, Mr. Shaw pulled Alex into a rough hug and kissed the top of her head. "The boys can Shift if there's trouble, but I don't want you to, not with the Were out there."

"Owen, what do you Shift into?" I got all bossy business, like I was talking to my Parkour pack.

"A Fox."

"Good. Connor, you and Owen should maybe Shift and head out. Then if there's a fight you can flank the Were and keep him out of it."

Mr. Shaw growled. "There won't be a fight."

I glared at him. "Mongers fight. It's what they do."

His eyes narrowed, and I thought he might have even huffed, but then he turned his gaze on Connor. "If it comes down to it, don't let the Were get teeth on you again. The second time takes twice as long to burn out."

Connor looked grim, but he nodded and shot a quick glance at Adam before he and Owen left to Shift. "Don't let anything happen to her." He meant his sister, Alex, and Adam clapped him on the shoulder.

"Be safe, Wolf."

I turned to the Bear. "We have pit traps and spear barricades about a hundred yards out between us and school. If you Shift, stay behind them. It's like a minefield.

Mr. Shaw gave us an approving look. "Good to know, but I don't intend to Shift."

In the distance we heard the crack of a big stick, and then a guy yelled something in a foreign language. Mr. Shaw and my mom looked concerned, but I knew. "That was the Were. He just hit a pit trip."

I turned to Archer. "If they see you, it's all the excuse they need to use force."

He looked grim. "With Walters in the group you're on the Monger hit parade yourself, love. And for that matter, so is Tom."

Archer was right, and the odds of walking away from a confrontation were looking bleaker by the moment. Even with the Were in the group, injured though he might be, Seth Walters was the biggest badass of them all. But then I had a sudden thought and spun around to Ava. "Can you look for the genealogy again?"

Her eyes went unfocused in an instant and I could feel the web of tension tethering us all to each other. She let out a breath and shuddered. "It's just like before. I can see the room with the computer and a lamp on a desk. It's the same desk I saw before, but this time the book isn't there. Or at least it isn't visible."

"What else about the room?"

"The window. It's arched, like one of those big old warehouse windows in high end lofts."

Tom grabbed Ava's hand and spoke in an urgent whisper. "Do it again. Let me See." We could hear crashing through the woods, and it was getting closer.

This time Ava closed her eyes, and it seemed like I could feel her focus reach out beyond us, beyond the school, out into the universe. None of us dared to speak. Then Tom's eyes popped open.

"I know that place. It's on the Thames. Seth took me there once, to a meeting with an East End gangster."

I spoke quickly to my mom and Mr. Shaw. "I'm going to take them out of here. If it's just you guys, Kelsey and the Shifters left, there's nothing the Mongers will want."

"Where are you going, Saira?" My mom asked, but the Bear already knew.

"He won't have left the book unguarded."

"But if Seth's here, he's not with the genealogy. We have a shot if we go right now."

A twig snapped too close, and I grabbed a stick from the fire pit. The tip was charcoal and still smoking from the fire Mr. Shaw must have taught the younger kids to make. I used it like a giant pencil to start drawing a spiral on the flat boulder under my feet. Buzzing filled my ears almost immediately, and I caught my mom's worried eyes on me. "You can go with us."

"I'll stay in case I need to get the others out."

The buzzing was getting louder and I turned to my … tribe, for lack of a better word. "I'm Clocking into the Bedlam cellar, just to get us into London. We can figure out where to go from there. If you want to come, grab onto me."

Alex and Ava were next to me instantly. Tom grabbed a shoulder, and Archer hooked his foot around mine and wrapped his arms around the two girls to hold them to me. It seemed like

Adam was struggling between the idea of staying and fighting Mongers, or running with us. The humming in my brain was sending waves of dizziness and nausea over me, and I reached my other hand to Adam. "Come with us. We need you."

My vision blurred, and I felt like I was fracturing into a thousand pieces. The hum was at a higher pitch than I'd ever heard before and barely drowned out the yelling Mongers as they crashed into the camp. I thought I felt Adam's fingers clasp mine just as everything went black and my stomach heaved into my throat.

The world was spinning.

And black.

And the thrum of an amplified rubber band sounded in my whole body.

I screamed.

And then I landed.

And puked.

And I wasn't the only one.

It should never have been so hard to clock through space. Time was the tough one. Space was just like a fast elevator ride to me. But not this time. Not with so many people hitching a ride.

My people. The sounds of groaning, a couple gasps of puke-in-the-mouth syndrome, and a dry-heave in the corner and I thought I'd identified all of them. It was dark in the cellar, but I could tell we'd hit the correct time because of the smell. "Say your name so I know everyone made it." My voice broke, and I knew I sounded bad.

"Archer." His voice was shaky and right next to my ear.

"Ava." She sounded weak, but okay.

"Tom." He was the dry-heaver in the corner.

"Alex." She sounded disoriented.

There was silence after Alex spoke. "Adam?" Had I imagined his fingers in mine? Did he come with us?

"Over here." He sounded … messed up.

"What's wrong?" I felt my way over to his voice. Waves of dizziness washed over me, and I could barely keep my feet under me. This wasn't good. But as bad as I was feeling, Adam sounded worse. I reached for him, and he grabbed my hand tightly.

"*That's* what you do? When you Clock?"

"That one was rough because I've never taken so many people before, but yeah, it sucks." It didn't sound like he was hurt, and I was relieved. I'd had a momentary, horrible image of part of him being left behind in the woods.

"I can't do that again. I felt like I was dying." He took a shaky breath, and I could feel Alex move to his other side. I hope she had his hand because he was gripping mine like a vise. "Like my soul was being ripped from my body and I couldn't hold onto it."

I needed my Maglite. I needed to make sure he wasn't in shock, because the clammy skin of his hand made me think his pupils would be like black holes and his face pale and sweaty.

Alex's voice gained strength as she calmed him. "You're fine, Adam. Nothing happened. Everything's okay. I'm here, baby, I'm here."

I let go of his hand and stumbled away, feeling awkward and intrusive. I could hear Archer's footsteps, and then the overhead lights clicked on suddenly. He and I were okay with the sudden light, but everyone else was blinking like bats.

"What is this place?" Tom was the first to recover his vision, and he scanned the old Bedlam cellar with startled eyes.

"Now it's the Imperial War Museum, but this used to be the main cellar of Bethlem Royal Hospital. Otherwise known as Bedlam." Archer was calm and confident. He had clocked almost as much as I had, and he had also just spent a week down here with Bishop Cleary.

"Should we get the bishop?" My head was clearing and I was starting to get my balance back, but I didn't like how long it had taken.

He shook his head. "Unless we need him, it would be better not to involve Cleary in anything illegal."

"Right. And we probably only have as much time as it takes Seth to get back to London. Tom, we're in Southwark. Are we close enough to this gangster building to walk, or do I need to clock us someplace closer?" The idea of clocking again so soon was not something I relished, and I saw Adam shudder.

Tom considered for a moment, then nodded. "We're close."

I looked at Archer. "Discovered any other exits from here, or do we have to go through Guy's Chapel?"

"No, there's an outside door. Cleary got the key from the Museum so he didn't have to tell them about the tunnel."

He led us to a door that must have been put in since the War Museum took over the building. Adam was still shaky, but at least he was walking under his own power, clutching Alex's hand. I didn't let anyone see how hard I worked to keep my hands steady.

Archer reached above the door to the lintel and pulled down a key. He met my eyes. "Old habits."

"I'm not complaining."

A park surrounded the War Museum, and it was deserted at that time of night, which was good. I didn't think our little tribe would go unnoticed if anyone was out. Archer pointed across the park. "The river's that way."

Tom strode off toward it, and we all kept pace. Ava walked with Archer and me, while Alex and Adam stayed back a few feet to talk quietly. In a few minutes we got to a bridge and Tom turned left, heading along the riverbank. "I don't know exactly where it is, but I think the building is between Lambeth and Vauxhall Bridges."

He slowed as we approached an older brick warehouse that looked like it had been converted to expensive lofts. There was a security camera aimed at the front door, and an entry keypad instead of a key lock. I looked up. The second and third floor windows were the big arched kind that didn't open. The top floor had the only windows that looked accessible, but even I flinched at the climb up vertical brick walls necessary to get there. The building next to it was a modern concrete and steel thing, and looked even harder, if not impossible, to scale. Archer and I shared a despairing glance, then he took off around one side, and I started for the other. I was careful to avoid the camera range of the entrance security eye, and we met at a service elevator entrance at the back of the building. Of course it was securely locked and had a solid metal door.

I eyed the big power box under the fire escape. It wasn't a good option, but it was the only one I could see. Scrambling to the top of the box was only mildly challenging. The real problem was the distance between my outstretched arms and the bottom of the fire escape ladder.

"It's too far, Saira." Archer's voice was an urgent whisper below me. I didn't look down, concentrating instead on the mortar between the bricks and the distance I'd have to climb. I still wasn't a hundred percent after that jump with five people clinging to me, but at least the dizziness had passed.

I flexed my fingers and reached up for the first brick. This climb was going to suck.

"Saira! Wait!" Ava's whisper was too loud and I cringed. The girl clearly had no concept of stealth mode. I let go of the brick and glared down at her, just barely hanging onto a whisper of my own.

"What!"

"You can't do it. You won't make that climb." Okay, she also must not have spent enough time with me to know that 'can't' is the fastest way to 'oh, yeah? Watch me' in my world.

She said something to Archer that I couldn't hear, and I saw him go a little pale.

Then Ava did something that got my attention more than any amount of warnings would have. She looked up at me again, saw me glaring down at her with my hands on my hips for emphasis, and she left.

Just like that.

"What did she say to you?" It's very hard to whisper a yell.

"I can't watch her die."

The dizziness came back with a vengeance, and I put a hand on the bricks to steady myself. "I can do this climb." I wasn't sure how convincing I could sound, so I added anger to punctuate the declaration.

He looked up at me for a long moment, then shook his head. "No, something's wrong. You've been … off since you brought us all out of the St. Brigid's woods." I remembered then that Archer had his own brand of Sight, and a lot of it seemed to be wrapped up in me and my well-being.

He didn't move, and he didn't take his eyes off me. I finally crouched down and jumped off the box. It was probably only about eight feet off the ground, but Archer had to steady me when I landed. He made it look like he was just holding me in his arms, but we both knew I would have fallen if he hadn't caught me.

I looked in his eyes, slightly terrified at the realization I would have failed. "I can't do the climb."

He shook his head. "Neither can I."

I looked back up the side of the building, at the sheer walls with tiny handholds in the brick mortar.

"We need a thief."

A Thief

"Ringo could do it." I said it with a sort of fatality in my voice, but somehow the words lit a little fire that started to burn in my brain. Archer must have smelled the smoke because his eyes found mine and locked on.

"It's a very bad idea."

"Probably breaks all kinds of time travel rules."

"Your mother did it though."

"And she didn't have a guide."

He stared at me for a long moment, and I watched the full range of protective instincts run across his expression. The last one was resignation, and I knew he wouldn't try to stop me.

"You're still shaky."

"I'll be fine."

"I can't go with you. I'm already there."

"I know." There was a temporal rule we'd discovered when I tried to take Archer to 1888. Because he was already there … then … whatever, living out his natural life, we ended up slipping back a little further, to 1861, before he was born. The rule was explained as 'no one can be in the same time as themselves.' Since Archer had existed steadily since 1861, the last of the nineteenth and whole twentieth centuries were pretty much off limits to him for Clocking.

He thought for a moment. "It's late March." His expression fell. "I'm back in Epping with the Missus. I needed to hunt every day to eat, and I tried to stay out of London."

I didn't touch that. I didn't want to know. "It's okay. I can find him on my own."

"You could take Arman."

I could tell how much it cost Archer to suggest that, and I put my arms around his neck with my face about an inch from his. "You're awesome. But he can't travel like we do. He's still freaking out from a local trip. One back to 1889 would send him over the edge." I kissed him softly on the lips, and his arms tightened around me. "I'll go alone, and I'll be back within an hour whether or not I find him."

I almost laughed when I recognized the pungent scent of the river in Victorian times. The lapping of the water against the pillars of the London Bridge felt like home, and the only people I saw on the street were the ones stumbling out of pubs. As long as I kept my head down and walked fast, I thought I could disappear into the background of the wharf.

But then again, I used to think there was no such thing as time travel, and look where that got me.

I was just about to turn into an alley when someone bumped into me, hard. I'd been so focused on listening for the sound of footsteps behind me that I forgot to look up, and whoever it was came at me from above.

"Oy! Watch where yer goin'!"

"Sorry," I mumbled, trying not to let the guy know I was female. Instantly, three more toughs materialized out of the shadows, and the certainty that life in the next five minutes was going to get very interesting walloped me upside the head.

The ringleader seemed vaguely familiar. His cap was slung low over his eyes, and he had the wide stance of a guy who didn't often have to run for his survival. When he spoke again I knew. He was one of the thieves I'd first encountered with Ringo. The guys he'd been proud of having ditched when he went to work for Gosford at the river.

"You'll not be needin' yer hock-dockeys then."

This was not going to go well for me; that much was clear by the shoulder-to-shoulder stance of the ones closest to me. Not that I had a clue what hock-dockeys were, but I didn't think they were planning to leave me conscious while they took them.

Two options instantly flashed through my brain. Well, three, but succumbing to their fists wasn't so much an option as a price for failure. I could stand up to them and reveal I was female, in hopes that at least one of them was raised not to hit a girl, or I could run and take my chances. I didn't know if Victorian sensibilities included rape, but I thought it would be a stretch to imagine any of them was gentleman enough to back off just because of a difference in plumbing.

Right. Run then.

The toughs, including a Nervous Nelly who couldn't stand still on his pegs, pretty much had forward and backward covered. So my options were limited to up and down. My eyes flicked above me and I flinched. Someone was there, calmly crouched on a window ledge as if waiting for an escape-to-the-roof attempt.

Which left down.

"Yer not movin' fast enough, nib-cove. I'll be 'avin' yer upper-ben too fer me trouble."

Yeah, right. What he said. Marble-mouth would have made me laugh if I wasn't so sure I'd die before the sound made it past my lips. With another quick glance up to see the Roof-Tough hadn't moved, I dropped to the street, and in one fluid motion of my leg, swept the feet out from under Nervous Nelly. He went down like a bowling pin, taking out Rough and Tumble next to him. Marble Mouth lunged for me, but I was already up and dancing to the side away from his grasping hands.

Even with two down, the alley was too small to stay out of their reach for long, and when Roof-Tough dropped down behind me I knew I was screwed.

Except Marble Mouth's eyes narrowed as he looked past me at Roof-Tough. His voice was an angry growl. "Yer dead, Keys."

Keys? Ringo!

I felt him take a step closer and mumble in my ear. "There's a bottle on the step behind me. Break it and arm yerself." My heart slammed in my chest at the sound of his voice. If I was going to die a bloody death tonight at least I'd have the company of one of my best friends.

"I've done with ye, Lizzer. We've no more at stake wi' t'other. The lad's a mate, and ye've no call to harm 'im."

"Mate o' yers is enemy o' mine, Keys." Lizzer spat the words as his toughs regained their feet and arrayed themselves around him. I felt the step behind me and never took my eyes off Lizzer as I reached for the bottle. It felt heavy, like a wine bottle, and Ringo's voice mumbled at me again. "Smash it on the wall when 'e moves." I gripped the neck of the bottle tightly and felt every muscle in my body coil.

"Ye'll let us by or ye'll get cut." There was an authoritative tone to Ringo's voice I'd never heard before, and I had to remind myself he was only sixteen.

Lizzer barked out a laugh as he lunged. I swung the bottle at the corner of the brick wall, and the bottom shattered off, leaving a jagged weapon in my hand. Ringo had been standing just behind me, so I hadn't seen him until he blocked Lizzer's lunge with a swing of a knife. Lizzer dodged the blade in my direction while the toughs jumped in, and I swiped the bottle up in front of me.

Lizzer's eyes went wide and then he howled.

"Bastard cut me!"

Crap! I was the bastard who cut him with my makeshift weapon. The toughs froze at the sound of their leader's outrage, and Ringo and I saw the opening at the same moment. We didn't even have to say the word, we just ran.

When we'd lost the toughs we doubled back on rooftops and dropped down to the dormer ledge of Ringo's loft. I really looked at him for the first time. He'd grown to about my height, which was tall for Victorian times, and he was wearing workingman's clothes. I found his bright green eyes under the brim of his cap. "I wondered when ye'd be back to see me." He looked down to make sure the alley below his building was empty, then quickly slipped the window casement up. "After ye, M'lady." The grin in his voice was unmistakable and did a lot to calm the adrenaline jitters from our near-death altercation with Ringo's old gang. I climbed into his loft and gasped at the change.

The basic layout was the same as when I'd stayed there, but there were things now that made it feel like a home. A rug on the wood floor. A pretty shawl thrown over a new settee against a wall. Books stacked against the walls and covering every surface.

"Those aren't just for show, are they?" I indicated the stacks and Ringo grinned.

"I'm teachin' Charlie to read now."

I knew Ringo had given Mary Kelly's little sister a place to stay after the Ripper claimed Mary as his last victim, but I hadn't realized they'd set up house together. Looking at the pride on Ringo's face gave me an interesting insight on how he'd spent the past three months.

Even more striking than the books, there was art on the walls where they had been completely bare before. I studied the drawing closest to me. At first glance the scene seemed like an ordinary scene of a boat docked at the side of the Thames. But then I looked closer, and a set of eyes peered at me over the side of the boat – otherworldly eyes from some vaguely magical-looking creature. And a giant squid-like sea creature was about to wrap its tendrils around the boat from under the water. Also, the fisherman in a nearby boat had pointed ears and a long tail just barely visible behind him.

"This is so cool!" I was in awe at both the skill and the imagination of the artist.

"That's a compliment then?" A girl's voice made me spin around in surprise, and my face split into a grin.

"Charlie! These are yours?"

She nodded, and her expression was somewhere between trepidation and pride. She was wearing a simple skirt and blouse, very different from the boy's clothes she'd worn when we first met.

"I love them." I'd moved on to the next drawing, which was a marketplace full of little hints of magic all throughout the scene. "You're very skilled, your style is fantastic, and your imagination rocks the planet!" Whether or not she understood what I was saying, she had to be able to hear the amazement in my voice. She finally smiled.

"I'm not sure about skill or 'magination. I just draw wha' I see."

"Are you kidding? You have an awesome imagination. These are incredible!"

Ringo's adult voice sounded so odd coming out of his mouth. "She's serious. It is what she sees, Saira." He shut the blackout curtain across the window and looked at Charlie. "I'll need t' lay low fer a bit. Lizzer an' me got into it a bit jus' now."

I looked from Ringo to Charlie and back again, torn between the conversation at hand and the magical drawings. Typical me, the art talk won.

"These aren't just made-up creatures?"

"Not to me, they're not." Charlie's tone was tentative. Ringo's news had shaken her. "Ringo can't see 'em, so I don't actually know what's real, but I've been able to see things like this my whole life."

It actually wasn't the idea of the creatures that intrigued me as much as the idea that they could be hidden from most everyone ... except Charlie. "So, do these creatures ever do anything, or are they just masquerading as real people?"

Charlie visibly relaxed. I imagined it must be hard to admit this to anyone, especially because she was an underage orphan in a world where Victorian nuthouses were the equivalent of the pit of despair. But obviously Ringo knew. And now I did too.

"This 'un," she pointed to something vaguely like a house elf that was pulling an apple off a market cart, "actually stole the apple, but the cart vendor thought it was the little boy behind 'is ma. 'E made the boy cry." She looked around at some of her other drawings. "Mostly they just try to stay out of the way, though."

"Do they know you can see them?"

Charlie looked sharply at me. "If I say yes then I'm starkers for talkin' to the things I see, not just mad for seein' 'em."

Ringo's voice was gentle, and he looked at Charlie with a tenderness that made me realize he was sixteen going on about twenty-six. "Yer saner than me an' Saira put together. Not that it's sayin' much." His smirk took the seriousness away, and his confidence seemed to give her permission to speak.

She finally took a deep breath. "I learned to 'ide it. Annie didn't want to hear nothin' 'bout what I saw, and if I wanted a place to sleep, I kept my mouth shut."

"So she couldn't see them?"

Charlie shook her head. "No, but I think our ma could. She never said nothin', but I 'member her lookin' at the creatures I saw. Lookin' at them and then turnin' away."

"I'm going to ask around at school and see if anyone else there can see creatures. And I'm sure you probably don't think this, but it's really cool what you can do."

"Cool?" Charlie looked confused, and I forgot she wasn't as well-versed in my 21st century-speak.

"She means ream."

Right, that. I turned to Ringo. "I actually don't have time to stay and hang out, as much as I want to." I included Charlie in that statement. She was as skittish as a barely-tamed cat, but I liked her, and I'd promised to be a sister to her. "Archer and I need help."

Ringo's ears perked up immediately. "'Ow is 'e?"

He thought I meant the Archer he knew. "Staying away until he gets things under control. But I mean in my time. We need a thief."

A whole book of emotions filled Ringo's face. The ones I could identify were excitement, probably at the prospect of time-traveling to the future, and something that looked like chagrin. I loved that word and had never actually seen it in person, but it was definitely chagrin I saw on Ringo's face. "I don't vamp no more."

"Vamp?"

"Steal. Thieve. Lift. Min. Nail. Mizzle."

Right. A whole Victorian vocabulary lesson about stealing. Kind of like the thousand words Eskimos have for snow. I looked steadily at him. "I know you don't steal anymore. But you still have the skills, and we think we've found the Descendants genealogy."

He stared. "The one Archer did for Wilder?"

I nodded. "The Mongers have it."

His face darkened. Ringo knew enough about Descendant politics to know how much that sucked. "Where is it?"

"In a brick warehouse by the river, between Lambeth and Vauxhall bridges. It's four stories tall, but the big, arched windows on the lower floors don't look like they open."

"Two floors of arched windows?"

I nodded.

"I know that place. Been there with the lads." His expression darkened and he studied Charlie for a moment. "Lizzer'll kill me if he spots me in the next coupla days. I need ta go, ri'? It'll keep ye safer if they don' spot me."

"Ye can do that? Ye can take someone with ye?" Charlie's eyes were on mine.

"Yeah. I've never taken someone from the past forward before, but my mom did it when she was pregnant with me, so I think it can be done."

She looked at Ringo with an odd expression on her face. "Ye have to go, of course. And I was fine before I came here, I'll be right enough when yer gone."

A flash of hurt in Ringo's eyes was gone so fast she didn't see it. But I did. "Charlie?" She turned reluctant eyes to me. "I know what it feels like to be the one left behind. It hurts, and you get mad to cover up the neediness you promised yourself you'd never feel." Something shifted in her gaze. Opened. "I'll bring him back to you, I promise."

She didn't say anything, just nodded. I thought she might be silent so he couldn't hear her fear. But Ringo spoke to her in a

113

voice that broke a little. "Ye ha' food and coal fer a fortnight, and Gosford'll help ye if you need it." He touched her arm softly, then went to a drawer and slid some metal tools from it into his pocket. And when his expression was carefully neutral again he finally looked at me. "Ready."

THIEVING

Ringo held my hand tightly as we Clocked, and it comforted me as much as it did him. I might have been breaking an unwritten rule of time travel by bringing him forward, but following rules wasn't really my strong suit anyway. I was starting to get better at not puking with every trip, but I could tell Ringo was going to need a minute. He clutched a tree for support as he struggled to keep down his dinner, and when he looked up, Archer was standing in front of him.

"Old friend." Archer's voice was full of emotion as he looked at the former street urchin and thief who had become like a brother to both of us.

Ringo stared in surprise at the hundred-and-fifty-year-old Vampire in front of him. "God, ye haven't aged a day, have ye?" He looked closer. "Ye've changed though. Seen things, I guess."

Archer and Ringo clasped each other in a warm embrace. Archer held on to Ringo's shoulders and looked at him, almost like a father would look at a son. "How is it you already look a man?"

Ringo's eyes held Archer's. "I reckon I've seen things too."

I couldn't explain why their reunion was so moving to me. Maybe it just felt like the band was back together, but in any case, I got all warm and fuzzy seeing them like this.

Archer turned his gaze to me then, gathered me in his arms, and gave me one of those kisses that melted all the purple polish off my toenails. "Thank you for coming back safely."

I smiled. "Well unsafely just wouldn't do, now, would it?"

He burst out laughing at the expression of shock on Ringo's face. "Don't worry, her virtue is still intact."

I caught a glimpse of the man Ringo might be when he was fifty as he gathered himself up and said stuffily, "'Ow anything can be left of it after that kiss, I don't know."

Impulsively, I kissed my friend on the cheek, and it made him blush. "Come on, we have to go."

We didn't give Ringo time to do more than suck in his breath at the 21st century as we ran back to the warehouse. "Bloody 'ell!" He said it under his breath, but I knew the car had nearly scared the poop out of him. I suppressed a giggle as he leapt backwards off a grate when a tube train passed beneath us. He was keeping it together way better than I would have, but he was a professional, here to do a job, and the questions could wait.

I didn't spot our friends when we got back to the warehouse, but I could feel Tom close by. They materialized from the doorway of a building across the street, and I gestured toward the back of the warehouse. A few moments later, Tom, Ava, Adam, and Alex joined us.

There was frank curiosity in everyone's gazes as they caught sight of Ringo, and for his part, he was in total survivor mode. I recognized it from my own repertoire – size people up in an instant, but never let them catch you do it. I could see the wheels turning as he figured out who was who from my previous descriptions.

"You guys, this is Ringo." I spoke in a whisper and was about to launch into individual introductions when Ringo stuck out his hand to Adam.

"Yer Adam. And this is yer twin, Ava? It's good to finally meet ye." They were surprised at his confidence, but shook his hand gamely before he turned to Alex.

"Ye must be Alexandra. I'm Ringo."

Okay, that one surprised me. I didn't think I'd ever described Alex more than just in passing, but he killed it with his next introduction.

"And yer…Tom? Cousin to the twins, no?

I stared at Ringo. "How did you know them?"

Ringo smiled, and I could tell he liked being smarter than me. "The twins were easy. Ye said Adam was big and Ava had the look of a fairy." He shrugged as if it was all self-explanatory. "And I figured ye wouldn't be here thievin' with aught but good friends."

"But Alex and Tom? I didn't tell you about them."

"Yes, ye did. Ye said Connor and Logan had an exotic half-sister whose mother was a famous ballet dancer." He shrugged again. "Ye'd have to be blind not to see the dancer here."

He turned to Tom. "And Tom here doesn't flinch when 'e sees Archer. The others try not to, but it's still there. So 'e either doesn't know 'im and I've given up the game, or 'e's the bloke ye went back to the Cotton Wharf Fire wi', and that makes 'im Tom Landers."

"Good God, man, did she quiz you on us before you came?" Adam was impressed, and I could see he'd finally recovered from his Clocking nightmare.

Ringo smiled. "Nah, I've just been waitin' to meet ye all. I'm only sorry Connor's not here with ye."

That brought me right back to our purpose. "Right. There's only a couple hours before dawn, and we need to get that book. You know this building, Ringo?"

He looked up past the electrical box I'd nearly fallen from an hour before. "That's new. Takes all the fun out of it, that does."

I glared at him, only half-joking. "Okay, *Keys*. You're on then."

Ringo narrowed his eyes at me. "I can get in, but no one else is comin' wi' me. So ye'd best describe what yer lookin' for."

"He's right. The alarm system's sophisticated and the book is portable." Archer sounded as unhappy with the realization as I was. It's one thing to ask him to open the door, it's another thing entirely to ask him to steal it for us.

Ava stepped forward and reached toward Ringo. "Take my hand. I can show you."

117

He did, and only the slightest widening of his eyes betrayed his surprise at the vision she sent him. That whole touch thing the Seers had going on was very cool, but until tonight I hadn't known it was more common than just passing dreams along. It was a conversation I hoped to have in more detail with Ava when we got through this.

"Right. Green leather binding. Tooled scrollwork on the cover. Got it."

I had a bad feeling in my gut, and I turned to Archer. "I'm recovered enough. I want to go with him." My voice was low enough that no one else but Ringo heard me. Archer's expression was solemn, then he locked eyes with Ringo.

"You can show her the hand and footholds?"

Ringo studied the side of the building. "She can do it on 'er own, but yeah, I'll show 'er."

Ava caught wind of our conversation and looked grim. "I still don't like it, Saira. Someone gets hurt."

"But it's different now that Ringo's here, right?

She nodded slowly. "It's different." When she didn't say anything else I scampered up to the top of the electrical box. "Whistle if someone comes, okay?"

Ringo joined me up there, and I could see Adam directing the others toward hiding spots around the building. Good, we'd have lookouts. Archer was the only one still standing under the electrical box, and I wasn't sure he was going to move at all. Ringo looked at me with a grin.

"Ye up for it?"

I flexed my shoulder out of habit, and Ringo squinted. "Still hurt or just testing it?"

"How … ? Never mind. You're worse than the Seers. I'm fine."

"Good. I'll race ye." Ringo scampered up the side of the brick building as if it was a jungle gym. Instantly I could see where I'd gotten my first handhold wrong, and when I followed his lead my confidence snapped back into place. I was really glad he was doing the climb with me.

At the first window ledge we paused for a breath. I looked out at the view and saw there was a car park the next lot over. It was the high concrete building that had seemed unscalable from the ground. The streets were deserted and London felt almost silent.

"It's so big and bright." I looked over at the awe in Ringo's voice. He was gazing out over the view with a wondrous expression on his face and awe in his eyes. I nudged him to keep climbing.

"Come on. Let's see what else I can impress you with."

He started up the next piece of wall, which was easier than the last because of the frame of brick that surrounded the half-moon window. We didn't stop at the second ledge but kept climbing. The roof was paneled almost completely in industrial skylights, and Ringo knew right where to find the latch to open one pane. The creak was from a bad gothic movie and I winced at the noise, but the room below us was dark. I hoped there weren't any overnight tenants in the place, or we were screwed.

Ringo went first, and I watched how he dropped down to a cross-beam and then tight-rope-walked across. Looked easy enough, as long as my balance wasn't still whacked from the multi-person Clock. Ringo must have felt me hesitate because he came back across and whispered up to me. "You're tall enough. It's only a couple inches if you hang."

Okay, I could do that. Not making it wasn't an option. So I pulled my sleeves down over my palms to avoid cuts from the metal window frame and lowered my body down.

"Right then, I've got ye." Ringo's whisper was only a little louder than air, but I could feel his presence in front of me. So I let go. Strong hands steadied my shoulders lightly and then were gone almost immediately. I appreciated that. It didn't feel so much like I had to be helped, and my legs were solid enough I could follow him across the beam. Then it was an easy climb down the wall to the top floor. So much light came in through the skylights we didn't need to mess with anything electric.

Ringo signaled toward the stairs, and we descended another floor. Both of us kept to the outside of the wooden steps, away from the creakiest boards, and within a few minutes he had jimmied the lock on the front office where the arched windows overlooked the river.

"It's either this or the one next door." Ringo moved through the office with the certainty of a practiced thief, looking through desk drawers and behind paintings for a hiding spot. But I knew Seth Walters, and if this was his office there's no way he would have hidden the book. So I walked straight over to the bookcase and opened the glass front. There, on display for everyone to see, was Bishop Wilder's genealogy with its finely tooled green leather binding. The arrogance of the man would have been astounding if I hadn't expected it.

"Got it. Let's go."

Ringo poked his head up from under the massive desk and flashed me a grin. "Look what I found."

He held up a man's gold ring, set with a blood-red ruby the size of a beetle.

"Put it back!" My whisper was almost a shriek. Something about that ring screamed power, and I wanted nothing to do with it.

"Why?"

"It's bad enough we're taking the book. If that went missing too our lives would be worth exactly crap."

Ringo looked speculatively at the gemstone winking in his hand. "He's that bad, huh?"

"Slick and Wilder are cut from the same piece of jagged rock." I hadn't called Seth Walters 'Slick' in a long time, but his office felt as slimy as he was, and it fit frighteningly well.

Ringo's expression was serious. "Right." He popped back under the desk and emerged, dusting himself off, then held his hand out for the genealogy and shoved it in the front of his waistband under his sweater. "We're off."

Once Ringo was back through the skylight he leaned in and hauled me up until I could pull myself out. He was just so elastic. I had to step up my own game to stay with him.

When we were back out on the roof, Ringo tensed. I instantly froze in place and listened. A scuffing sound on the pavement. Not damning by itself, but since my friends had all hidden themselves until we returned, it was worth investigating. We crept to the front edge of the building and dropped to our stomachs to look down. What we saw wasn't good.

Seth and four goons were just entering the building. It would take them about three minutes to get up to Seth's office, and if he was as observant as I thought he was, about thirty seconds to realize the book was gone. Three and a half minutes to get off the roof and away before someone came after us. Assuming they didn't post a guard outside the building.

We looked at each other with grim expressions, then went for it. We clung to the edges of the roof as we inched around to the back of the building. I only breathed again when we were down at the third floor window ledge. The alley below was too silent and it made me jumpy. And jumpy wasn't good for scaling sheer brick walls. At night. With no ropes, light, or safety net. I didn't look down.

Ringo got my attention with his little 'chhhtttt' sound. More effective than a shout for pushing me out of my head. He indicated with sign language that he was going to drop down to the electrical box first, and that I should wait five seconds before doing the same. He gave me a plan, and finally the running dialogue of death and destruction in my brain shut up.

I concentrated on following Ringo's hand and foot placement exactly, and in barely thirty seconds he dropped quietly to the electrical box. The alley remained silent as I counted to five, but I almost shattered eardrums when I dropped into an iron grip. It was Archer, and I just barely restrained myself from reflexively slugging him. He whispered in my ear that the others had slipped across the wall into the parking garage and were waiting for us to join them.

Which was all well and good, except a hamburger-nosed goon chose just that moment to burst out of the back door into the alley.

Archer's arm darted out to grab Ringo by the collar before his feet left the top of the electrical box. Hamburger-Nose was a Monger, as evidenced by my instant fight or flight reaction to his presence. Of course the fact that he was holding a knife didn't really help matters either. But still, it was three to one, and since one of our three was actually immortal, our odds didn't suck.

While Archer and Ringo were shooting rapid-fire hand signals to each other about how they were going to take Hamburger-Nose out, I did some plotting of my own. Being a chick is an occasional disadvantage, but being an armed chick gave me back a little edge. And I had spotted a paper-bag-wrapped wine bottle in the alley across from where we crouched on the electrical box.

Archer caught my eyes and said very clearly in his silent way, 'stay here.' Of course I nodded, and of course I had no intention of staying out of the way while my two favorite people got into a fight with a hamburger-nosed Monger piece of trash.

So, the moment Archer and Ringo flew down off the electrical box to tackle Hamburger-Nose, I took my own flying leap across the alley to the wino-trash. And in the same exact moment that I smashed the bottom of the bottle off on the brick wall, Slick and three other goons erupted from the building. The odds were most definitely not in our favor.

Archer was angry. Very angry. I couldn't tell if he was pissed at me for jumping down or at the two guys he threw punches at as he dodged their knives. Ringo was doing a fair job with Hamburger-Nose, but that left another goon and Seth Walters with nothing to do but cause trouble.

So I decided to cause it first. "Help! Police! Heeeellllp!!!!"

I seriously had never called for help in my life, but if nothing else, my fishwife screeching caused Beefy, the bigger goon fighting with Archer, to pause long enough to get a smash in the nose from an iron fist.

122

"Saira! Get out of here!" Archer's voice was a feral growl, and if I had been the least bit intimidated by him I would have run for my life.

"I'm not leaving you."

I held my broken bottle out in front of me like a knife and swung it just wildly enough to keep the ferrety goon by Seth at arm's length. There was a gleam in Seth's eyes, manic or crazy or just plain enjoying himself, and I didn't like it. Not even a little bit. Because it was directed at me.

"Someone taught you to glass, I see. I suppose I should expect a little gangster from you, considering where you come from." I would never get used to the oil slick that spewed from Seth Walters' mouth every time he opened it, and I shuddered. Ferret dodged in to grab the bottle from me, but I slashed it quickly and he jumped back out of range before it cut him. He was clearly no stranger to glassing, himself.

"I assume you have my book?" Seth was starting to circle me while Ferret kept me busy.

"You read? I didn't think you knew how." A flicker of annoyance crossed his features, and I knew I was playing with fire. Piss him off and he'd be even more dangerous. But piss him off enough and maybe he'd make a mistake. I struggled to keep my eyes on him and not let them dart toward Ringo. I couldn't see him anywhere, but I didn't make the mistake of underestimating Seth Walters anymore. Last time I did that, someone got shot.

"The coppers are on the way!" Adam's voice rang out, and I saw two figures leap over the back wall to join the fray.

Seth saw his opportunity and grabbed the broken wine bottle from my hand and spun it to face me with the jagged edge. "My book!"

Adam and Tom both lunged for Seth, but he stepped behind Ferret and they took him down instead. The sound of flesh hitting brick was horrible, and it was all I could do not to run to them. But I had a very jagged problem to deal with, and Seth's tightly controlled fury was directed straight at me.

I felt, rather than saw, Archer's attention shift toward Seth. The Monger must have sensed it too, because in an instant he was behind me with the glass bottle at my neck. Crap!

"Give me the book, Sucker."

The death glare shooting out of Archer's eyes would have rendered lesser mortals a pile of ashes. Unfortunately, Seth Walters was meaner than a rattlesnake and apparently wasn't fazed by the lethalness of an angry Vampire.

"I don't have it."

Ringo had finally managed to kick Hamburger-Nose in the face, which did little to improve his looks, and was about to step forward when Adam lunged for Seth's legs in a modified tackle.

Archer jumped forward to pull me away from the jagged edge of glass in the same instant as Seth went over with a roar of surprise. He twisted toward Adam as he fell, aiming the bottle right at Adam's chest. Somehow Tom threw himself forward at that moment, causing the broken glass to miss Adam and gouge him instead.

To add to the chaos, sirens jolted the air around us. With a final growl of scary rage, Seth rolled off the tangle of boys and glared at me in Archer's protective hold. "Your life just became worthless to you, little Clocker. It belongs to me now."

And with that, he and his goons slithered back into the shadows and were gone.

Archer and I immediately rushed to Tom and pulled him up. Blood was gushing down his face and it looked like one eye was missing. I choked back a scream and realized that the blood came from a piece of glass that had broken off the end of the bottle and lodged itself just over his eye.

"Archer, you and Ringo have to go." The sirens were right outside the building on the street, and I knew there was no way to explain a Vampire and a Victorian to the police.

Adam got to his feet. "The girls are in the car park. Take the book to my parents' house. We'll meet you there."

Archer clutched Tom's shoulder tightly. "You'll be fine, Landers. It's just a scratch." Tom smiled feebly and tried to blink through the blood, failing miserably. Archer kissed me quickly, and he and Ringo leapt over the back wall just as the police flashlights rounded the corner.

 Seers

It was full daylight by the time they finally let Tom out of the emergency clinic. Adam and I had been questioned for hours while they cleaned and stitched the cuts on Tom's face, but we'd managed to whisper a simple story to each other in the back of the police car.

We'd been out free-running when we came over the back wall just as some thieves were trying to breaking into the building. We described Seth and his goons as accurately as we could without giving anything substantial away. In the end the police seemed satisfied that we'd been the victims of random violence, and let us go with a warning about our nighttime activities.

Tom's wounds were a 'greater-than' symbol over his left eye. They covered the cut with a huge white bandage wrap, and he looked like a blast victim.

We were all exhausted, but Tom was grim-faced and silent on the ride to Adam's family home. I tried to ask him about his pain, but he just turned toward the window as if no one had spoken. Adam at least got a look.

"Thanks for … you know."

"Getting in the way? Yeah, no worries." Tom's voice was a weird, flat monotone, and Adam watched him for a long time after he turned back to the window. I reached over and squeezed Adam's hand quickly before we pulled up in front of the most beautiful Georgian town house I'd ever seen.

A house I knew.

"This was Lord Devereux's house!"

Adam was paying the driver and Tom had already gotten out of the taxi. I stared at the town house through the window with my jaw and eyes wide open. I'd only been there once, at night in 1888, but it was unmistakably the town house where Archer tried to lodge me when his rooms at King's College were off-limits. The one his father had owned.

I don't know if Adam heard me, and Tom didn't seem to care, but the coincidence was too much. I couldn't wait to talk to Archer, although if he was inside, he was out cold. Literally.

I unpeeled myself from the cab and climbed the steps to join Adam and Tom. A butler-type guy answered the door and nodded to each of us. Millicent Elian, the current head of the Elian family, had a driver named Jeeves, but this guy was so much more Jeeves than the real Jeeves that I would have handed him a calling card if I'd had one.

"Hey, Earnie. Is the fam upstairs?"

Earnie? "They're in the drawing room, sir." His monotone was of the 'I'm just barely tolerating your insolence' variety until he directed a question at Tom. "Can I get you anything, Mr. Landers?"

"No thank you, Earnest." Tom's monotone was much scarier because his voice sounded so … dead.

"Actually, could you have the extra bed in my room made up for Tom?" Adam caught Tom's eyes. "Then you can duck out to sleep when they start in." Adam's voice was surprisingly gentle, and I heard the level of their friendship in it. Tom closed his eyes as if steeling himself, then nodded.

"Right away, sir." Earnest wasn't quite so annoyed anymore, and I thought he must know Tom pretty well. People who knew Adam either loved him or hated him, but even through Tom's quiet reserve, he was a little shy, a little haunted, and always likeable. I hadn't known him before he was sucked into the Monger crowd, but since then I'd always felt a little protective of him. I knew I wasn't the only one.

Adam took a deep breath and squared his shoulders. "She knows we're here anyway; we might as well get it over with." He was talking about his mother, Camille Arman, the head of the Seer family and one of the most intimidating women I'd ever met. She was barely five feet tall, and yet between her French spike heels, her French pixie haircut, her gorgeous French clothes, her impeccable French accent, and her stunning French style, she was positively terrifying.

So, naturally, when Adam opened the door to the drawing room, I blurted out, in the dumbest possible way that makes a person wonder at their own stupidity for years after, "Does Archer know you're living in his house?" Yeah, painful.

Besides feeling like a totally uncouth Neanderthal in the face of the epitome of elegance that was Mrs. Arman, I'd even managed to make Adam stare with my rudeness. And that was saying something.

"Hello, Saira. Boys. Thomas, you need sleep. I've had the bed made up for you in Adam's room."

I looked at Adam quickly, hoping to get a grin or something comforting from him, but no. He was still staring at me like I was eight-legged and hairy. So I took a deep breath and turned to face the woman whose perfection made me quake.

Mrs. Arman had a signature boots and jeans look, like I did, but her look was nothing like mine. Adam and Ava's stunning mother wore dark, perfectly tailored jeans that probably cost a rent payment on the Venice loft we used to live in, pointy-toed, spike-heeled, red-soled boots of a designer variety I could only covet from magazines, and a simple, perfectly fitted white silk shirt. And if that wasn't enough, she was already three moves ahead of everyone, all the time, even her own remarkable family.

"To answer your question, Saira. Yes, I was aware of the house's pedigree. In fact, your Mr. Devereux sold the house to my great-grandmother, personally. She knew his mother, you see. They were distant cousins, I believe."

Of course they were. Archer was part Seer on his mother's side, but she had died when he was born and he never knew her or, I thought, her family.

128

"This was the Sucker's house?" Now it was my turn to stare at Adam. I couldn't find any obvious anger in his tone, but I didn't like the question, and neither, apparently did his mother.

"Adam, you will refrain from such inappropriate language, please. Mr. Devereux is our guest and will be spoken of courteously."

"I'm sorry, mother. It's a habit and I'll break it. Did they all make it back okay?"

"Yes, darling. Your sister and Alexandra are asleep in Ava's room, and Mr. Devereux is also resting." I noticed she didn't say where Archer was, and since Vampires are totally vulnerable during the day, that was a big deal.

"And Ringo?" I tried for polite, but I blurted again.

Mrs. Arman smiled, and it was the kind that lit up the whole block. No wonder she controlled the world and everyone in it, with an expression like that in her arsenal. "I left him in the game room with my husband."

I stared at Adam. "Tell me you don't have video games in your game room."

He winced, and then burst out laughing.

"Oh, God. His head's going to explode." I couldn't decide whether to freak out or bust up. Mrs. Arman decided it for me with her delighted grin.

"Quite likely, but they were both giggling like schoolboys when I left them."

Laughter won. "You realize I'll never be able to take him back to his own time."

"Why? He can keep his mouth shut, can't he?"

"He's sixteen, Adam. Video games? Really?"

"Come on. We better rescue my dad." Adam kissed his mother on the cheek before heading toward the door. "I'm going to catch a couple hours of sleep so I can be conscious when Archer gets up. I imagine we're all going to need to talk."

"Thank you, darling. It's lovely to have you home, even if you do look like something the dog unearthed. Consider a bath first?"

He sighed tolerantly. "Yes, Mother."

"Saira, darling. I've put you in the Green Room. Adam can show you the way."

"Thank you, Mrs. Arman." I followed Adam out of the drawing room, and he whistled when the door closed behind us.

"The Green Room's the old master bedroom. You must be pretty important."

"You have no idea."

In the game room it was clear that nothing short of a panzer tank was going to tear Ringo and Mr. Arman away from the role playing game that looked like a high-tech, digital version of Dungeons and Dragons. Ringo's eyes never left the screen, but he did engage his brain long enough to let me know Archer had the genealogy and everyone was fine.

When Adam dropped me off at the Green Room door we were both proper zombies. Adam brushed my hair absently with his lips, then stumbled off down the hall toward the family bedroom wing, and I went inside the room for 'important' guests.

The minute I was inside I wondered why Mrs. Arman had sent me there. The big, four-poster, heavily-carved wood bed looked like it had come with the house, and I understood perfectly why Archer was asleep on it. It would have been his room if he'd never sold the house. Except Mrs. Arman wasn't the type of woman who allowed unmarried teenagers to share beds in her house. I mean, Alex was sleeping in Ava's room, and Tom was in Adam's. So why did I get to curl up next to Archer? Granted, the only thing on my mind at that moment was a shower and a coma, but I didn't think Mrs. Arman had ever done an ill-considered thing in her life.

I was much too tired to process anything other than the hot water controls on the shower. There was a pair of pajamas that looked like they might be Ava's hanging on the towel rack, and I gratefully left my filthy clothes on the bathroom floor as I crawled under the covers of the big bed and wrapped myself around Archer's back. He didn't stir at all, and about ten seconds after my head hit the pillow, neither did I.

130

THE GENEALOGY

My hair was hanging in a wavy sheet over one shoulder, and I was wearing a midnight blue cloak over a matching long dress. The hood of the cloak hid my face from view, and I could just see the tips of my combat boots under the skirt.

Good to know I hadn't completely gone to the dark side.

And yet, as my vision-avatar was being escorted down a long hall toward a heavy wooden door at the end, I had the feeling that maybe I had. There were two guards behind me, and I was following a black-robed man whose face I had yet to see.

But I knew him.

The way he moved, powerful and yet freakishly graceful, like he was gliding on rails, was the dead giveaway. If I hadn't been so terrified, I might even have winced at my bad pun.

Dead indeed. The man leading me down the hall was Bishop Wilder.

We reached the wooden door, and one of the guards leapt forward to open it for us. The White Tower loomed into view outside the door just as Wilder turned to my vision-avatar and gave me a disconcertingly friendly smile. "After you, my Lady. I hope you'll appreciate the lengths I've gone to for your comfort."

"What. The. Hell."

I must have said the words out loud because I could almost still hear my voice in the room when I sat bolt upright in bed. The big four-poster bed in the Green Room. With no creepy bishops in sight. I automatically looked down at my clothes and was absurdly happy about the blue Smurf P.J.s I had on. Then I spotted Archer. He was still lying in bed as if he was sleeping, but his eyes were open and staring at the ceiling. It almost seemed like an afterthought when he finally looked at me. And smiled.

"Cute pajamas."

Really? He just saw my vision-avatar-booty waltz through a door with Wilder like a party guest, and the blue Smurfette winking at him from Ava's tank top had all his attention? I mentally slapped him and then got over it when his voice shifted. "The long Elizabethan gown isn't really your style, though."

"Elizabethan? Wait, how do you know that?"

Archer pointed to a painting above the fireplace across the room. I gasped and got up to look closer.

The painting was of a young, beautiful woman, with long gold hair, wearing a crown on her head.

"Elizabeth Tudor on the day of her coronation." Archer spoke matter-of-factly, as if it wasn't insane to be looking at this portrait in a private home.

"Why do they have it?" My voice came out in an awed whisper, and Archer chuckled.

"It's a copy of the original, painted at the same time, but specifically for the Seer Family. Camille's great-grandmother was very proud of this portrait and hung it when she took ownership of the house."

"Elizabeth was a Seer."

"So it seems. And you'll notice the style of the dress? Obviously this one is much more grand, but it's from the same period."

I looked closely at the dress and jewelry. It looked like most everything was gold except a bit of silver at her wrist. But Archer was right, the style of the dress was similar enough to the blue one I'd been wearing in his vision.

I turned back to him, looking through narrowed eyes. "You knew Elizabeth was a Seer when you had that vision of Ringo. Do you still deny it's her?"

He sat up and sighed. "It's getting harder to ignore the logic."

"You just saw me there too. Why is it so hard to believe it was a true vision with Ringo?"

"I saw you, but as a separate person. I wasn't looking out at the scene through your eyes. That's the difference." I rewound the memory and realized he was right. I'd been looking at myself in third-person. 'Avatar' hadn't been wrong.

Archer ran his hands through his hair, making it all messy and adorable. "At least we got confirmation we're going to the Tower."

"We?"

"You, me, and Ringo at least."

"How do you know you're there?"

Archer looked as if it took every ounce of patience to stay calm. "The first and most obvious answer is that I go where you go no matter what. And since I clearly wasn't born yet in the 16th century, there's nothing to prevent me from being there."

He had a point, so I bit back my automatic bristle-mode and waited for him to finish.

"Second, and perhaps equally obvious, is the fact that I'm the one having the visions. And since Seers don't have visions of things that happened in the past, it can only mean it will happen in my future."

My eyes went wide. "That's actually really brilliant."

He smiled wryly. I guessed it was sort of a backward compliment. I forged ahead to cover my blush. "I wonder if the Armans have ever thought that through?"

Archer raised an eyebrow. "If I were to guess, I'd say yes. Otherwise, why would we have been allowed to share this room last night? Camille Arman is almost as Victorian as I am in her ideas of acceptable unmarried behavior, so us sharing this vision must have been her motive."

"Ah, excellent point. I wondered about that."

He eyed my borrowed P.J.s again. "Lucky for you, I remain trustworthy."

"Because the Smurfs are so sexy."

"You have no idea."

I popped out of bed and said brightly, "Well okay then. Time to get up and face the Armans." I bolted for the bathroom and discovered my clothes, that I'd left strewn on the floor, had been cleaned and folded in a neat little pile on a chair. And as much as it creeped me out that someone dealt with my filthy clothes, I was very grateful to pull on something clean.

I thought about my reaction to Archer as I was getting dressed. I didn't think I was a prude. Not really. But then again, having no experience at all with the physical aspects of a relationship beyond kissing also didn't qualify me as particularly expert. In fact, if I was honest with myself, something usually best done in small doses, one of the few things I was actually expert at was running away. I sighed and twisted my hair into a quick braid, swished some toothpaste around in my mouth, and turned my back on the face I saw in the mirror.

Everyone had assembled in the drawing room, and what a fascinating group it was. Ringo was grinning from ear to ear as he described the flash-bangs he'd thrown at an evil mage in a role-playing video game. Archer and Adam were laughing at his enthusiasm, and Mr. Arman chuckled happily at the sight of so much animation. Alex sat with Adam, who held her hand easily. She didn't look nearly as comfortable with the display of affection as Adam obviously was, and she kept darting her eyes to Mrs. Arman, who talked quietly with Ava in the corner. Tom was the last to come in, looking drawn, as if all the angles in his face had sharpened with lack of sleep. I caught his eye and patted the couch next to me, but he pretended not to notice and veered off to sit against the wall near the guys.

As if by some silent signal everything got sort of quiet at once, and Mrs. Arman stepped into the center of the room.

"I trust you have all somewhat recovered from your ordeal of last night?"

All of us nodded. Except Tom. He sat motionless against the wall.

"I've informed Jane Simpson where you are, and she's letting your parents and teachers know you're safe." Her eyes landed briefly on me when she said that, and I realized she was talking specifically about my mother. I felt guilty for not having called her the minute I had access to a phone. Though realistically, the police station might not have been a comforting place from which to hear from one's daughter. I nodded my thanks and Mrs. Arman continued, her eyes still on mine.

"I'll save the lecture. There will be a time in all of your lives when you experience the same fear and concern for someone else's safety that we have felt for yours. And perhaps then you'll remember this time, and might even find it in yourselves to apologize to the people who love you."

That was probably the most effective non-lecture from a parent I'd ever heard. And if the squirminess of guilt in my own guts was any measure, it was one I wouldn't ignore.

Then she turned to Tom, and her tone softened. "Tom, I think you want to say something?"

He looked startled. "No, I don't."

She spoke gently, like she was coaxing a child into trying something unfamiliar. "It's much better to say it than let it fester, my dear, because if the anger doesn't go, it will become part of you."

Tom shook his head, clearly miserable at all the attention she'd put on him. "Really, there's nothing."

"I'm angry." Adam's voice cut through the thick silence in the room. "I'm angry that bastard keeps hurting you."

"It wasn't really on purpose. I just keep getting in the way." Tom's mumbled voice was painful to hear, and I got hit with a wave of guilt. I was the reason Tom had gotten hurt both times. Seth Walters had been aiming for me when Tom took a bullet in the shoulder, and it was my dumb idea that gave Slick the weapon to cut Tom's face.

But Mrs. Arman shot me a warning look before I could speak, and then she redirected the conversation.

"You were successful, I understand. You located the missing genealogy book and retrieved it, an endeavor not without considerable cost, as most valuable things often have. I would like to see the book, if I may?"

It lay on the table in front of Archer, the green tooled-leather cover looking worn, but still beautiful. He stayed motionless, as did everyone else, and I was in awe of his confidence. "While it is true we brought the book here to your home as a place of safety, it was an action designed to liberate it from Walters and his crew, not necessarily deliver it to new owners."

Camille Arman looked at Archer for a very long moment. She was clearly unused to being blocked from anything, and although he hadn't said no outright, the pleasant smile on Archer's face spoke as clearly as if he'd said the word.

"What is your plan, then, Mr. Devereux?" Frost laced her voice, and I shivered.

"My plan … our plan … is to determine Bishop Wilder's intention in having me compile the genealogy, to understand why the Mongers are willing to steal and maim to keep it, and hopefully decipher some clue as to what Wilder is doing in the sixteenth century."

I almost clapped.

The rest of the room's occupants looked stunned.

Except Ringo. He just grinned at Archer and winked at me like the urchin he used to be.

And with that wink, I knew exactly what to do next. I stood and went over to a portrait of the Arman family that hung over the fireplace. It was painted in a style reminiscent of presidential portraits of the twentieth century, sort of time-warp-locked in the sixties. And everyone in it was gorgeous, even though the twins were probably about ten years old. Camille Arman was wearing a stunning silver cuff bracelet that looked like it was covered in ancient scrollwork, and I pointed to it.

"Is that Aislin's bracelet?" Because the silence wasn't thick enough in the room. I knew I'd just busted Ava, but

136

circumstances being what they were, I hoped her mother could forgive her.

To her credit, Mrs. Arman didn't miss a beat. "Yes, it is."

I turned to face her. "Can you direct your sight to March or April, 1554 to find Elizabeth Tudor in the Tower of London?"

Mrs. Arman's eyes narrowed at me speculatively. "There are history books for that sort of thing, Saira."

"Like Archer said, we believe Bishop Wilder is there. With her."

She took a breath. It bothered her, but she hid it. "And what would you do about it if he is?"

"I don't know, exactly. But Archer has seen me and Ringo there, so I'd like to know what I'm taking us into."

This was news to Ringo, of course, since the only time we'd had alone we'd been running, stealing, or fighting, not chatting about Archer's visions-that-might-have-been-dreams. "Yeah, that'd be good to know. Since I've been invited an' all."

"And is that something you know how to do? Get back to a specific time and place in history?"

Adam raised an eyebrow at me and I crossed my arms in front of me, either defiantly or protectively, I wasn't sure. "It can be done." I tried not to sound twelve, I really did.

And I failed, if the raised-eyebrow look I got from Mrs. Arman was any indication. It was the kind of look that said 'indeed' in a way specifically designed to make one feel like the world's biggest idiot. What was it about this tiny, impeccably-dressed, rich Frenchwoman that made me feel so totally inadequate?

"Mum can't look into the past, even with the cuff."

I stared at Ava, remembering why I loved that girl so much. I didn't think the force-of-nature-and-good-shoes that was her mother would ever have admitted that out loud to me.

"Because it has already happened." Even as the questions raged through my brain, I already knew the answers. I turned to Archer. "And because I'm taking you back there with me, your visions haven't happened yet. That's why you're having them."

"Does that mean you'll let Saira take you back in time to use the cuff, Mother?" Adam's voice unexpectedly filled the space, but the look Mrs. Arman turned on her son would have withered plants on the spot.

"Certainly not. The girl has no idea how to get there, and I don't have the slightest intention of putting myself at risk for a goose chase."

"I'll go with her." Ava surprised me again with the strength it must have taken to say those words. "Loan me the cuff, and I'll help her figure out what the bishop is planning."

"You'll do no such thing."

Ava looked at her mother with very clear eyes. "You can't stop me, Maman."

"Don't be ridiculous, Ava. Of course I can. I am your mother and the head of this Family."

"And I'm the next in line for head. I'll take it to the Council if I have to, but it won't look good to have your daughter openly defy you in front of the other heads. You and I both know there are enough Seer Families vying for power that the slightest sign of dissent will leave you scrambling."

"It's what my father's been waiting for." Tom spoke quietly from the corner. Everyone's eyes swiveled to him, but he clammed up and didn't say another word.

"I'll find out how to get there even if I have to use my mother's necklace."

"Do you really think she'd allow you to go back five hundred years into the clutches of the man who tried to kill her? Because that's what we're discussing. Sending our children to their deaths. We won't do it, Saira. No parent would."

Archer stood and picked up the genealogy from the table. "Camille, James, thank you for your hospitality. It's been a pleasure to see these rooms again." He held his hand out to me and nodded to Ringo, who stood to join us.

Mrs. Arman was motionless, and she looked like she was barely restraining herself from leaping up to stop us. "Where will you take the book, Archer?"

138

"Someplace safe from Mongers and anyone else who would use the information in it against Descendants."

I mouthed the words 'thank you' to Ava as I followed Archer and Ringo to the door. But then I stopped and found Mrs. Arman's eyes. "I understand, Mrs. Arman. I know what it feels like when someone you love is in danger. The Mongers want mixed-bloods, and Wilder just wants blood. And when it puts people I love in danger, I have to do whatever I can to make it stop."

Her expression didn't change and I didn't stick around to see if it would. Archer tucked the genealogy into his coat and held my hand as Ringo opened the front door for us with a flourish.

"After you, my not-a-Lord and Lady."

I grinned at him, absurdly happy considering the conversation we'd just escaped. "Video games? Seriously?"

He and Archer burst out laughing as we stepped into the clear, crisp night.

LEAVING A MARK

"I was thinking I'd leave a message for Doran at Whitechapel Station."

"How?" Archer seemed amused, but not surprised. Ringo, on the other hand, was mystified until I explained that my vaguely-related cousin Doran seemed to be the only Clocker left who knew all the rules of time travel.

"You didn't actually think I'd come out unarmed, did you?" I pulled an orange paint marker out of the inside pocket of the sport bike jacket I had nicked from Archer's wardrobe.

"Another of yer fancy pens?"

"Yep. Let's go."

It was still early in Vampire night terms, and the foot traffic was all pub and club-goers. One of my favorite things about London was the pub on every corner. I wasn't much of a drinker, considering I was still four years away from legal drinking age in California, but I liked the idea of a neighborhood gathering spot. A place you knew you could find your friends if, you know, you had them and they lived in your neighborhood.

Since the band was back together it seemed a natural thing to go running. Archer and I were more Parkour runners – all about getting from A to Z without detours. But Ringo was evolving into a free-runner. Maybe it was a day of first-person video games, but he had suddenly developed some stunners. Londoners weren't typically too excited to be dodged and danced around as we traversed the city, but Ringo actually got applause from some street musicians when he executed a particularly impressive series of flips across the concrete caps of a guard rail. I didn't even stop to think about things like taxis and buses and electric lights, and what they must be doing to Ringo's head. I was having too much fun.

We finally made it to the Underground entrance on Whitechapel High Street, and I darted inside while Archer bought us all waters at a kiosk. They joined me in the alcove a couple of minutes later, just as I was putting the finishing touches on my message to Doran.

"Clocker Tower? Why there?" Archer handed me cold bottled water, and I took a long drink.

"He found me there before, and it's a place to hide Ringo." I turned to Ringo, who was playing with the plastic bottle cap, twisting it on and off. "Unless … I promised Charlie I'd take you back."

He looked up in surprise. "Are ye mad?" He held up the water bottle. "I've held my tongue 'cause there wasn't time before, but the questions need answers and I'm about done bein' patient."

I poised my finger over Doran's spiral. "Right then. To school?"

Archer picked up Ringo's hand and clapped it on my shoulder while he wrapped one arm around my waist and sighed. "I suppose it's faster than taking the train."

The Clocker Tower was empty, as usual, when we landed back at St. Brigid's. I was shakier on my legs than when I'd just brought Ringo with me, and it was clear that ferrying the extra people was more difficult than where and when I traveled them. Ringo's grip was still tight on my shoulder, and I could tell he was keeping it together by the skin of his teeth. The tower was dark, but that never bothered me, and I made my way to the desk for an extra Maglite I kept there. I clicked it on and handed it to Ringo.

"Here. I have a pack of batteries for you, too."

"Thanks, Saira." The way he said 'thanks,' and the grip he had on the Maglite made me think it was a comfort to him. I'd given him mine when I travelled to 1888 to find my mom, and it was probably the one thing he understood of all the modern things that had assaulted him in the past twenty hours. I knew he needed time to process all of it, but we still had a couple of things to do.

"Will you be all right here for a few minutes? I'm going to get us some food and a change of clothes for you." Archer and Adam were both much bigger than Ringo, but I thought he might fit into Connor's clothes. And worst case scenario I could give him a pair of my own jeans.

"I'm fine. Ye've no need to care fer me like a child. I can manage."

I bit back the snappy comment I was about to make when I looked at his eyes. They were sunk into purple sockets, and his skin was pale from lack of sleep. "There's a door to the upper floor hidden in the wardrobe, and you might like the view. I'll be back in a minute." I didn't tell him about the mattress on the floor because he'd deny he needed it, but I was fairly certain he'd find it on his own.

Archer headed toward the door. "I'm going for a change of clothes too."

Ringo waved his hand at us dismissively as he headed toward the wardrobe. "Be ready to talk when ye get back." He found the door and was already up the stairs when we left the tower.

I stopped in the deserted hallway. "Where are you really going?" I knew a change of clothes was not top on Archer's list of errands tonight.

"Shaw's office."

"Me too."

"Lead the way."

I took Archer down the back staircase leading from the closed wing. It was after lights out, but I didn't want to take a chance any of the staff were roaming the halls. As I suspected, there was light under Mr. Shaw's door. I knocked softly, and within moments the door was yanked open. Mr. Shaw didn't seem surprised to see us, but put his finger to his lips as he let us inside.

"Have you seen your mother?" He sat across from us.

"Mrs. Arman said she called her."

"She did, but I think she'd prefer to see you with her own eyes."

I knew he was right, but part of me wondered if my mother and I were on the same 'do something' team. Somehow I thought she might still be on the 'stay hidden and safe' side of the equation, and frankly, I didn't want the fight.

Archer's voice matched Mr. Shaw's quiet tones, and it felt like we were all sharing secrets. "What happened in the woods last night?"

"They were there for Alex and Adam. Apparently a Monger whelp had seen her arrive yesterday."

"How did they explain Walters being there?"

Mr. Shaw's voice was bitter and hard. "Monger enforcer. He said he was just doing his job. The Were took off into the woods a few minutes after they got there, but Connor and Owen had already made it back to school. So in the end, you guys were in the most danger, not us."

We gave Mr. Shaw the rundown of our own adventures, and he squinted at us twice. Once to realize I'd brought Ringo forward, and then when I described how Tom had gotten cut. At the end of the story, Archer pulled the genealogy out of his coat and set it on the table.

"So that's it, huh?" Mr. Shaw's eyes were locked on the dark green leather cover of the book. "I'm surprised you didn't leave it with Camille."

Archer smiled grimly. "As persuasive as she is, Camille Arman is too political for my taste. I'd prefer to leave the genealogy with you if I may, at least until we need it."

I'm not sure who was more surprised, me or Mr. Shaw. The expression on Archer's face told me that he'd given this a lot of thought.

"I compiled the book, so I know what it says, but not what it means. I'm hoping your scientist's eyes can uncover the truth behind Wilder's mission."

143

Mr. Shaw contemplated Archer for a long moment. "Was Wilder already a Vampire when he commissioned this book?"

"I believe so, yes."

"Any idea when he was turned?"

"None. Bishop Cleary and I did an exhaustive search on Wilder's background, and we believe he was still within his natural life when I knew him. The number of records surrounding his youth and education would be too difficult to fake."

"Well, that counts for something."

"How?" I'd never really considered Bishop Wilder's personal history as very relevant. He was just a nasty piece-of-work old guy who messed with people I cared about.

"If, indeed, Bishop Wilder was ingesting blood in the attempt to synthesize the genetic component of that blood, the genesis for his theories is an important factor to determining his intent."

"In English, please?"

Mr. Shaw smiled faintly. "How he got the idea might tell us what he's trying to do."

"Right." I looked at Archer. "Was he a scientist?"

He shook his head. "A theologian and a third son."

"What year was he born?"

"1830. In Cambridge. His father was a Peer and had a fairly decent-sized estate. Apparently Wilder applied to Christ College in Cambridge, but was denied entrance. Something to do with his father's politics. So he studied at King's College, and essentially just stayed there, teaching as he went up the ranks of the church."

Mr. Shaw thought for a long moment, then got up and pulled a book off a shelf. Archer reached over and picked up my hand, his fingers exploring the small cuts and rough patches of skin from my climb up Slick's building. Our fingers looked good twined together.

The book closed with a thump that snapped me out of my hand-gazing trance. "Charles Darwin," Mr. Shaw announced with finality.

"Marie Curie," I said, with just as much certainty.

The look both guys gave me made me laugh. "What? His non-sequitor gets a pass, but mine gets the 'she's finally cracked' look?"

Archer ignored my self-deprecation and raised an eyebrow. "*On the Origin of the Species* was published in 1859."

"Wilder's father might have known Darwin when he studied at Cambridge."

Archer shook his head, his eyes widening. "When I first got to King's College, Francis Galton was lecturing on eugenics, much of which was based on his cousin, Darwin's studies. Bishop John Wilder had just taken over the theology department at King's, and I remember seeing him at the lecture. That was in 1883."

"Were you already working with Wilder then?"

"Not for three more years."

I'd heard of eugenics, but it was usually associated with Nazis and selective breeding, so I didn't really follow the logic. "What does eugenics have to do with whatever it is Wilder's trying to do?"

"You mean besides all the horrors that have been committed in the name of eugenics science?" Archer scoffed, and I realized he had a pretty strong opinion about something I hadn't given a lot of thought to.

"Well, yeah. Wilder wasn't around after 1888, so he wasn't the one sterilizing people he thought shouldn't breed." I'd read enough on the subject that I could contribute to the conversation, but Archer way outclassed me in the Victorian science department.

"Not that I wouldn't put it past him, but no, I think his interest must have been in the arena of positive eugenics – selecting the traits one wants and breeding specifically to achieve them." Archer suddenly reminded me of the student he'd been when I met him.

"But Vampires don't breed, right?" I looked at Mr. Shaw instead of Archer for confirmation. That wasn't a conversation

145

we'd ever had before, and I was trying to treat it like scientific theory, not boyfriend fact.

Mr. Shaw shot me a strange look that I deliberately didn't read into. "Their cells are in a state of permanent stasis, so no, but that's not what he's talking about."

Archer clarified. "If the idea came more from the Darwinist school of thought, Wilder could have intended to treat his own blood much like a plant or animal breeder does, combining the genetic traits from others to see what skills he could acquire."

Mr. Shaw contemplated Archer for a long moment. "So, was the genealogy a way for Wilder to find potentially interesting genetic traits to exploit, or was it a Monger political power play?" His voice rumbled quietly in the room.

Neither of us had an answer for him, and the Bear picked up the book with gentle hands, then looked at me. "Your mother must know some of the people listed in here."

"She's in there herself." I remembered Archer telling me that a very long time ago.

"Are you?" Mr. Shaw's voice was quiet, like he didn't really want to know the answer.

Archer answered quietly. "I kept Saira's name out, but it was in my personal notes."

I held my hand out to Mr. Shaw. "May I?" He handed me the genealogy and I opened it carefully. The stiff, vellum paper crackled under my fingers. I turned the pages slowly, catching glimpses of other family names I itched to read, but continuing until I found the Elian Family tree.

It wasn't a big one, and had only two or three different branches every generation. My finger moved down near the bottom of the page. There was my mother, Claire Elian born in 1850, and her sister, Emily, 1852. And next to my mother's name, in the same handwriting, was the name William Shaw. There was no notation about his family and no date. Just the name.

"I knew the significance of his family name, of course. The Shaws have their own tree in the Shifter section. But at the time I wrote that, I was ignorant of the mixed-blood moratorium, and it was all still just an academic exercise, a scavenger hunt to track down the obscure connections between people. It wasn't until I connected the first Ripper victims to Clocker Families that I realized how dangerous the knowledge in this book could be." Archer's voice was so quiet, and in that moment I got that he'd been carrying the guilt of this genealogy with him for more than a hundred years.

I turned the page. There were no further Elians. The Clocker Family tree ended with my mother and Emily. "But Emily had a child, didn't she? I mean she's Millicent's grandmother."

"Actually, your aunt Emily was pregnant with Tallulah when your mother went back to see your father in 1888. But Claire didn't go to Elian Manor to see Emily then for obvious reasons. I began keeping an eye on your family soon after you left, but as far as I know, I didn't see Claire again."

I stared at Archer as the cold pit of certainty hit my stomach. My mother stopped traveling because of what Wilder did to her. She never met her niece, Tallulah, or her grandniece, Millicent. Nor did she see her sister Emily again. I knew my own part in that, and it felt like a piece of ice I would carry with me forever. But the full extent of the fear and horror that Wilder's abduction of my mother had left with her didn't hit me until I realized what it cost her.

I closed the genealogy and put it back on the table in front of Mr. Shaw. I started to shake and I thought it might be rage. It must have shown in my eyes when I looked at Mr. Shaw because he tensed. "She has to go back. She has to travel again."

"But he said she didn't." Mr. Shaw sounded confused.

"That's not how it works. He doesn't remember it because she hasn't yet. But if she does, his memory will open up to include it."

Archer nodded. "It is true that there have been gaps in my memory. They used to worry me; a sign of having lived too long. Then I realized they were holes to fill in with memories of Saira. Things she hadn't done yet."

That was a startling bit of information to Mr. Shaw, and he chewed on it for a moment. Then he sighed. "I don't think anything I say is going to erase your mother's fear. The fact is, I can't protect her there, or rather, then. And there's no real closure for her. She survived, yes, thanks to you. But Wilder almost killed her."

"And he's still out there." I said it out loud, but I knew it was the key to unlocking my mom's terror. She hadn't said it, but she knew, like we did, that Wilder had escaped the Bedlam cellar cave-in. And he'd done it through a portal because he had her blood. I caught Archer's eye as I stood up to go.

"I'm going to see my mom first, then I'll raid the kitchen and head back upstairs."

"You're staying here in school?" Mr. Shaw sounded hopeful, but wary, and I nodded.

"I need to talk to my cousin, and I asked him to meet us here. But I'm not sure how long we'll stay, and the Mongers can't know about it. I'm sure Seth Walters will be by daily looking for us and this book."

Mr. Shaw's eyes narrowed, then he nodded. "Where--?"

"Clocker Tower."

"Right. And you?" He looked at Archer expectantly.

"Wherever she goes."

Mr. Shaw nodded again, apparently satisfied. "Will you leave a note or something if you leave?"

That made me smile. He couldn't help himself. "Top drawer of the desk. But I'll go see Mom now too."

Mr. Shaw stood and wrapped me in a tight hug. It was as unexpected as it was comforting, and I hugged him back. "I'll keep the bastards away on my end, but you guys don't go swimming into their nets either, okay?"

"I don't swim." Archer delivered the line so dryly that Mr. Shaw and I both stared at him for a second. And then I saw the gleam in his eye and I started laughing. I gave him a quick kiss on the cheek and headed for the door.

"See you in a bit."

I was sort of dreading the conversation with my mom, and after Archer took off for his cellar I had to make my feet point in the direction of her rooms. But there's only so long a free-runner can procrastinate before the urge to really move overrides snail tendencies.

I scratched at my mom's door. She was a light sleeper so I knew she'd hear it. The door opened almost immediately and she pulled me into her arms.

"I was sure they'd taken you." She spoke into my neck, since I was almost a head taller than my mom. I could feel her tremble with the effort of keeping her tears back, but she managed it, and I was glad. I already felt horrible for not calling her the minute I could, and guilt made me nauseous.

Our voices were quiet and we sat close together, partly for noise, but also because I think she wanted to touch me, to confirm I was actually there.

"Mom, I'm okay."

"Are you? Because Camille said Tom had gotten hurt."

My voice was choked when I answered. "I thought I could do it myself. I thought I could keep them away. But it was my stupid weapon they used on him. If I hadn't broken that bottle…" I'd been being tough and capable for so long that the tears, when they came, burned like acid down my face.

My mom pulled me into her arms and held me. She didn't try to shush my sobs or wipe my tears or tell me anything was going to be okay. She just held me and stroked my hair and was my mom. I had no idea how much I'd been missing her until that moment.

Because crying sucks and sobbing sucks all the air out of a room, I made myself stop. Not before the snot joined the party, but Mom handed me a tissue wordlessly and waited until I could breathe without gasping.

"Guilt is sort of pointless, isn't it?" It's true, my mother should have been a Seer the way she could read minds. I nodded and swiped the last of the tears off my cheeks.

"I get headaches when I feel guilty. How about you?"

"Nausea."

"Did Camille feed you?"

I smirked. "We walked out before dinner."

"Hungry?"

"I will be, when my stomach unclenches. I was going to raid the kitchen."

My mom stood up. "I'll go with you."

There had been times in my life when the lines between adult and child had been blurry. When she disappeared for a week every few years and I had to take care of myself, I was the adult. When I faced down Jack the Ripper and Bishop Wilder to save her life, I was definitely the adult. Crying in her arms right now I'd been able to be the kid, which was as unsettling as it was comforting. But as we snuck our way to the enormous kitchens of St. Brigid's, I felt like we were friends.

We whispered to each other as we filled up a couple of cloth bags with bread, cheese, fruit, and some leftover chicken pasties. I filled her in on Ringo's presence and on the conversation we'd had with Mr. Shaw. She told me about yelling at the Rothbitch in front of Miss Simpson, the Rothchild brats being suspended from school, and the Were being sent away by the furious headmistress.

Then I asked about the Clocker necklace.

My mom looked at me for a long moment. "It's in a safe in the keep at Elian Manor. Why?"

"Because I think I need to get to 1554."

"No."

And just like that I went back to being the child.

I packed up the cloth bags and slung them across my body, refusing to speak until I had my temper back in check. She might talk to me like a kid, but I wasn't going to lose it like one. No matter how much I felt like throwing a tantrum. She sensed it too, because she started trying to justify the 'no.'

"Even if I would allow it, Millicent would never let the necklace out for something like that. It's too dangerous, and you're the last—" her words faltered, so I finished for her.

"The last Clocker. And if I don't have kids we're all S.O.L."

She watched me with worried eyes. I guess maybe she realized that saying no to me was pretty much a guarantee of defiance. But I didn't give her anything; no expression, no anger, nothing. Which scared her more than a tantrum would have. But hey, if she didn't trust me with the proven way to travel, I didn't need to trust her with my plans.

"I have to go. I'll see you later."

"Saira ..."

I hesitated just long enough not to be rude, but she must have changed her mind because the words got hung up somewhere else. "Good night, Mom."

I saw her wince when the sadness returned to my voice.

PREPARATION

I slipped away from my mother's rooms and tried to define the awkwardness our relationship had become. I was in a strange gray area with her. She'd raised me in America, where legal adulthood was age eighteen, and it was still pretty automatic for both of us to think that way. But in England I'd reached a weird adulthood at sixteen. I could legally work, pay taxes, get insurance, have sex, and I had to pay full adult fare on all public transportation. The full-fare thing chapped me the most.

But it all came down to the fact that I had been making decisions for myself for a very long time. She was my mother, so I would always give her the courtesy of listening, but she couldn't choose for me, and her word was no longer law where I was concerned.

On the heels of that thought came the realization that I probably needed to figure out how to pay my own way if I was going to be so openly independent, but I tucked that away to contemplate later.

I didn't run, the food bags were too heavy. But I was as quick and quiet as I could be as I crept into the boys' wing of the dormitories. Connor shared a room with a kid named Max, so I was counting on his Wolf senses to hear me tap the door with my fingertip. He answered, squinting into the dim light of the hallway, hair spiked up all over his head. His eyes widened fractionally at the sight of me, and he gave me a lopsided smile.

"I need a pair of your jeans, some socks, a t-shirt, and a sweater. You might get them back, but maybe not, so don't give me your favorites."

And this is why I loved Connor the Wolf. He thought about my request for about half a second, disappeared into his room, and came back less than a minute later with everything I'd asked for.

"There's an extra pair of socks. They're new. Came two to a pack."

"You're awesome, thank you. Come up to the Clocker Tower when you wake up. There's someone I want you to meet."

He yawned hugely and nodded, already closing the door to go back to bed.

After quickly grabbing my own bag of stuff and a pair of combat boots I didn't wear much anymore, I made it back to the Clocker Tower just as Archer was rounding the corner. I took the key inside with us and locked the door.

The main tower room was dark and silent, and we crept up the stairs to the upper room. Just like I figured, Ringo was crashed out on the twin mattress. Asleep he looked like the boy he probably hadn't been in a long time, and I resisted the urge to tuck the duvet around him. We silently made our way back downstairs and closed the wardrobe door behind us to muffle the noise of our conversation.

I dropped down to sink into the big old Chesterfield sofa my mother had moved into the tower during the five minutes she thought it would be her office. The art studio upstairs had sort of always been mine. I kept the twin mattress on the floor covered in a quilt and an old, super soft duvet for the times I just needed to be alone. Archer had never spent any significant time in the Clocker Tower with me before, so having him here felt like hanging out at 'my place.'

Archer sat next to me and put his arm around my shoulders to draw me into his chest.

"Did you see your mother?"

I nodded. "She told me I couldn't have the Elian necklace."

153

Archer tipped my chin up to look at him. "You knew that would happen though. It's why you left a message for Doran to meet you here."

I sighed. "Knowing something doesn't always take away the wish for a different outcome. The whole conversation did make me realize something though."

"What's that?"

"I need a job."

He laughed quietly. "Because saving Immortal Descendants isn't enough?"

I chuckled. "It doesn't pay the bills. And if I'm not going to do what my mother and Millicent want, I better be able to pay my own way. Because it's just a matter of time before they cut me off financially."

"You know, of course, that everything I have is yours." His voice got softer, and I looked into eyes that gazed back with total seriousness.

"I know you say that, Archer. And I know you probably mean it too."

The corner of his mouth quirked up wryly. He knew what was coming, even before I'd formed the words in my head.

"I need to know I can take care of myself in all ways; financially, physically and emotionally. Because if I can't count on myself to do it, I'll never be confident enough to accept anyone else's help."

"So by your logic, you have to give up your resistance to accepting my physical help."

"Huh?"

"I've never met anyone more physically capable in my life. You can clearly keep yourself safe, so it shouldn't be a problem to accept someone else's help with that too."

He was teasing me, but I also knew he meant it. I'd been resisting any and all safety conversations pertaining to me, but what was I really afraid of? That accepting help might mean I was weak and unable to take care of myself? I knew that wasn't true, so what was I holding onto so hard?

I nodded. "You're right. I'm sorry."

That surprised him. "I'm right? Would you mind repeating that in front of witnesses?"

I laughed and snuggled up against him. He held me close to him and I let myself relax into his arms, breathing in the warm spiciness of his skin.

"Part of me wants to ignore the visions," I whispered into the dark, and Archer stilled.

"Mine?"

I looked into his eyes. "If we don't go back, he'll never get Ringo."

"But he's not after Ringo."

I closed my eyes against the truth of Archer's words. "I know. But why is it our problem to solve?"

He kissed my closed eyelids. "Believe me, if I thought you actually meant that, I'd agree wholeheartedly."

I smiled ruefully. "It's not who you are either. You don't run away when something's not right."

"Hmm, let's see. Vampire with a conscience. Oh, the irony."

His hand absently played with long strands of my hair that had escaped the braid, so I sat up and quickly unbound it. He smiled when I moved back in for more grooming, and his fingers worked through the knots in the most luxurious way. If I could have purred, I would have.

"It seems you must be part feline after all." Doran's voice drawled from the darkness near the painting of the London Bridge. Archer must have heard him arrive, but I jumped a mile.

I realized in an instant that Archer and Doran had never met, because Archer's body was coiled and wary in a way that's actually really dangerous for the other person. Doran was either clueless or didn't care, because he stepped into the ring of lamplight around the desk with an easy smile.

"You wanted me?"

Archer tensed more than I thought possible given his already coiled stance. To me, Doran's arrogance was just annoying. But then again, stupidly handsome usually went hand-in-hand with arrogant in a way that wasn't usually charming. Adam was the exception to that rule.

"Teach me how to travel out of default range."

"Getting tired of the Victorians?" Doran's eyes never flicked to Archer. Not once. I wasn't sure if I actually heard Archer growl, but I could feel it, and the hair on my skin stood on end.

This pissing contest wasn't going to end well.

"Doran, I believe you know who Archer is. Archer, this is my distant cousin...ish, and occasional teacher, Doran."

"Oh, we're much more distant than cousins. And practically the last Clockers left if you believe the rumors." Finally, Doran's eyes landed on Archer. "You've held up well, Sucker. A lot of you lose your humanity. Too much time among the riff-raff and you start to hate them."

Archer was wound more tightly than I'd ever seen him before, and I wondered why he let Doran push his buttons. Or, for that matter, why Doran was doing it. I was just about to redirect the obvious disaster that was this conversation when Archer answered.

"Since I began as human, I remain one. There's no mystery there. You, on the other hand ..." There was nothing but pleasantness in Archer's tone, and Doran's mouth curled up in a tiny smile before he looked down at the desk still laid out with food.

"I'm starving. May I?" Doran reached for a slice of cheese with a questioning glance at me. I nodded and he popped it in his mouth. Somehow, the tension that was boiling between the two men was down to a simmer, and I let myself breathe again.

"Doran, where do you live when you're not dropping by to chat?"

He tore himself a piece of bread and looked at me with a smile. "I have a little place on an island in the Adriatic. But a better question might be *when*."

I raised an eyebrow. "You don't live in this time?"

He grinned at me. "I like how you called it a default range. It's sort of how you live, by default, because you don't know anything else."

He wasn't going to distract me from his non-answer. "This is my native time. What's yours?"

"Is it? I think *default* suits it better." He popped the last bite of his bread in his mouth and perched on the edge of the desk. "So, the same thing applies to travel. It's all in your mind, and the default range is just the place you don't have to think about." Oddly, Doran included Archer in his gaze. Considering how rude he'd been to him before, it almost fascinated me more than what he was saying. Almost.

"Saira, you've been Clocking place-to-place, right?" His gaze was back to me and I nodded. "So that visualization is the same principal used in out-of-range clocking. The tricky thing is getting a precise picture in your head."

"But it's not always a picture for me. At least it wasn't when I got us to Epping Wood when Archer and my mom were hurt."

He cocked his head at me. "Your mother painted that cottage in Epping, didn't she?"

"Yeah."

"You needed safety and comfort. Your subconscious chose Epping even if you weren't aware you were doing it."

"Then how could my mom clock forward when she was pregnant with me? She'd never been to the future. She didn't know what it looked like."

Doran shook his head like he couldn't be bothered. "Claire needs the necklace to focus, you don't."

"I don't?"

The man sighed as if *I* was exasperating *him*. "I wouldn't be here to explain things if you did."

"Because you're doing such a good job of it." I muttered it, but they both heard it. Archer smirked, and Doran burst out laughing.

"Okay, in simpler terms. Like the place-to-place Clocking, you need to fix an image in your mind. But you also have to fix a specific time. Photos are only good for the last hundred years, more or less, so paintings will be your best guideposts. Imagination works too, but I wouldn't try it for cities. It's hard to imagine how chaotic some things really were at certain times. It's how a lot of us lose ourselves *between*."

"*Between*? That … vomitous nothingness has a name?" I couldn't keep the shudder out of my voice.

Doran shrugged. "It's between time and place, so yes. But too long *between* and you know you've got a problem."

I stared at him in growing horror. "Does the time *between* get longer the further I Clock?"

Doran shrugged. "Everything's relative *between*. Just make sure your picture's solid and you'll be fine."

"So, if I want to go back to 1554 I have to find a painting that accurately depicts a certain scene? Because if it's not accurate enough and I picture it wrong in my head, I could get lost in time?"

He nodded thoughtfully. "That's about right."

"Oh. My. God! No wonder there are no Clockers left!"

Doran smiled at my outburst. "It's not as bad as that. They just weren't strong enough. As I said, it's a combination of visual and mental. You have the mental; find the visual." He grabbed an apple from the desk and took a bite as he jumped off and strolled back to the painting.

"Nice message, by the way. I liked the orange."

I opened my mouth to say something - ask another question, yell at him, cry, whatever I could do to make him not disappear - but I was too late. Doran was gone.

"I hate him!" I couldn't help it. I did yell.

Archer moved to my side and wrapped me in his arms. I was shaking with fury. "The guy is an asshole. He has everything I need wrapped up in his little pea brain, and he doles it out in the tiniest bites like I can't process any more than the morsel he gives me. And none of it ever makes any sense!"

"I agree he's an ass, but he did make sense."

158

"There's no reason I should be able to do what other Clockers can't. What my mom can't!"

"Saira, we know you're different from other Clockers, even if it's just by nature of your mixed parentage."

"That should make me a weak Clocker because I'm only half, not one who's able to Clock off the default range just because I say so."

"Right. That." He sighed and held me at arm's length to face him. "It makes me crazy that you can apparently do something so … imprecise. Something that relies so completely on whatever image you focus on in your head. It's probably a function of your artistic skills, but also something more, and it's like pure fantasy to me."

I scoffed. "That anything could seem like fantasy to you is awesome. It implies that things like vampires and time travelers and shape-shifters are just normal, everyday things, and not remarkable in any way."

"You are remarkable. Everything about you is so far outside 'normal' it takes my breath away." Archer's gaze held me as effectively as his hands did. And my insides fluttered a little in anticipation of his kiss. Did that ever get old? The anticipation? And then he did, and I felt it all the way to my toes. Made me all breathless and wobbly.

"My point is, as much as I may dislike the guy, I think I trust what he says. Doran says you can travel anywhere you need to go as long as you have a strong image in your head. So we just need to find you an image of London in March, 1554 to take us there."

"Yeah, 'cause that's easy."

He laughed at the irony in my voice. "Actually, there might be something hanging in Lambeth Palace from that era. Or the Antiquities Society. I think there's a painting of Queen Mary that might have some background scenery."

Inspiration hit. "Or the attics of St. Brigid's." He stared at me and I grinned back. "You mean all this time you've been living in the cellar you've never explored the attics?"

"It never occurred to me."

159

"Me neither. But Olivia took us on a little free-climbing tour the other day, and they're like this repository for all the personal stuff that got stored or left behind."

My eyes narrowed as I pictured a room in my head. I snorted. "Doran's an ass."

"I think we've already established that."

"No. I mean, yes, we did, but he painted the scene I need and he didn't say 'go up to the attics and find my landscape of St. Brigid's.' No, he just smiles his stupid little panty-melting smile and disappears."

"Panty-melting?"

"Yeah. Good thing mine are cast iron."

"Right. Good thing." I loved Archer's droll tone. "So, to the attics then?"

I shook my head. "Huh uh. It's too dangerous in the dark, and there's no way in from inside without the keys. Ringo and I can go in the morning."

He led me back to the sofa and pulled me down across his lap. "You know one of the things I miss the most? Daylight. Doing things people do in the daytime."

"You mean things like climbing around on rooftops?"

He smiled at me and smoothed the hair back from my face. "Anything with you, but yes, climbing around on rooftops was more fun during the day. The view was better."

I laughed. "You didn't climb around on rooftops before."

He pretended hurt. "Of course I did. I was a boy once."

"Hmm. I wasn't. What's my excuse?"

"An underdeveloped sense of self-preservation?"

I smiled up at him sleepily. "That's what I have you for." My eyes were closing almost against my will, but before I fell into full oblivion I caught the look of surprise that flitted across his face, and then a tenderness that I'd never seen before as he gazed down at me.

And my heart did a funny little dance in my chest as I drifted off to sleep.

DISCOVERIES

Archer was gone when I woke up. I wasn't too surprised by that; he was totally vulnerable during the day when he was out cold, and who knew the visitors we'd have to the tower? But I had to admit it stung a little.

I used the bathroom down the hall to scrub the sleep from my face and teeth, and came back to find Ringo digging into the bread and cheese I'd pilfered from the kitchen. He looked up with a grin when I walked in.

"What're we doin' today?"

I smiled back at his tousled head and excited tone. "Roof climbing. You'll need these." I tossed him Connor's clothes, and he was back a minute later looking almost like a modern teenager in jeans and a black sweater.

"The trousers are strange, but I think they'll take knocks better'n wool. And what's 'E=MC two?'" Ringo lifted his sweater and revealed Connor's brainiac humor T-shirt underneath.

"It's E equals MC squared, and it's Einstein's theory about mass and energy and momentum. Connor could tell you. Here, I think these will fit." I tossed him my old boots and he stared at them in his hands. "Sorry they're old, but they still have good tread on them."

Ringo quickly put them on and laced them. He seemed to wiggle his toes inside and then stood up with a grin. "These are the best boots I've ever 'ad on my feet." He bounced up and down on. "I think I might just be able to fly in 'em."

I laughed at his enthusiasm. "If you weren't flying before then I'm really in trouble. Keep eating, you're probably still growing."

Ringo took a massive bite of an apple, the kind boys can take, barely chew, and somehow not choke on, and nodded. "What else are ye goin' t'show me?"

There was a knock on the door and my eyebrows shot up. It was six a.m. Ringo indicated the wardrobe but I shook my head. The only people who knew I was here would understand.

I opened the door a crack, then pulled it the rest of the way. Connor stood in the hall, looking just as tousled and sleepy as Ringo did. His eyes went past my shoulder as he stepped inside the tower room. I closed the door behind him and made introductions.

"Connor, this is Ringo." Connor's eyebrows almost shot off his face. "Ringo, Connor."

Ringo stepped forward with a huge smile on his face and his hand outstretched to shake. "Connor the Wolf. These are your clothes? Thanks so much for the loan of 'em."

Connor shook his hand tentatively, his shocked eyes never leaving Ringo's face. "You're here. I mean, how? Why?" Connor turned a helpless look to me and I laughed.

"I don't know about you guys, but I need coffee."

Ringo got a dreamy look on his face. "Ye have real coffee here? None o' that chicory horror they pass as coffee?"

Connor was still staring at Ringo. "You coming, Connor?" He nodded mutely and I shook my head, laughing. "You should take the stairs. We're going by the roof."

"Why can't I go by the roof too?"

"You're not awake and you're a runner, not a climber."

Connor's eyes narrowed at me and Ringo gave him a cuff on the shoulder. "We'll race ye, 'ow about that?"

"To the kitchens?" Connor gave me the wolfiest grin I've ever seen on his face. "Go!" He bolted through the tower door and Ringo leapt for the wardrobe. I followed him up the stairs as he worked one of the windows open in the upper tower. We got

162

out to the roof thirty seconds later, barely out of breath. The view was spectacular, but it was just a backdrop for the run.

"Which chimney?"

"That one." I pointed to a chimney stack on the far side of the building. The fact that Connor had to take hallways and staircases was the only thing that gave us a fighting chance.

Ringo skated down the pitched tiles as if he was on wheels, and since I'd never done that particular move, I let him lead. He went up and over a pitch, and I mapped his route in my head as I followed. Each slanted roof became a skate incline, and each pitch was a hurdle to leap. He only surprised me once, when he slid under a rail instead of vaulting it, and I just had enough time to keep my momentum and do the same.

It was an exhilarating way to start the day.

I moved into the lead on the fire escapes down the back of the building, but we dropped to the ground outside the kitchen door at the same moment. Ringo opened it and stepped back with a flourish so I could enter first, and about one second later, Connor ran breathless into the room. His face fell for an instant when he saw us, but then his expression changed to awe.

"You have to take me up there with you."

"Anytime." Ringo grinned from ear to ear and I knew how he felt. The breathless high I always got from free-running was like adrenaline mixed with laughter. Annie was the only one in the kitchen, and she stared at all three of us.

"What're ye three doin' here so early, and who are ye?" Annie was a little breathless too, but I thought it was from surprise.

"My name's Ringo, ma'am. I'm a friend o' Saira an' Connor, an' I was 'opin' for a bit o' yer coffee this mornin'."

Ringo was a natural mimic, and usually sounded like a cross between Archer and me whenever we'd spent time together. But his accent was thicker than I'd ever heard it, and I guessed he dropped the extra letters for Annie's benefit, because her expression instantly softened into warmth. "O'course ye can. How do ye take it?"

"Oh, black, ma'am, but only 'cause I never ha' cream an' sugar."

Annie poured a huge cup of coffee for Ringo and added three sugar cubes and a big dollop of fresh cream. I poured my own black coffee, and Connor poured himself a mug of milk. Ringo's eyes lit up charmingly as he accepted the mug from Annie.

"I think I may 'ave died an' gone to 'eaven, ma'am. Thank ye very kindly."

"It's me pleasure, Ringo. Anytime." She was beaming right back at him, and I realized I was in the presence of a master.

"Annie, it would be really good if no one else knew Ringo was here. Especially the Mong… any of the Rothchilds' friends."

She made a tsking sound. "None'll hear it from me. I've nothing to say to those chits anyway."

"Thank you. And thanks for the coffee."

"No worries, Saira. Ye know where the pot is when ye want more."

The three of us went back outside, and between us and a combination of handing up mugs and climbing ladders with them, we made our way to the roof to watch the sun finish rising. Connor gulped his milk and looked over at Ringo seated on the other side of me.

"When did you get here?"

"To yer school, or to the twenty-first century? Actually, it's last night to both."

"We went to London to try to steal Wilder's genealogy from Seth Walters. I needed a thief's help, so I asked Ringo."

"Did you get the book?"

I nodded. "The Mongers are pissed."

Understanding dawned in Connor's eyes. "Hence the roof run. You need to stay invisible for a bit."

"Maybe longer than a bit. I don't really see this blowing over anytime soon."

"What are you going to do?"

164

I finished my coffee and stood to dust off my butt. "First things first, I need to get a painting from the attics. Wanna come?"

"Are you kidding? When Olivia told me about it I was so jealous."

The boys stood, and Ringo slugged the last of his coffee. "Best I've ever 'ad."

"Tell that to Annie. That was some of the most impressive charming I've ever seen you do."

"S'easier to get 'em with honey than vinegar. Got me the cream an' sugar too. Show us yer attics so I can get to the interrogatin' business of our day."

Connor shot me a questioning look.

"We haven't had time for explanations, and he's building up a list of questions for us."

"Ask away. I know more than Saira about most things anyway."

I punched him and he ducked away laughing.

"Right then, what the heck are them big, noisy carriage-type things. They're damn fast, and I can't figure out how they move with no horse to pull 'em."

Connor described the history of the automobile, then proceeded to answer every one of Ringo's questions in amazing detail. He knew things about electric lights, combustion engines, solar power, and air and space flight that I'd never even heard of. I was as captivated by his information as Ringo was, and we deliberately took our time getting into the attics just to keep Connor talking.

"And how come, when I play a video game, the little picture people can move around inside the box, doin' everything I tell 'em to do?"

I held up my hand to stop Connor before he could launch into a three-hour lecture about computers. "Hold it. I need one of you guys to help me carry this painting." I'd unearthed Doran's landscape of St. Brigid's and double-checked the back. Yes, the date was definitely 1554, and it seemed like the grass and trees

165

were just starting to get green. Maybe, hopefully, it depicted Spring since Elizabeth was brought to the Tower in March of that year. In any case, I could look outside right now to get an exact picture in my head, since things were just beginning to bud.

The frame was heavy and it took both of them to lift it out. I was able to pop the canvas out of the ornate frame so they could be carried separately. Connor wondered why I bothered to bring the frame.

"I don't really want to advertise why I've got it, so if it's hanging on the wall as a piece of art, it'll be less remarkable than if they stumbled across it in a closet or something.

He considered that a moment. "Okay, I'm definitely book-smarter, but you might have me on the street-smarts."

"Oooh, thanks for reminding me." I set off down the hall in search of the rooms filled with wardrobes. If we were going back to the sixteenth century we needed to dress the part. "Ringo, you too. And I need to find something for Archer that'll fit him."

The guys followed me as I opened wardrobe doors and pawed through clothes.

"What, exactly, are you looking for?"

"Clothes that would work in 1554."

The astonishment on Connor's face would have been comical except I was too focused on digging through a ridiculous number of old, stale-smelling clothes. "I think jerkins and doublets for the guys …" I looked at Ringo speculatively. "Yeah, your clothes weren't peasant clothes in Archer's vision. They were more like upper class servants."

"So I have that to look forward to, do I?"

"You have no idea." I whispered under my breath as I turned back toward the wardrobes.

"What's a jerkin?" Connor was still looking at me like I just said Star Trek was better than Star Wars.

"It's one of those sleeveless jacket things, probably leather, that went over the tight-fitting long-sleeved doublets."

"And you know this because …?"

"Because my mother's an artist and I practically grew up in museums."

"Right. What are you going to wear?"

"They didn't make dresses long enough for me, so I'm not sure."

"What about this one?" Ringo pulled a long green-skirted gown out of the wardrobe. It had a gold brocade bodice with really long bell sleeves, and a white chemise underneath. And it was long enough.

"Crap."

He looked at it oddly. "What? It's nice enough."

"Yeah, but that means I have to wear it, and it's fricking hard to run in skirts."

At least we were in the right wardrobes. I pulled out a dark green doublet with a soft leather jerkin and held it up. "Think this'll fit Archer?"

Ringo nodded and Connor raised an eyebrow. "What's he wear on the bottom?"

"I guess hose." I looked inside the doublet and saw loops hanging down on each side. "I think the stockings tie to the inside of the jacket to keep them up."

Ringo held up a pair of long woolen socks. "You mean, these?"

"Yeah. See if you can find some extra long ones for Archer."

I rifled through the section I had open and finally pulled out a really soft yellow doublet with a light tan jerkin over the top. My stomach sank at the memory of Ringo's head being forced into the cesspit by Wilder and the disgusting mess dripping down the light-colored fabric. "This is yours. But we should find you an extra one too."

Ringo shrugged and continued rifling through the stockings for ones that would fit both him and Archer. But Connor looked at me carefully. "Why?"

I was a coward. I didn't want to be the one to tell Ringo we'd seen him tortured. So I just shook my head and opened a trunk to rummage further. I held up a gorgeous pair of silk, high-heeled slippers that looked practically doll-sized. "Think they'll fit?"

Both guys stared down at my size ten combat boots and burst out laughing. "Hey, be nice. I'd blow over in a stiff wind if my feet weren't so big."

Connor held out his hand. "Let me have them for Olivia. She's a girl, she likes shoes, right?"

I handed them over, and he stuffed them in his coat pockets.

"Do ye have any coin?" Ringo had found a bag and shoved several pairs of hose into it.

"You mean money?"

"'Course. How're we goin' ta eat?"

Right, well, there was that. "I don't think we're going to find sixteenth century coins among all this stuff, so we should bring things to trade then, I guess." The thought of finding valuables from the 1500s overwhelmed me.

"Personally, I don't think people left a lot of jewelry and treasure up here for us to pilfer." Connor poked around another wardrobe and quickly shut the door when a snarling wolverine stole practically leapt off a hanger at him. Okay, not really, but that's what it looked like.

"Pssh. Ye don't need baubles fer food. A coupla fancy pens and pots o' ink, an' maybe some ribbon or fine fabric an' yer very wealthy indeed."

I stared at him. "You're a genius."

"Wow. That's just awesome." It was clear that Ringo's stock with Connor was pretty much off the charts.

Ringo shook his head, presumably at our narrow minds. "Ye both, with yer 'lectric things an' 'vision boxes and whatnot are very far removed from what really makes a man rich."

He was totally right, and I looked around at all the stuff in the attic room through a different filter. "Ringo, would you go hunting for trade goods for us? Preferably things that can be stuffed into pockets and small satchels?"

"An' who are we stealin' it all from?"

168

That gave me a moment's pause. Until I looked at the clothes in my hands and smelled the musty scent of stale fabric and mothballs. "No one. Whoever they were, they left them here at St. Brigid's a long time ago."

"When ye leave things like that, ye've no more need of them." He nodded at the heavy brocade gown he'd hung from a hook on the wall, then left the room.

"Wow. We must seem like spoiled brats to the guy."

"Ringo's not like that. He just calls it as he sees it. C'mon, help me find a bag to put all these in so we can get out of here. This place smells like no one ever took a bath."

Ringo popped his head back around the corner of the room. "No one ever did."

Connor was very reluctant to leave the Clocker Tower to go to science class, but he finally had to admit that no amount of our company could make up for a telling off from his uncle, Mr. Shaw.

I snuck down to the kitchens when everyone else was in class and there was less chance of running into Mongers. It didn't take much convincing for Annie to pack us a huge meal once she heard it was for Ringo. Annie was in her thirties, so the way she went doe-eyed at the mention of his name was a tad unsettling.

While I was downstairs I borrowed Ava's iPad from our room so I could do some research on Elizabeth. As far as I could tell, the twins and Tom hadn't come back from the Arman's house yet. It made me a little nervous, mostly because I didn't know where we stood with the Arman family at the moment.

When I got back to the Clocker Tower I walked in to find Miss Simpson having tea with Ringo. It was possibly the last thing I expected, and yet looked totally normal. Ringo stood up when I came in, and Miss Simpson smiled serenely at me.

"Ringo and I were just discussing his friend Charlotte."

I looked at him in surprise. I guess he wasn't breaking a confidence by talking about Charlie's 'gift' since she basically lived a century ago. He met my gaze directly. "She's not a freak. Others can do the same things." He looked to Miss Simpson for confirmation and she nodded.

"I've known two other otherworld seers in my life."

"Otherworld seers? Is Charlie a Seer then?"

Miss Simpson shook her head. "She's not specifically of my Family's line. However, it does take a bit of Immortal Descendancy to have the gift."

"She has Clocker on her mother's side. At least that's what Archer found out when he was putting together the genealogy."

"Speaking of your Family, Miss Rogers would like to see you this morning. I believe your lessons have been somewhat neglected?"

"Yeah, sorry about that. I haven't really been too present."

"No worries, dear. But now would be an appropriate time to resume them."

Of all the things for which now was an appropriate time, history lessons with Miss Rogers was at the bottom of my list. But arguing with the headmistress was even lower, so I smiled at them both.

"I'll see you soon, then." I turned to leave the room.

"Saira?" Miss Simpson's voice stopped me before I could close the door.

"Yes?"

"Stop by Mr. Shaw's office to make sure he has several doses of the smallpox vaccine on hand."

I stared at her, stunned. "Smallpox was eradicated in the nineteen seventies."

"Yes, but it was alive and well in the fifteen hundreds."

Right. Not only did Mr. Shaw have the vaccine for an extinct disease, the headmistress of St. Brigid's school had just given us tacit permission to travel back in time.

I didn't quite trust myself to speak as I left the tower.

TIME STREAM

I sprinted through the halls to Miss Rogers' cozy study. I knew I was taking a chance that a Monger kid would spot me, but everyone was in class, so I made it without incident. Miss Rogers was already waiting for me with two cups of tea poured and five dice on the table. We always played Yahtzee while we talked, which she claimed kept her brain occupied enough so she could access the buried memories. Considering the history and random bits of Clocker lore she came up with, I didn't doubt it.

If Miss Simpson was the grandmother I wished I'd had, Miss Rogers was like the slightly batty great-aunt. She had been the only Clocker teacher at St. Brigid's before my Mom came to teach history. Miss Rogers was a quarter-time — a crude way of saying she was one-fourth Clocker and not actually able to time-travel herself. I loved her though, and the nuggets of wisdom she dropped were always generously given, as opposed to my stingy cousin Doran, who horded information as gleefully as Golem did his precious ring.

I filled Miss Rogers in on the last couple of days, which sounded fairly action-packed when I relayed the events out loud. Her eyebrows raised with interest at the idea of meeting Ringo, and shot up in horror at the thought of him being tortured by Bishop Wilder in Archer's vision.

When our tea was gone, Miss Rogers picked up the handful of dice and began rolling.

"So, why, exactly, are you planning to go back to 1554?"

I stared at her. "Because there's a crazy man with access to Elizabeth Tudor who has no business being in that time."

She considered me thoughtfully. "You've heard of the grandfather paradox?"

I remembered Mr. Shaw had told us about it in class one day. "If a guy goes back in time and accidentally kills his grandfather before he's had a chance to meet his grandmother and have kids, how could he exist to go back in time?"

"Precisely." Miss Rogers was in teacher mode, and her eyes sparkled even as her voice got all clipped and matter-of-fact. "And extrapolating on that is the idea that time is inert. That is to say, it resists anything that threatens to change its path or progress as it's been laid out."

I must have looked confused because she simplified it for me. "Think of time as an actual stream. If you throw a pebble in the water, or say, for example, a Clocker goes back in time, the stream might ripple a little, perhaps even in a way such that people sense something isn't quite right, but ultimately it will resume its charted path with only the smallest interruption. However, if you throw a big enough boulder into the water – say, someone goes back in time to kill Hitler before he could start World War II – the water in that stream is going to split around the boulder and create a second stream. The first stream will be the timeline that we know happened, where sixty million people died. But the second stream, in which the madman is gone, would contain all the lives and families and accomplishments of all the people who lived. It seems the timelines inevitably must rejoin at the moment the killer left his or her native time. What do you think would happen?"

It was almost unthinkable. "Mass extinction."

She nodded. "It's what's been theorized."

"Forget Wilder, every time *I* go back I'm risking … that?"

"My dear, your extended Family has been traveling since the beginning of our history. No person has ever caused that kind of time stream split, nor, I believe, would anyone ever want to. It could make for a very uncertain future to return to if one were to

172

disrupt the past enough to cause a split. No, I believe it would take a massive historical anomaly to split time, and the inertia of time itself would seek to prevent such a disruption. Why else would there not have been time stream splits every time one of our Family went back?

I shuddered. "Maybe we're all just really lucky."

Miss Rogers spoke gently. "Or maybe everything I've just said was theoretical, and the fact that it hasn't happened yet means that it can't." She resumed rolling. "I believe I have a Yahtzee."

By the time Archer joined us in the Clocker Tower that evening, Ringo and I had sorted through all the treasures we'd gathered. Archer came down from the upper tower, which meant he traveled by rooftop too. He had dressed all in black, with light wool combat-style pants and a t-shirt under a light cashmere sweater. And with his slightly longish dark hair, fair skin, and blue eyes he was basically irresistible.

I leaned back into him as his arms circled my waist. He scanned the desk-full of odds and ends in front of us. "What did I miss?"

I nodded over at the painted landscape leaning against the wall. "We found the scene Doran painted, picked out some clothes, and Ringo went shopping though the chests up there for things we could trade."

Archer left my side to kneel in front of the painting. "It's St. Brigid's."

"Yeah, in 1554. He dated it on the back."

"But it's not London."

I shrugged my shoulders. "It's only a forty minute train ride. How long could it take us?"

"Two days. If there are no bandits. And *if* we have horses."

I stared at Archer. "Crap."

He raised an eyebrow with a smirk. "But since he presumably painted it for you to use, he must have a reason for us to start at St. Brigid's."

I sighed at Doran's general, irritating smugness. Why couldn't the guy just tell me what he wanted instead of leaving clues like scurrying little cockroaches for me to step on?

"Well, I think that's the lot of it." Ringo had packed a canvas messenger bag with everything we'd sorted through, and it was a strange mix of odds and ends. Velvet and silk ribbons, hairpins with little seed pearls attached, several knives, and a set of old-fashioned leather-working tools. There were old fountain pens that Ringo had removed the ink cartridges from and turned into dip pens, several bottles of ink, and some wooden paint brushes from an artist's kit. I'd found some sewing kits and took all the buttons, needles, and thread from them, and a tablet of airmail paper, the really thin kind people used to use when letters were the main form of communication.

"If you have any bars of soap, those would be useful." Archer stated the obvious in a way that made me shudder at the thought of a soapless world.

"Right. Good point. And not just to sell. Remind me to grab them from one of the bathrooms when we go to Mr. Shaw's office."

"Why are we going to Shaw's?"

I turned to look at Archer. "Ringo and I need smallpox shots. You're probably immune."

"Ahh, yes. And Mr. Shaw just happens to keep the vaccine for an eradicated disease on hand?"

"Apparently."

"Why am I not surprised?"

I loved Archer's very dry sense of humor.

His attention shifted back to the desk. "We'll have to be careful trading this stuff." Archer picked up one of the sewing needles. "This is steel and probably finer than anything the royal tailors had access to. We don't want to be brought in for theft just because we have things like this on us."

"Saira'll have to sell 'em then. Or you. Nothing about me is posh enough to get away with it."

174

I looked straight at Ringo. "Unless you want to get sent to prison."

He scowled at me and stuck out his tongue. "Excrement and blasphemy!"

I barked out a laugh. "What?"

There was a wry, resigned expression in Ringo's eyes, despite the twinkling that never left them. "As ye like t'say – crap and damn."

We had time to kill until lights-out when we could go down to Mr. Shaw's office. Ringo filled the time playing with Ava's iPad. I showed him the pocket version of Minecraft, and he spent an hour building an elaborate fortress just to blow it up with a well-placed explosive trap. Archer and I went up to the roof of the tower and sat on the cold slate tiles watching the clouds cover and uncover the stars.

I told him about my conversation with Miss Rogers, about the theory of inertia and the possibility of a time stream split.

Archer's tone was mild. "If Wilder killed Elizabeth Tudor before she could become queen, that would be a fair-sized anomaly."

I turned to stare at Archer. "Are you kidding? That would be the mother of all splits. Can you imagine? No world exploration. No patronage of Shakespeare? If Elizabeth died before becoming queen, the English crown would have gone to one of Jane Grey's sisters, whose husband would have taken over, leaving England totally vulnerable."

"And the Spanish would have come in to hand England to the Pope."

"Or the French Catholics." I contemplated the ramifications of a history I couldn't even imagine. "Devereux is French though. Your family would probably be fine."

Archer shook his head. "My ancestor was Robert Devereux, a cousin to Elizabeth through his mother, Lettice Knollys. My family would have been summarily executed."

"Are you serious? You're actually related to Queen Elizabeth?"

175

"Very distantly, through the Boleyns."

"What about your mother's people?"

"I never knew any of the Foss family. When I killed my mother, they wanted nothing more to do with us."

I forced his eyes to meet mine. "You didn't kill your mother, childbirth did. There's a huge difference."

"Not in the outcome. Dead is dead." The bitterness in his voice hurt my heart.

"But you lived, and that counts for everything."

Archer wrapped me in his arms and we sat there in silence. I finally spoke. "What would have been different if your mother had lived?"

He scoffed. "What wouldn't have?"

"For example?"

He didn't even have to think about it. "My father wouldn't have hated me."

There was nothing I could say to that. I never met Lord Devereux and only knew him from Archer's stories. And he wasn't a hero in any of them.

"It doesn't matter. He's long dead now and I can't change what happened." Archer stood and held his hand out to help me to my feet. "Besides, if he hadn't hated me I wouldn't have run away to King's College to escape him. And I never would have met you."

My heart actually ached for him – for the little boy who thought his father hated him, and for the man who never felt his dad's approval. I wondered what was worse: having an emotionally absent dad, or never having one at all.

The school had shut down for the night, and we headed out for Mr. Shaw's office. At the last minute Ringo grabbed our bags. He slung his own over a shoulder and handed ours to each of us. "Ye never know what yer gonna need."

I couldn't argue with that at all, though I thought carrying around a five-hundred-year-old musty smelling dress was a little overkill in the being-prepared department. I almost left it behind, but Archer stopped me. "Take it." The worried look in his eyes said there was something he wasn't telling me.

So I took it, as well as one last long look at Doran's painting, before we left the tower.

The halls were eerily quiet as we made our way downstairs, and my own survival instincts started to kick in strong. The school had always been a place of relative safety for me, but something was off tonight, and I thought Ringo's plan to be prepared was a good one.

The light was on in Mr. Shaw's office, and he opened the door almost as soon as we knocked. He locked the door behind us and then answered my unspoken question.

"Monger whelps were a bit restive today."

Archer nodded. "They're planning something."

Mr. Shaw looked surprised. "You've seen that?"

"I've seen them running through St. Brigid's with torches."

My eyebrows hit the ceiling with images of ogre-hunting villagers in my brain. Archer gave me a half-smile. "The electric kind." Oh, right. British for flashlights.

"You're here for vaccinations then?"

I nodded, but Ringo looked blank. "What's them?"

"Shots."

His eyes widened.

Mr. Shaw interrupted me efficiently. "It's a kind of medicine I'll give you just into your skin. It stops things like pox before it can ever take hold."

This time Ringo's eye-widening was accompanied by a look of disbelief. "Ye can stop the pox?".

"It's completely gone in this time because of shots like these." Mr. Shaw was getting two doses ready as he talked. Ringo eyed the needle and syringe with wary respect.

"Me mam had the pox. It's why she sent me away when I was small."

"How small?" It struck me that Ringo never spoke about his parents.

He held his hand out about waist-high. "'Bout five I think."

I gasped. "Who did you live with?"

Ringo looked at me funny. "Weren't no one. I jus' took to the streets. By the time I finally figured out she died, the landlord took whatever was left for back rent."

My face must have had shock written all over it because Mr. Shaw tapped my shoulder to bring my attention around to the needle in his hand. "Let's get this done."

I nodded mutely, not trusting myself to be intelligible. Mr. Shaw prepped a strange-looking, multi-pronged needle, and Ringo watched with complete fascination as Mr. Shaw carefully jabbed my upper arm several times. He checked my face quickly, and I held my expression totally neutral. It took a lot because I was still reeling from the knowledge Ringo had been a homeless five-year-old. I noticed Archer behind Mr. Shaw watching the process with an unusual amount of tension in his face, and I wondered what he was reacting to.

"Okay, that's smallpox, and here's a measles booster." A smaller needle went into the fatty tissue in my arm; I remained impassive. When it was done Ringo stuck his arm out preemptively.

"Give me the shots for pox and anything else you have." His voice sounded so eager Mr. Shaw had to stifle a grin as he prepped his arm.

"I've prepared smallpox, measles, and influenza type A. We think it's what contributed to Mary Tudor's death in 1558, which means it was already likely brewing in 1554. It should also keep you safe in the 1918 Spanish Flu outbreak."

The shots Mr. Shaw was giving Ringo would save his life during his natural lifetime too. The thought made me feel a little sick.

The flu shot was just going in when someone banged on Mr. Shaw's office door.

"Shaw! Open up!"

And I realized why my stomach had twisted. It was a Monger voice.

MORGAN

To his credit, Mr. Shaw didn't flinch as he finished Ringo's shots. We looked wildly at him, but he just put his finger to his lips to keep us quiet.

He clicked off the desk lamp and leaned over me as he stood to answer the door.

"Ward yourselves." Mr. Shaw's whisper was so quiet I almost didn't hear it. A chasm opened in my guts. Could I ward all three of us in such close quarters? I moved closer to Archer on the sofa, then pulled Ringo to the other side of me so I was sandwiched between the two of them.

Mr. Shaw grabbed the genealogy off his desk and tossed it into my lap. The pounding outside his office door intensified.

"Shaw, damn it! We know you're in there!"

There were three of them. Three adult Mongers just a few feet away, and I would have climbed out of my skin to get away from them if I could have. Fight or flight was definitely the trigger for my wards, and I could feel it slam up around all three of us. The cold threatened to freeze all the blood in my body, and the only comfort I could feel at all was Archer's thigh pressed against mine. It was a very small thing to hang onto, but I grasped at it with everything I had.

Mr. Shaw's eyes widened very slightly at our sudden invisibility, then he grunted to himself and opened the office door.

Seth Walters and the Rothbitch were there behind a big, nasty piece of work with a scarred face and wild, gray hair.

Something about him looked familiar, but in a rough, barely civilized kind of way, and I wondered if he'd been one of the toughs in the fight outside Walters' office. But then he spoke, and I knew without a doubt he was somehow related to Bishop Wilder.

"What took you so long, Shifter? Hiding something?"

There was something oddly cultured in his low, growling voice, and I mentally dubbed him Silvertongue. Different than Wilder's Silverback, but clearly of the same family.

"You hammer on my office door well after hours and then have the stones to hurl accusations at me?

"I think you have something that belongs to me." Silvertongue strode into the room without waiting for Mr. Shaw to step out of the way. I held my breath, but the ward hung tight around us and the chill from it seeped into my bones.

He couldn't see us.

I could feel Ringo tense up next to me. I'd told him about the wards I could do, but I didn't think he really believed it until now. But the Mongers ignored the couch, and Silvertongue started prowling around the room, no doubt looking for the genealogy that was hidden in plain sight on my lap.

"Get out of my office." Mr. Shaw's voice deepened into one of those hair-raising growls that only a Bear-Shifter could do.

"Where's my book?" Silvertongue's tone of voice signaled a pissing contest. My nerves faltered, and I could feel the edges of my ward begin to slip. The air must have moved or something, because the Rothbitch looked over at the sofa. But Archer gripped my hand in warning, and I pulled the ward above our heads with all the mental power I had left. It held, but barely, and the Rothbitch looked back at Mr. Shaw.

"I don't know what you're talking about, and I want you the hell out of my office." I could see the space around Mr. Shaw begin to shimmer. He was about to lose it and Shift right in front of three Mongers. I didn't think Shifters did that, at least not on purpose, and I could hear Ringo's heartbeat pick up speed. I was a little shocked no one else in the room could hear it because it sounded like a metronome to my ears.

The Rothbitch put her hand on Silvertongue's arm. "The girl's clearly not here, and if he has the book we'll get it through the Council. Let's go."

I could see that Seth Walters had been scanning the bookshelves and all the available surfaces in the office the whole time they were talking. He turned to the others. "She's here in the school. Raven's friend saw her."

"Get out of my office, and get off this property, Walters. You've been warned about coming to St. Brigid's already. I would be quite justified throwing you bodily out of this school."

Seth's hand twitched toward his pocket and I imagined a gun nestled in there. It didn't seem possible that Archer could get more tense. Seth Walters was a coward, but it seemed he wasn't a complete idiot because he backed toward the door.

"The girl is mine, Shaw, and I *will* find her."

"I'll be sure to tell the Council that when I speak to them next week." The air was still shimmering around Mr. Shaw, but his voice had gone a little quieter, as if he was struggling to stay in control.

Silvertongue glared at Seth. "Enough, Walters." Seth's eyes narrowed but he was silent. It was so out of character even Shaw looked surprised. Silvertongue's voice went hard. "I want my book, Shaw. I can make things very unpleasant around here if I don't get it."

The Mongers stalked out of the office, and Mr. Shaw strode across the room to slam the door behind them. He turned the deadbolt and I let go of the ward with a gasp.

"Good God! *That* was a ward?" Ringo's whisper was shocked, and he rubbed his hands over his arms as he stood up to pace. "I'm nearly numb with cold. It seeps into yer bones, no?"

"You three have to go." Mr. Shaw's voice was ragged, probably from keeping himself together when his instinct was telling him to Shift.

"How long do you think they'll be wandering around?"

"No. You have to leave this *time*."

Something in Mr. Shaw's voice scared me. Maybe it was fear I heard, and that made me mad. "I'm not afraid of them."

Mr. Shaw took a deep breath, and I could see him struggle with his temper. But his voice was calm when he spoke again. "Saira, there's something only you can do, and the more I discover, the more I believe it's a job that has to be done. Wilder is up to something, and I don't know if there's a direct correlation, but that man was Domenic Morgan."

Archer interrupted Mr. Shaw. "Morgan was the name of the man Wilder's sister married."

Mr. Shaw looked startled, then thoughtful. "That could be relevant."

"What does Domenic Morgan have to do with anything?" Fear had begun to creep into my voice again, making it wobbly.

"Until tonight, I've always known Domenic Morgan to be a quiet man. He's a bookkeeper for the Council, and I thought he was the least Monger-ish of all the Mongers I'd ever met." Mr. Shaw's gaze locked on mine. "He has changed. Almost overnight, it seems. He's never been so aggressive and ... entitled."

"What do you think happened?" Archer hadn't made the leap yet, but I had. And when Mr. Shaw looked at me, I knew he had too.

"Saira, you had this conversation with Mildred Rogers."

"You think Wilder made himself powerful in the past and it's affecting things now?" My voice squeaked on the question, and I felt my own heart kick start in time with Ringo's. "Could he have caused a time stream split?"

"Several of us have been getting a crash course in the theoretical consequences of time travel. Your mother and Mildred don't think there's been a split. Maybe this is more like a ripple effect."

"What does Miss Simpson think?"

Mr. Shaw looked steadily at me. "She believes information is the key to understanding. Without information, we're all flying blind into what looks to be a hurricane."

Nice and cryptic. Because apparently straightforward is too hard for Seers. I took a breath. "What else could it be? What if Domenic Morgan's just having a really bad day and was in a mood?" I was grasping at straws.

Mr. Shaw looked me straight in the eyes. "Have you ever seen Seth Walters take a back seat to *anyone*?"

Oh, God. He was right, and my head started to pound. I looked at Archer and Ringo. "We have to go." Ringo's eyes widened to match mine, and Archer just nodded.

"I know."

My head whipped around to Mr. Shaw. "Can we get back to the Clocker Tower?"

Archer put his hand out to stop me. "My cellar's closer. Less exposed."

Wow. Okay, that was huge. Archer just revealed his hide-out to Mr. Shaw, and to his credit, Mr. Shaw didn't bat an eyelash. Archer whispered to me. "I'm glad you finished your spiral there."

Mr. Shaw was already moving for the door. "I'll keep working on the genealogy, but I can't really get a message to you if I find something."

"I'll try to come back fast so you don't have to." I gave Mr. Shaw a quick kiss on the cheek, but he grabbed me for a solid hug.

"Be safe and come home to us, Saira," he whispered into my hair, and I had the sudden sensation of having been hugged by my dad.

Ringo and Archer shook hands with Mr. Shaw, and he held onto Archer's hand a moment longer than strictly necessary. "All of you come back safely."

Archer nodded solemnly, and Mr. Shaw unlocked the door. He stepped into the hall and listened for a long moment before finally gesturing for us to emerge. None of us said a word as Archer led the way down the back hall to the kitchens. I grabbed a last, quick look at Mr. Shaw before we turned the corner and were out of sight.

He looked sadder than I'd ever seen him.

St. Brigid's School

We made it down to the cellars without being seen. Once we were inside the secret room and the door safely locked, Archer quickly gathered a few things from his room while Ringo admired all the books his friend had surrounded himself with.

Meanwhile, I suddenly had a pressing need to repack my canvas satchel. Because if I wasn't busy, I'd have time to think. And I'd just become very nervous about taking two of my favorite people on a mad journey to a time I'd never been to and was only theoretically able to visit. And I was even underselling myself on the nervous bit. 'Terrified' was closer to the truth.

But there were only so many ways a bag could be re-packed, and soon my eyes wandered over to watch Archer. And he managed to shock the hell out of me.

"What are you doing?"

He looked up from the thread he was biting off with his teeth. The thread that was attached to what looked like an old wool blanket. He held it up proudly to show me. He grabbed a cord on either side of it and pulled, gathering the blanket onto the cord. "It's cold in March. You needed cloaks."

I stared at the cloak in shock. "You made that?"

"This one's for Ringo. I made yours before dawn this morning."

He handed the cloak to Ringo who tied it on around his neck. I had to admit, when it was on him it didn't look so much like a blanket. "Cheers, Mate. I always wanted to be Robin of Locksley."

Archer smiled back. "We're a couple years too late to play Robin Hood, sorry."

Ringo wrapped himself up in the cloak. "I'll be fair warm in this. Thank ye."

Archer looked at him critically and nodded. "It'll do." Then he picked up a long piece of brown wool the color of milk chocolate that was lying across the bed. "I had a bit more time with yours. The stitching's rough in places, but the material's finer than most might wear so it'll tell the story you're a lady."

He held the cloak up for me to put on. He had stitched together a hood, and he'd lined the cloak with something soft and olive green that took away the itch of the pure wool. I turned my back and he fastened it around my shoulders, then put the hood up to check the fit. I felt like a minstrel or a mage from one of Ringo's fantasy video games.

"You made this?" Even I could hear the awe in my voice, and Archer smiled.

"I told you, tailors are among the people who stick to regular business hours, so I had to learn to sew."

"This is gorgeous."

"I'm glad you like it." Archer pulled on his own black cloak, one that he'd had for over a hundred years. "Should we change here or when we land?" He was all business, and I was grateful for the practical distraction from the fear that still churned in my guts.

"I vote when we land. Unless ye think we're coming in amongst people?" Ringo turned questioning eyes to me. I shook my head.

"I'm going to picture the landscape, but the portal is here, in the cellar. And hopefully the old spiral I repaired was actually here when the school was built."

Archer nodded. "We can stash our clothes there in case we need them again. Everyone has good boots?" He looked at our footwear for confirmation. Then he searched my eyes and his voice softened. "Ready?"

I took a deep breath and tipped my head. They both slung their bags over their shoulders and joined me at the spiral. Ringo held my left hand, while Archer's arm snaked around my waist from the right. I began to trace.

I wished I'd spent more time studying the painting that was currently propped up against a wall in the Clocker Tower. I wondered if the Mongers would find it, or if they'd think anything about an old landscape of the school. My brain darted around to all the things we'd left in the tower, and I had to force it back to the image of St. Brigid's in 1554. I concentrated on emptying the trees of their leaves, adding some white puffy clouds in an otherwise gray sky, and feeling the sensation of the beginning of spring in the air.

The roiling waves of nausea were the first indicator that we were going. The tightening of grips on both my hand and waist was the second. I had a sudden moment of panic as I realized not only was I trying to jump off the 125-year time ring pattern, but I was carrying two extra bodies with me. And anyone extra meant a tougher period spent *between* times. I forced the panic to its knees and refocused on the scent of cold spring air in the dark cellar, and pictured the newly built school above us.

I counted every heartbeat that we were *between* and nearly lost my breath entirely from the shock when we finally emerged, gasping, into cool darkness. It was an alive darkness, not the total absence of everything that was the space *between* times. There was nothing in my stomach to lose, and I realized none of us had eaten in hours, so although we were all sucking air in a similar kind of shock, none of us was actually hurling. Which was nice.

I dug a mini Maglite out of my back pocket and shielded the business end with my hand. When the light clicked on I could just see where we'd landed, and it was clear the secret wall had already gone up. The bricks were covered in plaster with a Clocker spiral that looked recently carved. I unshielded the light, but still held it pointed toward the floor so I could get my bearings without blinding everyone.

Archer and Ringo had collected themselves and were starting to look around too.

"It's still St. Brigid's," Archer whispered.

"Let's check the other side of the wall."

I aimed the Maglite at the wall and found the latch exactly where I expected it. The shelves swung very easily to the side and I realized they must have just been installed. There were baskets on the other side full of potatoes, and what looked like a whole side of beef hung from a hook in the ceiling. I shuddered at that, but grabbed a couple of meat pies stored on a shelf and handed one to Ringo.

He looked at Archer. "Do you need to eat?"

Archer's gaze was locked on the side of beef, and he tore it away to meet ours tensely. "Tonight. I'll just need an hour."

I turned to Archer. "Can you hunt right now so we don't have to wait?"

He paused for one brief moment, then nodded curtly.

"Let's leave our bags in the hidden room and go explore." I looked at Archer. "We'll meet you back here in an hour."

I reopened the sliding shelf door, and we stashed our bags out of sight. Both Archer and Ringo refused Maglites, and reluctantly, I left mine behind too. It would be bad enough if any of us were caught in our clothes from the future, but they might just look foreign. Future technology was another thing entirely. My knife went in my pocket though, and I noticed both guys had theirs too.

Just before we went back into the food cellar Archer grabbed me around the waist and kissed me hard. It was a kiss that took my breath away, and Ringo's cough finally broke Archer's hold on me. He searched my eyes for a long moment, then flew up the stairs in that way only he could. And I remembered how very otherworldly he was.

"I don't think he likes you to know he has to hunt."

"I think you're right." Both Ringo and I were whispering. "Shall we go see if we landed in 1554?"

I was just barcly able to make out the glint of light in his eyes as we neared the top of the cellar stairs. He didn't speak, just nodded and gestured for me to go first.

There was a moon, and I could tell it was probably just after midnight, but it wasn't great for remaining invisible. We stayed close to the building and I went straight for the kitchen door. Ringo stopped me with a hand on my arm, put his finger to his lips, and pointed up. I shook my head. There was no fire escape, of course, and I reached for the door again, but this time he grabbed my arm and shook his head.

"What?!" I whispered in my most exasperated silent tone. Ringo leaned in close to my ear. "Cooks sleep by the fire or in a room right off the kitchen."

Oh.

He pointed up, but slightly around the corner, and I moved to the side to look. There was some scaffolding left in place, presumably to finish the decorative work around the window, and it was much more climbable than even a fire escape ladder would have been.

Up until then I'd just been acting on instinct. But finally my brain engaged with a mental 'snap.' "Where, exactly, are we going?" Ringo's hearing hadn't been damaged by too much loud music, and despite being ten feet off the ground already, he had no trouble hearing my mousy whisper.

He dropped down to face me. "I don't know. Where should we go?"

I thought for a long moment. My first instinct was to go back up to the attics where we could possibly find some more useful stuff. But that was a bad idea. If we had actually made it back to 1554, the attics would be servants' quarters, and people have a tendency to make a lot of noise when you startle them in bed.

The library was a possibility because there's never a bad time to be in a library. But really, the place I most wanted to see was the Clocker Tower.

I told Ringo that and he gave me a 'duh' look. I hate the look almost as much as I hate the word, or sound, or whatever it is that is designed to make someone else feel stupid. "That's where I was goin'."

Of course he was. I actually couldn't be annoyed at Ringo. If anything, he was too good at most things, and I bet if he had been born in a different time or in different circumstances, he'd have been one of those Renaissance guys who never 'work' a day in their lives because they love every job they do. Archer was that kind of guy too. It's probably why they got along so well.

I climbed the scaffolding up to the second floor window casement. We catwalked the ledge from there over to the drainpipe and then scooted up that to the roof where we stopped to catch our breath and take in the view. There was enough light from the moon to see that it was a very different scene than the one we'd last looked at. The big tree at the west end of the building was missing. Just like in Doran's painting, it hadn't even begun to grow. That and the scaffolding were starting to give me confidence I'd landed us in the right time period. The big crap shoot was whether it was the right month, or even if it was spring time. I could see our breath in the cold night air, and the trees were still bare of leaves, so I was hopeful it was March or April. But there weren't too many ways to find out for sure that didn't involve asking someone.

An owl took off out of a copse of trees a ways away and it made me jump. Ringo and I looked at each other but didn't say what I knew we were both thinking.

Archer was hunting.

Silently we picked our way across the roof tiles until we got to the Clocker Tower. The best way in was from the upper floor, so we had an eight foot section of stone facing to climb. Without the fire escapes it was actually pretty tricky, so I stood back and watched where Ringo gripped and stepped. He only had to backtrack on himself once, which was pretty amazing because I probably wouldn't have tried it if he hadn't mapped out how it could be done. I followed quickly, and we were able to slip into the dark tower room without making any noise.

The only thing visible inside from the window was a desk and a chair, but I had dropped to the floor and was halfway across the room when I realized there was a bed against the far wall. The shock of that discovery was further amplified when someone who had presumably been asleep in that bed sat bolt upright and said, "What the bloody hell are you doing?"

"Ahhh!" I couldn't help it. I yelled. Crap. There was nothing stealthy about the noise I'd just made, or about Ringo hurtling across the room to tackle the guy to the ground. The noise of two bodies hitting the wood floor was like a WWF takedown.

"Stop it!" I yelled at them in the loudest whisper I had. Ringo instantly froze, and the Bloody Hell guy shoved him off and stood up shaking himself like a pissed-off dog.

"What the bloody hell are you doing in my bedroom?" The guy was about as tall as me, and I couldn't see his face clearly, but he'd slept shirtless and he was broad-shouldered with tight, ropy muscles. I concentrated very hard on his face so I didn't have to notice his body.

"We're just passing through, mate." Ringo's voice was wary.

Bloody Hell stilled. "When did you come from?"

When? The guy was a Clocker. Which made sense, given that we'd just shocked him awake in the Clocker Tower, but wow. Somehow I hadn't really factored in the idea that there might have been lots of Clockers in the fifteen hundreds.

"Sorry we woke you. We'll get out of your way." My voice was still a whisper, but Bloody Hell jumped.

"You're a bloody lass." The shock in his voice made it loud, and I shushed him automatically.

"And you're a bloody idiot," I whispered fiercely. "You'll wake everybody up."

I realized how ridiculous that sounded after I'd said it, considering that we were the interlopers. But maybe Bloody Hell did too, because the smallest smile tugged at the corners of his mouth.

"You're dressed like a man." His whispered voice was back down to normal, and his eyes took in my clothes in a frank assessment that made me rethink the choice of them. Granted, climbing over rooftops in full skirts was a daunting prospect, but the gaze of shirtless Bloody Hell guy was the red tag special in the highly-uncomfortable department. It made me snarky.

"Yeah, well, you're not dressed."

"I was asleep."

"Not anymore."

"Clearly." His delivery was almost as dry as Archer's usually was, and I looked over to see how Ringo was taking our exchange. He leaned against the wall, arms crossed in front of him, watching Bloody Hell with a look of intense dislike. Which surprised the hell out of me.

"Put a shirt on." I'd never heard so much menace in Ringo's voice. I glanced sharply at him, and so did Bloody Hell, who glared at him with an 'I'm-the-man-here' stare.

The guy's shirtlessness was actually starting to get to me, and I broke one of my own cardinal rules by turning my back on him. I'm not overly modest, but I'm also not immune, and Bloody Hell was practically naked.

I could hear cloth rustle, and then Bloody Hell's actual voice. "I apologize to the lady if I've offended."

I spun around to face him. He was wearing a linen shirt of the Shakespeare in Love variety and it suited him. His dark hair was tousled and curly, and despite a long English winter his skin had the color of Italy or Spain. And I'd seen from his previous shirtlessness that there didn't seem to be tan lines.

"We're sorry for busting in on your sleep. It didn't occur to me the tower would be a bedroom."

"It's not generally, but my father is the headmaster, so it was the way to get my own room. Who are you?"

His gaze flicked briefly to Ringo, but he directed the question at me. Ringo was like a statue in the corner, and I couldn't tell if it was active dislike I felt coming off him or just mistrust. I decided first names couldn't hurt, and so far Bloody Hell didn't seem to be the alarm-raising type.

I held out my hand to shake. "I'm Saira, and this is Ringo."

After a moment's surprise, Bloody Hell took my hand and shook it. "My name is Henry. Henry Grayson. And since I've never seen clothing like yours, I'm going to assume at least one of you is a Clocker?"

"Since you're asleep in the Clocker Tower I assume you are?"

Henry winced. "Technically, I suppose. But since I haven't yet reached the age of majority, I'm still merely a student."

That confused me. "But you were born a Clocker, right?"

He looked at me oddly. "Until I've proven I can travel, I merely have potential."

Fascinating. "And you're allowed to travel at what, eighteen?"

"Nineteen, actually. Next month."

It occurred to me we were speaking at normal volume, and I had no idea who might have been woken up by our grand entrance. My voice dropped back down to a whisper. "What's the date today, Henry?"

The silence stretched out until it filled the room. Finally, Henry spoke. "March 31st. Year of our Lord, 1554."

I rapidly calculated from what I'd learned in my mom's history class. Lady Elizabeth Tudor had been in the Tower of London for thirteen days. I sagged in relief, but Henry must have taken my reaction for disappointment.

"You are from 1679, are you not?"

"1679? Why would you … oh, right. A century and a quarter per ring."

Now it was Henry's turn to look confused. "When else could you have come from?"

Not touching that one. "So when you travel next month, you're going back to …" Mental math. Not really my strong suit. "1429?"

Henry's expression was proud and he nodded. "My birthday was foretold as a triumphant day for England."

192

"There's a prophecy about you too?" I threw Ringo a look and he shrugged, still stony-faced. "What are the odds?" I muttered under my breath. I knew exactly what the odds were. Doran sent me back to St. Brigid's to meet Henry, instead of leaving me a painting of, say, the queen's apartments in the Tower of London. My fists balled up at my sides. Ringo continued to watch with careful eyes, and when my gaze flicked to the window, he nodded.

"Well, Henry, it's been interesting to meet you, but we have to go."

Henry moved as if to stop me, and Ringo was beside me in a flash. Henry's arm dropped to his side at a look from Ringo, but his voice held a plea. "Don't go. Please. There's much I'd learn from you if you're willing."

My eyes narrowed. This guy could probably teach me things, given his Clocker student status, but I had a feeling I was walking a big historical anomaly line with him. And I had no interest in messing with time like that.

"Sorry. If we come back to St. Brigid's maybe I'll catch you again." I headed back over to the window.

"Let me help you then. Why are you here?" Henry's tone sounded a little desperate. He'd gone from totally cocky one minute to rattled the next. Weird.

I turned to face him. "I can't tell you that."

"If you won't let me help, perhaps I could make introductions? I know people at court."

That got my attention. "Court, like the royal court?"

He nodded. "My mother is Mistress of the Robes to the queen."

My mouth dropped open a little. "That's knowing people."

He got a little of his swagger back. "You see. You're pleased you met me now."

"Yeah, not so much." I was already halfway out the window, and Ringo had my back. "Sorry we woke you, Henry. Good luck with your Clocking trip, and happy birthday next month."

Ringo pulled himself up and out of the window quickly, and we dropped down to the main roof level, out of sight of the Clocker Tower. Henry's whispered shout could just be heard on the wind. "Send for me if I can help you with your mission."

I knew he couldn't see how much those words startled me. "Mission? What are we, 007 agents?"

Ringo's voice was quiet and grim. "I don't trust Henry Grayson."

I looked quickly at my friend. Ringo's instincts were usually good. I hadn't gotten the same vibe from the Clocker guy, but maybe I was just blinded by muscles and bare skin. "At least we know the date. But maybe we should find Archer and leave now in case Henry decides to raise an alarm about us being here."

"My thinking exactly."

We made our way back across the roof and down the scaffolding. I didn't know if clocks even existed in this time, and pitch black is pitch black, so I was at a loss for how much more night we had.

Archer seemed to reverse-melt from the trees when we dropped to the ground. He had our bags in his hands.

"We should go."

Ringo clapped him on the arm with one hand. "Did ye see it, or do ye just know things?"

Archer's expression was grim as he scanned me up and down like he was looking for an injury or something. "I didn't like the way he looked at you."

Wait, what? He just got jealous from a vision? If my eyes rolled any further in my head they'd fall out.

Archer pulled his cloak out of his pack and draped it over his shoulders, then started walking. I sped up to catch him. "Did your vision tell you which way we need to go to get to London?"

"I know the way."

"On foot?"

"Yes, on foot."

"You couldn't have mentioned this before?"

"You didn't ask."

194

I held my tongue. Just barely, but somehow, I managed it. For a minute.

"He didn't look at me any different than any other guy does."

"Indeed."

ON THE ROAD

Just before dawn I decided I was too tired to be mad anymore. I don't know what it was about Archer's jealousy, but it tweaked some raw nerve I had – something to do with not being trusted, I guess. We'd made it to just outside Brentwood as the sky began to pale at the horizon, and I was ready to crawl into a hole and sleep for a week.

Archer knew of a Tudor house with such a hole – a priest hole accessible from the outside of the manor, designed to hide Catholic priests from over-zealous Protestant mobs. I'd stopped being surprised by the random stuff he knew a couple of hours before when he regaled us with the time he'd spent at Bletchley Park during World War II. It's where he met Professor Singh, whom he called Ravi, one of the very few Anglo-Indians working in wartime intelligence. The code-breakers had worked underground, where night and day didn't matter, and the only news of the outside world they received was related to the war. And so Archer and Ravi had bonded over the made-up world of movies, where musicals had been as far away from death and destruction as they could retreat.

The priest hole, he said, was one he'd used after that war. The country had still been reeling from its losses and Archer had wanted to escape the carnage of London. He had deliberately stayed away from anything to do with Immortal Descendants, which had probably been a good thing since the Mongers had gotten really strong then. But he'd been lonely, and he'd finally decided to take a road trip to see which Elians might be at St. Brigid's.

I had stayed quiet while Ringo peppered him with questions about warfare. That Archer had lived through things I'd only ever read about in history books was hard enough to fathom, but that he'd been so alone made my heart ache for him.

His walking pace slowed as the manor house came into view. It was one of the first buildings we'd seen up close, since we stuck mostly to the woods as we walked. A big, white house crisscrossed with black beams, it looked like a very grand farmhouse to my architecturally untrained eyes.

Despite total exhaustion, all three of us went into stealth mode as Archer led us around the side of the house to some cellar stairs. The door at the bottom was smaller than usual, but made of thick timbers, and I wondered how such an obvious entrance could be a priest hole.

But Archer didn't open the door. He knelt on the stone landing just outside it, and felt around the edges with his fingers. Then, with a grunt of effort, he pulled the biggest piece up and carefully laid it down off to the side. Under that stone were the square edges of a wooden frame, and a ladder descending into the darkest hole I've ever seen. He looked at Ringo.

"I'll go first."

Archer dropped through the hole without using the ladder. I started down more tentatively. I wasn't a big fan of jumping blind, which probably would have made anyone who knew me laugh. I seemed to do it a lot.

Strong arms caught me at the bottom, and Archer's whisper barely carried in my ear.

"We're not alone."

Not even my night vision could help me see in this pit, so I tried something different. I reached out with my instinct – whatever it was that hated Mongers and trusted my friends. I imagined that sense drifting out like invisible fingers to touch whatever else could be in that hole with us.

And it did.

I'd never consciously tried to *feel* anything but Mongers before, but whatever that instinct was, it found someone whose fear was so strong I could practically smell it.

Ringo had shifted the stone into place and dropped down next to us. Apparently he had no issue with blind jumps. But before I could say anything, Ringo froze in place.

"Who's there?"

"Whoever it is, they're scared."

I realized the darkness worked to our advantage. We were still dressed in our modern clothes because walking was easier in jeans than in heavy skirts, and Archer still carried my dress in his bag. So, instead of lighting up the priest hole and giving ourselves away, I tried a different tack. Honesty.

"My friends and I are going to stay until dark. We won't bother you, and we won't tell anyone you're here. I'm sorry we scared you, but we need to rest. So please, if you don't mind, don't murder us in our sleep, and we'll be on our way at dusk."

Archer's chuckle was low in my ear and he gripped me tightly in a hug. I felt safe in his arms, and it may have helped that some of the fear coming from the far side of the hole went down a couple degrees. I hoped our unknown companion was more like a quaking Chihuahua than a cornered pit-bull, and I dubbed him Pancho to make myself feel better about our chances in the dark.

I felt my way over to the wall behind the ladder and sank down with my back against the dirt. I refused to think of the creepy crawlies that could wriggle out of the earthen walls and into my hair while I slept. I was just too tired to care. Archer settled in next to me and reached out for my hand. I guessed his recent feeding was what made his skin warmer than normal, and I felt almost like a regular girl holding hands with my boyfriend. The part about hiding in a hole under a manor house in the sixteenth century, not so much. But maybe this was about as normal as my life got.

Ringo settled in a little ways away. I could feel him wrap his arms around his knees and stare into the darkness. I knew he was taking the first watch so I could sleep, and probably mostly so Archer was safe while he went unconscious.

The far corner of the priest hole stayed completely silent, and within a couple breaths, I nodded off.

The sound of whispered voices dragged me from a dream. Ringo was speaking quietly with Pancho, and I could tell they'd been talking for a while.

"Yer ma hasn't been back since?"

Pancho's whisper sounded young and, I thought, male. "The family sends food in once a day, and takes the chamber pot, but I've not been out in a fortnight."

I gasped, and I could feel the fear spike across the room. Definitely a Chihuahua. I felt a little bad for him. "You're being held down here?"

"They're hiding the lad from the queen's men." Ringo answered.

"Why?" I directed the question at Pancho, but he still wasn't talking to me.

"'Is family's hip-deep in 'igh water with 'er Majesty. From what I gather, 'is name'll get 'im the Tower on a good day, or the ax on a bad 'un."

"How old are you?"

There was silence from the corner. Finally Ringo answered. "'E's twelve."

I sucked in a breath. "You haven't been out of this hole in two weeks? Are they nuts?"

"It is treason to harbor a Wyatt."

I felt sick. "The Wyatt Rebellion. Thomas is in the Tower right now."

"How do you know my brother?" Pancho's voice trembled, but he sounded brave too.

"I don't." I was going to fail at this time line protection thing. Badly.

"Your manner of speaking is very strange. You must be from France, or Spain perhaps. A spy."

199

Again with the 007 business. "Not a spy. Just passing through."

Pancho sounded resigned. "It wouldn't matter. Even death would be better than living like this."

"Dude, you're twelve. You don't get to talk like that."

"Some lives have been lived through in twelve years." Ringo, with his own sixteen years, had just told a bigger truth than any philosophy book I'd ever read.

I pulled Ringo close so I could whisper in his ear. "Let's take him with us." I sounded like Dorothy asking the Scarecrow if we should take the Cowardly Lion along for an adventure. Too bad there actually was a wicked witch, and his name was Wilder.

Ringo nodded. "It's a risk, but none should live in the dark like this."

My voice was as silent as I could make it. "His brother will die in the Tower."

Ringo was quiet. Then, "Right. Are ye going t' ask 'Is Lordship, or just do what you will?"

That startled me. I actually hadn't been going to ask him.

"We're in this together. We should all agree."

"Good. Then I agree." Archer's whispered voice came from behind me. I hadn't realized he was awake and I reached for him. He clasped my hand and brought it to his lips to kiss. "Since you were going to do it anyway."

Apparently the living lie-detector part of his Seer abilities wasn't color-blind in the dark.

I spoke in a normal tone, since everyone was awake now. "Okay, Pancho, do you want to come with us?"

"My name is Francis."

"Great, Francis Wyatt. Too much information." If we actually had been spies, the kid would have given himself away six ways to Sunday. He must have realized it too, because he was silent. And losing more of his fear to anger. Good. Angry would work better than afraid in the long night of travel we had ahead of us. "We're going to London, to the Tower." Pancho gasped so I continued quickly. "We need to see someone who's being held there."

"Thomas."

"No, not your brother. But he's there too. If you're disguised, maybe we could get you in to see him before ..." I sighed. Crap.

"Before he is put to death." The resignation in his voice prickled with pain.

Okay, not pulling any punches with this kid.

"Right. I don't know how we're going to get into the Tower, or for that matter, if you even want to see Thomas before he dies. But if you stay here you'll either become some stunted, twisted bitter thing in the dark, or you'll die. And sorry if I don't believe in expiration dates for twelve-year-olds."

"I want to see Thomas."

"Okay, so you're with us." And I'd just increased our likelihood of failing by a factor of four. Oh well, sometimes it's not a choice.

The sound of the rock above us being dragged up cut through the dark with a sharp edge. Pancho whispered frantically. "The houseman is coming with food for me. He will have a light with him."

The fear was back, but Archer turned on his horse-whisperer voice. "Francis, listen to me. We're going to hide. When the light comes down the ladder you won't be able to see us, but we'll be here with you. School your face and your voice so the houseman sees nothing amiss."

"Yes, sir."

And just like that, he calmed. The flickering light of a candle lit up a circle of dirt floor, and I quickly grabbed Archer's and Ringo's hands. The ward went up with an immediate dip in temperature around us, and I shivered in my cloak. I could feel Archer press himself against me, but body heat was useless under a ward. I set my teeth against chattering and concentrated on keeping the ward around us while heavy footsteps creaked down the ladder.

Instead of looking at the houseman struggling with a plate of food as he descended the ladder, my eyes were locked on the spot in the far corner where I'd felt Pancho's fear. The candlelight very gradually revealed the form of a lanky boy, his arms wrapped around his knees and his face buried in the crook of his elbow. He had red-orange hair and freckles on the backs of his hands, the kind that attempt to shield fair skin from the sun. A ginger Chihuahua. He sat in a nest of tangled blankets, and his fine clothes were a wrinkled mess.

"Yer alrigh', Master Francis?" The houseman's voice was gruff, but it sounded like he actually cared about the answer.

Pancho looked up, squinting and blinking at the dim light. "I live in a hole, Roderick. I haven't seen daylight in weeks, nor have I moved beyond the ten paces of this room. I am alive, yes. But certainly not living."

Fascinating. Pancho actually had a backbone when he wasn't freaking out. I was glad to notice his eyes didn't flick over to where he'd last heard our voices.

Roderick set the plate of food down and traded out an empty bucket for one in the corner that must have been full of waste. He sounded genuinely contrite when he spoke. "I'm sorry. Ye knows there's naught I can do fer ye. Not while the Mistress fears them soldiers'll be back."

"I am certain my mother's sister will always do what is best for her."

Roderick paused, apparently unwilling to speak out against the lady of the house. "Can I get aught fer ye tonigh'?"

"What is the time?" Bless him. Pancho had a brain.

"Tis after nine. T' house is shuttin' down, but I can bring ye sommat else from the kitchen?"

"No need, Roderick."

"I'll see ye tomorrow then. Good nigh', Master Francis."

"Thank you for taking care of me."

Roderick looked sad as he shuffled back up the rickety ladder. The light was gone and the stone scraped back into place.

I dropped the ward, and Archer wrapped his arms around me to get warmth back into my skin.

"Are you still here?"

"Nice going, Pancho. I'm impressed."

"He will not return tonight."

"So, we give Roderick ten minutes to settle back into the house, and then we go." Archer's voice was steady and confident. "Bring your cloak and perhaps a blanket. Otherwise we travel light as we're on foot."

"I have two horses in the stable. My mother's man who brought me was sent away on foot. The price of my care, I suppose."

"But if we take them both, won't they assume you had help to escape?"

"Why would I not take what belongs to my family by rights?" There was certainty in his voice, total confidence in the order of things. Privilege was the only life this kid had known, and I wondered if the time he'd spent in this hole had tempered his expectations about life yet.

"I'll see that all's clear and come back for ye." Ringo's voice was low and businesslike, and he was up the ladder with barely a sound. The stone slid back with some effort, but even the small amount of moonlight coming in was a relief after the complete absence of light in the priest hole.

I was already starting to climb when Ringo's whisper carried into the darkness. "It's clear. There's a dog in the stables, but I've made friends with him, so I'll meet ye there." My muscles were stiff after the night of tramping through the woods, but I guessed Pancho would be much worse off than me until he got used to moving again.

Archer sent me up, then helped Pancho climb. His ginger head popped up above the stones, and I grinned at the expression of shock on his face when he saw me.

"But you are a girl."

"Yeah, and?"

His eyes were huge in his freckled face, and I thought he would grow into them pretty well when he got older. If he got older.

"And girls do not—"

One eyebrow went up, and the look on my face was clearly daunting because he wisely shut his mouth and just blinked at me. I helped Archer put the stone back in place, and then he stood to face Pancho.

"I'm Archer, this is Saira, and our friend in the stables is Ringo. Now, take us to your horses, if you please, Francis." The deer-in-headlights look was starting to fade from the kid's eyes, and he had the presence of mind to nod to me before he led us away from the manor house.

Ringo was playing with a big wolfhound when we found him in the stables. The dog probably looked fierce when he was on the job, but with his tongue lolling out and the big grin on his face as my friend wrestled with him, he looked like an overgrown puppy. Wiping dog kisses from his face, Ringo smiled at Pancho.

"Ye're probably the fastest one in yer family, eh?"

Pancho pulled himself up to his full five feet proudly. "I can beat every one of them except Thomas. But he is a man, so he hardly counts." Standing next to Pancho, Ringo looked full-grown. It was disconcerting.

"Well, good. Strength and speed'll help ye get strong again after yer time in the hole."

"I'm guessing these are your mounts over here?" Archer had gone to the end of the stables and was leading two small creatures from their stalls that looked more like ponies than horses. Pancho's grin lit up his face as he went to the dark brown one and rubbed its nose.

"This fellow's Clyde and that's Bess."

"They can't hold two of us each." Either these horses really were ponies, or the last five hundred years had seen huge advancements in horse-breeding.

Pancho spun angrily to face me. "They can too! Clyde is stronger than any other horse in my father's stables, and Bess

204

carried Tucker, who's fatter than all of you put together, for three days to get here."

Archer rubbed Bess' nose. "She's a lovely girl, Francis. Help me with tack for them and we'll be on our way."

Pancho looked stunned. "I don't do tack. Grooms do."

Ringo let go of the dog he was rolling with and stood up to brush off. "It's time you learned then. Lord Devereux is a patient teacher."

If eyes could have bugged out of a head, Pancho's had at the mention of Archer's title. The little brat apparently realized he was way outclassed in present company, and to his credit, he wisely stepped up to Archer and followed his lead with the horses.

I pulled Ringo to one side. "I'm going to look for a food storehouse, or else I'm breaking into the kitchen."

"Already done." Ringo opened the bag at his hip to show me two sausages, some cheese, and some bread. "Found these too." He tossed me a wizened apple and I took a happy bite.

"I knew there was a reason I kept you around."

"Nah, ye just need someone around who's better than ye at some things."

I stuck my tongue out at him, then looked over at Archer, patiently teaching a spoiled nobleman's kid how to tack up a horse. "I'm not sure the name Pancho fits the entitled little aristocrat."

"It's perfect. Makes 'im sound daring and full 'o courage. 'E'll come to like it."

A few minutes later we were leading the horses away from the manor house and out into the night. Archer and I walked next to Bess, while Ringo and Pancho whispered around Clyde. When we were out of sight of the house, Archer pulled me up behind him on the horse, and we took off down the dirt track at a gallop.

Pancho was right; those horses were strong. They carried us through the night, and it wasn't until just outside London that we finally dismounted at an inn to stretch our legs and give them a rest.

I sucked in a breath as soon as my feet touched the dirt courtyard. Riding is *not* easier than walking. My feet tingled while they woke up, and Ringo was doing a similar shifting dance as he worked the blood back into his legs. Archer and Pancho were fine, but I had yet to find anything Archer didn't do well.

He was a good guide too. He and Ringo communicated directions through hand signals most of the way past thatched cottages and farmlands. It didn't really hit me then that we were almost five hundred years in the past, and that everything my eyes took in I'd only either read about or seen in paintings.

Archer went to wake up the innkeeper to get a room for us with the trade goods we brought. Ringo and Pancho took the horses to be stabled, and I clung to the shadows of the courtyard, staying as invisible as I could. Archer and I had a quiet discussion about my wardrobe before we arrived at the inn. He said I'd blend better if I had the dress on. I said I would only blend if I was lying on a brocade bedspread at the Madonna Inn. His eyebrow went up in one of those gestures full of unspoken conversation, and I blushed and wisely shut my mouth until we stopped to rest.

Pancho almost went for the one bed, which was covered in scratchy wool, not shiny brocade, but then looked at Archer and stopped before he claimed it. I'd been listening to Pancho's accent long enough that I did a decent impression of it to ask the innkeeper's wife for two bedrolls. I had just pulled my hair from under my sweater and unbraided it when she tapped lightly on the door. I didn't think, I just answered it. And despite being dressed like a guy, and covered in all the grime the dirt road and the back of a horse could lay on me, my long hair gave me away. The woman's eyes widened in shock, and then narrowed dangerously as she handed them to me with a disapproving glare at the three males behind me. I sighed as I closed the door.

"Apparently I'm this century's version of a hooker. Awesome." I tossed the bedrolls to Ringo and Pancho and crawled into the bed. Archer was sitting on the edge of it, unlacing his boots. "I should just cut off my hair and travel as a man. It would be easier."

Again with the eye-bugging. Poor Pancho.

"Not if you have any hope of getting to Lady Elizabeth in the Tower."

"Right." I muttered under my breath as I yanked a brush through my hair. "Can't just go in over the walls like a normal person."

"My mother's second husband was the Lord Lieutenant of the Tower until the queen had him arrested. I used to play there when I visited her." Pancho's voice was small, and he watched me warily.

I stopped punishing my hair for having knots and stared at him. "You know the Tower of London?"

He nodded and swallowed.

A huge grin split my face, and I leapt up to go for my bag. Pancho jumped out of my way like I was going to hit him. I paused and considered him. I could feel the edges of his fear around him like an aura. Weird.

"You don't need to be afraid of us, Pancho. We're not going to hurt you."

He wrestled with the fear. Tried to pull it back. I was fascinated that I knew that. It felt like a kind of animal instinct, maybe from the Shifter in me.

"Why do you call me Pancho?"

I looked him in the eyes. Always best when you're about to give it to someone straight. "Because you remind me of a scared Chihuahua – which is a kind of little dog. My neighbor in L.A. had one called Pancho, and just like him you get cocky and proud to cover it. I give nicknames to people, and I say them out loud to people I like. And your name is Francis. I can't say that with a straight face."

Archer struggled not to laugh while Pancho processed what he could understand of my words, since I didn't bother to explain my words. His expression was like a loudspeaker for every emotion he had. I watched him fly through anger, indignance, resignation, until he finally settled on a kind of pride. The kid was twelve, and if he didn't screw it up with arrogance, he might be a pretty cool guy when he grew up.

"Just so ye know, I wasn't born with the name Ringo."

Pancho watched Ringo grin with me at our private joke, then he finally nodded.

"So, what shall I tell you about the Tower?"

GETTING IN

There weren't enough window coverings for Archer to sleep safely through the day on the bed with me, so we made a nest for him under it. I draped my cloak over the front so he was in a kind of dust-bunny cave. I sincerely hoped I'd beaten the bedding enough that any unwelcome guests of the microscopic variety had gotten the word their invitation was revoked. Pancho probably thought we were certifiable, but he didn't demand an explanation. Not that I'd have given him one anyway. He was still passed out cold when I woke up in the late afternoon, but Ringo was lying on his bedroll studying the map of the Tower I'd drawn with Pancho's help.

"Seems the river might be our best bet for gettin' in unnoticed."

"So one question is, did they keep the princess in the Bell Tower like modern history says, or in the Royal Apartments, like Professor Singh believes?"

"They don't know in yer time?" Ringo seemed shocked.

"I did a bunch of research online before we left, but everyone has a different answer, and everyone believes his information is correct. The thing the Professor said, and I believe it, is no matter how mad Mary Tudor was at her sister, she still always treated her like a princess of royal blood because of their dad. It makes me think Mary wouldn't have had her put in a cell."

"Well, they're on opposite sides of the common, so one of us should do some scoutin' before we all move in."

I looked at the details on the map that Pancho had so carefully pointed out: the guard towers, the garden, and all the best hiding places for children's games.

"I never studied up on Thomas Wyatt, so I have no idea where he was held before his execution."

Ringo looked over at Pancho, who slept curled up like a cold dog. "Do you know the actual date?"

I nodded. "April eleventh."

"So 'e's got a week."

We were each lost in our own thoughts for a moment before I finally asked Ringo the question I hadn't asked myself yet. "Do we trust him?"

He considered the sleeping boy again. "'E's young, so the arrogance of 'is station is only a habit, not yet who 'e is. And 'e holds 'is lordship in 'igh enough regard 'e won't openly defy 'im. But 'e was in that 'ole a long time for bein' twelve years old. Darkness can change a person."

"I guess the question is, can his time in the darkness inspire loyalty to the people who got him out?"

"Only if 'e believes 'e couldn't 'ave gotten out without us."

Ringo slipped out to find us some food, and I tackled the knots in my hair with a wide-toothed wooden comb from our trade goods stash. Archer emerged from under the bed, and I was surprised to see that the light had faded to dusk outside. He took the comb from me and smoothed out the last of the knots, an unexpected luxury that made me feel pampered. I braided it tightly while he brushed the dust-bunnies off his clothes and regarded Pancho, still curled in a tight ball on the floor, with humor and pity. "Has he even moved?"

I shook my head and held my hand out to Archer so he could pull me up. "I think the poor kid moved more last night than he has in two weeks." I kissed Archer lightly and his arm snaked around my back to hold me tightly against him.

"I could get very used to spending so much time together." There was a low, rumbly quality to his voice.

I grimaced. "Considering my general state of unwashed-ness, I'm not sure how flattered I should be."

He laughed and kept my body pressed against his. "Flattery is definitely not my intent."

No, given the intense way he was looking at me, I'd say flattery was way too tame for what he had in mind. My breath caught in my chest, and my heart pounded as Archer's mouth moved closer to mine. This wasn't going to be a quick kiss hello.

"Where am I?"

Nope. It wasn't going to happen at all. There was regret in Archer's eyes as he let me go and turned toward Pancho, awake and blinking blearily from his pallet on the floor. Recognition seeped into Pancho's eyes and he looked around the room. "And Ringo?"

Just then, Ringo opened the door juggling a tray with a jug of ale, some bread, cheese and meat pies. "'Ere. Get the ale for me. I think I spilled 'alf of it on some blighter's coat downstairs."

He distributed three cups to us and set the rest of the feast on the floor for a picnic. I grabbed the meat pies before Ringo and Pancho could take them. "How now!" Pancho sounded indignant.

"Road food. Eat the cheese now while you have use of a knife."

"Are you not eating, Milord?" Pancho looked up at Archer, who stood by the window looking out over the yard.

Archer shook his head. "I have no hunger." His gaze went to Ringo. "Did you check on the horses?"

"Still there."

"Good. We'll leave soon, then. And it's time for the dress, Saira."

I shook my head emphatically and swallowed the bread and cheese I was gnawing on. "Not if we're still on horses. I'd rather carry it and take my chances."

"Does your father whip you for wearing trousers, or has he given you up for a lost cause?" Pancho's question caught me off

211

guard. He was plainly curious, and I almost laughed at the fact that those were the only options that occurred to him.

"My father is dead." My heart ached just saying the words, but it seemed to satisfy something for Pancho.

"That explains it."

"Explains what?"

"How you can travel with men. You are neither sister nor cousin, are you?"

"Definitely not related."

"Right. I thought not. So the only other possibility is that you're under Milord's protection. Perhaps you are his ward?"

I shrugged and decided to blow his mind a little. "Or his lover?"

Yep, that did it. Mind blown. Jaw unhinged. Eyes bugged. Made me smile only a little evilly, and Ringo shot me a look that said 'shut it.'

I got up and dusted off my butt. "Okay, I guess we're out of here."

Ringo shouldered his bag. "I'll get the 'orses."

"I shall help." Pancho wanted to get very far away from me and bolted out the door behind Ringo.

Archer sighed and rolled up Pancho's forgotten blanket. "Be careful how you wind him up." He looked me straight in the eyes. "And me."

I chewed on that as we slung our bags over our shoulders and left the room. I tucked my braid down the back of my sweater again, but that didn't stop the innkeeper's wife from shooting me a death glare on our way out. Ringo and Pancho had the horses already saddled by the time we got to the yard, and I pulled Pancho aside before we mounted.

"I was just teasing, before. Archer and I aren't…" I caught Archer's eye as he watched our exchange, and I took a deep breath. "We're together, but we're not lovers."

Pancho looked back and forth between us, his face flaming red. "Oh."

212

It took nearly all night to make our way into London, and when we finally passed the villages of Shoreditch and Spitalfields, the markets were just beginning to set up. I took mental snapshots and made notes of things to sketch later for my mom – a farmer setting a table with fresh cheeses, a forager unloading a saddlebag full of dandelion greens, two little kids chasing a chicken around the yard while their mother watched them, laughing delightedly. I realized that's what my mom had been doing all those years with her paintings of Victorian England – chronicling her travels for me. Another piece of resentment fell away and I breathed a little easier. And immediately choked on the stench of sewage.

I recognized the layout of one of the major intersections just outside Aldgate and realized it's where I would go back in time and first meet Archer in three hundred years. In this time it was still a rural village outside the wall of London, which rose up in front of us in a very imposing pile of Roman brick and stone.

Archer turned us from Whitechapel High Street onto Aldgate High Street and I suddenly understood why it was called Aldgate. Ald, for 'old,' and the gate part was unmistakable. Looming up ahead was a massive three-story fortress-like structure with two arches passing through it, one for incoming traffic and one for outgoing. The foot and horse traffic on the road at this pre-dawn hour was light, and I was fascinated to see a portcullis – one of those medieval spiked gates – raised above us as we passed through Aldgate and into old London. There were no guards that I could see, so I guessed the gates must only be manned if there was an army on its way.

We turned left almost immediately and followed the wall until it intersected the Tower and presumably ended at the river. The Tower of London was situated right at the end of the wall, and I could see the strategic advantage to this from the time both defenses were built.

Archer pulled up our horse, and Ringo and Pancho came up next to us. "It's only an hour until dawn. Either we go in now and bunker down, or we find an inn close by and plan for tonight."

213

I considered the sky, inky black in this world without electric lights. "I am clearly useless with innkeeper diplomacy, so if you and Pancho get rooms then Ringo and I can go down to the Tower and scout for the best way in."

Archer shot me a look that was loaded with 'no,' but I cut him off before he could protest.

"Seriously, I can't open my mouth without suspicious look, and Ringo knows the area better than all of us." I wrapped my arms around Archer's waist. "Just go. We'll be fine, and you can meet us down at the river as soon as you find a place."

It took remarkable self-control, but I didn't actually swing my leg over the back of the horse to dismount until I saw him nod.

Ringo was off his horse with one smooth motion and looked up at Archer. "Try the Crosse Keys or Bell Inn off Gracechurch Street. Shakespeare was supposed to 'ave done plays in the yards there." I stared at him, but he ignored me. "We'll head down to the little 'arbor just west of the Tower and work our way around from there."

Archer nodded curtly, shot me another look full of 'you better stay safe' directives, and turned his horse down Fenchurch Street. Pancho followed him mutely, and I spun on Ringo.

"You know Shakespeare?"

He actually rolled his eyes at me, the punk. "Ye'd have to be deaf, dumb, an' blind not to know Shakespeare. The 'amlet and Laertes' swordfight is the stuff o' which little-lad stick battles are made."

Ringo turned off the main road and headed toward the river. The smell of raw sewage clung to the air with rotting corpse fingers, making the wood and coal smoke from the buildings that lined the lane smell like heaven in comparison.

We walked in silence. A fisherman whistled quietly as he passed us on his way to the boats, and a drunk lurched out of a doorway to heave on the sidewalk. I kept my head down, but I had googly eyes as I took in the sight of Tudor England. Whitewashed, timber-framed houses crowded either side of the cobbled road, and signs hanging outside the stone-clad lower floors showed that most buildings had shops underneath to justify their existence.

It was like a movie set except for the smell. Raw sewage with a couple of dead fish thrown in for flavor. Not appetite-inducing at all.

When we reached Thames Street, Ringo turned left, and I saw the Tower head-on for the first time. It loomed up in front of us like a battle-ready fortress wearing armor with spikes, so different from the beautifully-lit, silk-bannered castle I explored with Archer in modern times. I shuddered at the thought of being imprisoned in such a cold, dark place.

A little inlet in the riverbank provided a harbor, and Ringo was headed toward a small fishing boat furthest away from the street.

"What are you doing?" I whispered into the silence as Ringo stepped into the little boat.

"Looking at options and checking its seaworthiness. Get in. I need yer weight."

If it were possible, the water actually smelled worse than the raw sewage running in the streets, and I battled between breathing through my nose, where I could smell it, and my mouth, where I risked permanent taste-bud damage. I read somewhere that at high concentrations, sewer gas actually temporarily disables the sense of smell, so I opted for inhaling through my nose out of self-defense. Still, I was very glad it had been hours since I'd eaten last.

The little boat dipped a little, but held fine. So I untied it from its mooring. "Can you get us closer to the Tower? We can scout for a way in from the river."

Ringo looked at me. "'is Lordship won't like it."

I rolled my eyes. "We're just *scouting*, Ringo."

He considered the river for a long moment, then grabbed a long pole from the dock and expertly maneuvered the boat out of the inlet. He finally spoke in a low voice when we were about twenty feet offshore. "Our best bet may be a sewage tunnel."

I winced at the ugly reality of what we were trying to do, then steeled myself against the inevitable. I was going to have to deal with the crap.

The walls of the Tower rose up from the river like a solid, unclimbable barrier. An arched gate was visible in the darkness. Water lapped at the steps beyond it, and I knew without a doubt that was the Traitor's Gate. They may not call it that yet, but they would. The sound of small waves against the solid walls sounded deceptively peaceful.

"There. Down low in the wall. Bars." Ringo's voice was a whisper as he pointed out the sewage outlet on the wall.

Oh, yay. Bars.

He ignored my snort of disgust and pushed the little craft closer. When the nose of the boat bumped the stone, he grabbed one of the bars and pulled us around so we were up against the side of the small, gated opening. There really were no hand or footholds in the solid face of the river tower, and based on the grunts and whispered curses from Ringo, no way into the sewer tunnel either.

Our scouting mission was starting to feel like a bad idea. "We should go back before Archer heads down to the river looking for us." I couldn't tell if it was just the smell making me feel gross or if it was something else, but I was sick to my stomach.

"Oy! You, there! Hold fast!"

The dark shape of a boat loomed up behind us, effectively pinning our small craft to the wall. I had no idea how many guys were in the boat, but at least three of them were Mongers. I could feel them. The crap was just piling on tonight.

"Can ye swim?" Ringo whispered directly into my ear.

"Yeah."

"Do it then. The inlet were we got the boat is a hundred yards that way." He nodded in the direction we'd come from and there was calm urgency in Ringo's whisper. It was weird to be ordered around by him, but I knew I was going to do what he said.

"Right. On three then?"

"No. Go now."

He gave me a little shove, and I tensed at the anticipation of impact with a river so full of sewage it stank like a train station toilet at midnight.

"Oy!" The yell behind me was one of outrage, and I didn't stick around to find out what they were going to do about it. I just hoped Ringo was right behind me because there was no way I was going to tread water in that cesspool. I grabbed a big breath of fetid air and dove under so I couldn't be seen, then swam underwater until there was no air left in me. I broke the surface with a great gasp that I immediately regretted.

The Tower walls didn't loom anymore. I'd managed to leave them behind in my mad underwater dash for the inlet. I searched the river surface for signs of Ringo swimming behind me, but spotted nothing breaking through the water. The inlet was only a couple boat lengths away, and I ducked under again to get there. When I finally hauled myself out of the revolting river, I could barely stand to gasp for breath because the stench on me was unbearable. Clearly, my sense of smell was still intact.

"Saira!" Archer's whisper was fierce and angry. I looked up into his face above me. Every muscle in it looked clenched and I could see his jaws grinding. He reached down to haul me up but I stopped him.

"Don't touch me. I reek."

He ignored me and pulled me to my feet. And I was grateful he wasn't totally disgusted by the horrible smell rolling off me in waves. But then he pulled me into his arms and that was too much for my conscience. I pushed him away.

"Don't. You'll stink too."

His expression was still unreadable, but I could feel the anger rising to the surface of his skin. His voice was controlled and tight. "Where's Ringo?"

"He was behind me. Didn't he make it back yet?" I scanned the river for signs of a swimmer.

Archer ground his teeth. "Ringo doesn't swim."

His words hit me at the same moment I spotted the boat with the Mongers in it. We both dropped to the ground, and I was very glad there was still some dark outside. My stomach was churning ice-water.

The boat skimmed fairly close to the shore and one of the Mongers called out to his buddies. "There's naught in the water. Perhaps 'e went ashore, aye?"

"Or drowned." Another guy growled.

"Well, we've got the one, anyway. Let's go back in."

I couldn't breathe as the boat turned around and headed back toward the Tower. I watched it land at Traitor's Gate where the guards disembarked, pushed someone up the steps, and went in.

"They've got him." The words came out in a desperate whisper.

"What did you do?" Archer almost shook me in his frustration. The accusation hung in the air between us, worse than the rot of sewage could ever be.

I set my teeth against the defensiveness that threatened to set in. "We had time. We were looking for a way in."

"You just couldn't do it, could you? You had to go in without me. And so close to dawn when I couldn't get to you if something happened. It's like Whitechapel all over again." He ground the words out through clenched jaws.

Whitechapel. Where I'd gone after my mother. And where Archer had almost died to save me.

A spark was lit somewhere in the region of my gut and I lashed out. "This is nothing like Whitechapel. I didn't withhold information. I didn't lie to you! You knew we were coming down here to scout. And I wasn't alone, I was with Ringo!"

His anger was a quiet, cold thing. "Right, and where is he now?"

The fire went out with a sputter and puff of smoke. And with that, a chill set into my bones. I stumbled. "Oh, God." Archer caught me in strong arms and pulled me to his chest.

He smoothed my hair back from my face as I began to shiver.

"I didn't know he couldn't swim." My voice was small, and Archer sighed.

"Well, he's found a way in, I suppose."

Wait, what?

And it hit me. It wasn't how I would have chosen to get any of us into the Tower of London, but at least for the moment, Ringo was inside the walls.

"And now it's time to get you out of those clothes."

For the briefest of moments I thought Archer had forgiven me and might even be coming on to me. Until he spoke again.

"You stink."

Pancho was waiting for us back at the Crosse Keys Inn. The remains of a meat pie sat in front of him on the table, and he was practically asleep in his seat. Archer propelled him toward the stairs, called out for another meat pie for me, and thrust the poor kid up in front of him.

A few moments later the Innkeeper pushed a meat pie into my hands and wrinkled his nose. "There's a well out back. Get the stench off 'afore ye sleep in me bed." I was about to protest that I had absolutely no intention of either a. sleeping in his bed or b. washing in cold water in an outdoor yard, when a breeze ruffled my clothes and the reek hit me like a sledgehammer to the face.

"Right. Do you have a towel I could use?"

He looked like he was going to say no, but then the Innkeeper finally shrugged and tossed me a dingy bar towel. Awesome.

I took a bite of the meat pie and stepped out into the big, cobblestone courtyard. There was a water pump at one end like something from Little House on the Prairie, and I finished the pie in a couple of bites so I had free hands to wash with.

The water was fricking *cold*. It took every ounce of willpower I had to strip off my stinking sweater and douse my whole body in the freezing stream. I scrubbed at my hair and skin as well as I could until shivering stopped my hands from working properly. I wrapped my hair up in a knot, then used the dish towel to put some circulation back into my skin. Archer found me outside, teeth chattering so loudly I couldn't even smile at my cloak in his hands. I'd left it behind on the horse and it felt like Christmas when he wrapped it around my shoulders.

"I think perhaps it's time to change into that dress now?"

My chattering teeth wouldn't let me tell him to go to hell, but he could see it in my face. He didn't smile exactly, but I could see amusement lurking under the residual anger.

"You'll learn to like dresses, I'm sure." He wrapped his arm around me to keep me from punching him and led me up the back stairs to the room he'd gotten for us. Pancho was already passed out on a pallet on the floor and didn't even twitch when I stepped around him toward the single bed.

The sun was just starting to pink the sky, and Archer hung his cloak over the small window to black out the room from the daylight. "If you wake before me, take Pancho with you to find out the gossip. Don't ask a man, he won't tell a woman anything of importance. But if you find a charwoman or shopkeeper's wife, she'll be full of news from the Tower. Just promise me you won't go in without me."

I must have looked away before nodding because Archer gripped my upper arms tightly and forced me to meet his eyes. "Promise me."

I had no choice. I promised.

My teeth finally stopped chattering when I was fully laced up into the dress Archer had been carting around England. I was still having fits of shivers, so he pulled me down onto the bed and wrapped me tightly in my cloak. I tried not to dwell on worry for Ringo, but it wasn't helping my chills. Archer settled himself behind me and snaked his arms around my body. He'd been angry, but he hadn't pulled away from me, and after a few more violent fits of the chills, I finally dropped off to sleep.

INSIDE

"So, are ye keepin' the princess in the Bell Tower or the Royal Apartments?"

The Yeoman Warder holdin' my arms behind me stumbled a bit.

"Are ye tryin' t' get yerself killed, boy?" 'Is voice was low and in my ear. "If ye were after breakin' the Lady out, fer God's sake, don't admit it out loud. Ye'll bring harm t' her as well as yerself."

"I was merely wishin' t' pay my respects with a nod in the right direction." The Yeoman Warder and four of 'is mates were marchin' me around the outer compound of the Tower. I recognized the Royal Apartments from Saira's map and tossed my head at it. "If she's there, I just want to walk a little straighter, that's all."

My guard was grim. Then 'e gave a quick nod. "Walk straighter then, and I won't fault ye."

I got a look at 'is face. 'E was not young, and there was more gray in 'is beard than black. But I made note of 'im. It could be useful to know where loyalties lay among the guards.

We went toward a white timber building in the inner court, just inside the walls. One of t'other guards knocked on the door.

"Prisoner for the Lord Lieutenant."

The door swung open and we were shown into the Lord Lieutenant's quarters.

"'E was found at the sewer gate on the river, Sir." My Yeoman Warder spoke to a man in full uniform sittin' behind a desk. The Lord Lieutenant of the Tower, if I had to guess. 'E looked up sharply and studied me like I was under glass.

"People don't generally break into a prison unless there's something inside that they want. What is it you want, lad?"

The Lord Lieutenant's voice was tired, but 'is eyes missed nothin' and I knew this one wouldn't be easily fooled. Didn't stop me from tryin' though.

"I work for the Lady Elizabeth."

Made 'im sit up at least.

'E looked at the men behind me. "Get her."

Well, this was going to be interestin'.

I tried to stay busy lookin' anywhere else but at the Lord Lieutenant, though I knew 'e was studyin' me closely. Too closely, it turned out. "To hear you speak I'd guess you were born not a mile from here, but you appear to have spent time elsewhere. Perhaps another court?"

"I've never left England, Sir."

"But your garments are like nothing I've ever seen. Finely woven, an odd style, and leather footwear of a nature I'd like to own myself, yet have no idea where to procure."

I looked down at the Lord Lieutenant's feet. 'E wore simple leather shoes that slipped on without ties, with soft leather soles. "My uncle was a cobbler, Sir. 'E tried 'is designs on my da, an' when they both died, I got these boots. 'Tis all I 'ave left of my da." I added the last bit in case the Lord Lieutenant was thinkin' of takin' 'em off my feet.

'E said nothin' more, but kept 'is eyes on me until the door burst open and a young guard tumbled in. "The Lady comes."

All eyes went to the door as a woman entered the chamber. She was young, but not a girl anymore, and the eye didn't know where to land with 'er. She wasn't pretty. That would be too common. She was … arrestin'. Pale skin like the finest, thinnest silk. Hair near to 'er waist the color of a copper kettle where the sun hit it. And practically bloodless. She's been ill, that was clear as day. I'd never bowed to a monarch before, but goin' down on one knee hardly seemed enough to show 'er respect.

The other men in the room all bowed at the waist, so I was the only one who saw 'er eyes never left mine. There was a question in them, so I did the only thing I could think of. I nodded, and smiled.

And she smiled back.

"I see you've brought Ringo to me. Thank you, Lord Brydges."

That brought me up short. The woman who'll be queen someday knew my name?

The Lord Lieutenant arched an eyebrow. "Ringo?"

She nodded in my direction like it was obvious. "My taster, of course. Obviously your kitchen staff have informed you that I can barely eat for fear of poison. I am, after all, completely at the mercy of my sister and her ... advisors."

Lord Lieutenant Brydges had nothin' but a rock and a hard place for company. I tried not to grin, but I've never had much luck hidin' cheek. His eyes narrowed at me and then he finally sighed.

"Of course, My Lady. We shall bring him to you with your meals."

"You'll do no such thing, Lord Brydges. Ringo will sleep on a pallet in my sewing chamber. You'll see that it's provided, please."

She held her hand out to me without another look at 'imself." "Come, lad. Tell me news of my household." She was almost as tall as Saira, and she tucked my 'and in her arm like I was a child. I suppose it wouldn't be seemly for 'imself to think of me as aught but young or 'e'd never allow it.

We were followed by the Yeoman Warder, but not handled by 'em now as the princess walked me across the compound to 'er apartments. She didn't speak until we were inside and the door closed.

She dropped my hand and stepped back to face me.

"If you're here to kill me, you'd better get on with it."

I jerked awake just as Archer clutched me to him. Another vision. Happening now, or about to happen? I turned to face Archer and saw he was conscious too.

"She protected him. How did she know?"

"She must have seen him, in her own vision."

I winced and scrubbed my eyes. "At what point did our journey to the past to save Ringo cause the harm in the first place?"

"You can't think that way. You'll make yourself insane."

I scoffed. "Right, 'cause that's not already a statistical probability." I sat up and swung off the bed. I forgot I was wearing the dress and instantly regretted the move because I got tangled in yards of fabric and almost landed on my butt. "Hey, where's Pancho?"

Archer was much more graceful in his leap up. I was perversely glad to see hair sticking up on one side of his head. Not so perfect with his Calvin-and-Hobbes-bed-head. "Gone, apparently."

"To bust us, do you think?"

Archer shook his head and ran his fingers through his hair. So much for Calvin. "No, he has too much to lose. If the wrong person recognizes him he joins his brother in the Tower."

"I was thinking about how to sneak him in. Could you find a dress that would fit him?"

A slow grin spread across Archer's face. "He would hate that."

I guessed I was forgiven for the moment, since Archer was playing with me again. Relief trickled through my veins, and I answered his smile with a devious one of my own. "I know, that's why it's perfect." I started to pace the room and got hung up on a chair. Seriously, this long skirt thing as daily wear was going to kill me. I picked up my still-damp jeans from the fireplace and sniffed them. Ugh! I didn't think the stink would ever come out.

"At what point do we just leave?"

Archer tried to hide his smile. He knew what I was really mad at. "Maybe he's just being a boy and exploring London."

"Or maybe I got supper for grumpy companions." Pancho appeared in the doorway holding a bag of something greasy. He handed each of us some sort of pastry-wrapped meat pie, though Archer broke his in half and handed them back to us. Pancho accepted it without question, but I looked at Archer with a raised eyebrow. He nodded briefly, then pulled on his cloak. "I'll go scout the Tower entrances while you two eat. I'll return as soon as I've found something." I knew the 'something' was more like 'someone,' and his gaze avoided mine as he closed the door softly behind him.

Pancho spoke after he swallowed a huge bite he'd taken. "I can get us in."

"Not through the sewer."

He rolled his eyes. "Obviously. Through the old Beauchamp Tower gate. Almost no one uses it anymore."

"It's not guarded?"

He shrugged. "It is a small gate. There is only one Yeoman Warder. We shall bribe him."

Of course. "Will he let us in at night?"

"I do not know. I have never attempted entry at night."

Right. I kicked off my boots and pulled my stinky jeans back on. Pancho's eyes got big at the sight of my bare legs, but I ignored him. When my boots were re-laced I felt better. I could tie the damn skirts around my waist if I had to climb or run. I was not going to rely on the casual confidence of a twelve-year-old Lordling.

I was trying to stay calm doing yoga stretches when Archer finally got back. He was barely in the door when I grabbed my cloak. "Let's go."

Archer grabbed my arm and pulled me to him. I met his eyes. "Thank you," he said. His voice was as warm as his skin.

"You're good now?"

He nodded. "Maybe a little tipsy, but fine."

"You couldn't find anyone sober?"

He laughed. "There isn't anyone sober. They don't have tea yet, and the river water is foul, so it's either ale or wine."

Oh. I hadn't thought about that. I was still drinking the last of the water we'd brought with us from the St. Brigid's storage cellars. Archer draped my cloak around my shoulders and fastened it at my neck, allowing his fingers to trail lightly over my collarbones. It raised delicious goosebumps on my skin, and he smiled. He kissed me softly and I might have melted a little, but then the business part of my brain kicked in and I pulled away.

"Let's go find Ringo."

Pancho was right about the one guard at the Beauchamp gate. He was asleep on a stump just inside, but the gate was locked and the keys were attached to his belt, just out of reach. I was already a couple of feet up the wall and looking for my next handholds when Archer passed me and signaled that I should get down. I glared at him, but his glare had teeth and was therefore scarier, so I did what he wanted and jumped back down to wait outside the gate.

It was a high wall, two very tall-ceilinged stories, but the stone and mortar was old and rough. It looked like exactly the kind of climbing I'd love to do if I wasn't carrying about fifty pounds of skirts on my body.

Archer made it over with only a couple hesitations, and I didn't hear him at all until he suddenly appeared on the other side of the gate, bent over the sleeping guard. Archer had a lock-pick's touch with builder's hands. They weren't rough, but strong and substantial, and yet he barely rustled the silk of the guard's jerkin as he pulled the keys off his belt.

I wrapped my skirt around the lock to muffle the click as Archer opened it. He had put the keys back on the sleeping guard's belt before I was done refastening the chain around the gate.

Pancho seemed slightly bemused by our nefarious break-and-enter activities, but wisely stayed quiet through the process. I knew we were going to have to deal with finding his brother at some point soon, but the only thing on my mind then was getting to Ringo. I whispered into his ear, "The Royal Apartments." He didn't hesitate, but stuck to the shadows of the Beauchamp tower. I had tried to spell it 'Beecham' on the map, because that's how Pancho pronounced it, but was corrected by him in that tone people reserve for little children and the especially stupid.

We clung to the edges of the buildings until we caught a dark shadow from the White Tower. Then, one at a time, we made a dash across the dirt courtyard to the other side, where a big stone building ran down toward the river. I'd only seen it on old maps because it didn't exist in my time. It was the Royal Apartments.

Pancho led us to the side closest to the White Tower. "The queen's apartment is up there," he whispered into my ear. That gave me a chill. Those were the same rooms Henry VIII had

226

decked out for Elizabeth's mother, Anne Boleyn, when she was crowned queen. And the same place she stayed right before he had her head chopped off. It made me wonder how the Lady Elizabeth was sleeping these days.

"'Ello mates." I nearly left my skin hanging on a shrub when Ringo appeared right behind me.

I wanted to hit him, so I threw my arms around him and whispered in his ear. "Scare me like that again and I'll murder you where you stand."

He gave me a strange look and stepped back from my hug. "Let's go in so we can talk." His whisper didn't carry beyond our little group. Ringo was good at the clandestine stuff and was nearly noiseless as he led us to a tree near the side of the building.

"Guards at the doors, so up we go." Ringo leapt up into the lowest tree branch and held out his hand. I didn't need it until my damn skirt got hung up on a knot and I had to reach down to free it. He dropped my hand as soon as I was stable, then reached for Pancho. I was already at the second floor window by the time Archer was off the ground, and I dropped inside the dark room to help Ringo push Pancho across the narrow gap. Archer and Ringo leapt easily into the room, and Ringo silently closed the mullioned glass window behind us. He put a finger to his lips, then led the way through a massive gallery to a tiny room off to the side. When the door was closed behind us he finally spoke in a quiet, normal voice.

"Got yer torch, Saira?"

In fact I did. It was the only good thing about the huge skirts. There were deep pockets to store things and plenty of fabric to hide the bulk. I knew it was a big risk to carry my little Maglite, but it was like my security blanket and I'd take my chances.

I set it, business-end down, on the floor and clicked it on. "Are there windows?"

"No. This is the pages' chamber. They don't get things like windows."

"Why would pages need windows? They're only ever in their room long enough to sleep." Pancho sounded genuinely confused.

I was about to bite back, but Ringo beat me to it. "Ye'd think differently if ye'd ever been one."

I shone the little light around the room. There was a woven rush mat on the floor, a longish table with some benches pushed up against the wall, and a couple of bedrolls stacked in a corner.

"What manner of fire is that?" Pancho was staring at the Maglite with fascination and fear. But his little noble superiority had annoyed me, so I ignored him. "Can this room be secured for Archer during the day?"

Ringo pulled a heavy iron key out of his pocket. "Took the liberty of borrowin' this once I'd found it. No pages here without the court, an' though the Lady takes 'er walks in the great hall, none think to look in the servants' rooms."

My eyes narrowed at him. "You've been here a day and you know all that?"

He looked away. "Been busy."

I looked him up and down. He wasn't hurt that I could see, but he was acting weird. "So it was true. Elizabeth actually came for you?"

Archer spoke authoritatively. "You can't call her that to her face, Saira, not even here. 'My Lady' is about the least title you can get away with until the queen declares her heir."

Pancho stared at Archer. "Why would the queen do that though? She'll marry and have her own children. It's why Thomas did what he did. 'Twas the only way to take England back from the Catholics."

None of us said anything. What could we say? 'Your brother's life was wasted because Mary will die childless in four years.' No matter how I felt about the kid, I wasn't cruel.

So, I avoided the conversation altogether and turned my attention back to Ringo. "Have you had much chance to talk to her?"

"Just long enough to convince her I wasn't the one trying to kill her."

Pancho stared. "How'd you do that?"

Ringo included me and Archer in his very direct gaze. The intensity of it made me squirm. "She described a vision where she saw me bein' tortured by a bishop. I told 'er I hadn't heard about the torture bit, but we'd come to stop the bishop hurting 'er."

My heart pounded in my chest. I felt about five inches tall. "I'm sorry, Ringo. I didn't ... couldn't ..."

"Couldn't be honest before askin' me to come wi' ye? Somethin' bein' dangerous is different than it bein' a foregone conclusion, don't ye think, Saira?"

I stood stock-still in the direct line of Ringo's fire. Archer came up beside me protectively. "I should have told you. It was my vision."

"But she knew it an' she did the askin'." Ringo directed his clear, laser-sharp gaze back to me. "I'm not sayin' I wouldn't 'ave come, but I should have known what I was goin' t' face." Ringo rubbed his head wearily and I knew a word or touch from me would be entirely unwelcome.

"Do ye know when she finally decided to trust me? When she asked what Immortal I was descended from. When I said none, she looked relieved."

What was left of my confidence pretty much pooled around my ankles. What the hell were we doing here?

"I'm goin' t' bed. You lot stay away from her apartment. Ye'll have to pass by me t' get to 'er anyway, an' I won't 'ave it. Not tonight."

He tossed me the key before he turned on his heels and left the room, taking a giant piece of my heart and crushing it under his feet as he went. My temper flared in self-preservation. I hated being wrong. Hated it with a fierceness that made me want to lash out at him for calling me on it. But the same instant the anger flared, it died and left me cold and shaky in its wake.

Archer put his arm around me, and all I wanted to do was sink into it and let him take away the guilt. But he couldn't, so I didn't.

"I'll be back." I left my Maglite on the floor where it gave a small glow to the room and made the pages' quarters feel almost warm against the chill that was creeping through my veins. Archer twitched, like he was going to step in my way, but then seemed to think better of it and let me go without a word.

Guilt is the one thing that'll send me into self-loathing, and thus I avoid doing things that make me feel guilty. But I failed this time. And the whole thing had very disturbing echoes of me trying to protect Archer from the knowledge that he'd become a Vampire. Ultimately, it was always the lie that really hurt.

Archer once said the aura of omission was a blue/green color and he'd seen it around me more than just a couple of times. What if I only told the truth, and I told the whole truth, regardless of who I thought might get hurt from it?

What if I just said exactly what I meant all the time?

The consequences of that couldn't be worse than how I was feeling now.

I wandered around the edges of the great hall. My wandering might have looked a little bit like lurking to the average person, but I couldn't help the instinct I seemed to have been born with. I supposed felines, like my large predator cat-shifting father, were more slinky than lurky, but I was feeling about as far from feline slinkiness it was possible to get. If I could have slithered, that would have been a little closer to the truth.

I was surprised to find a small chapel at the end of the Great Hall. I didn't think the royals would have wanted such a constant reminder of their sins as they drank and debauched their way through history. There were candles on a table just inside the door, and I took one back into the Great Hall where the embers of a fire still smoldered. I'd seen what it took for the innkeeper to light a fire with a tinderbox, so I got why they never really let things burn totally out. I lit my candle, went back into the chapel, and slotted the wax taper into a holder on the altar. The small room looked warm and pretty in the flickering candlelight, and I sat down on a bench to take it in.

The ceiling was the best part. Carved wood and painted with tiny stars, it felt like something out of a fairy tale instead of an unused chapel in a fortress that had become a prison. I leaned back and stared up at it, letting the beauty drown out the noise in my head.

"I believe you may have lost your way." A soft voice came from the shadows behind me. I spun to find the speaker, but saw no one.

Until she stepped forward into the flickering candlelight.

ELIZABETH

Elizabeth Tudor was reed-thin and maybe only an inch or two shorter than me, which made her look a little like a Whippet. Her long hair was loose, and she wore a dark blue gown with embroidered gold thread that was probably simple for her, but to my eye looked like a ball gown.

I realized I was staring, and I fumbled a bow that was a cross between a nod and falling in a hole. The expression on her face was a mix of imperious haughtiness, interest, and a little bit of humor in her eyes. Thank God for the humor, even if it was at my expense.

"My … Lady. I'm sorry. I'll go." I wasn't ready to see her yet. And absurdly, I wanted to honor Ringo's ban on talking to her tonight.

"You'll stay and tell me who you are."

Yeah, no question about it. This woman was born to be queen. There was absolutely no other option in the world but to obey her, and if I did my math right, she was twenty-three years old.

"My name is Saira Elian. And I'm …" I fumbled again. She didn't seem to have any love of Immortal Descendants, but my truth-telling vow kicked in and I took a breath. "I'm a Descendant of Time … and Nature." I didn't usually do that. Didn't own my mixed-blood status out loud. I had no idea what they did to mixed-bloods in this time, so it was a gamble. But I hoped being something that was outside the usual lines of Descendancy would work in my favor with someone who wasn't pleased with Descendants.

I had the sense that she was studying me, looking at me from the inside out. But she was a Seer, so maybe it was possible. The silence was totally unnerving and my confidence was beginning to puddle on the floor when she finally spoke.

"Why have you come?"

Her question couldn't have been more simple, but I had no idea how to answer it. The scary part was I'm not sure I ever really knew the answer, even before leading us here to a time when we could accidentally, yet epically, screw things up.

"You're in danger."

She stared at me like I was standing in front of her buck naked. "Of course I am. Now more than ever. They could poison my wine, murder me in my sleep. My sister could sign an order and my head would be removed quite permanently from my shoulders. Presumably none of these things is remarkable enough to warrant a visit from whence you came?"

"There's a bishop. Actually, he used to be a bishop, but he still uses the title."

"Your point?"

Sometimes imperiousness is just rude, but I didn't think saying that to the future queen of England was going to get me anywhere. "My point is Bishop Wilder is here, now. He wants something from you, and we're not totally sure what it is. My guess is he wants your blood."

She scoffed. "The queue forms to the left."

Okay, maybe I could like her a little bit. I smirked, and she answered with one of her own. But the humor was gone with my next words. "Your actual Seer blood. He's ..." – I thought vampire might be a concept too laced with mythology – "one of Death's Descendants. He has discovered that something in his own blood seems to allow him to absorb the powers of other Descendants when he ... consumes theirs." I was treading on the edges of too much information, or at least science that was way ahead of Elizabeth's time, but she didn't flinch. Her gaze stayed locked on mine so steadily that I thought she would be an awesome poker player.

"You believe he wants to drink my blood?"

Yes, it did sound ridiculous to anyone not brought up on old black and white Bela Lugosi movies. "He kidnapped my mother a few months ago and drained her of nearly all her Clocker blood. Drinking it is how he was able to come to this time."

Ha! Made her eyes widen a fraction. She was good, but I was better. I decided to put away the mental high fives and go back to honesty.

"You are clearly a powerful Seer. I don't know what you can do, but because Bishop Wilder has painted a target on you I have to assume it's because he wants your skills."

Her gaze was steady. "You've explained why this bishop is here, but you still haven't said why you are. Revenge, perhaps? For your mother?"

Well, that was interesting. Had I traveled back in time almost five hundred years to dish up a little payback? Put that way, there was a lot to pay back. My mom, Archer … my dad. "He killed my father too."

"Ah, so it is personal."

I felt like I was clenching the honesty card in my teeth. "Maybe, yeah. But not totally. I wouldn't have dragged my friends here to fight my battle."

"And the young man with you whom you disdain so much? Who is he?"

"Pancho didn't come with us. We picked him up on the way."

She made a dismissive gesture. "Not the Wyatt pup. The other one. Tall. And dark."

I stared at her. "I don't disdain Archer. I barely even know what that means."

"You seem to care little for his concerns, yet you expect he will follow you without question. He's clearly besotted with you, yet you choose the young and charming Ringo with whom to share your thoughts, though apparently, not even he gets the full extent of your honesty. You seem to care nothing for this Archer's heart when you ride roughshod forward without a thought for his desires."

My eyes felt like saucers in my head, and I was doing a fair imitation of a statue.

What. The. Hell?

I couldn't stop it: the explosion. It just … happened.

"You know, your Highness, or High-and-Mightiness, or whatever you're called, you don't know me. You don't know anything about me. Whatever you've Seen in your visions isn't who I am, and nothing, not even your royal blood, gives you the right to judge me on how I love people."

I managed to break free of the freeze-lock on my muscles and stomped out of the chapel as graciously as a three-year-old having a tantrum.

My heart was still pounding as I sprinted down the length of the Great Hall and slid around the corner to a long gallery. I stopped in a window alcove, sank to the floor, and clutched my knees to my chest.

The roaring in my head burned down to a dull throb.

I just yelled at the future queen of England. Probably the most powerful woman of her time, and I snapped like a pissy toddler who didn't get her way.

It occurred to me that if we survived this madness I should probably get out of Dodge and not come back when Elizabeth had some real power. I wasn't too high on her Christmas list at the moment.

But there was a tightness in my chest that still felt like anger.

Or was it indignation?

That thought made me oddly uncomfortable. Indignation always seemed like the last stand of the guilty, and I didn't want any part of her words to be true.

They weren't. They couldn't be. I didn't treat people that way. Definitely not the people who loved me.

My heart rate slowed to something that wouldn't make the charts blip as that last thought replayed in my brain. The people who loved me … who loved *me*. Why not 'the people I loved?'

Oh ick. Not. Going. There.

I forced my brain away from that train of thought. My self-protective instinct was throwing walls up around Elizabeth's words so I didn't have to see them or hear them or taste the bile that rose in my throat at the thought of them.

"Ye just had to do it, didn't ye?"

I was pretty sure that guilt leaves a stain, and on me it felt like a sunburn. I looked up to find Ringo glaring at me with his arms crossed across his chest. When had he stopped being a nineteenth century street urchin, and who was the young man that stood in his place?

All the fight fled from my body and I slumped. "If you're here to beat up on me, get in line." I waved half-heartedly and then dropped my head into my hands.

"How's that hair-shirt feeling? Itch yet?"

I looked up. He was still towering over me, but the glower had been replaced with something that looked a little like a smirk.

"Yeah, somehow I don't think a hair shirt's quite enough, do you?"

"It's a start."

I scoffed. "I'm screwing up, Ringo. I think I know what I'm doing, but instead I'm barreling around in the dark slamming into my friends and knocking them into cesspools."

Ringo winced. "Is that what happens, then?"

I clenched my eyes shut and took a deep breath, then looked up at him. "You want to sit?"

He slid down next to me, shoulder to shoulder. We both stared at a painting on the opposite wall for a place to rest our eyes that wasn't each other. I told him about Archer's visions, including the privy dunk and Wilder's sword-to-the-sternum trick to get Elizabeth to spill. And then I told him what Elizabeth said about how I treated Archer, and about blowing up at her and then running away.

We stared at the painting in silence for a long time. So long that I started analyzing paint swirls and brush techniques and trying to guess if it was a court artist or an apprentice who had painted the portrait of the lovely dark-haired woman holding a small child on her lap.

"Ye do a lot of running."

"It's how I stay alive."

"Nah, it's how them that're on their own stay alive. Ye've got people now. Ye don't have to run like that no more."

Said the boy who'd been truly alone for most of his life. I looked at him for the first time since he sat down, and I knew he could see the fear swirling in my eyes. "But what if I forget how to run?"

"Can ye learn 'ow not to?"

I searched his eyes and saw tenderness and humor and strength and fearlessness there. All the things I'd come to expect from this boy-man Ringo had become.

"Do you forgive me?"

His eyes narrowed. "Depends."

"I won't keep secrets from you again."

"Good, but that wasn't my condition."

"Oh."

"No, don't take it back. There's no secrets between friends, Saira. Can't be if we're going to make it through this business."

"So what's your condition?"

He took a deep breath. "I asked ye once to consider marrying me if ye didn't go with his Lordship."

I felt like a trapdoor released under me and my stomach had just fallen through the floor.

"Ringo …"

His gaze narrowed again as he held my eyes locked to his. "Ye'd be settling if ye did it."

I couldn't hide my surprise at his words.

"I won't ever love ye like 'e does. I know ye too well."

I couldn't help it, I started giggling when the tears began to stream. Both reactions made me feel totally ridiculous. "So I'm too scary, and you're taking back your offer? Awesome." The last word barely came out, choked as it was by the beginning of teary hysterics.

Ringo grabbed my chin and forced me to look at him. He spoke softly, his eyes never leaving mine. "Saira, ye listen to me and ye listen well, 'cause I'm only sayin' this one time. I love ye, but I love ye like my sister. And because I love his Lordship as well, I'll never play that 'what if' game that leads to so much heartbreak. I've seen how he looks at ye like the moon rises on yer skin, and how he holds his breath when ye pass by so he doesn't reach out to pull you in just so he can smell the vanilla in yer hair. He loves ye with the whole of his past, present and future, and it's a thing someone like me, with such a small life behind and in front of me, can never compete with. Nor do I want to. Because ye deserve a love like that. Ye're a good person, Saira Elian, and ye should be loved like ye're the last woman on earth and he's the last man. Because I guarantee, fer him ye are."

Breath shuddered in my chest, and the tears ran with full volume down my face. I had no voice left and the words came out in a raspy whisper. "What if I don't love him enough, Ringo?"

His hand dropped away from my chin, and I felt the loss of contact like a cold chill over my skin. "Enough for what?"

"To let go."

Ringo stood up and dusted himself off. My arms tightened around my legs reflexively and the lead ball in my stomach held me rooted in place.

"And is it so great, what ye're holding onto?"

For once Ringo allowed his shoes to make a sound down the gallery as he walked away from me. It was the loneliest sound I'd ever heard.

THE PLAN

We were stuck in the pages' annex during daylight hours, mostly because we had no business being in the Tower of London, but also because Archer and daylight didn't mix. Sometime before nightfall Ringo popped in to bring us some food he managed to slip from the kitchens, but he was gone the next minute. I picked at a meat pie because I knew I should eat, but my appetite had pretty much flown out the window with my voice attached to its back.

Archer was still comatose in the far corner of the room. When I'd gotten back to the annex the night before, I couldn't manage more than a couple of words to anyone, and though Archer's eyes followed me wherever I went, I had trouble meeting them. Since I was such charming company I finally wrapped myself up in my cloak and pretended to sleep. Archer had settled in behind me just before the sun came up, and despite my best efforts to punish myself, I couldn't help nestling into the cavity his body made.

The weight of the silence in the pages' annex was crushing the breath out of me. Pancho had polished off his food and the remains of mine, and the sound of his chewing had nearly sent me at his throat.

"I'm going out."

Pancho looked over at Archer's sleeping form. "I'll need a minute." He burped loudly and wiped the back of his hand across his mouth. I did my best to ignore him. He looked up, surprised I was heading for the door. "I said wait."

"I don't want you with me."

Pancho stared, clearly at a loss for coherent thought. I did that to people, especially arrogant little entitled pricks.

"I need to find my brother." God, the kid was whiny.

I shrugged. "Go find him, then."

I needed to run, to lose myself in each move and get out of my head. I needed to be completely in the moment with no thought to spare for anything other than that. But the twelve-year-old looking out of Pancho's eyes reminded me I wasn't the only one who needed, and maybe doing something with a purpose would quiet the noise in my brain. I took a deep breath and leveled a gaze on him.

"Okay." I looked away from Archer's body so I could deny the guilt that crept up my spine. "I'll go find your brother for you. But until I find him, you need to stay here and keep watch over Archer."

Pancho's pout reminded me he was just a kid. "He doesn't need a minder, and in any case, I'm the one who knows the layout of this place."

"Right. And there are people here who know you. Don't end up in a cell here too, rotting away until someone remembers to feed you."

He flushed. That one hit very close to home. "Where do you intend to look?"

I shrugged. "I'm starting with Beauchamp Tower. They held a lot of political prisoners there."

"You do that often." Pancho watched me through narrowed eyes.

"What?"

"Speak as though it's already past."

I shrugged casually. "Habit." And one I clearly needed to break. "Don't let anyone but me or Ringo in, okay?" I swept toward the door, which was about the only thing big skirts and cloaks were useful for: the grand exit. "I'll be back." I almost did a Terminator voice and caught myself just in time. What the hell was wrong with me?

"When you find Thomas …"

"Tell him yourself, Pancho." I managed to add compassion to my voice. I think he got it because he finally shut up and let me leave.

Breathing came a little easier once I was out of the pages' annex. I hadn't realized how trapped I felt in there. I made my way down the gallery toward the Great Hall. Hopefully it was early enough in the evening that Elizabeth and her entourage were still embroidering or reading or whatever it was they did sitting by windows in their rooms. The future queen was about the last person I wanted to see at that moment.

So of course I did.

I slid around the corner into the Great Hall and practically bumped into a Yeoman Warder. The look on his face echoed the shock on mine. I almost made it out of reach, but his grab was fast, faster than I expected, and my wrist was caught in his strong grip.

"There you are, Saira. Did you find the needlework I left by my bed?" Lady Elizabeth's voice rang out clearly from across the Great Hall where she seemed to be doing laps with one of her ladies. Damn, she was good.

"No ma'am." I used the Yeoman's momentary distraction to yank my wrist out of his hand.

"Well, no matter. Come and walk with me. I do believe I've exhausted poor Courtney with my pace."

I didn't see a way out of this and crossed the hall to meet her. I towered over Courtney, who was practically Olivia's pixie size, and Elizabeth smiled at her fondly. "Thank you for the company. I'll meet you back in our rooms when Peterson is tired of allowing me my exercise." Courtney shot me a quick glance from under her long eyelashes, then ran across the room past the guard and out the door.

The height similarity between us made walking with her easy, and Elizabeth seemed to add speed to her stride as we circled the room. I was surprised when she didn't immediately speak because

I was expecting some well-deserved harsh words. Finally, I was the one to break the silence.

"I'm sorry about last night. It wasn't fair, what I said to you, and I apologize."

Her expression was bland, but there was an edge to her tone. "Fascinating that you believe a mere apology can absolve you of the gravity of your transgressions. I find apologies are most often an insincere attempt to make oneself feel better."

I hate it when people don't accept apologies. It makes me snappish and defensive, and I fought to keep my voice even. "I'm sorry you're surrounded by insincere people. When I need to take responsibility for doing something wrong, an apology is usually how I start."

"Are you responsible for the sincerity of my people?"

I stared at her, uncomprehending.

"You apologized for them, so by your logic, you must feel the need to take responsibility."

My jaw hurt from clenching my teeth against the frustration she inspired. I took a breath and composed my words carefully. "Lady Elizabeth, you called me in here, and I owed you an apology. If you don't want to accept my apology, that's fine, but I will not apologize for apologizing. That's just stupid."

"Of course it is."

My eyes narrowed, and I could feel another blow-up building. "If you're finished playing word games with me, I'm going to head out now. I am perfectly capable of making myself feel like crap. I really don't need your help doing it too."

A tiny smile played around her mouth. "I'm going to have to guess at the meanings of some of your words, but I do accept your apology."

I stared at her. "I don't know how to be around you. We're almost the same age, but you're practically the queen. And to be honest, you scare me a little." The corners of her mouth lost their small smile, and I was suddenly anxious to put it back. "So, I'd like to apologize in advance for every stupid, filter-less thing I say or do. I really don't mean to be offensive; I just seem to have a talent for it."

Elizabeth studied me silently as we passed Peterson, who stared straight ahead but met my eyes in a direct gaze for a second as we went by. I shuddered involuntarily and then realized why. Peterson's mouth had quirked up when he looked at me, and it was the sort of smile that I'd seen attached to predators' faces when they spot their prey. I forced my attention back to Elizabeth.

"Is Peterson your usual guard?" I spoke under my breath and hoped we were far enough out of earshot.

She flinched very slightly, but her voice was calm and direct. "He's been assigned to me since the day after I arrived."

"Only in the daytime?"

"From dawn until sunset."

"And then?"

"Then Alvin. But I won't allow my people to wander about when Alvin is working. There's something …" Her voice trailed off warily and I nodded.

"Predatory?"

"Yes." The word was a hiss of something that sounded like fear, but then she squared her shoulders and lifted her chin. "Do you know that until I was three years old, I was the beloved daughter, cherished by my mother and treated by my father as a bright new plaything. And then my mother lost the boy she carried and my father …"

I thought about the beautiful brunette woman in the portrait gallery, holding the bright-haired baby on her lap. It was Anne Boleyn with Elizabeth, who was three years old when her mother was beheaded by order of her father.

Elizabeth took a deep breath. "My father set us both aside to get his heir. His male heir. And I began to look over my shoulder a little bit more every day. Do you know how difficult it is to see forward *and* look back?"

She meant her Seer's Sight, and she waited until she was sure I'd gotten that before continuing. "Just before you entered my visions I began to see my own future very clearly. It's the first time I've known exactly what will come, and I must say, it has finally given me the peace I felt when I was a small child." Her eyes wandered across the hall to Peterson, who was cleaning his nails with the tip of a dagger. "I've stopped looking over my shoulder now that I know exactly how I'll die."

I stared at her. "You've Seen that?"

A tiny smile danced on her lips. "You said you are sometimes afraid of me, and, to be perfectly frank, it is something I am proud of. I have cultivated that ability to inspire fear as a way to ensure people don't take it upon themselves to steal up and plunge a dagger between my ribs. And yet, now that I know it will be a sword, not a dagger, that takes my life, I find I'm not so fond of fear, either inspiring it or feeling it. So I do wish you'd reconsider the advance apologies. I think I'll find them quite unnecessary."

We were circling around past Peterson again, and Elizabeth changed the subject with a speed that would have left me gasping if I hadn't anticipated it. "The littlest boy, I believe he's the son of the Lord Lieutenant, came to me in the garden today and brought the most beautiful posy of bachelor's buttons. How could he know they are my favorite flower? Since I was a girl I've loved picking the bright blue wildflowers and would weave them into crowns for all my playmates. The boys would refuse to wear them of course, and Robin always teased that I looked like a wild thing in the woods with flowers woven into my hair." Her smile turned sad at that memory, and her voice dropped again once we were out of earshot of Peterson.

"He's here you know, Robin Dudley. His brothers and father thrust poor Jane onto the block just as surely as if they'd held the ax themselves."

It was so strange to hear her talk about people I'd read about in history books: her cousin, Lady Jane Grey, who had been executed by Queen Mary for basically being a pawn in the chess game for the crown; and Robert Dudley, who she'd known since childhood as 'Robin,' and who probably became her lover after she was queen. "Have you seen him?"

"Robin? Oh, no. I don't even know where he's being held. I haven't seen him since we were young, though I do remember looking at him one day when I was about thirteen and thinking, 'when did he get so handsome?' Before then he'd always just been Robin, the boy who teased me about my hair."

"My mom used to say that boys only tease girls they like."

"Well, he was merciless, so he must have liked me very much."

She was trying to be light, but I wasn't going to let her slide on what she'd said before. "You don't die here, by the way. There's no sword in your future."

Elizabeth's clear green eyes were almost the same color as mine. In fact from a distance we probably looked pretty similar, especially if I ever wore my hair unbraided and loose like hers had been the night before. Her hair was more like copper and mine was a bit more golden, but we were close enough in height that our strides matched and neither one had to look down on the other.

"I will be beheaded here on Tower Green. Even now Bishop Gardiner is attempting to make my sister see the danger in letting me live. When Thomas Wyatt goes to his death, the head of the misguided snake will have been chopped, and the only one left for his supporters to see will be me. My sister will suddenly know fear, and with that my fate will be sealed." Her composure was firmly locked into place on her face, and I could imagine the queen she would be.

"My history says you're going to live to be the greatest monarch England ever has."

A small flinch and a hairline crack in her composure. "My fate is written, Miss Elian."

"I'm Saira."

She smiled, and we passed Peterson again in silence.

"One more turn, Milady." His voice was coarse, and there was a sneer behind it that made me loathe him on principle.

245

As soon as we were out of earshot again she whispered to me, and I almost didn't hear the question. "Are you a virgin, Saira?"

And because she startled me so much I blurted out the truth. "Yes."

"That's rather unfortunate."

I stared at her. "None of my ladies will tell me what it's like to lay with a man, and I had hoped that perhaps in your time it is a discussion women could have with each other."

I finally knew the proper definition of flummoxed, because the future queen of England had just done it to me. I couldn't even imagine what to say, and before my brain could make my mouth utter a single word, Peterson was on us like stink.

"Right. Yer done now, Lady. I'll take ye back to yer apartments, and ye'll stay in the rest of the night."

The Lady Elizabeth slipped her frighteningly regal posture back on and took my arm as we left the Great Hall. I wasn't sure how I was going to get out from under Peterson's glare, but she solved that problem for me just before we turned up the stairs.

"Saira, please check the kitchens for me. I believe I must have left my needlework on my lunch tray."

"Of course, Milady." I dipped into the kind of curtsey I'd seen in movies and walked down the hall before Peterson could tell me not to. I heard her ask Peterson the time as they headed upstairs, and I tucked myself around a corner out of sight until his answering voice receded.

 DUDLEY

I'd discovered that besides pitch black, the time of day I was least visible was dusk, maybe because people were heading in to deal with evening meals, and whatever came out at night hadn't emerged yet. I clung to the side of the Royal Apartments until I could sprint across to the base of the White Tower. Across the common I could see Yeoman Warders heading toward the Lord Lieutenant's Lodgings, presumably for shift changes, and I ducked behind a cannon until two other Yeoman Warders passed headed toward the Royal Apartments. They were probably replacements for Peterson and whomever he worked with. The big guy reminded me a little of Lurch from old Addams Family reruns, so I dubbed his short friend Uncle Fester. Lurch turned to scan the green, and he seemed to be listening to something Uncle Fester couldn't hear. I shrunk deeper into the shadow of the cannon when his eyes seemed to seek me, like he could hear my heartbeat or something. And then I knew with the certainty of twisty guts that Lurch was at least part Monger, and the other part was something I didn't even want to think about.

Lurch must be Alvin.

I figured I had about five minutes before Peterson left the Royal Apartments, so as soon as the coast was clear I crept along the base of the White Tower and then darted across the open commons to Beauchamp tower. My luck was holding with visible guards and only hitched slightly when I got to the tower door. Locked. Go figure. But just behind St. Vincula's chapel were the guards' barracks. If I made it there without being seen, I thought I could get up to the roof to enter Beauchamp tower from the top.

I clung to the shadows at the base of the wall until I reached the barracks closest to St. Vinculas. The walls were timbered, shadowed, and relatively easy to climb as long as my skirt stayed tied around my waist. I was glad that I hadn't changed out of my jeans since my makeshift rinse in the courtyard of the inn. If I thought about my general state of griminess too long I'd gross myself out, so I put the idea of clean underwear back in the drawer until I could get a tub of water bigger than my mug. Instead I concentrated on putting hands and feet where they could keep propelling me up.

The only tricky part was getting onto the roof of the barracks, and it tested my grip in a way I didn't entirely like. If Archer had been awake when I left he would have been a good climbing partner for this. But I was avoiding Archer because the things I wasn't saying to him were too loud in my head, which was why I slipped out in the first place.

Once I made it to the barracks roof, the scramble to the guards' walk of Beauchamp tower was easy enough, and the scrapes on my palms weren't deep enough to open the skin. Open wounds were a bad idea in this time, especially with the prevalence of raw sewage everywhere.

There were people down on Tower Green, and I ducked below the ramparts to crawl across the wall. The door at the top of Beauchamp tower was unlocked, and I took a moment to unwrap the heavy skirts from around my waist. If I ran into someone in the tower I hoped I could pretend to be a servant or something. It was weak at best, and I pulled the hood of my cloak up as if I could hide from my own feeble plan.

I slipped down the stairs to the top floor of the tower. Bad plan number two hit me upside the head as I looked down the long, pitch-black hall. How was I supposed to find Thomas Wyatt in a space with no exterior windows and no obvious light? Crap. I inhaled sharply and picked a side of the hall to start on. I held a hand out at hip height to run along the wall and stopped at the first indentation of a door. I felt around for a handle and, shock of shocks, found a big iron key sticking out of the lock. Lazy Yeomen had just made my life much easier.

I turned the key and the door opened with a loud creak. Not a very well-used lock then. The room had a little light coming in from the archer slits in the wall, and I could just barely see it was some sort of storage room. Not what I was looking for, so I re-locked it as quietly as I could manage, left the key in the door, and moved on down the hall.

The second and third doors also had keys, but held empty cells. The fourth lock moved soundlessly, like it had recently been oiled. I opened that door cautiously and immediately saw candlelight flickering inside.

A man looked up from the thing he was carving into a stone wall. His expression registered surprise at the opening door, and shock when he realized it was a girl opening it. He stood so suddenly I jumped, and he held his hands out in front of him as if to calm me. One hand held the blunt knife he'd been using on the stone wall, and I suddenly recognized the carving.

"You're Robert Dudley."

If his eyes had opened any wider his eyeballs might have fallen out. He seemed to realize that possibility because he narrowed them warily. "And you are here for what reason, Milady?"

"Oh, I'm not a lady. I mean, not like that. I'm Saira." I was also babbling. He was handsome in a bearded, sixteenth-century way, but that wasn't why I was so weirdly flustered. Robert Dudley was searching my face in a way that was so ... probing. He could have had his hands on my naked body and it wouldn't have felt as intimate as that look. Damn.

I took a deep breath to get my nerves under control. If this was the way Dudley looked at women, how could Elizabeth not have hurled herself at him every chance she got? There was something like it in the way Archer looked at me, like I was the most fascinating thing in the room. But I'd never felt quite so much like food under Archer's gaze. Which was definitely a good thing considering what he ate, but still. It made me feel like freaking Venus on the half-shell, and suddenly I knew what I had to do.

"I've come from the Lady Elizabeth."

If I thought he was hungry looking at me, it was nothing compared to the look of the starving man at the mention of Elizabeth's name. "Is she well? They've said she was ill and I've worried for her safety."

Wow. The guy was head over heels in love with her.

"She's fine-ish. Convinced she's going to die, but that's probably nothing new."

Dudley's face practically crumpled with distress. That's what it was, pure distress at the idea that Elizabeth could be anything other than perfectly happy.

"I would see her if I could. That she's here in this wretched place has torn my heart from my body, but that she knows even a moment's fear is more than I can bear."

Dude. Have a little drama with your angst.

It was time for these two to get over their bad selves and hook up. So, I came up with what I hoped wouldn't be crappy plan number three.

"Can you get out of here?"

"Not without two guards. They allow me one hour on the ramparts at midnight. The sun has become a distant memory to my tortured eyes."

Good God, this guy needed his own Greek chorus.

"Okay, fine. She'll come to you. I'll let you know as soon as I've figured out when I can make it happen."

Dudley looked like the sun had just risen on my face. "You're an angel."

"Or something." I was getting nervous that no guards had come by, and I definitely didn't want to be caught in Dudley's cell. "Where's Wyatt, and how often do the Yeomen Warders come by here?"

Dudley's eyes narrowed dangerously. "Say the rumors of an affair aren't true. You cannot imagine I'd tell you the whereabouts of that scoundrel? I'd rather die than facilitate a meeting between my Lady and the dog who put her at such risk."

Wow. The guy turned on an emotional dime, and I blinked when I realized what he was actually saying. "Dude, Elizabeth doesn't even know Wyatt, much less have a thing for him. The guy's going to die, and his little brother wants to see him, that's all."

I forgot to speak in sixteenth-century words, but Dudley was seriously annoying with his instant conclusion-jumping. I got a grip on myself and lowered my voice. "Just tell me what I need to know, and I'll make sure you get to see Elizabeth."

Dudley's eyes did their undressing thing on my face again, but this time I was immune. He took his sweet time, but finally answered the question. "I know not whence you've come, but my desire for news of my Lady Elizabeth overrides my fear. Guards leave me to my own devices from late afternoon until my midnight release." He paused dramatically, and I bit my tongue. "And the Wyatt dog is kenneled down there." He threw his head in the direction I'd been traveling down the hall. "He whimpered pathetically on his way down the corridor this morning."

Right. I suddenly felt bad for Pancho, and wasn't sure I really wanted to go in search of a guy who had been whimpering this morning. But I squared my shoulders and sucked up a little courage.

Then I nodded toward the carving Dudley had been doing in the stone wall. "I like your work, by the way. It looks like it'll hold up well." Little did he know.

The compliment seemed to surprise him. "Many thanks."

I backed out the door and was just about to close it. "Milady?" Dudley's voice was nearly a whisper. "I've never been more than a childhood friend to her. How can you know she will come?"

"She remembered the bachelor's button flowers you used to tease her about, and she called you Robin. She'll come."

The look of longing that crossed his face was too much and I closed his door and turned the key in the lock as silently as I could. The guy was clearly in love with her. I hoped Dudley knew how to reserve that look for just one woman, because every woman should feel adored and revered like that. Especially the future Virgin Queen.

The moment the door closed my senses were plunged into darkness again. But this time it was different. If I was canine, my hackles would have raised up in an automatic fear response to an unknown threat. But I didn't have hackles to make me look big and scary. I had a functioning brain and four other senses to help me figure out what the hell was in the dark hall with me.

WYATT

I ran down an instant mental checklist. Eyes? Useless. Ears? I couldn't hear anything. Not one thing, and it made me ridiculously nervous. The way my heart was pounding with instinctual fear I should have been able to hear someone breathing, or even blinking for that matter. Nothing. Taste? Residual meat pie, and dry mouth. Ick. Smell? The only sense I had a shot with, if I could get past the scent of my own terror. It was clear that whatever was with me in the dark was something 'other.' Regular humans didn't provoke this kind of fight or flight reaction in me – so instinctual I had to fight my own responses to assess what I was facing. It wasn't Monger though, whatever shared the darkness with me. My guts were curling with regular fear, not the vomitous kind Monger proximity inspired.

I took a tentative, silent, deep breath, and instantly relief flooded my veins. The very faint, very warm smell of spice tinged the air, and my knees nearly gave way with the suddenness of my certainty.

Archer.

"You scared me." My voice was barely a whisper, more of a breath really, but he heard me. He wrapped his arms around me protectively and breathed into my ear.

"I'm sorry."

He was tense. I heard it in his whispered voice and felt it in the arms that held me.

"What's wrong?"

"Not here."

I turned to face him, still wrapped in his arms. I couldn't see him through the soupy darkness, but I could sense the tightness running through him. I tried out my sixth sense on him, the instinct that had told me he was something 'other,' but he was closed to me. I finally broke the long silence.

"Help me find Wyatt?"

"Yes."

I let out a breath and then turned to continue down the dark hall. I went past the next door, then tried the one after that. Another empty cell. Archer trailed behind me, not touching, but always there. His presence was comforting in a way I didn't realize I'd wanted. It was probably one of those things Ringo would bust me on if I ever admitted it out loud.

Finally, near end of the hall, I hit another easy-turn lock. I opened the door slowly and Archer moved up right behind me. The room was nearly as dark as the hallway had been, but someone was there. I could hear shallow breathing coming from the far corner, and the stale smell of sweat and sickness drifted through the cell.

"Wyatt?" Archer's voice was a low rumble, and I could hear the person in the corner shift. "Thomas Wyatt?"

I felt fear roll out from the corner, and heard a short gasp as he sat up. "It's him. Wyatt, we're here in the Tower with your brother, Francis. He wanted to see you." I made my voice soft and as feminine as I could manage. I had the sense this guy was beyond freaked out.

A sob caught his voice. "He can't see me. Not like this."

"Do you have a candle?"

He hesitated. "They've taken the light."

Damn. I'd left my Maglite tucked behind a table in the pages' annex. The jeans would be bad enough to explain if I was caught. The flashlight would have been impossible.

Archer shifted slightly behind me, and then I heard a match scrape against the stone wall. The smell of sulphur bit the air and he produced a candle stub from an inside pocket of his cloak and lit it, using my body to block his actions from Wyatt. Matches hadn't been invented yet, so hopefully he wasn't paying attention. Archer held the candle out to me, and I flashed him a grateful smile. His face remained expressionless.

I turned back toward the corner where Wyatt lay huddled.

"Oh my God." I couldn't keep the horror out of my voice, and Wyatt flinched. The candle flickered with the sudden trembling of my hand. The guy was a total mess.

It wasn't just a beating; that would have been cleaner. This was the stuff of Cold War spy novels. There was a web of systematic cuts along every piece of exposed skin I could see. Some of them were angry red and weepy, and others had burn marks crisscrossing the incisions like a sadistic game of tic-tac-toe.

I moved toward him, but Wyatt shrank from me like the monster under the bed had just come out to play. My hands went up in a gesture of harmlessness, and Archer quietly took the candle from me so I could kneel down next to him.

"What did they do to you?" I carefully reached forward to pull aside the collar of his tattered shirt. The cuts were deep and seemed to be in a pattern. Wyatt flinched, but let me pull the collar back far enough to see the cuts wrap around to his back. Those weren't delicate slices, they were brutal whip marks with torn edges of skin pulled so far apart they wouldn't heal even if he was going to live long enough to get them properly tended.

"I've betrayed her." Wyatt's voice was a whisper of agony that I barely heard, but which snapped Archer's attention around like lightning.

"Who? What did you do, Wyatt?"

He looked up with haunted eyes, and I could see that physical pain wasn't the only thing going on behind them.

"Bishop Gardiner has a man …" He took a deep, ragged breath as if he was trying to gather strength. "A man wearing the robes of a bishop with the eyes of the devil, he made me … talk."

None of the espionage novels I'd ever read could have prepared me for the horror of real torture.

"What did he want?"

"Evidence against the Lady Elizabeth. Of treason."

"And he got it?" Archer's voice had a hard edge. It was weird and didn't fit with the compassionate, totally protective guy I knew. Wyatt flinched again.

"I signed where they told me to sign."

Archer stepped backwards, drawing the candle light away from where I still hovered near Wyatt. "Did you ever hear a name of the other bishop? The man who did this?"

Wyatt was silent long enough I wondered if he was still conscious.

"Gardiner called him Wilder."

I had to run to catch up to Archer. He was flying up the spiral stairs to get outside, and I'd barely had time to lock Wyatt's door behind us before he was gone. The night air was cold and silent, and I could see my breath in the darkness.

Archer didn't drop to the barracks roof, but instead kept going along the battlements until we were over a part of the Tower I had only seen in modern times from the tube stop at Tower Hill. Maybe because it was behind the guard barracks it didn't seem to be guarded as rigorously as the rest of the complex was, and I felt like we were actually alone.

"Archer, wait." My whisper was nearly silent, but I knew he'd hear it anyway. He stopped and turned to face me. His expression was as unreadable as a mask. "What's going on?"

"Wyatt never signed a confession against Elizabeth Tudor in our history." Archer's whispered voice was angry.

"But it's the thing we came here to get." I was exasperated with his anger. History may not have recorded that confession, but we both knew what his vision had revealed. "Wyatt just confirmed what we already knew."

He ran his hands through his hair in a way completely at odds with his normal composure. "It's really happening." He squeezed his eyes shut tightly, then opened them. His angry glare was tinged with panic. "It's not just a theory being handed down in a classroom. Time isn't correcting itself. Wilder's actually changing things, Saira, and no matter how hard I try to shake it,

256

no matter how much I convince myself that three people from another time can make a difference, I feel powerless to affect this."

I stared at Archer. "That's just it. *Wilder* set this thing in motion, and he's as much out of his time as we are. If anything, that makes this three to one. The only difference is we don't want to cause a time stream split and he either does, or he doesn't care." I glared at him to make my point. "But we do care, and that's why we're here."

I stepped forward, into range of Archer's arms. He stayed motionless so long a sinkhole opened up in my chest, and I almost turned away so he wouldn't see the tears that threatened. But then, finally, he reached for me and pulled me in. I breathed in the spicy scent of him and felt the sinkhole fill with something not-quite solid. But at least the hollow, sick feeling was going away.

I looked him in the eyes. "What we just learned doesn't change anything. We came here to find that paper and keep Elizabeth alive, and that's what we're going to do."

His arms tightened around me the instant before he let go, like he'd just tucked some piece of emotional baggage back into a closet. I'd seen him do this before and it scared me a little. The door would close on whatever was bugging him, and when the smile quirked his mouth I knew I'd probably never glimpse the bothersome thing again. And he was doing it now. First the door closed, then the smile didn't quite reach his eyes.

"Well, since we're out here anyway, let's take ourselves on a tour. Maybe Ravi will give you a job when we get back home and you'll be able to put all this knowledge to good use." He tried to sound light-hearted but I could hear the tension still anchoring his voice.

"You want to run?"

"No. I want to fly." Archer took off running across the battlements. He leapt up to a window ledge at the end of the line and scrambled up the tower. And in his cloak he truly did look like he was flying.

I ran, and he flew. It's what we did when we turned away from the things we saw in the mirror. And since I knew the move, had invented my own version of it, I shrugged off the sense of unease his unspoken baggage had left and took off running after him, with wings on my feet and the first hint of lightness in my body since we'd come to the Tower of London.

An Assignment

When Archer and I returned to the Royal Apartments, dawn was only about an hour away. We kept a sharp eye out for Lurch, and since Uncle Fester was snoring with exceptional talent at the main entrance, we slipped up the same tree we'd used the night before and entered the unlatched window in complete silence.

Pancho was curled up asleep in front of the smoldering embers of a fire in the pages' annex. I covered him with the blanket he'd kicked off and sat at the long table across from Archer. He slid a tankard of ale across to me and I took a sip. It tasted like a sweet beer. I grimaced. "This is all there is to drink? I'm going to dehydrate if it's my only option."

"Let's scavenge up a pot and we can boil water."

"Maybe I can find some chamomile or peppermint out on the grounds to make tea. And if I can find arnica or St. John's wort I'll try to make a salve for the cuts on Wyatt. It won't save his life, but it'll help with the pain and infection."

Archer put his hand on my arm to stop me from heading out the door. "Saira, I need to say something."

I tried not to read too much into the seriousness of his tone and waited expectantly.

"When I wake up and you're … gone, I …" He looked away. "I panic."

Well, that was unexpected. I reached out to touch his arm, and he met my eyes. "Every time it happens I feel helpless and weak because I can't fight the sleep, and then I get angry because there's nothing I can do to change it. If anything happened to you while I was down …" He took a deep breath.

There was something in his eyes that I couldn't decipher – something I could only describe as shame.

Pancho stirred on his bedroll and then rolled over, so I grabbed Archer's hand and pulled him with me out of the room.

I scanned the Great Hall quickly, then dragged Archer across the room to the tiny chapel on the other side. I closed the heavy wooden door behind me and did a quick search of the room to make sure we were alone. I stood in front of him and made him look at me.

"Last night in this very chapel, the Lady Elizabeth basically told me I treat you like crap." Eyes wide but mouth shut. Smart. "And then I called her a bunch of completely inappropriate names and ran away like a two-year-old. 'Cause I'm grown-up like that."

One corner of Archer's mouth quirked up in an almost-smile, but he quickly got it under control. "And then, when I was feeling sorry for myself, and making up all kinds of excuses about how over-protective you can be, and how everything's fine with us, and she doesn't know me at all, Ringo came along and doubled-down on all of it."

Now Archer was just listening. I pulled my courage up by its bootstraps and put on my big-girl panties to say the next words. "And they were both right."

I narrowed my eyes at him. "Go ahead. You know you want to say it."

"I love you."

Well, that pretty much rocked me back on my heels. Not what I expected him to say.

"That's what Ringo said too. Did you know he once asked me to marry him if things didn't pan out with you?"

Archer's eyes narrowed dangerously, and I planted my fists on my hips. "But he took it back last night. He said he would never be able to compete with the way you feel about me and didn't want to try."

I could see a whole herd of thoughts go stampeding through his brain, but his eyes never left mine, and I forced another lungful of air into my chest. "The thing about you is you've got everything so handled. You know exactly what you're doing, you're good at all of it, and you don't make mistakes. It's intimidating." He snorted, but I ignored him. "I know, you've had a hundred and twenty-five years to practice, and you've got a couple extra skills running through your blood. But I only have seventeen years under my belt, and since I was twelve I've had to manage on my own enough times that I earned a few stripes and kept myself alive. So I know I can do it; I'm used to doing it. When you get overprotective on me, I feel like you don't trust me. And then I do to you what I always did to my mom. I run."

I closed my eyes. "There's a part of me that's afraid to love you without reservation, because it would be so easy to let you take care of me … but then I'd have nothing left of myself."

"Saira." He waited until I looked at him. "You carry my heart with you always – carelessly sometimes, especially when you put yourself in danger, but it's the reason for my protectiveness. As long as you are safe my heart only need fear your rejection, not your injury or death."

"But that's too much responsibility." I didn't know if I was talking about Archer or myself, and I practically whimpered.

He reached for me and pulled me down to a bench, where I let him cradle me in his arms. My emotions were a tangled mess and they were squeezing the breath from me. Archer spoke into my hair, and I heard something different in his voice. Something lighter.

"And when you are happy and well and in my arms, I am more than myself. I am you too. I have felt your heart reach for mine before you remember to pull it back and protect it from me, and in those moments I am the biggest, strongest, best version of myself because you love me."

Oh.

I looked up at him, our faces inches apart. "I'm so sorry I hurt you." I was whispering, and he heard what I meant. I had hurt him in the past and probably every day since then.

"Then stop."

Stop. Stop hurting him. Stop running away. Stop holding myself back like I could only exist inside the protective shell I'd built to keep me safe and alive and … free. I guessed that was the real question my brain had been grappling with. Did I give up freedom when I chose to love Archer? Yes. The freedom to be with anyone else, freedom to do what I wanted without thinking about another person's feelings or wishes, freedom to be completely, unapologetically selfish. But were any of those freedoms worth losing him over?

When I focused on him again after my mini mental debate with myself, he was smiling. "What?"

"I love it when you do that. There's a moment, when you come to a decision, that your eyes clear and you look at me with the intent to share something true."

"You're right." I inhaled. "This is true. I'm terrified to give you all of me. Totally and completely terrified that it's too much, that I'll lose myself, that I'll suck at it." He couldn't help the tiny tug at the corner of his mouth, and I had to look away so I didn't smile back. Yet.

"But I'm going to try."

"Do or do not. There is no try." I stared at Archer in complete shock that he had just pulled a perfect Yoda voice out of his back pocket.

I threw my arms around his neck and kissed him with every single cell in my body. He growled deep in his chest and kissed me back. And I felt the emotions untangle in my chest, and air fill my lungs.

And I could breathe again.

I woke up about midday and carefully slid out of Archer's arms. He would be out for another four or five hours, and I resolved to be there when he woke up. Pancho was sitting morosely by the fire, poking the ashes with a stick.

"I found your brother last night."

His face lit up with so much hope it made my heart ache for him. "Can you take me to him?"

"He's afraid to see you. They've hurt him pretty badly and I don't think he wants to you remember him that way."

His hands balled into fists and his voice was fierce. "They'll pay for hurting Thomas."

"They're going to do worse than hurt him, Pancho. They're going to kill him."

There was a pause while Pancho digested that. It wasn't news, it was just unwelcome.

"I have to see him then. He cannot die believing he is alone here."

"You're going to feel helpless. And seeing him is going to tear your heart out. It did mine, and I don't even know the guy. Are you strong enough to deal with that?"

Pancho studied me like I was a puzzle to be worked out. "While it is clear you're without morals or decency and have no liking for me at all, what is unclear is why you would feel sympathy for my family, or indeed, why you would care about something that in your mind is a foregone conclusion."

My eyes narrowed at him. The little jerk just couldn't leave superiority in his back pocket. "I'm going out to find herbs to make a salve for his wounds. Archer and I will take you to him after dark."

And despite the fact I wanted to verbally rip him a new one, I realized it was completely pointless. Pancho was twelve, and his ideas about right, wrong, and true were carved in the stone of privilege and rank. Frankly, I had better things to do.

So I left.

I'd seen the kitchen gardens behind the Royal Apartments, and assumed there were probably bigger gardens elsewhere on the grounds, but I needed to find Ringo before I ventured out on my own in the daylight. There was no one in the Great Hall, so just for practice I ran the length of the building and found the servants' staircase to the upper floor. The Royal Apartments were laid out in a way that probably made sense to the original builders, but was totally counter-intuitive to me. The ground floor contained the storerooms and kitchens, upstairs was the Great Hall and the various public rooms, including the little windowless pages' annex we occupied, and above that was the private queen's apartment. I hadn't been up there yet, but I figured it must suit Queen Mary to put her sister in her headless mother's rooms.

I spotted Peterson in the hall outside what must be the queen's apartment and made a quick detour into a drawing room before he saw me. The furniture was covered in sheets and the place looked nicely haunted, even in full daylight. The walls were paneled in elaborately painted wood, and in less than a second I spotted the door hidden in a panel as if it had been outlined in black sharpie. I loved stuff like that.

There was no handle to the door and it seemed to open into the room I was in, so I hunted around the ridges and swirls in the paneled wood until I found the loose piece, then pushed. I probably needed to make a lot of money in my life, because I wanted my house to be full of secret doors with hidden latches. Maybe even a dumb-waiter or two, and definitely a windowless keep so Archer had a safe place to sleep.

That pulled me up short. Since when did I ever imagine life beyond a couple months from now? And how was I so sure Archer would be in it? I shook my head as if to clear all future thoughts from it and focused on making it to Elizabeth's rooms without being spotted.

The next room was furnished more simply, and I stopped in the open door. Someone was using this room. It didn't have that deserted feeling of the one I'd just left. Then I spotted Ringo, up in the heavy cross-beam rafters. He was perched and watching me. There was no smile on his face, even when he knew he'd been spotted.

I quickly scanned the room, then hiked my skirts around my waist and ran for the opposite wall. A table stood near a heavy wooden chandelier. I was able to jump for it and swing close enough to the bracket holding a big beam into the wall. From there it was a quick scramble up and across to plop down next to Ringo.

"I didn't think of the chandelier. Nice touch."

I followed his eyes down to the still-swinging fixture. "Flashy, but not smart. Gives too much away."

"Since when 'ave ye ever been subtle?"

Since when had I ever been anything but subtle? I had counted on my ability to blend in for my survival through new schools every two years and stealth-tagging on the streets. Although to be fair, ever since I discovered I was descended from Time, I hadn't been in my element anywhere. And St. Brigid's was one school I'd never blend into, no matter how much I tried to fade into the woodwork.

"I talked to Archer." I missed Ringo, and I knew this was still between us. "I'm trying." Then I heard Archer's Yoda impression in my head and smirked. "Not trying. Doing."

He studied me for a moment. "Doin' what?"

"Well, I promised I'd be there when he wakes up and not out searching the Tower without him, if that gives you an idea."

Ringo whistled like the cheeky urchin I first met on the streets of Victorian London. "Ye practically 'anded him yer leash, did ye?"

"Jerk." I wanted to push him off the beam but had to make do with sticking my tongue out at him instead.

"Ye know, 'is Lordship doesn't do so well with bein' taken care o'either."

"That's news? Even when Seth Walters shot him he slunk away and hid out until he healed." I scoffed. "Not that I could do anything for him anyway. The guy is practically indestructible."

He watched me carefully, like he was weighing how much to say. "Ye could. Do for 'im, that is. I did once."

"What happened?"

"Right after ye left with yer Ma, the Missus gave me the job of huntin' for 'im. I had to bring back whatever I could find, and even better if I'd trapped it alive. 'E needed the blood, see. The sickness was eatin' 'is own blood and starvin' 'im. She said it's why they're so dangerous at first. It's all survival for 'em until there's nothin' left for the sickness to consume. They balance out after that. Drink just enough blood to keep the sickness in check. Better if it's human though. They need less."

I felt a little like I'd been punched. I had done a very good job of being in denial about Archer's need for blood. I could deal with the mechanics of it, but I seemed to have kind of a moral squeamishness that made me want to hide my eyes. And Ringo wasn't letting me.

"No matter how many rabbits and foxes I brought 'er for 'im, the sickness was killin' 'im."

My breath caught in my chest. I'd chosen to save my mom, and I'd left Ringo the job of keeping Archer alive.

"The Missus always did a swift job of killing and bleeding the creatures I trapped. She'd give the blood to 'im and 'e'd gag and sputter and try to spit, but she always made 'im drink." Ringo's gaze looked very far away. "'E was dyin' though. 'Is eyes didn't see anythin', even when 'e was lookin' right at ye." He seemed to shake himself out of the memory and his gaze refocused on mine. "I had to do more. So when the Missus left a rabbit to drain, I slit a line in my wrist and let some of my own blood mix in."

I couldn't help the gasp that slipped out, and Ringo flinched. "No one knew. No one saw me do it. But it was the right thing. 'E got better after that. I did it one more time. The other wrist …" Ringo unwrapped one of the leather bands he always wore around his wrist. There was a red line, still welty, but healed closed. "'Is Lordship never knew, but you should … just in case."

Realization hit me like a two-by-four. "He has your blood in him. That's why he saw through your eyes. That's why you were in his vision so clearly." Ava had said it happened in families sometimes; visions that focused on blood-relations. And it had happened to Archer and Ringo. But Archer still doubted the truth of his visions because he didn't know he had Ringo's blood.

"You have to tell him."

Ringo shook his head violently. "'E'd never forgive me."

"Do you know one of the reasons I never told you about his vision of you with Wilder? Archer said Seers can't See out of other people's eyes, and his vision was from your perspective. *I saw what you saw* because I was touching him when he had the vision. Ringo, this explains it! This is why you're connected to his Sight. He didn't just drink your blood, it became part of him. Like my mother's Clocker skill is part of Wilder."

I swung down from the rafter and dropped the last eight feet to the floor. Ringo followed right behind me. "What are ye doin'?"

"I need to talk to Elizabeth. She Saw you both in that room with Wilder, but she Saw it from a different perspective."

Ringo put a hand out to stop me. "Ye can't just—"

"We have to find that room, Ringo. And I won't wait for him to take you there. I can't."

"Ye just said the vision's true, and now ye're on about changin' it?"

"It's possible. But it hasn't happened yet, so there's still time to do something. But I need to know what Elizabeth Saw."

THE GARDEN

Ringo left me just inside the door to the queen's apartment while he went to talk to her. She sat on a low bench by a window reading a small book while her ladies gathered near her with their embroidery. Except for Ringo leaning over to whisper in Elizabeth's ear, it could have been a painting in a museum. She looked over to where I stood and said something to her ladies, then got up and glided across the room to me. She was so pale her skin was almost translucent.

"We can speak in Ringo's chamber." Elizabeth's voice was quiet and sounded as weary as she looked.

Ringo joined us and closed the door between the rooms. He stayed back, but I knew he could hear everything we discussed. "Ringo said you Saw him in a vision with yourself and a bishop."

The weariness disappeared from her voice, and it was replaced by something sharp. "The vision in which your friend is tortured, you mean?"

I winced. "That one." Elizabeth's gray-eyed stare dared me to look away. I didn't take her dare. "Did you see Bishop Wilder hide a document in the room?"

"I did."

"Do you know where the room is?"

"I do not."

I held back my impatience with her curt answers. "I need to find that room."

Her eyes narrowed. "It is only a matter of time before we visit the place. Whether either of us will be able to reveal its location in the aftermath is another question."

"That's the point. We need to find it before you go. We need that document."

"Why?"

"I believe it's a confession they forced Wyatt to sign naming you a conspirator in his rebellion."

Storm-gray eyes studied me as if she was pulling apart every thought in my head. What she was looking for I didn't know, but I felt dissected.

"It won't change anything."

"It will change *everything* if that document gets out."

The weariness was back on her face. "No matter how many times I look, the sword is still committed to its course." She took a deep, shuddering breath. "At least my sister has the grace to afford me the sword."

Like her mother. It's what she didn't say. Henry VIII sent for a French executioner so Anne Boleyn's head could be removed by the sharp and accurate sword rather than the dull, less precise axe everyone else got. I stared at Elizabeth.

"You truly believe you're going to die here?"

A sad smile played at the corner of her mouth but was gone so fast I thought I imagined it. "And a virgin, no less."

"Not if Dudley has a say." I mumbled it under my breath, but Elizabeth grabbed at the words with both hands.

"You've seen Robin?"

I looked her squarely in the eyes. There was no point in dodging. "Last night. He's in love with you."

Something happened then that explained everything about her lifetime of incredible power over an entire country, maybe even all of Europe. Her face *transformed*. There's no other explanation for the glow that shone through her skin, gleamed in her eyes, emanated from the red-gold hair framing her face. In the space of a breath, Elizabeth Tudor transformed from prisoner to … goddess. She was stunning.

"He loves me?" The hope and uncertainty in her voice broke my heart.

"He burns with it." It was the only way to describe the fever he had for her. And the way she looked in that moment, she was probably in danger of the same thing.

She clutched my arm and my skin practically fused to hers. "Take me to him."

"Are you kidding? That's all the excuse Wilder would need to get you in his clutches."

She shrugged as if Wilder meant nothing to her. "I need to see Robin. *Please*, Saira. I must know that part of being a woman before they take it from me."

It was so far beyond the realm of bad ideas it was like it had sprung from my own head. The pleading in Elizabeth's eyes turned hard so suddenly it made me dizzy, and when she took a step back from me I felt cold.

"Take me to him, and I'll give you my vision."

The woman was a witch. That much was totally clear. Whether she was a good witch or a bad witch was the question skipping through my brain in Glinda's tinkling voice.

"I can't take you there until nighttime, and that's when Lurch … I mean Alvin … guards you."

She looked at me speculatively, then reached for my braid. I willed myself not to flinch back from her fingers as they quickly unbound my hair. She looked at Ringo.

"Get Courtney. Ask her for my lace cap – the one shot through with pearls." She looked critically at me. "And my blue cloak with the fox collar."

Ringo was gone for barely a minute before he and Courtney returned with the cloak and cap. In the meantime, Elizabeth had finger-combed my hair until it hung down my back in loose waves from the braid. She wrapped the cloak around my shoulders and closed it in front so my dress was invisible underneath. As she fixed the lace cap to the back of my head, she finally looked me in the eyes.

"Be me. In public. Go for a walk in the gardens. Courtney always accompanies me when I stroll the grounds. You and I are of a height, and when your hair is unbound the color is similar enough they will assume it is me."

I shook my head. "We don't look anything alike. The guards will know I'm not you in two seconds."

She smiled slowly. "They fear me. No one comes close, and if they did approach, pull your hood around your face and Courtney will glare with all the fierceness of a terrier. She excels at keeping undesirable company at bay."

I looked at the petite blonde lady-in-waiting, and she smiled politely. The barest hint of a canine tooth stuck out on one side of her mouth, and I suddenly wondered if she didn't actually have terrier in her.

"How will you get to Dudley's cell if I'm in the garden impersonating you?"

Elizabeth shot me one of those looks that had a 'duh' sound effect attached. "Ringo will take me, of course."

"He didn't come with me last night."

"Top floor, Beauchamp tower. Fourth room down the east hall." Ringo's easy voice drawled through the sharp spaces between us. I tore my eyes away from Elizabeth to stare at him. He shrugged. "What else am I goin' to do when ye and his Lordship sleep?" I narrowed my eyes, but I knew him too well to imagine I could ever intimidate him into making the safe choices. He grinned at me. "And ye do look a bit like Milady. Enough to pass from a distance. Especially with that angle ye both hold yer chins, like ye'd happily have my hide for a pair of boots."

"It's settled then. Courtney, take Saira to the gardens, but leave through the kitchen door where Peterson lurks. Then Ringo and I will follow the moment he has gone with you."

"And I'm supposed to just waltz past Peterson like I'm you?"

Elizabeth smiled. "As Ringo said, it is all a matter of bearing. Walk like a king's daughter and that is all they will see."

Easy for her to say.

271

But she wasn't wrong.

Courtney got us past Peterson with a flirty smile and an innocent question while I walked ahead to the gardens. Once inside the gate, I dropped the hood on Elizabeth's cloak and let my long gold-tinged hair be my disguise. My color wasn't the same as hers, but maybe in the overcast gray light it was close enough. After a few minutes Courtney joined me, asking 'Milady' in a loud voice what she could help me find.

"Actually, I'm looking for arnica, St. John's wort, and if there's any lavender left from the fall, that would be great."

Courtney looked speculative. "For a tea?"

I shook my head. "Medicinal salve."

"I suppose it is well to anticipate the effects of torture. Milady has never yet been wrong."

I stared at her, then realized she must be talking about Elizabeth's vision of Ringo. Her words gave me a chill, and I tried to shake the feeling of dread that was starting to settle around my shoulders.

Rosemary and juniper were easy enough to find. I discovered the tiniest heads of chamomile shooting through the first spring growth, and Courtney came back to me with an apron-full of arnica and St. John's wort. I knew the lavender was a longshot, and marjoram was pretty much out of the question that time of year, but after killing an hour in the garden I had almost everything that I needed.

"Does Milady have any almond oil in her chambers?"

"No, they didn't let us pack more than her personal clothing. I'll see if I can trade for some with Peterson though."

I looked down at Courtney in surprise. She was so fiercely protective of her Mistress I forgot she was tiny until I stood right next to her. "What would you trade?"

Her smile verged on wicked. "A kiss, of course."

I barely suppressed a shudder. "You'd do that?"

Her raised eyebrow made the grin even scarier. "I have been experimenting with a powder made from ground apple pips, but of course have had no one to try it on. If I coat my own lips with wax first, then the powder, and of course, don't swallow any pieces, I should remain unaffected. I shall need the oil first, because hopefully he will be somewhat - or maybe permanently - useless soon after I kiss him."

Wow. This chick was a whole lot of scary in such a small package. Apple seeds? Some small part of my brain vaguely recalled the word cyanide associated with them.

We made our way back up to the Royal Apartments, and I flipped the blue hood back into place before we approached Peterson. I shouldn't have bothered; his eyes were glued to Courtney's flirty smile.

"I'll be right with you Milady. I have a question I must ask Peterson first."

I didn't have to be told twice and was inside the kitchen door and swiping a mortar and pestle before Peterson could think to look at me. Ringo and the Lady Elizabeth weren't back yet, so I set to work in Ringo's room grinding up the herbs we'd gathered.

Courtney raced up to her mistress' rooms, then popped her head in with a smirk. "He took the bait, and I do not even have to go to his quarters with him." She shuddered theatrically. "I hate Bell Tower. It is always so numbingly cold there." Then she held up a tiny pot of something. "Let's see what happens." She was gone in the next moment. The girl was on fire, and I couldn't even imagine what her plan was. It was much better I didn't know.

Not even five minutes later Courtney was back, triumphantly holding up a small flask of almond oil. She tossed it on the table next to me and raced from the room. When she returned, her lips were red and puffy and looked freshly scrubbed. I stared at her in shock.

"What did you just do?"

"I had to wash it off my lips before it had a chance to work its way into my mouth."

"Is it really that toxic?"

Her smile was innocent and charming. "Peterson's going to have a nasty bump on his head if he wakes up. The man fell like a stone."

If he wakes up. Hopefully a person had to eat a lot of apple seeds to get a lethal dose. I tried to picture the mechanics of kissing someone without getting the stuff in one's own mouth and gave up for lack of imagination. Or maybe experience. Courtney picked up the flask. "Will it work?"

"It's perfect. I don't suppose there's a candle around?"

"I'll be right back."

I broke the beeswax candle she brought me into pieces, added a few drops of almond oil into the mortar, then moved the whole thing close to the fire. Courtney watched me carefully. "Did you apprentice with a midwife?"

"Who?"

"A midwife. The birthing woman?"

Oh, right. Not even on my radar. I shook my head. "I had a teacher …" I didn't think Mr. Shaw would be easily explained, so I went with the Missus instead. "A friend of my mother's. She lived in the woods and knew all kinds of plant lore."

And helped Archer survive the bite of a Vampire.

The sky outside was just beginning to darken, and I'd made a promise I intended to keep.

"I have to go."

"When Milady returns, where shall I say you are?"

I gave her a very small smile as I left the room. "Keeping my word."

Archer stirred when I pressed my front against his back and curled around him on the bedroll. Pancho was gone somewhere, hopefully not getting himself caught, and it felt right to be there, wrapped around Archer as he woke up.

"Hello." He rolled over and searched my face. I smiled.

"Hi."

"You smell like honey and tea."

"I was in the garden today. I made a salve for Pancho to take to his brother."

Concern clouded his eyes and I tried to erase the worry. "I was with Courtney, one of Elizabeth's ladies. And I was disguised."

He sat up. "Disguised as whom?"

"Elizabeth."

Archer took a deep breath, which told me he was choosing his next words carefully. I wasn't even sure he needed to breathe, so that was something.

"You say Courtney was with you?"

"Peterson is in lust with her, so he didn't have eyes for me at all."

"Peterson? Oh, right. Well, that's useful." I was shocked into speechlessness. No 'what were you thinking?' or 'don't you know how dangerous that was?' None of that.

"Thank you."

"For?" He looked genuinely mystified.

"Loving me."

He looked into my eyes for a long time before he kissed me, and his whisper was almost lost against my lips. "You're welcome."

And with the impeccable timing only someone named Pancho could have, he burst into the room, startling me so much I slammed into Archer's nose with my chin.

"Pancho!" I growled at him, a little because my chin hurt, but mostly because I wasn't ready for that kiss to end. Archer looked at me with a glint in his eye that made my cheeks flush.

"I'm not finished with that." His whisper went through me like a shiver, and I got an instant case of butterflies. That kiss wasn't just a kiss. It was a promise of something I didn't know nearly enough about.

Archer stood in a graceful motion and helped me to my feet. Why was it that when I scaled a brick wall I was all feline, but when I'd just been thoroughly kissed I turned into something much more bovine?

"You'll take me to my brother now?" Pancho was breathless. I scowled at his impatience, but Archer got to him first.

"An hour after full dark, when most of the Tower inhabitants have settled inside for the night."

Pancho didn't like that answer. "But *she* went out today. I saw her in the garden."

"First, what I do has nothing to do with you. And second, I was getting plants to make a medicine for your brother. So shut it, okay?" I turned to Archer and let go of the edge in my voice. "I need to head back upstairs to Ringo's rooms. I left the salve cooking away in the fireplace up there, and hopefully he and Elizabeth are back ..." I shot Pancho a quick glance and decided he didn't need to know everything. My voice dropped to a whisper. "Come with me?"

"To the ends of time."

Now, that could have just been a Victorian saying, or some poetic thing he'd picked up in the last hundred years, but it felt very personal and very ... true. My breath caught in my throat, and I decided then and there that I needed to know Archer Devereux for a very long time.

Archer finally tore his eyes away from mine and asked Pancho to find us some food. I knew he didn't include himself in that "us," but he was still maintaining the illusion with the kid that he was just like anyone else. Of course since it was Archer who did the asking, Pancho jumped right up without question. Had it been me – well, I probably wouldn't have asked.

When Pancho was gone, Archer pulled me into a hard embrace, kissed me hungrily, and then released me so fast I gasped. "Come," he said. "Let's find my young brother and his princess."

I held his arm. "Wait. You need to know some things." I quickly filled him in on the deal I'd made with Elizabeth. Time with Dudley in exchange for her vision. I watched his face closely, looking for signs of disapproval, but he mostly just looked thoughtful.

"I suppose seeing the vision through Elizabeth's eyes will give us an idea of how wild the goose chase we're on has been." He sounded speculative, and I took a bracing breath. He needed to know.

"The vision you saw was real."

He sighed. "We've been through this before, Saira. There's no way I could have seen things through Ringo's eyes. It just isn't possible."

"The twins do it."

"Ringo is the brother of my heart, not my blood."

"You have his blood in you."

Archer stared at me. Words seemed to have deserted him.

"You almost died when you were turning, and the animal blood the Missus fed you wasn't enough. No one knew Ringo added his blood to the mix you had to drink. He confided in me today. He's been afraid to tell you."

The grinding of his jaw was the only indication that he'd even heard me. Archer seemed to control his voice when he finally spoke. "Come. We'll find them and get her vision."

He took my hand as we left the pages' annex, and I was idiotically glad it wasn't me who had done the thing Archer wrestled with this time.

Ringo was alone in his chamber when we got there. He had pulled the mortar out of the fireplace, and it sat on the hearth, hopefully cooling enough to handle.

"How did it go with Dudley?"

Ringo's face went pink, and I realized I'd never seen him blush before. "You'll have to ask Milady."

"She's here though. You guys made it back safely?"

"She had an hour with Lord Dudley. No one seems the wiser."

Archer's gaze was locked on Ringo. I would have felt like a bug in a magnifying glass under that stare, but Ringo stood his ground.

"Ringo ..." The word strangled in Archer's voice, and I looked sharply at him. I could see Ringo brace himself. But just

277

then the Lady Elizabeth swept into the room with Courtney on her heels.

And I mean swept. The times I'd seen Elizabeth before she was always regal and very proper, if not tired and scared from being kept prisoner by her own sister. But this a very different woman. She held her chin at a proud angle and a smile played at the corners of her mouth while she studied me. Then she strode forward to Archer and put her hand out for him to kiss.

"Lord Devereux." She actually purred like a predator stalking a mate, and I wanted to throw a punch.

 Visions

Archer seemed startled, and I realized they'd never actually met face to face. He took Elizabeth's hand and grazed the back of it with his lips. It made me want to change trajectory and hit him.

"Lady Elizabeth. I'm honored." His tone was formal, thank God. If it had been low and growly I might have ended the Tudor line about forty years early.

Her eyes found mine again, and she seemed satisfied to find me seething. The predatory thing disappeared, and her smile was genuinely warm and friendly. "Thank you, Saira." The undercurrent of a secret laced her voice.

"You found what you wanted?"

A dreamy look flitted across her face. Just for an instant, but it was enough. "More than I could have imagined."

Archer looked sharply at me. I hadn't really spelled out that the future Virgin Queen had probably just gotten laid. That sounded bitchy, even for me, so I made a conscious effort to return her smile.

The dreamy look lingered in her eyes as she searched my face. "I finally understand, and I see that you do too." Wait, what? She knew I'd never …

"No, Milady. I don't think I do."

Lady Elizabeth hooked my arm with hers and walked me away from the others. We stood at the window and looked out over the dark gardens. "You love as if you've a choice in the matter, as if the bond between you was an option rather than a certainty written in the stars. Yet your heart knows differently.

You reacted as a wild thing does to a rival just now. It is a thing I never felt myself, until today. Now if another were to look at Dudley as I just did with Devereux, I'd fly into her face and likely scratch the eyes from her head." She took a deep, shuddering breath.

"It terrifies me to be so totally at another's mercy. I find that I have no wish to deny the insistence of my heart that he is the other half of my body and of my soul." Her hand touched my arm gently. "You have given me a priceless gift. Only one who knows love could have given it. I will go to the scaffold a woman now, and none can take it from me."

"You keep saying that, but you're not going to die in this place."

Elizabeth smiled sadly. "It's time I kept my part of the bargain."

She led me back to the table where Archer sat with Ringo, then looked up at Courtney. "Please see that we are not disturbed."

"Yes, Milady." Courtney obeyed without hesitation, and we took our places at the table.

Elizabeth included the guys in her gaze, but she spoke to me. "I told Ringo what I envisioned, but since that night, before I was taken from Whitehall and held in this wretched place, I have not looked for it again."

I turned to Archer. "I want to see her version of it. Something was off in yours; parts were blurry. She might have different details that will help us find that tower."

Archer looked directly at Elizabeth. "My Lady, I am only a small part Seer. I am unable to call up a vision at will. Is this something you can do?"

"If I have seen it before, yes."

Archer sat back, impressed. I guess I'd just taken for granted it was a thing all Seers could do. "Isn't it basically just a memory once you've already Seen it?"

"We're not telepaths, Saira. I can't project my memories into your head at will." Archer's tone was more patient than the words sounded, so I kept my bristling to a minimum.

"Okay. We need to be touching, right?" I reached over to Archer, then held my hand out for Elizabeth. Her skin was cool and so soft I wondered if she'd ever done anything rougher than hold a pen with that hand. Ringo completed the circle and I stifled a smirk. There should have been a Ouija board on the table in front of us.

Elizabeth closed her eyes, and after sharing a quick glance with Ringo, I did too. A heartbeat later a scene filled my head. Like I was watching the movie version of something I'd read, except this time the point of view was different. I could see Ringo and Wilder and the guard I realized with a shock was Lurch, Elizabeth's nighttime jailer – the creepy one who wasn't quite Monger, and maybe something worse. I couldn't see Elizabeth, and then I realized I was looking at the scene through her eyes. I felt like the worst kind of voyeur and hoped that seeing her vision didn't come with any emotions or thoughts attached. I wasn't ready to feel everything Elizabeth Tudor felt.

The scene played out exactly as it had in Archer's vision: Wilder torturing Ringo, wanting information from Elizabeth about the child of the prophecy, and then threatening her with the signed confession that he locked away in the window seat. I tore my focus away from the people in the room and tried to see the space itself. What was different from Elizabeth's perspective?

There. Under the other window. Faintly etched into the stone.

A spiral.

Abruptly, the scene in my head changed. Dusky light and green grass surrounded by the high walls of the Tower. I could only see straight ahead, so I must have been wearing some sort of hooded cloak. There were people crowding the narrow path, somber and silent, and every pair of eyes was on me. The crowd at the end of the path parted, and I saw it. A big, wooden platform, with an upright piece on top, sort of a stool, but solid, and without legs. Standing on top of the platform was a slight man leaning on something metal. Glittering eyes looked out at me from under a rough wool hood which covered his face. And then I saw it was a sword the man leaned on.

He was an executioner.

My eyes flew open and I threw Elizabeth's hand from mine. I was horrified and could barely keep the shriek down in my throat.

She looked serene. "I told you it was my fate. You chose not to believe." I wanted to slap the peaceful look off her face. No one should be that ready to die. Was that wrong, slapping the future queen of England? Except if her vision was right, she had no future.

Archer stood and was pacing the room. Ringo sat very still and held his body tightly, as if he was protecting himself from a blow. I wasn't sure what was more disturbing – the vision or everyone's reactions to it. I shook my head like a swimmer clearing water from her ears.

"That vision is wrong. I'm sorry, I know you have, like, mad seeing skills, but you don't die here."

Elizabeth hadn't moved, and she sounded like she was soothing a frightened little kid. "Lovely though it feels, your outrage will not change my fate."

She wasn't being reasonable, so I ignored her and turned to Archer. "Did you see the spiral? Under the window? We didn't see it before."

He contemplated that for a moment, as if he was rolling back the tape on the vision. Ringo was already there. "So not a cellar then."

I'd focused on the spiral, but he saw the window. I shook my head. "I guess it's not underground. We looked for that room in the wrong places."

Archer's voice was thoughtful. "The ground floor rooms are too visible to other people. Wilder wouldn't have hidden that confession someplace people had regular access to."

"Which leaves the towers." Ringo was already at the window. "So we need to go out."

"Maybe not." The others turned toward the excitement in my voice. "Maybe I can Clock directly into that spiral." I spun to face Archer even as his mouth opened. "Only long enough to figure out where it is, then right back out."

"How do we know you won't Clock right into Wilder?"

"I could wait and go in daylight." I hated that option and I knew Archer would too. He was already shaking his head.

"No. I need to be awake."

"Good, because I'd rather take you with me."

The surprise in Archer's eyes actually made me feel bad. Had he really been expecting me to just go off and leave him behind? I didn't like what that said about me and my disregard for his feelings, but hopefully this was evidence of me turning a new leaf.

"It is quite striking to me that you both believe one's fate can be altered. You continue to seek change that truly will not happen."

I squared my shoulders when I faced Elizabeth. "If you really believed that, you couldn't possibly be the queen I know you'll become. So please excuse my rudeness, but I'm going to say it anyway: knock the negativity off. It's not helping."

Bam. Just told the future queen to shut it. Which made me really badass or really stupid. Probably both, considering the grim line of her mouth and the way Ringo's shoulders stiffened. Amazingly, Archer didn't seem fazed. He held his hand out to me.

"We should go."

I took it and nodded to Ringo. "We'll be right back. If this goes well, maybe we'll have the confession with us and I can take you home."

He grimaced. "Here's hoping I dodge the privy bath."

"For so many reasons."

I followed Archer from the room, and he whispered as we snuck down the stairs. "I never realized how much your boldness … affects me."

Oh. Well. That pretty much left me speechless. I could only guess what my expression was from Archer's grin. "So, where to?"

"The chapel. It's private."

We stuck to the shadows and back corridors. I figured Lurch would be stationed right outside Elizabeth's apartments; that was one bad guy I definitely didn't want to meet around a dark corner.

The Great Hall was empty and the chapel deserted when we got there. I grabbed a candle, but didn't light it, then chose a spot set back from the door which gave us the best protection from casual observers.

"Watch my back?" I whispered to Archer as I crouched down next to an altar.

"Always."

I was getting used to this partnership thing. Maybe even taking it for granted a little. And liking it. Which was fascinating. And cool. And freaking scary.

I set my shoulders, pressed my back against Archer's, and used the candle like a wax crayon to draw a spiral.

The effect was interesting. The edges seemed to glow a lot faster around what were essentially invisible lines. I knew from experience that place jumps in the same time zone went quicker, with less likelihood of puking, and I concentrated on the image of the spiral under the window.

The hum and stretch hit fast enough that I braced myself for landing and hoped the room would be empty so we didn't have to stand up and fight. Then we were *between* spaces, and the feeling of Archer's back against mine was barely more than a memory. I fixed the image of the tower room in my mind, adding more and more detail to my mental picture the longer it took to land.

But it was too long. More than the two or three breaths it usually took. Longer than the journey to 1554 had been. My body was being pulled like a rubber band and the thrum of it hurt my head and left me boneless and raw. A thought was forming, so terrible I could feel the scream build in my throat. Had I screwed up? Was the vision I'd locked us on wrong? Did I just lose us *between* space, in the place completely devoid of every sense that made me human?

I reached out, or at least I thought I did. Nothing felt real, but I willed my hand to move. And then there it was. A solid thing. Like a force field, only denser and bone-chillingly cold, and … repellant.

There was no air in my lungs. No air *between*. I had to get us back. Back to the chapel where I could breathe and scream. I forced my brain to switch gears, to ignore the stretching and pulling that threatened to rip me apart, to find the echo of Archer at my back and focus on the dark chapel where he was real and solid.

And then the nothingness was gone, replaced by the blackness of a dark room. And Archer caught me in his arms and gasped with a breath he didn't need. I could feel him tremble even as his strength kept me from breaking apart.

Breathing was hard. Sobbing without breath was harder.

And I couldn't get enough air in my lungs to scream.

"What" *gasp* "the hell" *sob* "was that?"

Archer didn't answer. I dragged my gaze to him. He couldn't. His eyes were squeezed shut and he swallowed convulsively like it was the only thing keeping the puke down.

The cold was still seeping out of my bones and it made the fireless chapel seem tropical by comparison. The only other time I'd been so cold was in the Elian Manor keep.

I gasped. "The room is warded. That's why we couldn't Clock in."

Archer's grip around me flexed and I knew he understood, even if he didn't have the power of speech yet. I felt safe. And warm.

The opposite of cold.

I knew which tower held Wilder's secret.

Tower Run

I refused to do this in skirts.

If we got caught we were screwed anyway, so I braided my hair tightly, shoved it down the neck of the sweater I'd co-opted from Archer, and laced boots over skinny jeans. Archer's nobleman's outfit was almost as bad as my skirt, so he changed into 21st century jeans and boots too. Ringo was fine in whatever he wore, though I don't think I'd seen him take off my old boots since he put them on his feet.

Rubber soles and dark clothes. Free-running gear.

The room with the spiral was warded. It was the only explanation I could find for our failure to get in. And Courtney had complained the Bell Tower was always so cold. It was the one place we hadn't searched, and the blueprints of the upper floor Professor Singh had shown us were so similar to the vision we'd seen – now from two different angles – of the room where Wilder would torture Ringo … unless we changed it.

Unlucky for us, the Bell Tower was basically inaccessible. It was a corner tower, with sheer stone rising up three very tall stories from the ground outside the walls, and inside the complex they'd built the Lord Lieutenant's lodgings right in front of the entrance. Which pretty much meant that every guard in the place checked in there during their shift. The one thing we had going for us were battlements on either side of the Bell Tower. Granted, they were designed to keep marauders out, but we were already in, and we had skills.

We left Pancho with firm orders to stay put, and went down the tree. I could sense Lurch like a dead rat decaying in the walls of the Royal Apartments, but his pervasive presence cleared the minute we were outside. The guy was dangerous, and it made me nervous that I couldn't pinpoint what he was.

"There's a man on top of each tower. They usually face out, unless it's shift-change time, then they watch for their replacement." Ringo's whisper carried just far enough for us to hear him. Archer nodded as he scanned the darkness.

"Shift changes in about an hour. We have some time on this side of the walls."

I shook my head. "I don't think we can get close enough from the inside because of the Lord Lieutenant's lodgings. We should stick to the shadow of the wall and when the shifts change, scale the outside of Bell Tower."

Archer gaped at me. "That's a nearly impossible face?"

"We do it in two steps. First to the battlements, then across them and up the tower to the upper window."

"Show me." Ringo's whisper challenged. If I couldn't defend it, the plan wasn't worth a damn anyway.

Step one: to the battlements. There was a section of wall between Lanthorn and Wakefield Towers that I'd scouted earlier, where the garden walls met the walls of the inner ward. It was far enough away from the corner towers that we had a good chance of staying invisible in the deepest shadows. Hand and foot placement was everything though, and it felt good that Archer and Ringo hadn't stopped to assess my route. They were right behind me as our fingers dug in and our boots bit the edges of the stones. We stuck to the corner where two walls met and I was glad for the extra surface at my back. That piece of wall was only one story high, but it had been a straight up sheer climb. I tripped over a chunk of brick and caught myself quickly before crouching in the shadow of the low battlement wall to catch my breath.

Archer knelt beside me. "What's next?"

I nodded at Wakefield Tower ahead of us. "We have to get past that and the Bloody Tower before we have a clear shot on the battlements to Bell Tower. Or if we think that's too exposed, we could also drop to the other side of the wall, hug the shadows, and scale the whole thing in one go." There was a bridge between Wakefield and the Bloody tower, and crossing it put us in the direct line of sight of the guards on top of each.

Archer snuck a glance over the wall. "We're above the main river gate to the Tower, with the same risk of exposure. I think we should stay up high."

"Ringo, are you up for the sprint?"

I could just make out his grin in the shadows. "'Course I am. Just wish I had one of them flash-bangs to make the guards look the other way."

Video game tactics. Not a bad idea.

"How far can you throw this in that direction?" I handed Archer the chunk of brick I'd tripped over and nodded back toward the White Tower, which stood tall and intimidating in the center of the complex. There were some low-lying quarters between us and the tower, and I thought a noise coming from there might be less likely to pinpoint. Both Ringo and Archer immediately understood my plan.

"Get ready to run."

Archer pulled his arm back like a major league baseball pitcher and hurled that chunk of brick so hard my own shoulder ached with the effort of it. A few seconds later a piece of white exploded off one of the corner towers of the White Tower, and the echo of the hit sounded like a shot.

Men's voices yelled from every tower rooftop in the complex.

I stared at Archer. "Damn!"

He shoved me in front of him, and all three of us sprinted past Wakefield Tower, across the bridge, and past the Bloody Tower. We kept going right across the battlement toward the Bell Tower, and I could hear guards calling to each other as they ran toward the White Tower. I figured it was only a matter of time before they mobilized at the gates to protect against intruders.

Below us was a walled garden that must have grown the food for the Lord Lieutenant's Lodgings. I saw two small flashes of something pale running on the garden paths and thought for a second that we were busted. But there were no other calls of warning, and we continued our mad sprint across the narrow battlements behind the Lord Lieutenant's Lodgings. This was the really stupid part of the non-plan because we were in full view of anyone who turned toward the perimeter walls. I crouched as low as I could so I was hidden at least part of the time. I felt like we were ducks in a barrel with every gun trained on us, except maybe they didn't have guns yet, and maybe they were still all looking at the White Tower.

The sheer stone walls of Bell Tower loomed in front of us.

And so did a very big problem.

"What the hell?" There was a gap between the tower and the battlements, as if the wall was unfinished or it was under repair. It was different than what I remembered from my date-night stealth tag run with Archer in the modern Tower.

"There's no purchase between the battlements and the window."

Ringo had pulled ahead and was already scanning the walls above him. Archer wasn't out of breath, of course, but I was gasping air into my lungs so fast it burned. There was a tiny window ledge near the very top of Bell Tower, but the stone walls under it were built with tightly fitted stones. The slight curve of the face added to its impossibility, and the only variation I could find in the stone was a lip where the battlement might someday connect to the tower, and a small gap behind a badly wedged stone about chest-height.

Impossible. But then again, I believed in impossible things.

I ran down a list of our assets. Ringo was light and agile. Archer was strong. And my hands were the smallest.

Right.

"I'm open to options, but here's what I see. I'll jump the gap and wedge my hand behind that rock. Archer, use me as an anchor and climb on my shoulders. Then Ringo, you climb us both and Archer will throw you up to that ledge."

Both guys stared at me like my hair had suddenly turned hot pink.

"Are ye daft?" and "Not bloody likely!" Their voices mingled in whispered outrage. I was right, though, and they'd see it soon enough. The question was, did I wait for them to get it on their own, or point out the obvious? Pointing out the obvious was much more fun, so I put on my most patient smile.

"Of course I'd love not to be on the bottom of the human pyramid, but I'm not strong enough to throw you up to the ledge, Ringo, and you're a better climber than me if Archer misses. Besides, I'm the only one with small enough hands to wedge into that handhold."

Archer was shaking his head grimly. "I don't like it. Any of it. There's too much risk."

Ringo's whisper was almost silent. "I'll just steal it somehow when Wilder's done with me. This isn't worth either of you getting hurt."

I tried very hard to stay calm "You're not getting tortured by that freakshow. We're here to change things, so that's what we're going to do. And unless you have a better idea, I'm jumping."

I gave them about two seconds to come up with something before I backed up and launched myself at the wall. I heard the sharp intake of breath and a stifled grunt of surprise right before I hit. Every fiber of my being was focused on trying to force my hand into the fissure in the rock before my body could rocket backwards off the lip and into the abyss below me. And in the split second after I wedged my hand into the gap, I made a fist and locked it in place.

Effing OW! Rock climbers were insane if they did this on a regular basis. The fist-lock business had seemed like a good idea, except for the fact that I was pretty sure my hand was going to detach at the wrist and leave me stuck with a nickname like 'Stumpy' for the three seconds I'd have left to live. Before I hit the ground and shattered into a million stupid pieces.

"Saira? Are you alright?"

"No."

I made the mistake of looking down, and then I realized that my very bad plan had no exit strategy. It was about thirty feet off the wall on the outside, with a bunch of crazy, pitched roofs full of guards on the inside.

"Crap." I adjusted my feet so there was a piece of ledge available for the guys to aim for, found a chunk of loose mortar to dig into with my other hand, and tensed my fist-lock. "Do it, Archer." My whispered voice sounded mad, probably because I was.

He hesitated and I think I might have growled. So then he jumped.

"Shit balls!" Damn, it hurt. His hands clutched at my waist, and his hips pushed mine into the wall. I was going to have bruises, that was for sure. To Archer's credit he stabilized really fast and didn't pull us both off the wall. He also whispered in my ear, which gave me a chill all up and down my skin. "I'm so sorry, my love."

I gritted my teeth in anticipation of the weight on my clenched fist. "Just climb me."

"A rain check, perhaps?"

Okay, that made me laugh. A little. For a second. Until Archer's foot found my thigh and his other one hit my hipbone. "Bloody hell." I couldn't get enough breath to actually say it, but I'm pretty sure the scream inside my head was loud enough for him to hear.

A lifetime, or maybe thirty seconds later Archer was standing on my shoulders. Based on the scrabble noise I heard above me, and the pieces of mortar that fell on my head, he had found a place to grip.

"Are you okay?" His whispered voice was full of concern.

"Shut up." I needed to concentrate on staying locked to the wall, and sympathy was very distracting.

"Brace yourself, Saira." Ringo's whisper sounded strained. He was nervous, but I knew it wasn't nerves for himself.

"Just do it." I clenched everything, and I could feel Archer try to lift his weight off my shoulders as Ringo landed behind me. His hands clutched my waist, and he almost stepped away from my back right off the ledge.

"Sorry. Sorry." If I could have broken concentration long enough to roll my eyes at his embarrassment I would have.

"Climb or I'll push you off." I ground my teeth with the effort to stay attached to the wall. Ringo chuckled softly, and in one fluid movement pulled himself up to my shoulders.

"Pardon me, Ma'am."

I gasped with relief. "You're excused."

His weight was still on my shoulders as he climbed Archer, but I only had to focus on my locked fist and burning thighs. Keeping my knees from buckling became the center of my entire being; the lives of my two best friends literally rested on my shoulders. No pressure. I might have squeaked. It probably sounded like pain because Archer tried to lift his weight off me again.

"I just need a better grip so I can send Ringo up."

"It's fine." My fist was starting to numb, and I tried to feel the edges of the stone biting into it just to know it was still closed.

And then I pictured what Archer was about to do.

And my knees started to buckle.

Oh, God.

Archer spoke through gritted teeth. "I have to push Ringo about five feet straight up for him to catch that ledge."

With one hand.

I was going to be sick.

"You ready?"

No. Except he wasn't talking to me.

"Do it."

Crap. I locked every single muscle I still had control over and braced myself. Archer seemed to double in weight as he launched Ringo off him. It took everything I had to stay attached to the wall. The skin ripping off my hand was making it slippery, and I didn't think my muscles could hold on much longer.

"Aaaahhh!"

Ringo's voice sliced through the night, and I expected to see him fall past me to the yawning darkness below us. But somehow he didn't fall.

Crash. The sound of breaking glass dared me to look up. Archer was struggling to keep his hold on the tower above me, which was bad. But even worse was the sight of Ringo, his eye socket bleeding and rapidly swelling, dangling from one hand on the narrow ledge while the other one flopped around searching for something to grab.

What the hell happened? Had he missed?

"Ringo!" I didn't think I had any voice left, but apparently it was enough for him to shush me. My fist was beginning to let go and my knees wobbled dangerously.

"I'm going to fall, Archer."

"No. Don't let go!" Archer's whisper was urgent, but I could barely hear him through the buzzing in my ears. I locked eyes with Ringo and his mouth set into a grim line.

"No." I saw his mouth move. Saw the word instead of heard it, just as he swung himself up to the ledge and slid into the window.

"I'm sorry." I met Archer's gaze and a moment of complete connection passed between us. And then a strip of skin tore off my hand and my fist let go. I could feel the backward momentum on my body and saw my own terror reflected in Archer's eyes.

"Nooooo!" Archer let go of the tower wall and plummeted with me toward the blackness below. It might have taken two seconds, maybe three, and I don't think I took my eyes of his the whole time.

Bloody hell, this was going to hurt. I hadn't seen the ground below us, but I assumed it was stone. Worst case I was dead. Other worst case I was brain damaged. Pretty much anything else would probably kill me slowly, but maybe I'd survive long enough to tell Archer how much I loved him.

SLAM!

We landed together, in a tangle of limbs. That I was aware of it meant maybe I wasn't dead. I hurt. I couldn't breathe. My eyes were still tightly shut, or I was blind. All the breath had been knocked out of me, but then I gasped and found the air again. I touched my head, feeling for blood. I didn't break my skull. Or my arm. I hadn't landed on rocks. That was something. I tried to roll over, and I rolled off instead. Off ... Archer.

"No, no, no, no." I slid the rest of the way off Archer's body. Somehow he landed first. Broke my fall. Saved me.

It was so dark there, I couldn't find his face. I felt his body with my hands, found his back, his shoulders. Nothing moved. Was he dead? *Could* he die?

I was afraid to move him. Afraid to turn him over. What if his neck or spine was broken? How was I able to move and I couldn't even feel his muscles twitch?

"Archer." I found his ear, smoothed his soft, dark hair back from it, leaned over and whispered. "Don't be dead. Please, don't be dead."

"Okay."

"Oh!" I crouched down to find his face. "Can you move?"

"Probably." His voice sounded pale. Was that possible? Could sound be pale? His definitely was. Which meant he was hurt. Badly.

"Can you feel your legs?"

Archer's voice got a little color back, or maybe texture. It was soft and low and the sound of it was like velvet around my heart. Even his groan sounded good to me as he rolled himself over and laid on his back. His eyes found mine in the dark. "I'll live."

I started to cry. And laugh. "You broke my fall with your body."

"Good."

I kissed him through my tears and his arms went around me. He felt so good. So *alive*.

"Saira?"

"Yeah?"

"You need to move away from me now."

294

Nothing like a cold dose of … something cold. I leapt backward, or at least moved as fast as my very sore body could go.

"Did I hurt you?"

"You're bleeding. I can't …" His voice was a bright red growl and I suddenly remembered. He wasn't alive. Not in any medical sense of the word. And my blood was making him growly.

"Do you need … to drink?" My hand felt like raw hamburger meat and I knew it would be easy to give him access to the human blood that healed him.

"No." The word was sharp and pointed.

My voice was small. "I want to help you."

He sighed and shifted his body so he could lean against the tower wall. It hurt him to move, but he could do it. "It's too dangerous. I don't want … your power."

To Clock. Because if he had my blood he might be able to do what Wilder did.

"Oh."

Archer raised a hand with effort and touched my face gently, then he looked up. "Did Ringo …?"

My gaze followed his up the side of Bell Tower. The battlements were so high above us, and the upper window where Ringo had hung by one hand seemed impossibly far away.

"He made it inside."

A man's head was visible as he leaned out the window, and a voice that made the blood freeze in my veins said nauseating words. "Ah, you've come."

It was Wilder.

# ESCAPE

Wilder had Ringo.

No!

"Bring them to me." Wilder spoke to someone inside the room as he pulled his head inside.

"We have to go, Archer. We have to run."

"I won't leave Ringo."

I scanned his body, which should have, by all rights, been broken beyond repair. As it was, he was definitely damaged. "You can't fight him. Not yet. You have to heal first, and we need to go, Archer. Now." My whispered voice was urgent and I stumbled to my feet.

I heard a door slam somewhere inside the tower just as Archer finally pushed himself to his feet. He moved slowly, painfully, but I wasn't exactly winning any races myself at the moment. Breathing was hard, and I might have bruised some ribs, but I didn't think anything was broken. The way Archer held himself so tightly, I couldn't say the same for him.

There were guards on the Tower grounds. Lots of guards. Our earlier diversionary rock throw had brought them out in force. But they seemed to be focused toward an imaginary threat outside the walls, and with some fairly clever cat, mouse, and Monger dodging, we managed to stumble and weave back to the Royal Apartments.

Lurch burst out of the building and sprinted toward the Bell Tower, and I was more certain than ever that some dark and demonic connection between Wilder and Lurch existed. We slipped into the building through the kitchens, and I grabbed a linen dishcloth to wrap around my still-bleeding hand.

We were silent all the way upstairs, and we got to the pages' annex without meeting anyone on the way. Pancho was asleep on a pallet by the far wall, bundled in every blanket we'd managed to scrounge up for ourselves. Archer closed the door softly behind us, and I heard a thud.

I spun to look at him, really look at him. He had fallen back against the door, and the wall was the only thing holding him up.

And he looked like he was dying.

"Archer!" I shouted my whisper as his legs collapsed under him. There was a line of blood from his ear to his collar, and that side of his face looked like a piece of very raw steak. The blood had congealed as the superficial wounds closed, but there was internal bleeding too. I was sure of it.

I rushed to his side to help him to his sleeping pallet, but he flinched away from me. "Don't ... touch my ... blood."

"I don't care about that."

He got himself over to his pallet and collapsed onto it.

"You need blood, Archer. This is bad. You need it to heal."

His face was a mask of pain, and he wouldn't look me in the eyes. "My body will fix itself if I sleep."

I glared at him. "Just take some from me, damn it! So what if it gives you Clocking skills?"

He finally looked at me. "I ... won't be ... like him." He ground the words out, and I gasped at how much they hurt me to hear.

"So, you're going to sleep? They'll come for Elizabeth, you know. If you go down now, I'm on my own." I was angry, and Archer turned away from it. Which made me want to hurt him more. "I pretended to be her before, maybe I can fool them again."

Archer stared at me in horror. It made his voice stronger. "It's too dangerous. Ringo is bait. Even Lady Elizabeth is bait. Wilder wants you and he will ... kill ... you." His voice was raspy and I could hear a sucking sound in his chest.

"God! If you won't take my blood, then Pancho's ... anyone's!"

"No one I care about. I just need ... rest. Don't go ... to Wilder." There was so much fear in Archer's eyes. I couldn't stand that it was there because of me, and I started to cry.

"I've never seen you so hurt, Archer. I don't know if you can heal without blood."

Archer reached for my face and his hand cupped my cheek. "Do not let them take you. If they come for ... her ... you have to hide."

A sob caught in my throat as I looked at him. "You promise you won't die?"

The corner of his mouth quirked up. "You can't ... get rid of me that easily."

I wiped the snot and tears from my face as I studied his. The wound on his cheek was a little less angry. "I trust you."

The sucking sound in his chest and quieted and his eyes met mine. "I trust you too."

Archer was asleep almost before I left the room, and Pancho had never even moved. I slipped into Ringo's room through the interconnecting doors. It was empty and the fire had gone out.

Courtney met me when I knocked. "I need to see Elizabeth."

She scowled at me. "The *Lady* Elizabeth is sleeping."

"Wake her up, Courtney. It's important."

She was actually going to tell me 'no.' I could see it in her eyes. So I narrowed mine. "This is not a game. If you want your mistress to live past tomorrow, you need to wake her up *now!*"

Apparently I was scary, because she spun to head into the sleeping chamber. She left the door open behind her, so I took it as an invitation. The fire in the sitting room was lit, and I huddled next to it on a low stool. I was shaking, and I'm not sure what was nerves, fear, adrenaline, or just cold. I looked down at myself and saw tear-stains, filthy jeans, shredded boot leather, and a damaged hand wrapped in blood-stained linen. Awesome. Way to dress to meet a princess.

I would have scoffed at my own joke if I'd still had a sense of humor.

"I imagine you changed nothing and have managed to bring yourselves to the notice of the guards. Well done. When shall I expect them to come for me?" Elizabeth's voice was tired. Tired of me, and probably tired of waiting for a sword she thought was inevitable. I would be, except I didn't think anything was a foregone conclusion. *Everything* could change. Everything.

"Wilder has Ringo, and he knows we're here. Which means he'll come for you soon, maybe even tonight."

"You are so certain of something you did not previously believe would come true." There. There was the sarcasm I'd been expecting from her.

"He's being held in Bell Tower. It's where they'll take you. We've seen it's only Wilder and Lurch in there with you guys. If you surprise them, you could kill Wilder. I could create a diversion to give you time. Ringo would help if you freed him first." I hated the desperation in my voice, especially since it rolled right off her back.

Elizabeth was shaking her head, and there was something that looked like pity in her eyes. "We both know how this ends, Saira."

"It doesn't end that way!" I yelled at her. Courtney stiffened protectively in the corner. I hadn't even noticed her there.

"Yet it is the only vision of my death I've ever seen. And now it's the only thing I *can* see."

"But it's not how you die." I could feel desperation choking me even as something tugged at the edge of my brain. "Wait. Where's the cuff? The silver one from Aislin?"

"I'm sorry, I am not familiar with a cuff of Aislin." Her voice got very formal, like I was giving away family secrets. I suppose, in a way, I was. Not that I cared.

"I've seen it in a portrait of you. Your coronation portrait. You had a silver bracelet on one wrist. Aislin's silver cuff."

She didn't crack. Not a muscle twitched in her face until she spoke. "Well, since I have clearly not been crowned queen, it also may stand to reason that I do not possess this cuff of which you speak."

I clenched my eyes shut. Crap. It was hard to think.

Then I flung them open again. "I have to go back and get you Aislin's bracelet. You can see every possible future with it, and you need to see the one where you live!"

Elizabeth watched me for a long moment, and then finally, offered me her hand. I wasn't sure if I was supposed to shake it or kiss her ring, so I stood and took it tentatively. "You will do what you must, Saira, and so will I. And despite our differences, I know you as the woman who gave me the gift of my Robin. God go with you on your journeys, and perhaps we'll meet again."

It was as formal a kiss-off as I'd ever heard, and the part that really sucked was that she truly believed it.

"You're selling out, you know. You could have a life with Dudley. You do, actually, in the version where you live. You just have to choose it." I saw the flinch then, the very slight widening of her eyes at the mention of a future with her lover.

But I couldn't press this point home with her because the sound of heavy footsteps coming down the hall outside her rooms was the only warning we had. I darted back into Ringo's room just as the door swung open to Elizabeth's. There was no time to close Ringo's door, so I leapt up onto the table and into the rafters as extra insurance against being found.

"Lady Elizabeth Tudor." The man's voice was deep and gravelly and reeked of dead rat. I knew it was Lurch speaking by the shudder that went down my spine. "You will stand for the bishop."

I hadn't seen her sit. That was a tactical play worthy of a queen and guaranteed to remind everyone exactly who she was.

The scene unfolding in the other room was invisible to me, but the voices were clear. "My Lady Elizabeth, I would have thought you'd be surprised to find men in your rooms in the hour before dawn. One could almost imagine you expected us." That was Wilder, and the hair on my arms stood straight up. I pictured the flash of him I'd seen out the window earlier. Unmistakably a silverback gorilla, gray and powerful, but now feral and more grizzled. The irony of his name wasn't lost on me.

"And you are?"

"Bishop John Wilder, second to Lord Chancellor Gardiner, Milady."

"I expect that gentlemen, even strange ones, will behave appropriately in the presence of the king's daughter." Elizabeth's voice remained strong, but I could feel the force of will it took for her to keep it that way.

There was a rustle of paper. "In that case, I will most appropriately inform your Ladyship that you have this day to commit your soul to God. The time for your execution, for the conspiracy to commit treason against your rightful monarch, has been set. By order of Her Majesty, the Queen, I will escort you to your fate at sundown."

A sudden wail of horror filled the room, and I realized Elizabeth's ladies were there with her. I clutched the rafter for support as waves of dizziness washed over me. It was happening.

"Shall we, Milady?"

The door to Elizabeth's rooms opened, and footsteps disappeared down the hall. The minute they were gone, Elizabeth's ladies began wailing again. The sound of helplessness grated on my last nerves.

Just as I dropped down from the rafters, Courtney appeared at the door between the rooms.

"You and your friends will save her." It wasn't a question or a request. More like an expectation. I applauded her determination to keep Elizabeth alive.

"We will."

AISLIN'S CUFF

I raced down the stairs to the Great Hall, thinking furiously of a plan. I didn't have one. What a surprise. And then I shocked myself by stopping in the pages' annex. Archer was dead to the world as his organs stitched themselves back together, but Pancho was just waking up. He looked as surprised to see me as I was to be there.

"If Archer wakes up before I'm back, I need you to give him a message for me. Can you do that, Pancho?"

He nodded mutely, wide-eyed, and probably freaked out by the whirlwind that had just flown in. "Tell him …" Tell him what? That I'm leaving him here in the sixteenth century, and if anything happens to me he's trapped here forever? "Tell him I'm going to bring back Aislin's cuff, and I need him to know that whatever happens, I'll find him."

I looked over at Archer curled on his side, his sleeping face looking so young under the blood and fading bruise. I wasn't alone because he really would be okay. I started for the door. "Mistress?" Pancho's voice startled me and I stopped.

"Yeah?"

"My brother … he says a thousand thanks for the healing balm." Pancho's chin trembled and I realized that his night had been spent with Wyatt in his prison tower. The traitor who had sealed Elizabeth's fate with a signature on a phony confession. The only thing I had left for Wyatt was pity.

"I just made the stuff. You're the reason he feels better, Francis. Your bravery, and your love."

I bolted before the tears spilled down his cheeks. I didn't think he'd appreciate me seeing him cry.

The chapel was empty and totally dark. I needed to get a grip on all the thoughts whirling around in my brain, and at a minimum, figure out where to land.

St. Brigid's. The Clocker Tower. Okay, breathe.

With the image of the round room with the London Bridge painting firmly locked in my mind, I started tracing my candlewax spiral. The last time I'd tried to skip to another spiral hadn't been good, and I had to force myself past the unsettling thought that I might not make it. At the last turn of my fingers I remembered to picture the modern electric lights in the tower room, just so I didn't accidentally end up skipping over to St. Brigid's in this time.

The hum and stretch were almost welcome as I tried to calm my nerves about this jump, but *between* was jarring and horrible, just like always. And just like always, I had to hold down the dry heaves as I crumpled to the stone floor in a heap. Stone floor. My eyes flew open. My tower. The painting. Electricity. The ticking heartbeat of the clock, and black night of pre-dawn lingering outside the window.

I gasped in relief and stood on shaking legs. A plan. I needed one. Badly. How long had I been gone from this time? We left Mongers at St. Brigid's who had never been so strong. Had Wilder managed to actually split time? Had I come to the right future?

Despair seemed pretty pointless, so I chose action instead. I needed boots that weren't torn to shreds and a pair of jeans that didn't stink of Thames slime. And Ava. My room was a place to start.

I didn't meet anyone in the corridors and didn't hear anyone moving around, but I took the back stairs just in case.

The door to my room was locked from the inside. Huh? Ava didn't lock doors. Even though I'd never used a key on our door, I swept the upper frame for one. Ava wasn't lazy like most people who hid keys, but she could See things and might have known I was coming. There it was.

I unlocked the door quietly and slipped inside. The curtains were closed and it was too dark to see whether Ava slept in her bed.

"You came back." Her breathy voice sounded a little jumpy, as if she hadn't been completely sure it was me.

"Can I turn on a light?"

"No. Wait, here." Ava fumbled at her nightstand and found her phone. She flipped on the flashlight app and propped it against a book.

"Why are you afraid?"

"They're hunting you."

"Who is?" It wasn't news, but until a couple hours ago I'd stopped feeling like prey. The feeling came back full force with her words.

She stared at me. "Everyone."

Well, that was new.

"Tell me what happened."

Ava took a deep breath and sat up in bed. She looked tired, and scared. And suddenly I realized how much I'd missed my friend. I waved my hand at her. "Scootch." She did, and I kicked off my shredded boots to sit next to her on her bed.

"You stink." She wrinkled her nose daintily and I leapt off her covers.

"Sorry." I quickly stripped out of my gross jeans and my underwear that didn't bear thinking about and tossed them in the garbage bin. I wanted a shower, but clean clothes would do for now, so I was back on Ava's bed in under a minute.

"Things started getting weird right around the time you guys left." Ava's voice had lost some of the shake, but she still spoke in low tones. "That bookkeeper, Domenic Morgan, took over as head of the Mongers, and for whatever reason, Rothchild let him."

I stared at Ava in shocked silence. She might as well have said Rothchild's head was cut off and Morgan's grew back in its place. "How could that even happen? Mr. Shaw said the guy was nobody."

"He *was* nobody. But now the Mongers all line up behind him. The only hold-out is Seth Walters. He's still doing his own thing, but I don't think it's sanctioned by the rest of the Monger hierarchy."

"Mongers hunting me isn't new though. You said 'everyone.' Who is everyone?"

Her eyes searched my face. "You remember the conversation we had about Aislin's cuff at my parents' house?"

My stomach lurched with dread. "Yes."

"The cuff is missing."

I almost screamed, but managed to strangle the sound into a hiss. "Nooooo!"

My horror seemed to answer something for her, and the worry in her face relaxed just a little. "Saira, they think you stole it."

"Clearly I didn't."

"We've all Seen you with it."

"We, as in all the Seers?"

Ava nodded, the worried expression was back.

"I didn't steal your cuff, Ava." I twisted my braid like it was full of worry beads. "It's what I came back for."

She moved a little away from me. "What do you mean, you came back for it? You were going to take it?"

Now it was my turn to stare. "According to you all, I already did."

She ignored me. "But Saira, Aislin's cuff has been in my family since, well, Aislin. You've seen the coronation portrait of Elizabeth Tudor wearing it. An outsider can't just take it."

"That's the thing. I need to take it to Elizabeth. She doesn't have it."

"Of course she does. She was the head of the Seer Family for forty years."

I shook my head. "She showed me her death. I saw her walking to the scaffold at the Tower. Elizabeth Tudor believes she's going to die, Ava. I need her to see a different future."

Ava stared at me in growing horror. "What have you done?"

"*I* didn't do anything."

She backed away even further, and her voice came out in a whisper. "Did you cause a time stream split by going back? Did you change history?"

It was the thing Clockers could do that scared me the most. And hearing Ava say it out loud made me defensive and mad. "Someone else has Aislin's cuff, Ava. Not me. But I need to find it, and I only have …" – I looked at the clock – "about eleven hours to do it."

I got off Ava's bed and rummaged through my dresser for things I wanted to take back. Anachronistic things, of course, but if the time stream had actually split like Ava thought, how much worse could I make things? I didn't even bother mentally answering that. There wasn't really a quantifier big enough. Googleplex? Apocalyptic?

I unwrapped the bloodstained linen cloth from my skin-stripped hand and winced as it peeled away the fresh scabs. Mr. Shaw made better green medicine than I did, but I wasn't even sure he was still on my side. That thought just made me tired.

"What happened to your hand?" I was a little surprised Ava was still speaking to me, considering she had pretty much accused me of bringing about the end of the world as we knew it.

"Stripped all the skin off it trying to keep Ringo from getting captured." I pulled a fresh long-sleeved t-shirt over my camisole and grabbed the thickest, blackest cashmere sweater I could find from my collection of Archer's clothes. "Didn't work. Wilder got him anyway."

"Wilder has Ringo?"

I nodded in defeat, and Ava threw the covers off herself to get dressed. "C'mon. We'll find Adam and figure this thing out."

I looked at her, surprised and relieved. "I need to see Shaw too."

"It'll be hard to get him away from my parents and my uncle, but I'll see what I can do."

The Armans and Phillip Landry were here? "What do they want with Shaw?"

"They knew you'd be back."

We agreed to meet in the Seer Tower, which no one but the twins used anymore. Because maybe the warded tower room could block the Seers' visions. Ava couldn't back that up, but since wards could block physical sight, maybe they could block the mental kind too.

I still didn't have a plan, and I didn't know where to even begin looking for Aislin's cuff. Why couldn't they See it with the real thief? Why was it only with me in their visions? My other giant problem was the time stream. Somewhere in the deep recesses of my brain I knew something was very, very wrong. I had to find my mother and Miss Rogers and Doran, if he could be coaxed out of hiding. I needed to talk to anyone who could help me figure out what was going on.

The corridors were still clear as I took every back way I knew downstairs to my mom's rooms. Her door wasn't locked, and she was having her early morning tea curled in a chair by the fire. She looked tired, and ... fragile.

"Hi, Mom." I made my voice as soft as I could so I didn't startle her. She jumped anyway, and when she saw me about ten years fell off her face. She held her arms out to me and I folded myself into them.

"Oh, Saira. You're back."

I let her hold me a long moment before I finally untangled myself and perched on a stool near her feet. "I can't stay long though. This isn't done yet."

Something flashed in her eyes as she studied my face. I braced myself for the hammer but she surprised me. A lot.

"Do you need the necklace?"

I shook my head. "I can focus without it."

"I should have given it to you before. I've been so afraid you never got to where you were going because you didn't have it." Her voice choked and I gripped her hand. It was cold and felt a little brittle.

"I'm okay, Mom." Then I took a breath. "Actually, maybe I'm not."

"They think you have Aislin's cuff." There was no accusation in her voice. More like fear.

"I don't, but I need it. I need to take it to Elizabeth."

She studied me in surprise. "Elizabeth Tudor? You've met her?"

"I'm pretty sure by now Wilder has her. Probably for the same reason he wanted you."

My mother gasped. "Is he bleeding her?"

"According to a vision she and Archer both had, he was questioning her about her visions. But it seems like he's driving her toward execution. That would give him a whole lot of access to her blood, wouldn't it?"

"When were you?"

"April, 1554."

"So she's a prisoner, but she still has some power. And Lord John Brydges wouldn't have allowed unfettered access to the queen's sister."

"Elizabeth has seen her own execution. She believes she's going to die at the Tower."

Now it was my mom's turn to stare. "But she's a Seer."

"They're not infallible, Mom. Seers think I stole the cuff, remember?"

"Well, isn't that what you came back to do?"

"More or less. But that's not what I mean." What did I mean? The thought weighed heavily on me, and I finally said it out loud. "What if there's been a time stream split? What if Wilder already changed things so much he caused a split before I got there, or … what if it was something I did?"

My mom did a classic British Lady thing to buy time before answering. "Do you want some tea?"

I sighed. There was no way around that particular stalling tactic. "Yeah, sure." She got my favorite mug out, a giant one with a chicken on it, and she poured me a cup of tea. Then she went to her bookcase and pulled a small, cloth-bound book off the shelf. The cover might have been brocade or velvet once, but most of the fabric had worn down to something vaguely red. "I found this book at a London shop in 1886. The bookseller said it was one of the Katherine Parr translations of Prayers and Meditations." She opened the fragile tie and held it out to me.

I turned the parchment pages carefully. They were brittle with extreme age, but not faded. There were notes in the margins in tight handwriting, but most of it was illegible. Just inside the front cover was an inscription to Elizabeth from Katherine.

"It was Elizabeth's?"

"The bookseller thought it might have been from Katherine Parr's household, but because of what's painted in the back, they discounted the idea that it could have been Elizabeth Tudor's, despite the fact that Katherine was Elizabeth's last stepmother, and the one who took her in after Henry VIII died."

Inside the back cover of the prayer book was a beautifully painted design inset with the initials 'C' and 'E.' I looked up at my mom in surprise. "Those are your initials."

She smiled sadly. "I've always held on to the belief that the prayer book belonged to Elizabeth Tudor, and somehow she knew I would one day find it. She was so strong, and so … alone. I like to think she left me a sign that I could be strong in my aloneness too."

"Mom … " I traced the blue and gold letters with light fingers. What could I say that could make any of the last seventeen years less painful? She'd left the love of her life behind to save me.

"Elizabeth was alive when you left?" My mom's voice was quiet.

I nodded mutely as I closed the book and handed it back to her.

"Time hasn't yet been split then."

"But Mr. Shaw and Ava said the Monger guy, Domenic Morgan, came from nowhere and has taken over. He's related to Wilder through his sister."

Mom shrugged. "That could be circumstantial; anything's possible with Mongers, although Bob is certainly not prone to exaggeration or false concern." I didn't miss the note of pride in her voice when she talked about Mr. Shaw. "My understanding about time is that it takes something really big to actually split it."

"You mean like ending the Tudor monarchy?"

She looked down at the book in her hands. "That would probably do it."

"Well, an hour ago she was still breathing."

My mother looked me straight in the eyes. "Then you might have to keep her that way."

"No pressure."

"Only the fate of the modern world. You're up to it though, right?" She smiled, and I recognized my mom again. The young, vital one I remembered from before Wilder.

I put my mug down and hugged her again, hard. "Thank you, Mom."

"I love you, Saira."

"I love you too." I kissed her cheek and straightened up. "Can I take a quick shower here before I go in search of Aislin's cuff?"

She crinkled her nose. "I didn't want to mention it…"

"But I stink. Yeah, I know. The sixteenth century can do that to a person. If I had time there's a lot I'd do before I go back. But if Elizabeth can see the future where she lives, she might actually stand and fight. And if there's one thing I'm learning it's that people have to want to change their own fate for it to happen."

"Some people go their whole lives without learning that lesson."

"Yeah, well, some people haven't tried to keep a princess alive through sheer force of will. And believe me, no one's will is stronger than Elizabeth Tudor's."

"I wouldn't mind meeting her."

310

"You want to come with me?"

Her smile faded and I rushed on before she could say no. It bothered me more than I could admit that she still wouldn't Clock. "Actually, never mind. This place needs all the good guys it can get to keep the bad guys at bay."

She looked serious. "Be careful, Saira. There are those of us who forget who the real enemies are."

I ticked off on my fingers. "Wilder. Mongers. Anyone who hunts mixed-bloods or Vampires just because. Anyone I'm missing?"

"As long as that cuff is missing, maybe the Armans? And I'm sure Millicent would put herself on that list if she got her hands on you. She's been storming around Miss Simpson's office fairly regularly since you left."

I grimaced at the thought of running into the head of the Clocker Family. "It's a pretty personal list though, huh? I bet if you asked Seth Walters who's on his list of enemies it would be very different."

"Something to keep in mind."

 **SEERS**

After the world's fastest shower, I slipped out of my mom's rooms and down the hall. I was headed toward Mr. Shaw's office, but had to change direction when voices came from that hallway.

"I'll meet you in a few minutes. I need to see Shaw first."

Crap. I thought I recognized the voice. Phillip Landers. Tom's dad. Which meant he must be talking to Mr. or Mrs. Arman. In a moment of pure instinct, I slipped into an unlocked classroom.

Olivia looked up at me in surprise. "What are you doing here?" she hissed. She was reading at a table by the fireplace with a blanket around her shoulders.

"Hiding. What are *you* doing here?"

She looked worried. "The same."

"What's going on, Liv?" I locked the door and crossed the room to sit next to her. Our voices were barely above a whisper.

"They've sent the non-Family kids away. I'm still here because of my aunt, but Miss Simpson wants me to stay out of public view as much as possible, at least while the Seer head is here looking for you."

I winced. "Why'd they send kids away?"

She shrugged. "Family politics. Call me crazy, but I'm actually here for the education." She looked really worried. "You should go, Saira. They're all looking for you, and it's really serious."

"Yeah, I heard. As soon as I find what I'm looking for, I'm out of here."

312

"You need a Seer." The irony wasn't lost on either of us.

"Like a fricking hole in the head."

She laughed, but there wasn't a lot of humor in it. "Seriously. Go to Miss Simpson. She's always been on your side."

I gave her a quick hug. "Maybe I will. For the record, I didn't do what they said I did."

She smirked. "You're guilty anyway as far as they're concerned. You might as well do whatever it is and get the benefits."

I grinned. "Say hi to the Wolf for me."

The smile on her face told me volumes about how she felt about Connor, and I slipped out of the room with a little lightness in my heart.

Olivia was right about going to see Miss Simpson, but it was a big risk. She was a Seer and the headmistress of the school, which could mean that she put the rules above the students, or it could mean the opposite. In my limited acquaintance with Miss Simpson, she *had* always been on my side.

Only the reading lights were on in the library, but the morning was gloomy outside so it felt dark and deserted. Miss Simpson was in her office, and so was someone else.

Someone on my list.

"I must insist that you detain her until I can come and take her home." Millicent's posh accent directly conflicted with the nastiness of her tone. I slunk back into the stacks, out of sight, but not out of earshot.

"Don't be ridiculous, Lady Elian. We do not detain students at St. Brigid's. Saira is our student, her mother is her guardian, and this is not a conversation I need have with you again. Are we clear?"

Miss Simpson's words and the way she stood up to Millicent struck me like a slap. And propelled me toward her office door. I knocked lightly.

"Come."

Miss Simpson stood across the desk from Millicent, and both of them had expressions that would have worked in a boxing ring.

She didn't look surprised to see me, but Millicent did, despite the flat tone of her words. "You're safe then."

"For the moment." I squared my shoulders and faced the woman who was the de facto head of our Family. "I appreciate your concern, Millicent, and I'm sorry if I've worried you. I'm only here for a short time though, and your presence will probably draw the Armans, whom I'd prefer to avoid. So if you don't mind, I need a minute with Miss Simpson."

The shock on her face was so filled with indignation it looked painful. "Saira—"

I tried Archer's horse-whisperer trick and dropped my voice to something low and calm. I even added a polite smile. "I'll come by Elian Manor when I get back, and I'll tell you everything then."

She opened her mouth again to speak, but no sound came out. If I hadn't been so determined to keep the upper hand I'd have been shocked at my own audacity. She finally found her words as she swept from the office. "Plan to stay for dinner then. I expect it'll be a long night."

The door closed behind her with a controlled slam and I just barely resisted the urge to laugh. From the shine of her eyes, so did Miss Simpson. But reality came crashing in when I saw the lines of tension around her mouth.

"It wasn't me. Aislin's cuff. I didn't take it." She knew. I could see it on her face. She led me to a seat across from her. "Why are you letting them hunt me?"

A small sigh escaped her. "The best part of being a teacher is giving my students the tools to navigate their lives. The hardest part is then letting them do it. I haven't had much influence in shaping you, Saira, so I will give you what I can. There is a knot tangling the threads of time and you alone have the skills to unpick the knot."

She stood and locked the door. And when she turned back to me her expression was serious.

"The Dream remains for none to See,
And time of War is what shall be.

314

Unless the child, Death by her side,
Can choose the path to turn the tide."

Miss Simpson's voice had whispered into me, and her words felt imprinted on my soul. I shuddered and her voice returned to normal, but her expression was still grave.

"I don't want to be the child." My own voice sounded small and frightened and I cleared my throat. "What if every path I choose gets people hurt?"

"Accepting that your fate is your choice is a place to start, my dear."

The irony smacked me upside the head. I hadn't fully accepted that I could be the 'child' because I couldn't imagine that my fate could ever be so big or important. But here I'd been demanding that Elizabeth choose a big life, and I hadn't given myself the same mandate. If I *chose* the job of fulfilling the Prophecy of the Child, I might actually be able to pull it off. Maybe. If I was really lucky and a little bit crazy. The ramifications of choosing that fate were massive.

"If I find the cuff, may I please take it to Elizabeth?"

I don't know why I felt I needed Miss Simpson's permission, but the seriousness lifted from her face and she smiled in a way that dropped about fifty years. She was beautiful. "Yes, dear. You may."

She unlocked the door and turned to me as I stood to go. "I'm sorry that there's fear, and that fear has taught intolerance. But it can change. *You* can change it."

Cryptic words, but they sounded kind of like a blessing, so I took them. "I don't suppose you know where it might be, do you?"

"It will find you, Saira. But knowledge of a path doesn't make the path any easier to choose."

Well, that was good to know, even if it was couched in a warning. I hugged Miss Simpson goodbye and slipped out of her office. I was late to meet the twins, and I hoped Ava had somehow gotten a message to Mr. Shaw that I needed to see him.

My hand was throbbing, and despite finally getting clean, I was afraid it would infect with some sixteenth century bacteria I had no immunity to.

Finally, there were kids in the halls to dodge and I had to take the long way to the Seer Tower. The secret entrance behind the bookcase moved freely again. Someone must have fixed it since Mr. Shaw forced his way through it a few months ago.

Adam and Ava were already in the old headmaster's office in the Seer Tower, but I was surprised to see Tom there too. The bandage was off his head and the cut above his eye was healing well. The scar would probably look good on him when it faded. "Hey, guys."

A big grin split across Adam's face, and he buried me in a huge hug. "You're back."

"Not for long."

"Ava told us. Obviously the cuff is missing and everyone thinks you took it. But now I can see you didn't. Not yet anyway."

Tom came in for a quick hug too, which surprised me. He'd always been so reserved. I caught a really quick flash of something off him. Like part of a vision. Of the cuff. And me holding it. I stared at Tom in shock. "That's what people see?"

He looked guilty. "You caught that? I'm sorry. I didn't mean to …"

"Does that happen often? That flashy vision-thing?"

He shrugged. "You learn to deal."

"I've seen enough Seer visions to know I'm really glad not to be one of you guys."

Adam groaned. "I'll take my visions over your time travel any day."

"Yeah, you don't do so well with Clocking, do you, big guy? Finally, something the great Adam Arman sucks at."

"Oh, the places my imagination could go with that statement."

I hit him. Not hard, just hard enough to remind him I *could* hit. "Practice restraint."

He grinned. "That's not what Alex says."

316

"TMI, Adam. Seriously." Ava was laughing and it felt really good to be with my friends.

"Tell her I said hi. I missed you guys."

"Spill everything. You know you want to." I really did. I liked this 'having friends' thing. A lot. So I gave them the abbreviated version of the last ten days. Ava's mouth hung open.

"You really think Elizabeth doesn't have Aislin's cuff?" It was back to the cuff. Never mind about the death threat scheduled for sundown tonight. But I guess they'd been living and breathing Aislin's cuff since it had disappeared.

I included all three of them in my gaze. "I've been thinking about this. What if I'm the reason she gets it in the first place? What if she never had it until I brought it to her?"

"Doing a little timey-wimey thing, huh?"

I leveled a gaze on Adam. "Doctor Who breaks all time-travel rules, and you know it. I'm serious about this. Your family is freaked out because they think I stole the family relic that once belonged to Queen Elizabeth I. Except I'm telling you, she doesn't have it. What if the whole reason it's gone now is so she can get it? Because without that cuff and what it can show her, she's going to walk passively to her death."

"It's not like she's going to step in front of a car or throw herself off a bridge, right? Why can't you save her?" Trust Adam to put me on the hot seat.

"Who am I, the guardian angel of time? Believe it or not, I've been trying to change what she sees. But all you Seers seem to think what you see is what's written in stone. And no matter how hard I try, the only fate I've had any luck changing is my own."

"And you think the cuff will show her a different fate?" Adam sounded skeptical, but Ava saved me from making stuff up.

"Aislin's cuff shows the wearer every possible fate, not just the one we would normally see."

"You mean 'make this choice and that happens?' Like a 'choose your ending' kids' book?" She nodded and I could see the shock on Adam's face. "How come I didn't know that?"

"Only the heads know, and they've always kept it pretty secret. Otherwise people would be wanting to Sec with the cuff all the time."

"Well, why shouldn't they? Because if there really are a whole bunch of different outcomes possible, then the visions we usually See are just b.s." Adam was really bothered by this, and I knew he took the whole fate and vision thing seriously.

"I don't think they're b.s." I held his eyes with mine. "I think they're like guides. If you know an outcome, you can choose the steps to get there. Kind of like when you're free-running. You can See the way that'll get you where you want to go. But if the outcome you See isn't what you want, I do believe you can change it. Make different choices. Go another way." Adam looked like a lost little boy. He was usually so completely confident that everything was the way it was. And when things happened to shake that certainty up, it took him time to get his balance again.

Tom had been silent since he'd given me the quick hug hello, and he looked like he was finally going to say something when voices from just outside the office carried through the door.

"Crap! It's the parentals," Adam whispered, and the panic on his face told me he wasn't expecting them. "You have to hide."

I looked around the room. "Where?"

"Up in the tower."

"No way. That room's warded."

"Then I don't know, go out the window or something."

I looked out at the sheer drop below. "I'm not Spider Man."

Adam was freaking out. "Seriously, you have to hide. Do your warding thing. Whatever. Just don't let them find you." His whisper took on a panicked note as he turned toward the door. It began to open just as Tom grabbed my arm and whispered in my ear, "I have Aislin's cuff."

WARDS

Well, that was unexpected.

My See-Monger friend, the only other mixed-blood I knew – who was afraid of heights and had weird, flashy visions when I bumped into him – stole Aislin's cuff and let them blame me.

The door to the office swung open and without conscious thought I felt a ward come up. Tom still held my arm so the ward covered both of us. I felt him move in closer to me under the protection of invisibility, and part of me wanted to push him away. But I didn't, and when I saw who entered the room, I was glad I hadn't.

"Do you have her? Is she here?" The way Phillip Landers spoke to Ava and Adam was like he expected to see them. Was it a planned meeting? That thought made my stomach hurt.

"Of course she is. What, you can't see her?" Ava's voice was full of scorn for her uncle, and I was stunned that sweet, lovely Ava had it in her. Tom's grip tightened on my arm and I resisted the urge to flinch away. Ava turned to her mother. "You've already convicted Saira and you expect me to be on your side?" Ava pushed past her parents and left the room.

"Come back here, Ava." Camille Arman had a perfectly cultured voice that sounded expensive and bossy.

"Let her go, Mom. You guys have been doing this for a week, and we're both sick of it." Adam had lost the panic from his voice and was back to casual indifference. Good for him.

I could feel Tom's heart beating next to my arm. I had slowly moved us back against the wall and my shoulder was pressed against his chest as the Armans and Mr. Landers spread out around the office. The multitude of mirrors on the walls cast weird reflections and made the room feel crowded with enemies. I could only hope that our images weren't visible in those Seer mirrors.

The last time I'd seen Adam's dad he had a goofy grin on his face from a marathon session of video gaming with Ringo. This was not that guy. His expression was serious, and I got the sense he was here as back-up for his wife. Adam got his height and surfer-build from Mr. Arman, and I knew it probably pissed Mr. Landers off to have such a handsome brother-in-law.

Like his sister Camille, Phillip Landers was short and dark-haired. They were both striking, but what was petite and powerful on Camille was just small and annoying on her brother. The twins had filled me in on the drama of the older brother who believed he should rule the matrilineal Family, and the younger sister who had firm control over the vast Seer clan. The Seers made my small, dysfunctional family seem like a poster child for healthy relationships.

"She's here now. The light is right, we're gathered together just as I've seen. The girl and Aislin's cuff are in this room." Mrs. Arman had always scared me, but now she practically had sparks shooting from her eyes.

"You know what, Mom. I'm out too." Adam looked and sounded disgusted with his mother as he headed for the door.

"Adam, you come back here this instant!"

Adam did turn around, but this time he was the one on fire. "No, I'm done. Saira didn't take the cuff, and even if she did, she would have had a reason. But you've been witch-hunting her and turning this whole place upside down just like the Mongers did in their search for the Sucker. I'm not going to be that guy, Mom. I won't be part of anything that shoots first and asks questions later."

"Don't be ridiculous, Adam. Of course we're not condemning the girl without a trial. But we've all seen her with the cuff and you must admit, it's the only thing that makes sense. She's taken a valuable Family heirloom and we just want it back."

Not for a second did I believe that's all Camille Arman wanted. Based on her expression, I figured she'd have me cheerfully drawn and quartered even *after* she got her precious silver cuff back. Despite the fact that I didn't steal the damn thing in the first place.

Adam was about to launch another attack but he was interrupted by the very noisy, very timely arrival of Mr. Shaw barreling into the room. I saw Ava beckon to Adam from behind Mr. Shaw. Adam didn't want to leave, but he finally took her silent advice, and Mr. Shaw clapped his big hand on Adam's shoulder as he passed him. It was the first sign of real friendliness I'd seen between them.

I could feel Tom holding himself tightly behind my shoulder. His body heat was the only thing keeping the frigidness of the ward from overtaking me completely, and I struggled to hold it up.

"What the bloody hell is wrong with you people!" Mr. Shaw was in full Bear mode, despite the human form he currently wore. Mr. Arman was tall, but Mr. Shaw topped him by at least three inches and probably fifty pounds of pure muscle. "I heard what young Arman said to you and he's absolutely right. This isn't who we are, and it's certainly not who we're on the verge of war to become."

Phillip Landers stepped forward. "This has nothing to do with you, Shaw. You can leave now." He looked like a terrier facing a pit bull, and it would have been funny except it most definitely wasn't.

"It has everything to do with me. You're in my school, hunting my student, and intimidating your own kids into helping you."

"They're our children first." Mrs. Arman still sounded imperious, but she wasn't quite so bossy with Mr. Shaw.

"That's right, they're your children. And yet you hound them and spy on them and make them choose you over their friends.

321

What kind of parents are you? What kind of example are you showing them? You're just bullies, all of you. Adam compared you to Mongers, but he's wrong. You're worse. At least Mongers are honest about their witch hunts."

Mr. Landers had gone still with rage. "You dare compare me to a Monger? You know what Walters did to my family! You know what he did to my wife! I let his half-Monger bastard call me 'dad' for God's sake. How dare you compare me to something so unspeakably vile."

And just like that, I dropped the ward.

And slapped Phillip Landers.

The room was utterly silent, except the slamming of my heartbeat was like the ticking of a time bomb in my ears. I wanted to kill Landers in that moment for what he had just done to his son.

"You don't deserve him." I spat the words and it seemed to unlock the freeze frame that held the room.

Landers looked behind me at Tom, and his face flushed an angry red. Then he grabbed my upper arm, hard. "Give over my cuff."

"Oh, it's yours now? I thought *she* was the head of the Seers." I indicated Camille and my voice was low and fierce as I tried to pull my arm away. "Take your hand off me." But his grip was hard and he yanked me to him. And with his other hand he hit me across the face.

Damn, he hit hard.

I could feel blood well at the corner of my mouth and tears automatically fill my eyes, which pissed me off almost as much as being hit had.

Apparently it pissed off Mr. Shaw too.

"You've. Gone. Too. Far." Mr. Shaw just managed to get the words out before he rage-changed.

I'd seen Mr. Shaw transform into a Bear before and it was a fairly terrifying thing. This was like that, only ten times worse. Because he was pissed. The Bear went straight for Landers, who tried to use me as a human shield. I twisted out of his hands and

322

started for the door, but Mr. Arman caught me, and his grip was much stronger than his brother-in-law's.

"Put her in the tower!" Camille was furious and more than a little panicked at the proximity of a massive, enraged Bear. Mr. Arman half-dragged me to the tower door and shoved me inside. As he slammed the door shut I realized Tom was already there. He must have slipped away to hide there from the mayhem in the office.

And then the deadbolt clicked into place.

"Crap!" I pushed against the door, and instantly the freezing cold of the wards seeped into my bones. Not only was it a locked room, it was a warded room, which meant I couldn't even clock us out of it.

I pounded on the door and yelled, "Hey! Open up!" But all the sounds from the room on the other side of the door had gone silent, and I realized this room was warded against everything. A very effective hide-out ... or prison.

Tom's face was pale and he looked like he was going to be sick. I grabbed his arm and dragged him upstairs to the tower. "Here, lie down." He sat on the floor of the bare tower room and put his head between his knees. His breathing seemed ragged and shaky, and all my own anger faded in the face of what he had just heard.

"I'm so sorry, Tom. No one should ever have to hear something so ... nasty."

He gulped another couple breaths of air. There were bags under his eyes, and he looked like he'd been tormented a lot longer than just the past ten minutes.

"You can have the cuff if you take me with you."

The cuff. I glared. "Why should I? You've been letting me take the heat for the theft for days and now you want to come with me? How does that make you trustworthy?"

"Whether or not you believe me, the truth is I took it because I saw you'd need it. I didn't know when you'd be back, but I saw you come back for the cuff."

Huh. Interesting. "Why didn't you just let me ask for it instead of turning me into a criminal in the Seers' minds?"

"Families don't just hand over their treasures, Saira. There's no way you could have gotten it by asking."

He may have had a point, but I wasn't going to give it to him. His breath shuddered and he put his head between his knees again.

"Tom, what's going on? Why do you want to go?"

His eyes found mine. "You heard my fa—Phillip. I'm the half-Monger bastard he barely tolerates. You knew I was mixed blood because of how you react to Mongers. I didn't want to believe you, but honestly, I knew it too. I just didn't realize... my mother..."

"Was forced."

Tom scoffed. "It's a pretty big secret to keep in a Family of Seers." He got to his feet and brushed off, then wandered over to the window and looked out at the midday sun. I felt the ticking clock and I knew I had to get out of that room soon. "I don't know why they didn't see my mixed blood. Maybe it has something to do with not seeing things you don't want to."

I snorted. "Oh, awesome. So truth is relative with Seers too? Well *that* makes me feel so much better."

"I don't pretend to know much about how my Family's gifts work. But I think I can do something most of them can't. Maybe because of my mixed blood." He took a deep breath. "I specifically See Mongers. I see what they'll be doing, and if they're close, I can See exactly where they are."

My eyes narrowed. "So you're like a road map to Mongerville."

The ghost of a smile hit his lips. "Something like that."

Fascinating. And potentially useful.

"This Wilder guy's a Monger, right?" he asked.

"Yeah, underneath the Vampire beats all that warm and fuzzy heartlessness."

"Thanks."

324

"Oh, shut up, you're only half heartless." I grinned at him and the ghostly smile got a little more substantial. "And I'm like a nearly extinct half beast, so we're even."

"But you see my point, right?"

"I see how you can be helpful to me. But I still don't know why you want to do it."

Tom sighed. "You know all those flashes you get whenever you touch me?"

"Yeah."

"They're full of Mongers."

"Ick."

"Exactly. You remember I told you they were getting stronger?" I nodded. That felt like a lifetime ago, or maybe even a whole timeline ago.

"Well, they've gotten even more powerful since you went back. And I heard what you said about maybe Wilder causing a time split."

"It may not be a proper split yet because Elizabeth is still alive, but it seems to be heading down a really dark path."

"That's the thing. If all the changes I've been seeing in the Monger camp are from things he's causing, he needs to be stopped."

"What did Mr. Shaw mean about us being on the verge of a war?"

"Did you notice how quiet the school is right now?"

"The halls were noticeably empty. Is that what you mean?"

"The heads of Families felt we were all at risk of exposure to the regular population, so they made Miss Simpson send all the Ungee kids away."

"Well, that's weird and isolating."

"I'm pretty sure your grandmother would have yanked you out of school too, if anyone knew where to find you."

That got a giant eye-roll. As if Millicent had any say over me anymore, since all I had to do was threaten to Clock out and she shut right up. "Why? This place is a fortress."

"Exactly. St. Brigid's is one of the most defensible buildings in England. The whole place can be locked down like a stronghold, and the Mongers know it. The Armans used the theft of the cuff as their excuse for hanging around here since you left, but really, it's Descendant politics. As many Descendant adults as they could get to help keep the school out of Monger hands, the better."

I stared at him. "Then why do they have me locked up?"

Tom's look was tinged with pity. "Don't underestimate the power of a good bargaining chip."

"Seriously? There's no way they could use me like that. Simpson and Shaw, not to mention my mother and Millicent, would never let them."

"They'd be within their rights if they found Aislin's cuff on you."

I stared at Tom in growing horror. "So that's it? You're working with Mongers again?"

He looked startled. "What? No!"

"You stole the cuff to plant it on me so the Armans had justification to trade me in?"

His eyes widened. "I told you, I want to go with you. I took the cuff for you, not to trap you with it."

I studied Tom for a long moment. I thought he was telling the truth, but if I was going to bring him with me I had to be sure.

"How did Seth Walters get you to See for him?

I'd managed to catch Tom off guard. "He said he had proof my mom had an affair with someone else, and he'd make sure my da... Phillip found out about it unless I worked with him. But he said it like it was still going on and it never occurred to me ..."

"The guy's a pig."

"You're telling me nothing I don't know." There was bitterness in Tom's voice that made me cringe, and there didn't seem to be a lot to say after that.

Just for fun, I tried to draw a spiral. I didn't even get the slightest glow from the edges, and definitely no hum in my ears.

The windows had a magnificent view, but two of them didn't open, and the one that did led to a 20-foot drop down to the pitched roof of the nearest attic wing. I wasn't kidding when I told Adam I wasn't Spider-Man. It was the kind of drop that needed an extension, and then something to keep you from flying off the roof below with sheer forward momentum.

I was exhausted, but too cold to lie down and sleep. The time bomb kept ticking away, and the longer I stayed locked in this room, the less chance I had to keep Elizabeth alive. The memory of her execution vision gave me the zoomies, and I started pacing.

Finally, Tom got sick of my constant motion. He told me to sit on the floor with my back to his and my arms curled around my knees. His body heat at my back kept me from going hypothermic in the warded room, and I finally slipped into something resembling a coma. It wasn't enough sleep to make up for the night I'd missed, and was just enough for me to be completely groggy and disoriented when the sound of the bolt being thrown back jolted me awake.

THE BEAR

"Ten minutes." Mr. Arman's voice rumbled from outside the door as Mr. Shaw stepped through it. He quickly held his finger to his lips to keep me from speaking as he climbed the stairs. The door closed behind him and the bolt shot into the lock again.

I flew down the stairs and threw myself into his arms. I didn't even realize he carried me back up until he finally put me down on the floor in the tower room.

"Now then, show me that hand." His voice was gruff and full of emotion.

"How'd you get them to let you in?"

"I threatened them. How else?" He winced as fresh scabs came off with the cloth around my hand. He caught Tom's eyes. "It wasn't right what Landers said. Not right and not fair. And so you know, not representative of how the rest of us feel." Mr. Shaw bent to study the skin on my hand, probably to give Tom a chance to compose himself.

"Thank you, Mr. Shaw." Tom's voice broke. I shot him a quick smile before he looked away.

Mr. Shaw led me over to the window to examine my hand more closely in the light. "You've got a bit of red starting at the edges. How did it happen?" He let go of my hand to fish around in his pockets. "Devereux and young Ringo are still intact, I trust?" Mr. Shaw pulled a tin of green medicine out and began slathering it on the open wounds.

"Hopefully. They were when I left." I told him in bold strokes everything that had happened since we left while he rewrapped my hand in a fresh bandage, also from his pocket. When I was finished, he turned to Tom.

"You have the cuff on you?"

Tom looked startled, but then nodded.

"Use it to figure out how to get her out of here."

"He's coming with me." As I said it I realized it was true. Tom needed a chance to make his own name, to get out from under the ones both his fathers carried.

Mr. Shaw looked speculative, but said nothing as Tom pulled the bracelet out from under the sleeve of his sweater. He took it off and looked into the convex mirror of the polished inside. I moved around behind him, but the only thing I saw were ghostly echoes of pictures. And then I touched Tom's arm.

Flashes of visions went past my eyes like old-fashioned newsreel. The Armans returning to the tower room and Mr. Shaw attacking them. Millicent in Miss Simpson's office screaming at the Armans. Mr. Shaw boosting us out of the window as we made our way to the attics. Doran looking in at the window at us trapped inside and shaking his head. Mongers striding in the front doors of the school to face a line of teachers. Wilder grinning at me from across Tower Green while a Monger rushed at me with a knife. A sword swinging down and slicing off Elizabeth's head.

Tom jerked his arm away from me and I gasped at the sudden loss of sight.

"Wow." I felt off-balance, like too much information had just downloaded into my head. Tom was just putting the bracelet back on when Mr. Shaw stopped him.

"No. Give it to Saira."

"It's my insurance," Tom protested.

"Her word is all the insurance you need. Give it to her."

Reluctantly, Tom uncuffed the bracelet from his wrist and gave it to me. Mr. Shaw helped me put it on and hide it under the sleeve of my sweater.

"Now, how are we getting you out of here?"

Tom didn't speak. Maybe he was still overwhelmed by all the different choices there were. But I knew. "We need a boost out of the window. Then I can hold Tom so the fall to the attic roof is doable, and you can drop me down after him."

"I don't like it." Mr. Shaw's voice was gruff, and I could hear the weird dad tones he pulled out when he was worried about me.

"Me neither." Tom sounded a little panicked, and I remembered from free-running lessons that he's afraid of heights.

I turned to Mr. Shaw. "It's what I do. I'll be fine. As soon as we get into the attics I'll Clock us out of there." Then I looked Tom straight in the eyes. "If you don't do this, I'm leaving you here. So deal."

He gulped and lost all color in his face, but then nodded. I got busy opening the window.

"Wait." I turned to Mr. Shaw. "Can I have the green medicine to take back with me?" He didn't even hesitate. He handed me the tin of green medicine and an extra bandage, both of which went into my back pocket with the bloody linen cloth from my hand.

"What else do you need? I brought my kit." He pulled out a small cloth roll and unwrapped it, pointing to things he named. "Aspirin, morphine, a scalpel, scissors, tape, antibiotics…" Then he emptied his other pocket. "A lighter, matches, a mini Maglite, spare batteries, and ether."

"Ether? Why are you carrying around a little jar of ether? Is it a narcotic?"

He shrugged. "You never know when you might need to knock someone out. Like a guard." He wrapped the cloth roll back up with the new additions and handed it to me. "The ether's highly flammable. Be careful with it." I nodded and stuck it in the waistband of my jeans, pulling my sweater down over it.

"You're pretty awesome, you know that, Shaw?"

He chuckled. "You're not so bad yourself, Elian."

The spring air felt like the hottest summer in comparison to the bone-chilling cold of the warded tower room. I climbed out on the ledge first, and Mr. Shaw insisted on holding onto my ankle just in case I suddenly decided to take a header off the roof.

Getting Tom to follow me out took a lot of coaxing and pushing and pulling, so I was glad to be anchored to something.

Tom finally sat on the ledge, but kept his eyes closed. I guessed the instinct to hurl himself off that some people have was actually pretty real for him. I got on my knees and Mr. Shaw held tight to my ankles while Tom grabbed one hand and one wrist, to make up for my injury, and slowly lowered himself off the window ledge. I finally understood the meaning of glacial, and more than once I was tempted to just let go and let him drop the full distance, but after about a decade, when we were both completely extended, it was time.

"You're going to land in a gully on the roof. Drop into a crouch first thing and that'll absorb some of the impact. I'm worried about the noise of breaking tile, so try not to scream and give anyone a reason to look up, okay?"

"You promise I can survive this?"

I considered the snappy comeback I would have made to anyone else and discarded it. "You can do it, Tom. You just have to see it in your mind."

"I did see it, remember?"

"Great, then do it just like you saw. Land, and then get out of the way so I don't use you as a body cushion."

He took a deep breath. My grip was starting to slip from his sweaty palms. "Okay." And then he let go.

To his credit, the scream he swallowed turned into more of a yelp when he landed, and he did okay on the tiles, but it looked like he might have twisted something.

"You okay?"

"I hurt my right ankle."

"Just a second. Move, and I'll be right there."

Tom shifted out of my landing zone and I leaned back up into the window. Mr. Shaw seemed surprised to see my face, especially when I took his big, ginger-haired one in my hands and kissed him on the cheek. "Thank you."

The gruff dad-voice was back. "Love you, kid."

I grinned. "Love you too." And then I extended down from his hands and let go.

The fall wasn't bad. I'd done that distance before, but usually onto the ground where I could take a step without hurtling off the roof. Tom looked like he nearly swallowed his tongue when I landed next to him, and his arm shot out to grab me when I threatened to take a step for balance.

"Thanks."

"Yeah."

"Okay, let me see your ankle." I knelt down next to him and gave it a cursory examination. "Well, if you survive this next bit, you'll live."

"Thanks." There was no smile on his face. Nothing but the grim line of his mouth.

Right. Absentee sense of humor. Got it. "Let's get down to the attics, shall we?"

"Yes."

And … we're down to monosyllabic answers. "Okay, wait here while I find the best window ledge to get to." I was across the roof before he could protest, but I doubted Tom had anything left but the sheer will not to vomit.

I was back in less than a minute. "I'll help you across this bit. There's an easy dormer to climb down and the window's already unlocked. I'll hold you so you can get inside first."

His ankle clearly hurt him as he hobbled across the rooftop, and I was pretty sure he just followed my directions with his eyes closed.

Behind us, in the Seer Tower, I could hear angry voices, and the Bear's booming yell over all of them. He said something about a spiral, and I hoped they believed we left through a portal instead of out the window. But I pushed Tom faster and we finally made it inside the attic with the window shut behind us.

It was a different wing from the one I'd visited with Olivia, and most of the box rooms seemed empty. A couple were still furnished as though they were maids' quarters, and one down at the end of the hall was locked.

332

"What are you doing, Saira? I thought we were spiraling out of here directly."

"We will. I'm just looking for any clothes that might disguise you in 1554." I looked at him closely. "Are you sure you still want to go back? I can wrap your ankle and give you an aspirin, but that's it for the painkillers."

"I'm not going to stay here. Not when I can do something there."

"Okay, then take off your shoe and let me stabilize your ankle first."

I wrapped my old bandage around Tom's ankle and tied it loosely. He stepped on it to try his weight.

"It's good. Better than before. Thanks."

"You're welcome. You want to help me look for stuff and we'll meet back here in five minutes?"

"Sure." We split off in different directions. I searched the furnished rooms, starting with the closets, which were empty. Then I rifled through drawers for any personal items that might have been left behind. I managed to scrounge a piece of candle and a linen handkerchief, but that was all. Tom was at the end of the hall waiting for me by the locked door, where he held up the key with a proud smile. "I've been practicing on locked rooms around school."

"Nicely done, Houdini." I was impressed. Apparently I didn't suck as a teacher of nefarious skills. He unlocked the door and pushed it open carefully.

I gasped.

Inside was an art studio. There were blank canvases propped against the wall, half-finished landscapes on various easels, and a table full of beautiful art supplies; oil paints, acrylics, pastels, colored pencils, pens, and brushes of all sizes and shapes. It was like one of my versions of heaven and I stepped reverently into the room.

"Lock it behind us but leave the key in the door." My voice was hushed like the way people speak in church, and I thought the comparison wasn't a bad one.

"Who works here?" Tom touched one of the brushes, and I resisted the urge to slap his hand away so he didn't get the oil from his skin on them.

The room was the last one on the hall, and the far wall was made of plaster. Swirled into the plaster, nearly invisible unless you caught it sideways to see the raised edges, was a spiral.

"It's Doran's."

I didn't bother to answer Tom's quizzical expression. I was too busy looking for clues to my cousin's world. There were no sketchbooks or inspiration boards or anything else to indicate his art came from anywhere but his memory or imagination. Some of the oil paints were so old they probably had arsenic in them, yet the acrylics all looked fairly new. There was a cobalt blue oil paint that I instantly coveted, and a metallic gold that looked like it was made from gold leaf. I pocketed both of those, and one small brush.

"What are you doing?" Tom had poked around a little, but mostly just watched me move carefully around the room.

"Leaving him a note." A Murano glass ink pen and a bottle of black ink stood on the table near a pad of drawing paper. My note informed Doran that I'd taken two of his paints and a brush, and would probably take the glass pen as well to give Elizabeth. I also told him I'd be back in 1554 if he wanted to find me, as there was the little matter of some tangled time that needed attention. Considering that my cousin had basically left me to deal with a deranged, Vampire-infected, time-traveling bishop on my own, he should consider helping me out. Although a frozen hell was likelier than Doran's assistance when it really counted. I really did try hard not to be snarky in my note, but I also didn't feel bad taking the pen and paints with me.

Tom finally noticed the spiral on the plaster wall. He pointed to it. "Hey, isn't that a—"

"Yep. If you're serious about doing this, you're going to want to hold on."

I stood right in front of the spiral and Tom hurried over to hang onto one of my belt loops as I began to trace the first spiral.

Aislin's cuff gleamed at me from my wrist and the hum started in my ears.

"Saira?"

"Yeah?"

'Thank you."

And just like that, we were gone.

CHOPPED

There was still about an hour before sunset, but the light outside the chapel's windows was strange. Overcast, like it was maybe going to rain. I had pictured the chapel perfectly in my mind, and somehow that seemed to make the travel easier. For me anyway. Tom was hunched over on the floor trying to keep the dry heaves at bay, but he was a puker, so it wasn't a shock.

"Come on. I need to change and get you out of sight."

"Change?" His voice was a little shaky.

"Clothes." I looked at the odd expression on his face. "I'm not a Shifter, you know. Only part."

He took a deep breath. "I didn't … I know." He looked around. "Where are we?"

"The chapel of the Royal Apartments. The building doesn't exist in our time."

"It's pretty."

People surprised me occasionally, usually when I didn't expect them to care about anything but themselves. The fact that Tom had noticed a room at all, much less thought it was pretty, that was one of those surprising things. It made me less grumpy with him. For the moment.

We slipped out of the chapel, and made it to the pages' annex with no issue. Which was odd to me. Before dark was usually the busiest, with people getting meals and setting up for night when the only light came from candles and fires.

Archer was still asleep, if it could be called that. It really was more like stasis. The bruise on his face was completely gone, and the sucking sound in his chest had disappeared. I touched his cheek softly but he didn't move a muscle. He was out cold.

The rest of the room was empty. "Where's Pancho?"

I wasn't talking to Tom, but of course it begged the question. "Who?"

"A kid we picked up. He kind of watches over Archer during the day." Tom's eyes were drawn to my sleeping Vampire, and I found myself wanting to put myself between them to protect Archer, even though I knew Tom was one of the few people from our time who accepted him.

I found my dress where I'd left it and tugged it on. I didn't bother turning my back to Tom because I left my camisole and jeans on underneath the heavy wool dress. He watched me with detached fascination. "How do you lace that up by yourself?"

"I don't." I turned my back to him and lifted my braid out of the way. "Don't pull too tight though. I'm a fan of breathing."

He did a credible job getting everything closed. "Thanks. I don't have anything for you to wear though, so don't go anywhere. I need to find Elizabeth and get her to try the cuff so we can figure out a plan to change things."

I topped the dress with my cloak and Tom seemed surprised. "You suddenly look like you stepped out of a fairy tale."

I nodded. "Yeah, I know. This one has a stubborn Seer and a villainous Vampire bent on drinking her blood."

He winced. "What do you need me to do?"

I looked at Archer and I wished I could wake him up and take him with me. "Can you hang here and fill him in on everything when he wakes up?"

"You don't need my help out there?"

I shook my head. "I'm just going to the queen's apartment. I'll be back soon."

With one last glance at Archer's sleeping form I left the annex, and despite the heavy skirts, I sprinted upstairs.

No one was outside the queen's apartment door.

Not good.

I slipped in through Ringo's room and found the door between the rooms open. There was no one inside either. There didn't seem to be any signs of a struggle, more like the women had just stood up and walked away.

It wasn't good at all.

I bolted back down the stairs and to the kitchens, meeting no one on the way, and when I stepped outside a heavy mist slapped me in the face like a wet blanket. I pulled my hood up and closed the cloak over my dress with a shiver. Something was wrong. As soon as I turned the corner, I realized why there was no one inside. Everyone was on the green.

Oh, no!

I sprinted toward the crowd gathered around the far end of the green. A small figure was running toward me in a panic, and I was just about to duck out of the way when I realized it was Pancho.

"They're gathering on the green! At the scaffold!"

Oh, God.

"I need to see him before they do it! I need him to know he's not alone." Pancho was nearly hysterical.

Wyatt. Of course. Wyatt would be executed on April 11, 1554. That must be it. I almost sagged in relief that all this wasn't for Elizabeth. Her vision was wrong, or she'd changed things already. That had to be it.

Pancho trembled and the tears started for real. My heart broke for the kid. He was trying to be so strong for his brother.

"Come on, I'll get you close. Pull the hood up on your cloak so it hides your face."

We ran toward the thickest part of the crowd, where they gathered around the scaffold. I expected the onlookers to be jeering or throwing things, but maybe that just happened in movies. These people were nearly silent as they watched the prisoner kneel in front of the block. His dark cloak hid his features, so maybe they were just waiting to see his face before they shouted insults at him.

338

We wove our way through about twenty onlookers before we got close enough to see the executioner. He was a smallish man, his hood covered everything except his eyes, and he leaned on a sword while Wyatt's cloak was removed.

Wait, that was a sword.

Wyatt didn't get a sword.

It wasn't Wyatt.

Long, reddish gold hair was swept to one side and bent toward the block.

Elizabeth's hair.

Elizabeth's neck.

No.

"No." The word was a whisper that died in my throat.

The sword raised up.

NOOOOOOO!!!!!

And slashed down.

The wet sound of the sword as it sliced through bone and flesh sent bile into my throat. I don't know if it was an actual scream that tore through me, but I couldn't breathe and I couldn't swallow.

All I could do was stare at the beautiful face of Elizabeth Tudor as her head rolled away from her body.

I might have blacked out for a second, but the thing I could finally focus on was Pancho's face in front of mine. He was terrified, and kept shaking me as if to wake me up.

"Go! Go find Archer! Wake him up! Tell him to come!" I might have whispered, or maybe yelled, but he heard me. Pancho's eyes searched mine one last time and then he ran for the Royal Apartments like his life depended on it.

A flash of silver caught my eye and Aislin's cuff taunted me from under the sleeve of my dress.

Despair welled in my chest. If only …

Wait.

I looked around me. The crowd was disbursing. People seemed to be in shock, and my own horror was echoed on several faces. I saw Courtney across the green, sobbing with giant, choking gasps while another of Elizabeth's ladies held her upright. Behind me was the White Tower, and I stumbled toward it, around the side, behind the corner tower.

I pulled Sanda's knife out of my boot, and with a shaking hand I started to carve a spiral.

Fixing a moment in time into my mind was pure desperation. It had to be the hour before dawn, the sky still dark and no one on the green. The edges of the spiral began to glow and I clutched at the moment in my mind with every ounce of my self-control. I had to go back. I had to fix this. I could do this if I had the time.

The jump was a short one. As if I'd skipped locations, not times. But I'd never gone back just twelve hours before. I'd never gone back to a time I had just left.

The fact that I hadn't skipped backward, past the moment when we first landed in 1554 told me I'd timed it right. The rules of time travel wouldn't let me be in the same time as myself, so I'd arrived after I left. It was pre-dawn. Elizabeth had a death sentence, Ringo was captured, Archer was in a healing coma, and I'd gone back to the present.

And somehow, I was still breathing.

I checked my wrist. Yes, I was wearing Aislin's intricate silver bracelet. That was the key to the unformed plan in my head.

I was still in my dress and hooded cloak, so I was able to slip back to the Royal Apartments without undue notice. Lurch was on duty and I almost lost my nerve. There was something so dark and evil about that guy. Demonic. That was it. I thought about what Charlie had said about being able to see the others, and I deliberately unfocused my eyes when I looked at him. But I didn't have Charlie's skill, I just had my own slightly animal instincts about predators and prey. And Lurch was most definitely of the predatory variety.

I concentrated on complete silence as I slipped into the first chamber and made my way to Ringo's room through the interconnecting doors. The one between his and Elizabeth's rooms was still open.

I crept up to the door and looked inside. Because I had no real plan, I was a little loathe to wake the princess again. But she was still up and sitting next to the fire while Courtney braided her hair. It really was kind of stunning that our coloring was so similar, since every painting I'd ever seen of her gave her bright orange hair. Maybe it was just odd enough that the artists played it up and made it as bold as possible, or maybe they just didn't have the right shade of gold to do us justice.

She turned toward the door like she was expecting to see me. "Did you find what you were seeking?"

"You knew I went?"

She spoke quietly to Courtney, who nodded, then left the room. Elizabeth waved me over to the fire. "I felt your return."

I was so tired, and when I sat down it felt like my bones melted. I unfastened my cloak and let it fall from my shoulders.

"Lady Elizabeth …" I took a deep breath, because I had absolutely no idea what to do or say. And then I realized I didn't need to know. I could just talk. "Okay, this is weird for me because I'm used to having the answers, or at least making other people think I do. But you're actually the perfect person to work this out with, because you're the greatest Seer on the planet."

I snuck a peek at her but her expression hadn't changed, so I continued. "I don't have a plan, and I need your help coming up with one. Archer's out until he heals, probably tonight, we need to rescue Ringo, and then we have to stop an execution. Your execution, to be exact. Because if we don't, time will split and a whole new timeline might be created. That could be very bad for everyone on it when the timelines rejoin, probably in 1888 at the moment Bishop Wilder went back in time."

She watched me closely. "I'm unfamiliar with the rules of time, but one of my teachers, Roger Ascham, was interested in temporal physics, so the concept of a split does make sense."

I tried not to let my jaw fall open. Didn't have as much luck with my eyes. "You understand that? I still don't and I've seen evidence it can happen."

Her gaze sharpened. "You have? When?"

341

"At home. Things are different. Not big differences yet, but it's pretty clear there will be." I twisted the silver cuff around my wrist. "It may not seem like a big deal to you, but if you don't become Queen Elizabeth I, my history will be pretty much unrecognizable."

Her short bark of laugh was bitter. "You say that, and yet nearly my whole life, despite an education tailored to a King's son, I have been assured I shall never be fit nor able to rule England."

I unclasped the cuff and handed it to her. "This belongs to you."

She held it uncertainly. "Aislin's cuff?"

"You know the story of it?"

"My mother's mother told me."

That surprised me. "The Seer line came through Ann Boleyn?"

She snorted. "My father was brilliant, but not wise. Though he made certain I was as much an orphan from the Sight as I was from a mother."

"Look into the concave part of the cuff. I watched another Seer get his visions from the smooth silver inside it."

"What will I see, Saira?"

I looked her in the eyes. "All the futures that could possibly be yours."

"And if I see those futures, what then?"

"Choose one."

The cuff had not stopped moving through her hands, as if she was memorizing the detailed carvings with her fingertips. Her eyes were still locked on mine, until finally she looked into the smooth interior of the silver cuff.

I resisted the urge to spy over her shoulder and instead concentrated on her eyes. They didn't go unfocused like Ava's always seemed to, instead they sharpened, almost like a hawk's when it saw prey. Something surprised her, then shocked her, then made her eyes narrow in anger. I was dying to know what that last one was, but from what I knew about history, the list was pretty endless.

I got up and went to the window. There was probably less than an hour of darkness left before dawn. I needed Archer to wake up. I needed Elizabeth to wake up. And we needed a plan.

Elizabeth was back to her absentminded exploration of the cuff's surface while she contemplated the flames dancing in the big fireplace. She looked up as I re-joined her.

"I'm afraid," she said.

I exhaled sharply. She got it. "Me too."

Tears sprang to her eyes. "What if I cannot accomplish all that I must to give England a chance at peace and strength and glory? What if I cannot live past this day?"

"I think you just choose your destination, then make sure that every step you take keeps you on that path." I was talking to myself as much as to Lady Elizabeth.

"Why does that sound so much easier than it likely is?"

"Probably because it's easier to know the right answer than to do what it takes to make it true."

"Perhaps it is as it was with Robin. The idea was a pretty one, but until I risked everything to make it real, I could never know the gloriousness of love."

"So, now we need to take a risk."

She smiled slowly. "May I keep this?" She indicated Aislin's cuff in her hands.

"It's yours. Just do me a favor and wear it for your coronation portrait?"

Her gray eyes danced with something that looked like acceptance. "I shall."

 SIGHT

We quickly laid out all our assets and liabilities. I told Elizabeth what I'd seen on the Tower Green, and I was perversely glad to see it bothered her. She'd been so blindly accepting of her fate before she'd looked into the cuff, and blind acceptance just pissed me off on principle.

I showed her things I'd found in Ringo's stash, and the medical items Mr. Shaw had given me. She was especially fascinated by the steel embroidery needles and the scalpel, and I knew I'd be leaving those behind with her when this was all over.

The highly flammable ether and the zippo lighter had a definite place in our arsenal, and even Courtney's ground-up apple seeds found their way onto our list of assets.

Elizabeth's fingers hadn't stopped moving along the cuff until one caught on something. "What is this?"

She showed me the small door and I shrugged. "Ava, my friend who is next in line to head the Seers, said it was a poison compartment. She used to pretend she was a princess, and it's how she would rescue herself from the bad guy."

Exactly one heartbeat later, we stared at each other with the same look of "that's it!" on our faces.

She picked up Courtney's apple seed powder. "Would this count as poison?"

"You have to ask Courtney. She kissed a guy to make it work."

Elizabeth's nose wrinkled delicately. "That might lessen its effectiveness, as I have no intention of kissing neither Mr. Alvin nor your Bishop Wilder."

"You're thinking of the Bell Tower?"

She looked me squarely in the eyes. "We've both seen it, haven't we." Not a question.

"I could go in your place. I've done it before."

"From a distance. And hooded. No, Saira. This is mine to do."

I looked sharply at her. "Then we should do it on our terms. Not wait for them to come to you."

We assembled weapons of needles, Sanda's knife, and the scalpel, and hid them among her skirts. Courtney mixed the apple seed powder into green medicine and packed it into the secret poison compartment of Aislin's cuff. She was careful not to touch it directly with her skin, and gave Elizabeth a handkerchief soaked in lavender water for cleaning her hands after she used it.

The plan was that Elizabeth would pre-emptively go to Lord John Brydges, the Lord Lieutenant of the Tower, to complain that her servant had been taken from her by Bishop Wilder. Since the only way into the Bell Tower was through his quarters she would sweep through the front door as if she owned the place, never giving Wilder the chance to come for her.

Once she was in the Bell Tower with Lord Brydges confronting Wilder, she'd work on getting Ringo released. As for the signed confession, that part was up to circumstance and she would play it by ear.

It grated on every nerve I still possessed that this whole rescue mission was squarely on Elizabeth's back. I had no control over any part of it, and would be lucky if I even got to know what happened. Lucky, because if I ever heard about it, Ringo and/or Elizabeth would have gotten out alive.

We were cutting it close, but I thought she still had a couple of minutes before Wilder and Lurch came for her. She gave me a quick hug that I wasn't expecting, then shooed me toward Ringo's room before she opened the door to the hall.

345

"Mr. Alvin. I wish to see Lord Brydges."

I had stepped back from the door, but was still close enough to hear the exchange. I held my breath.

"How 'bout I take ye to the bishop instead." The edge to his voice was like barbed wire, and there was a snide nastiness in his tone.

"You may do so when I've seen Lord John."

This time I could hear the leer in his voice when he spoke. "Or mayhap we'll just skip the Lord Lieutenant altogether."

Lurch reached into the room and snatched at Elizabeth's arm to pull her forward into the hall. She had just enough time to shoot me a terrified look before being pulled away from my outstretched hand. Lurch slammed the door shut behind her and we could hear her angry protests as he dragged her down the hall.

I looked at Courtney. "I have to go get the Lord Lieutenant."

"No! You'd be taken prisoner. Let me. He knows me as Milady's. I'll send him to her in the Bell Tower before the bishop can cause any harm."

"Any *more* harm, you mean." I said it under my breath because it didn't matter. Elizabeth's vision was playing out as she had originally seen it. My heart was pounding in my chest and I felt like I couldn't breathe, so I ran with Courtney down to the kitchen door to see her safely outside. There were no other guards on Elizabeth's rooms besides Lurch, so she was able to get out unseen. In her dark cloak, her figure was nearly invisible as she ran across the green in the barest light of dawn.

Then I realized there was another way I could See what was happening in that tower, and I raced back upstairs to the pages' annex. Pancho was curled up on a bench, and I envied him his twelve-year-old ability to sleep anytime, anywhere.

Archer was on his back and I lay down next to him with my head on his shoulder. His arm tightened around me reflexively and I could feel the pounding of my heart still to something resembling peace.

I whispered in his ear, hoping some part of his unconscious brain could hear me. "Show me the Bell Tower vision. Find Ringo and See him."

I scanned his face for any sign that he'd heard me. I traced his jaw gently with my fingertips and he seemed to sigh in his sleep. I closed my eyes, lulled by the warm spice that was his scent, and by the feeling of safety in his arms. And I would have slept except for the vision that suddenly filled my brain.

I spat in the bastard bishop's face.

Shock lit up Bishop Wilder's eyes and 'e slid the tip of 'is sword down from my neck to the base of me ribs, leaving a thin red line to mark the passage. 'E should 'ave run me through. The fact 'e didn't said 'e 'ad a worse fate planned.

"Shall we continue, Lady Elizabeth? I believe your lad, Ringo, can take more." The sudden grin on the bishop's face made my knees give way. The bishop pulled 'is sword back to grab for me 'fore I could hit the floor. Then 'e turned my head and pressed me down toward the privy.

Bishop Wilder's voice in my ear sent a chill through me. "Rest assured, young Ringo. I will have the name of the child, and then I will make your lady bleed."

I'd 'it the stones face first when I'd gone up the wall off Archer's back. The eye was swellin' shut an' I wondered what fancy medicine Saira might 'ave that could pull the filth of shite out o' the wound. Odd that I dwelled there at a time when I was goin' back into it. Maybe feelin' was too much, so thinkin' was all that was left. 'Is fist clenched and I braced for another dunk, but a poundin' on the door 'alted the push.

'E ground out a curse and the bit I could see o' the chamber told me dawn was comin'.

"See who it is," Wilder spat at the bastard Saira called Lurch.

'E threw me away from 'imself and I shifted my stumble toward the window. A slash of blood-colored light was wakin' the sky and I knew the bishop's time was runnin' out. Milady fumbled at her wrist, eyes locked on the bishop's every move. 'E wasn't watching 'er.

347

I could 'ear a man outside the door. 'E was blocked by Lurch from seein' inside, but I'd 'eard 'is voice before. It was deep and carried weight. "Stand aside, Warder. My business is with the bishop."

I edged closer to the window seat where the bishop kept Wyatt's confession. The bishop stepped up behind Lurch and whispered into 'is ear. Lurch nodded and drew back. The bishop slipped past 'im and out o' the room. "Lord Lieutenant Brydges. How can I assist you this morning?"

'E closed the door behind 'im with a firm snap.

Lurch turned to Milady with a leer and I itched to wipe it from 'is ugly mug. "I'm to keep you from shouting out to the Lord Lieutenant." 'E moved so fast I couldn't get there before 'is body was pressed against 'ers, and 'is filthy 'and covered her mouth.

I was 'alfway across the room when she did it. Milady bit down 'ard and drew blood. When 'e opened his mouth to yell, she swiped 'er fingers across it. I pinned 'is arm before 'e struck 'er face, but then 'is eyes went blank, 'is knees buckled, and 'e very nearly took us both down with 'im. I let go o' the arm and Milady wrenched 'erself out of 'is grip.

She was a fighter, that one. I could 'ave kissed 'er if she weren't a feckin' princess. But I 'ad a job to do. I made quick work o' the bench and pulled the box from it. 'Twere locked, but Milady drew a needle from the 'em o' 'er dress and handed it to me. The one eye 'ad closed properly now and the lock was slippery. But I'd earned the title 'thief,' one eye or no, and 'ad it open in the space of two breaths. I gave the paper to 'er and it disappeared into 'er bodice with a speed to rival mine on my best day.

Milady looked back at Lurch, the nerves showin' on 'er face.

"What now?" I tucked the box back in the seat and covered it. No sense raisin' the alarm first thing.

Milady stepped over Lurch's body and strode to the closed door of the tower. She pounded on the door with 'er fist. "Lord Brydges? I demand to be released from this tower at once!"

The determination in 'er voice was a thing to send men quakin' in their boots, and a bare moment later we could 'ear, footsteps in the 'all outside. The door opened slowly. 'Twere Courtney there, and 'er look of relief was wiped by a big grin.

"I think it is time for us to go, Milady. Don't you?"

348

"Yes!"

My exclamation startled Archer out of his vision … and his healing sleep.

"Saira?"

His eyes were clearing and he sat up gingerly. I slid back to his side. "Are you okay?" He still looked battered and so tired, but there was color in his skin again.

"What has changed?"

"Everything."

He searched my face. "You went back."

I nodded.

"Tell me."

There were only a couple of minutes before full dawn and I laid down next to him, our faces inches apart. "Elizabeth wants to live. She's seen a different future and we're going to make it happen."

Archer touched the cut that Phillip Landers gave me. "Someone hurt you."

"Phillip Landers. I'll tell you everything, but none of it matters here."

Frustration was written plainly across his face. I knew that feeling of helplessness. Knew it and understood the cost of it. "I can't be here when you wake up tonight. I'm so sorry."

"You're going back?" There was hurt in his tone, and maybe anger. I reached for his face and held his cheek in my hand so he had to look at me.

"I'll be out at the green. I've already done it so I can't change it. I'm bringing Tom Landers back with me and he'll be here to tell you the plan. Try not to eat him."

I'd succeeded in turning the shock to a smirk. "If it was Adam, I don't think I could make that promise. But I like Tom."

If he was making a joke he would be okay. *We* would be okay.

He stared into my eyes like he was willing the information to seep from my brain into his.

"I'm sorry I can't do this with you." He sounded resigned. And bitter.

"Me too. You make better plans than I do."

"Here's a plan. Ringo's safe now. Why don't you take him back?"

I shook my head. "Even if I wanted to, he wouldn't let me. They killed Elizabeth the first time. Neither of us will let it happen again."

Archer closed his eyes as if everything hurt, and I could tell the sun must have risen because he couldn't fight me anymore. I kissed him gently on the lips. "You have to be able to count on me. You always protect us when you're awake, trust me to protect us when you're asleep."

He forced his eyes open to meet mine. "I do trust you."

The thing was, I believed him. Because I knew how much it cost him to let me take care of myself.

"I'm choosing this, Archer. This is my fate because I say it is." The last piece of fear broke free and I let it go. "I love you, and we *will* get through this."

His eyes closed and I eased his head down onto the bedroll. I kissed his jaw before I rubbed my eyes tiredly.

Pancho sat up quietly and I knew he'd been listening.

"Tell me how I can help."

PLAN A

Elizabeth and Courtney were already back in the queen's apartment by the time Pancho and I slipped in through the interconnecting rooms. An older Yeoman Warder was on duty outside her door, someone I hadn't seen before. I wondered where Peterson was, and how long Lurch would be out, or if he'd even wake up.

"Where's Ringo?" No preliminaries, just straight to the thing that mattered to me most in that moment.

"He's gone to the kitchens to wash. Who is this?" Elizabeth's eyes were on Pancho.

"Lady Elizabeth, meet Francis Wyatt, youngest brother of Thomas Wyatt."

Pancho flinched. His brother was the reason Elizabeth was being held prisoner in the Tower of London. He bowed deeply. "My Lady. I am so very sorry my family has caused you such hardship and grief. Would that I could take it from you to carry as my own."

Wow. Those were some pretty words. I guess there was something to be said for a noble upbringing.

There was a look of anguish on his face as Elizabeth lifted his chin. "Your brother's actions were merely the timing of my imprisonment in this place. I have been a prisoner far longer than this, young master Wyatt. And in this moment, at least ..." Elizabeth looked at me over Pancho's head. "... I feel quite remarkably free."

Ringo walked in at that moment, scrubbing his hair dry with a piece of linen cloth. He had on a fresh shirt and pants, a magnificent black eye, and the only thing I recognized, besides the cheeky grin on his face, were my boots.

I was grinning too. "Who'd you steal the clothes from?"

He shrugged. "Alvin. Left 'im 'is stockin's though."

"That was generous." I gave him a hug despite the risk of hurting him, and the way he hugged me back let me know we were okay.

I pulled Mr. Shaw's green medicine out of my pocket. "Sit," I commanded. Surprisingly, he obeyed, and I was able to slather the ointment on the broken skin around his eye socket.

"Must've killed ye to let Mistress Courtney come for us, eh?"

He knew me that well. "I saw you through Archer. You were amazing. All of you." I included Elizabeth and Courtney in my gaze.

Ringo looked at Elizabeth with pride. "Milady was brilliant. Until the day I die I'll never forget the 'orror on Alvin's face to know 'e'd been bested."

Then his face turned serious again as he looked at me. "And his lordship? That fall broke bones, I'll wager."

My voice dropped to a strained whisper. "I thought he was dying." Ringo gripped my hand and I held his gratefully. "I was so mad that he wouldn't let me help ..." I met his eyes meaningfully and Ringo's expression told me he knew what I meant. I took a deep breath and let go of his hand. "But since I'm the reason you both got hurt, it's pretty hypocritical to be mad."

Ringo snorted. "Back to the hair shirt are ye?"

"I'm starting a collection. One in every color."

"And damned arrogant, too."

I looked at Ringo, startled. His eyebrow raised in a fair imitation of Archer's. "'I' think we'd blindly follow ye wherever ye tell us to go? Give us both a little credit, would ye? We're grown men. We know what we're on about."

The knots of guilt loosened in my stomach. "You're right. You're both right. And Archer's healing while he sleeps, like he said he would."

"Yer all witnesses, see? Saira Elian 'as admitted someone besides 'erself could be right."

There was relieved laughter around me, and I included the others in my gaze as I sat back and wiped my hands clean. "And since I'm not the most right person in the room, I have an idea that I want to run past you all. It's stupid and crazy and everything else that makes it a bad plan, but it's bold enough that it might actually work."

Elizabeth sent one of her other ladies for some food and ale, and we sat around the table in Ringo's room discussing every feature and every flaw of my plan.

The main thing, as far as I was concerned, was keeping time intact. Ripples we could deal with. Inertia would take care of that – I hoped. A full-on split was the thing my history couldn't handle. If Elizabeth hadn't been queen for forty-four years everything from religion to exploration to the arts would have been different. For God's sake, the woman was patroness to Shakespeare, Marlowe, Drake and Raleigh, none of whom would have had a chance in a Catholic England. And I told her so.

"You might be altering exactly what you wish to keep intact by telling me all of this." Elizabeth seemed a little overwhelmed by the highlight reel of her reign.

"Maybe. But maybe I'm just telling you to be extraordinary. Because according to my history, you will be."

"And if I choose not to be?" I could see the flash of defiance in her eyes and I bit back a smile. Because we were more alike than either of us would ever admit.

I looked her straight in the eyes, the way Mr. Shaw would have looked at me in the same situation. "Then none of this will have been worth it. We all will have risked everything for nothing. And that's not who you are."

The defiance was still there, but I knew the words landed with her.

353

Because they would have landed with me too.

Ringo got us back to business. "Personally, I like the flash-bang crowd-distractions of the plan. But gunpowder is locked in storerooms and under 'eavier guard than she is." He indicated Elizabeth, who had gone to the window and was staring out at the activity below her. I'd seen the view about an hour before, but the carpenters building a scaffold depressed me too much, and I'd stayed away from the window since then.

"I know that, but we can make some," I said

His eyes narrowed, and then gleamed. Ringo was definitely not going to say no to explosives.

I continued, "But we need saltpeter and sulfur. And those are going to be pretty nasty to collect."

I turned to Elizabeth. "Do you know where we can get an alembic?" Her eyes came into focus slowly. "It's one of those glass retort containers chemists use to distill things."

"The physik makes distillations. Perhaps we can get one from him?" She looked at Courtney for confirmation. Courtney nodded. "I bring him herbs sometimes. Show me how it looks and I shall ask him for one."

I drew one for her and she nodded. "I have seen such a thing in his chamber."

"Can you find some cinnamon too?"

She looked startled. "Not easily."

Oh, right. Not native to England. I pulled out the kit Ringo had put together before we came back in time, but kept Mr. Shaw's cloth roll tucked in my dress. "Take anything in there you think you can trade. I need about this much." I cupped the palm of my hand and her eyes got even bigger.

"Perhaps only the Lord Lieutenant's cook would have that amount on hand." She picked through the things on the table, then finally took a small paring knife, a needle and some embroidery thread. "These may do. I warn you, the alembic will be much easier to procure than the spice."

And so the day went as we searched for the supplies. I sent a very reluctant Pancho outside the walls, to the field where the

354

privies emptied, to scrape up the white saltpeter. Courtney left to trade for the cinnamon and some sulphur. I collected the urine concentrate from the privy myself. I wasn't going to ask Ringo to go anywhere near a privy for a long time.

Elizabeth had the most important job of all. She had her Yeoman Warder guard escort her to the Lord Lieutenant's lodgings where she made a plea for her life. The fake confession Ringo stole would have guaranteed the queen's signature on her sister's death warrant, but we hadn't changed what had actually happened in history. The unsigned warrant would still go to Lord Brydges, and he was the only one who could officially stop Elizabeth's execution. It was the key to keeping the historical damage down to the ripple variety, rather than full splitsville. It also helped make Elizabeth angry at the crappy hand she was being dealt, instead of resigned to whatever fate she thought she had.

And while Elizabeth and the guard were inside with Lord Brydges, Courtney and Pancho, disguised as one of Elizabeth's ladies, were setting up a kind of trip wire outside the guard's quarters. They used kitchen twine and a variation on the high-tension rabbit snare I'd learned from Alex. Pancho had grumbled about the dress but decided that trap-setting was worth it.

Meanwhile Ringo was stealing every glass jar and bottle he could get his hands on without getting caught. I felt a little bad that I'd been responsible for turning him back into a thief, but he just smirked and said he'd been getting bored anyway.

We turned the room beyond Ringo's into a laboratory, and once I had the alembic I taught Ringo how to light a fire using a Maglite battery and the piece of steel wool I had kept with me ever since Mr. Shaw's fire-starting class. Then we set the alembic up so the spout dripped into one of Ringo's stolen bottles. We made a best-guess mixture of the urine, cinnamon and charcoal dust from the fireplace, and my little white phosphorus distillery was in business. I knew I was playing with something much more dangerous than fire, but with Ringo watching avidly over my shoulder and Mr. Shaw's voice ringing in my ear, my confidence may have been a bit higher than common sense would dictate.

Pancho and Courtney returned first, and Ringo put them to work grinding up saltpeter and sulphur, while we planned the best way to test the ratios with charcoal for the most explosive gunpowder.

"There's a tunnel that connects the Royal Apartments to the White Tower. We could go down there to try out explosiveness," suggested Ringo.

"Because that's a good idea," I snorted, "explosives in an enclosed space. How are you going to light the gunpowder that we don't even know works?" Despite my dry tone, I couldn't help the little thrill of excitement I got at the word 'tunnel,' and I didn't want to be responsible for collapsing something with such coolness potential.

Ringo looked at me like I was missing a couple pages of the script. "A fuse, a'course. What else?"

"Show me the tunnel."

Mostly I just wanted to see the secret passage Ringo had found, but we really did need a way to test our concoction. The white phosphorus couldn't be tested. It was a one-time deal. But the gunpowder was all about ratios, and I had absolutely no idea if we were even in the ballpark of something incendiary with our mix.

The entrance to the tunnel was under the northern kitchens, where the storage rooms had been built. Ringo showed me a small doorway behind some stacked crates that led to a low-ceilinged tunnel. The structure wasn't particularly big or long, but the room it emptied into was much more interesting.

"We're in a sub-crypt of St. John's Chapel, under the White Tower." Ringo's whisper was dramatic and gave me a lovely chill. It was a fantastic space, with huge support pillars holding the arched brick ceiling. The only light came in through narrow slits near the upper corners, and I thought they must also provide the fresh air. We both instinctively circled the room, and Ringo was

356

the one who spotted the anomaly in the wall at one end of the chamber. "What's this?"

There was an uneven section in the wall, about chest-height, with the uniformity and size of a breadbox. I picked at the brick with fingertips, then resorted to using the tip of my knife to chisel it free. The piece looked like it had been added after the wall was built, and it didn't take much to finally slide it out in one solid chunk. I was about to reach into the black hole, but hesitated, the victim of one too many horror films of grabby arms and biting creatures. Ringo reached in and removed a dusty wood box carved with scrolling vines and flowers. The woodwork was beautiful and looked old.

Ringo held the box so I could open it, and I gasped.

"There's a jewel house right upstairs. Why hide the crown in the crypt?"

Ringo's eyes gleamed with the gold of the small, plain circlet topped with a cross I'd unwrapped from a piece of velvet. "Don't trust each other much, do they? Put it on."

I shook my head. Uh uh. "No way. People who try on crowns they have no right to lose their heads. I may be superstitious, but there's a reason Elizabeth is a prisoner in this place. And this crown is it."

Ringo looked disappointed. "So I guess we shouldn't give it to her either."

"Not a chance. We should tell her where it is though. I have a feeling there are probably only about three people in England who know about this hiding spot. And two of us are here."

I'd never heard anything about a secret stash of crown jewels being held anywhere else but the jewel house, but with the current political climate, she who controlled the crown might just control the kingdom.

I wrapped the hammered gold back up in the silk velvet cloth and replaced it in the case Ringo still held. He gave the box a last look of longing, then tucked it back into the recesses of the hole.

"Well, that was fun." I tossed my braid over my shoulder. "Makes me feel a little like Lara Croft. Well, except for the long

357

dress. And, you know … boobs." I smirked at the look of horror on Ringo's face. "The butt-kicking I can do though."

He shook his head. I was clearly a lost cause in the arts of feminine delicacy. So just for good measure I took a running jump past him through a doorway into the next part of the cellar.

This room had potential. It was in the middle of the underground cellar complex and had no light slits to carry sound up to the surface. But best of all, there seemed to be a well in the floor. At least that's what it sounded like when Ringo dropped a rock down it. I had clicked on my Maglite, and a quick tour of the space showed us the well was probably our best bet for explosives testing.

The carriage of sound was my biggest worry, but Ringo solved that problem for me. The cannons on the roof of the White Tower were fired twice a day, just after dawn and just before sunset. It wouldn't give us much time to fix things if the gunpowder didn't work, but at least the noise would mask a test.

As far as Ringo knew, the floor above us wasn't used for munitions storage. So, as long as we didn't accidentally blow anything up, we could probably get away with our plan. And once we found the right mixture of elements, we could get busy with our flash-bang distraction.

Elizabeth had returned to the Royal Apartments by the time we got back. She looked worried.

"Lord Brydges is stodgy and ill-tempered. He has no love for me or for Protestants in general, and I believe he blames me personally for the fact that the Tower is at present so crowded with prisoners."

"What did you tell him?"

She shot me a glare. "I informed him that despite my sister's current state of political crisis, under no circumstances would she sign a death warrant against me. And as I have done nothing wrong, to execute me on anything less than her full signature would be tantamount to murder, for which he alone would be responsible."

"Nicely put." I was impressed. Elizabeth in queen mode was scary.

She smiled and some of the tension shifted in the room. "Thank you for the preparation. I'm not sure I would have dared speak to a man like that otherwise."

I grinned back. "Well, apparently your brands of flirting and fighting are particularly effective during your reign, so get used to it."

"Flirting and fighting. I like that."

I left Ringo and Pancho in the laboratory measuring out different formulas for the gunpowder, and went in search of Courtney. She was in a little anteroom off the queen's apartment and was just finishing the alterations on a dress. She shook it out and held it up.

"Here, try it on. You're bigger than Milady around the shoulders, and I added some length to the skirt, but otherwise it should fit."

With Courtney's help I pulled my green brocade dress off and her eyes widened at my camisole and jeans. "What manner of undergarments are those?"

"The kind that allow me to run and climb."

She studied me with a critical eye as I struggled with the stays in the midnight blue dress she'd altered for me. "I think I must make a pair for Milady. For when she rides her horse."

I giggled at the idea of Elizabeth Tudor in a pair of jeans, and muffled the sound in the fabric of the dress as I dropped it over my head. Courtney helped me lace up the back, and when she was done, she made me twirl to show her the fit.

My way of testing the fit was to swing my arms in a circle to make sure I didn't tear out the back, and both of us were satisfied in the end. "Unbind your hair and I shall brush it out for you."

The braid I'd worn since my shower at home made my hair wavy. "Shouldn't I be wearing something on my head?"

"Unmarried women may go bare-headed, and a coif is worn out of respect. I hardly think Milady would be feeling respectful on this day."

When my hair was loose and brushed out I turned to face Courtney. She looked me over with a critical eye. "From a distance, just as with the garden, you have the right height and hair color. If you remain hooded until the end, none will notice."

"Thank you for this. It's actually a lovely dress. I'm a little afraid to get it dirty."

Courtney gave me a straight-in-the-eye look. "If she wore it today, it would not be dirt stains marring the fabric. Thank *you*, Milady."

She'd never called me that before, and I was conscious of the compliment.

I hadn't told anyone else what Courtney was doing because I was afraid they'd try to stop me. At least Ringo would, and maybe even Elizabeth. But I didn't see any way around it. Elizabeth couldn't go out onto that green. She couldn't put herself anywhere near the blade of that sword if we wanted to ensure the timeline, and her neck, stayed intact. There were still a million things that could go wrong and we had probably only accounted for about five of them. But if I had anything to say about it, Elizabeth Tudor's head would not leave her shoulders today.

Mine might, but the way I'd managed to avoid thinking about that, they'd have a tough time finding where I'd buried it in the sand.

The missing piece of my outfit was a cloak. I asked Courtney to bring me Elizabeth's finest one. It's the thing the spectators and guards would see, and for some people, would be the only way to identify me, since most people had probably never seen their princess in person.

When I returned to Ringo's rooms the Lady Elizabeth had a body double, and I was it. Pancho was lining up flasks of gunpowder on the table, and Elizabeth was coiling waxed twine into manageable piles by the window. When Ringo walked in with two bottles of white phosphorus I was worried he'd drop them. The look on his face told me he knew exactly what I was doing – and he didn't like it one bit.

"Ye're not goin' out there."

I narrowed my eyes at him. "You've been spending too much time with Archer."

"Maybe so. And I don't want to have to answer the question 'e'd ask."

I could have gotten mad. I was inclined to. But I knew he was right. If I was going to put him in an impossible situation with Archer, he needed to be able to defend himself. Elizabeth looked ready to launch herself into the discussion too, so I included all of them in my gaze.

"I'm taking Elizabeth's place on the block because I'm the only one who can. Courtney would, but no one would believe her height, and all her other ladies are too small. I know you hate the idea, but that's why you're my insurance."

I turned to Elizabeth and spoke directly to her. "Believe me, if I thought there was any other way to keep the time line intact, I would do it. But you can't die on the scaffold today. And when Wilder realizes he's been denied your blood, he's going to come after you himself. You're going to have to hide someplace where he can't find you."

"I will not have you fight in my stead." Her best imperious voice was on, but it was no match for mine since I'd put on her clothes.

"You will. And there's something you should see anyway, since you're going to be queen."

Ringo finally nodded his agreement. "Right. That's the first good plan I've heard since I walked in. And it's time I take these to the gentlemen who'll be 'elpin'. Pancho, ye comin'? We're off to see yer brother and give 'im 'is chance for a bit o' payback."

Elizabeth pulled a letter out of her skirt pocket and handed it to Ringo.

"Would you see Robin gets this, please? And tell him …" The worried look was back, and Ringo's expression softened.

"Ye'll tell 'im yerself, Milady. 'E's only droppin' flashbangs and won't be in the fray. And neither will ye be. When this is all over there'll be time to tell 'im anythin' ye like."

He bowed to her, tucked the glowing yellow glass bottles under his arms, and headed for the door.

"Be careful with those, Ringo. I need all your fingers intact if you're going to hold that sword."

THE SWORD

It was late when Ringo and Pancho returned. Pancho's eyes were red from crying, but we all pretended not to notice. Ringo bowed over Elizabeth's hand and kissed the back of it carefully. "From his lordship, Milady. He bids you strength and grace in the face of yer enemies, and stands with ye against all who seek harm."

He smiled a little wickedly. "And I can't give ye the other thing Dudley sent, 'cause then 'e'd 'ave to hunt me down and kill me."

Elizabeth laughed a soft and lovely laugh I'd never heard before. It transformed her face from striking and interesting to delicate and beautiful. No wonder she was able to navigate her early reign so effectively. Men would probably fall all over themselves to get a laugh like that from her.

It definitely went into the 'note to self' category as I figured out who I was going to grow up to be.

I gave Ringo a searching look. "Packages delivered?"

"And received with great enthusiasm by both parties."

"Wyatt and Dudley know their signal to drop the phosphorus?"

Pancho's voice broke the first time he tried to use it, so he tried again. "I shall set off an explosion under the Beauchamp tower that they can see, so they do not confuse the cannon fire for the signal."

"And then get the hell out of the way."

Pancho looked at me. "Yes, ma'am. No one will be the wiser."

"Good." I looked back at Ringo. "We should take Elizabeth downstairs now. It's almost time." Ringo and I had told Elizabeth about the crypt under St. John's Chapel, but we wanted to surprise her with the crown.

Ringo went into the hall to speak to the old Yeoman Warder. He was back a few moments later. "Yeoman Warder William has assured me that Milady's rooms are always very quiet, so any lack of noise 'ere will go unnoticed by 'im."

I stared at him. "How do you do that?"

Ringo grinned. "I met William when I arrived at the Tower. 'E told me I should bow to Milady in this direction if I was so inclined."

Elizabeth nodded. "Then I should do well to remember William when I am queen."

"'E'd appreciate it, Milady."

I indicated the door to the interconnected rooms. "Lady Elizabeth?"

Courtney marched forward. "I'm coming too."

"I'm going to set a ward. You'll feel the cold."

She pulled a fur off Ringo's bed and draped it around her shoulders, leveling a fierce gaze on me. "I'll not be leaving my Lady alone."

Clearly.

We were not a particularly stealthy group as we made our way down to the tunnel entrance. Pancho had taken a fuse and the book of matches, which I'd shown him how to light. He went out to hide himself under Beauchamp tower, but the rest of us traveled to the sub-crypt of St. John's chapel. I had left a long note for Archer outlining the steps of the plan and explaining what he and Tom should do when he woke. I signed it, 'I love you, -S', but I hoped he would be able to feel what was underneath the words.

The way to the sub-crypt was deserted, and Elizabeth was surprised to learn such a chamber existed under the White Tower.

"This is the part we wanted you to see, though." Ringo dug the brick patch out of the wall and pulled the carved wooden case out of its hideaway. Elizabeth's hands shook as she held the crown. It was a simple circle with four gold arches meeting in the middle where a hammered cross rose up to top it. A few roughly cut gemstones were embedded in the metal, but it wasn't quite the elaborate beauty I remembered from paintings.

"That this lies here gives truth to the turmoil of my country. There are those who mistrust my sister not to give it away to Spain, and so they have hidden it away."

"Don't let them hide this crown from you." I knew I was preaching to the choir the way Elizabeth's eyes flashed.

"It is a symbol of England's trust in its monarch. If I survive this night, I shall endeavor to be worthy of its proud display."

"I've seen your coronation portrait, remember? You may want to add a few more jewels though. And maybe some pearls." I kept my tone light on purpose.

Elizabeth smiled. "I love pearls."

"I know. And someday, when you buy your cousin's six-strand black pearls, you should probably hide them somewhere. Because in 1649 the crown jewels get broken up and melted down."

Elizabeth gasped in horror. "They dare!"

I grinned. "You're going to be a *great* queen."

Suddenly, above us came the sound of cannon fire. Ringo and I looked at each other in a panic. "They're early!"

Elizabeth's expression had turned to fear. "They fire cannons for executions too. They have signaled it is time."

"But it's *not* time yet!" My voice was tinged with hysteria and Elizabeth took my hands in hers.

"Saira, I owe you my life and the future of my people. My words are not nearly big or meaningful enough to convey the depth of my gratitude." She leaned in to kiss my cheek. "Thank you."

I took a deep breath. "Just make it worth it." The look on her face told me she would. "Okay, Ringo, I'll meet you in the tunnel." I turned to Elizabeth. "I've never warded a room before, but I know it can be done. So, I'm going to try for something I can leave behind to keep you both safe from anyone who wants to hurt you. But if you see Wilder or Lurch, you have to *run*. Or if you can't run, hide. Clear?"

They both nodded and Ringo stepped out of the room. I pulled a ward up and consciously *pushed* it out past the barriers of my skin. I kept *pushing* as I concentrated on filling the room with the magical barricade. I was shivering when I'd finished, and Courtney looked a little scared of me. "You feel that, right?" My eyes were on her and she nodded. "Okay. Wow." I was exhausted and more than a little shaken. But I didn't have time to be anything other than strong, so I found Elizabeth's eyes and felt her determination give me back a little strength.

She smiled at me. "You are the strongest person I know."

That, coming from Elizabeth Tudor, was the best compliment I could imagine.

William was still outside the queen's apartments, but had his back to the corridor as we slipped in through the connecting room. Ringo quickly helped me with the deep hood of my cloak, and I sat by the window with Elizabeth's other ladies arrayed around me. I hadn't bothered to learn their names since they all seemed afraid of us, but now I was relying on them for my life. If any one of them revealed I wasn't Elizabeth ... I couldn't even think about it.

Ringo kneeled in front of me and looked in, past the hood, to the grim expression on my face. "The plan is a good one."

I ticked off my fingers. "We're going to use explosives we haven't tested. We're relying on prisoners, a maid, and a kid to create diversions. And that's not even counting the executioner you're going to try to take down. Seriously? What's the worst that could happen?"

Ringo smirked at me. "From what you've told me, it's a game you play often."

Panic and laughter battled for dominance. Uncharacteristically, panic won. "But even if everything goes perfectly, what then? We don't have a plan for after." I whispered so the ladies couldn't hear, but the desperation still carried in my words.

"We don't need one. We'll have Archer then."

He had total confidence in a man he'd only known a few months. I felt like the Grinch whose heart grew three sizes with the love I felt for both guys.

He lifted my hand quickly and kissed the back of it before striding from the room. I picked up Elizabeth's prayer book from a table where she'd left it and absently flipped through the pages, just to stop my heart from choking me. There were notes in the margins, in Elizabeth's tight handwriting, and I turned back to the cover to examine it more closely. It was bound in red tapestry and had red fabric ties to hold it closed. Inside, the inscription was to Elizabeth from Katherine Parr, and I realized I held a book in my hands that would one day belong to my mother.

"May I borrow a bowl?" I asked the lady sitting closest to me, a pretty brunette whose name I thought was Hannah.

"Of course, Milady." She brought me a small painted dish and sat near me pretending to sew like the other ladies.

I pulled the cloth roll out of my dress and unwrapped it, then dug out the Murano glass pen and paints I'd swiped from Doran's studio. Dumping a little cobalt and a little gold paint into the dish, I used the pen like a very fine paintbrush on the inside of the back cover. I was conscious of the time and figured the guards would be coming for me any minute, but I still lost myself in the swirls and spirals of the design. When it was finished, Hannah leaned over to look more closely.

"The 'E' is beautifully wrought and Milady will think it very fine indeed. But what of the 'C'? What meaning does that have?"

"A personal one. I don't think Lady Elizabeth will mind." I wiped the paint from the glass tip of the pen. The sound of men's voices carried from the hall and suddenly the quiet tension in the room had shifted to agitation. I tucked a candle stub in my pocket and then quickly hid the cloth roll back in my dress. I had removed the antibiotics, which I left with the prayer book under Hannah's sewing. "Make sure Milady gets this. There are medicines in the brown bottle that will help fight illness."

I tugged the hood of the cloak further down, pulled some hair over my shoulder so it showed down the front of the cloak, and counted on expectation to mask me. The door swung open and three men entered the room. William was first, looking dignified and solid, followed by Lurch. He wasn't looking too hot, and I wondered idly how much cyanide it would take to kill a demon. But the third man walked in and the dead-rat stench of Lurch was overpowered by waves of ick rolling off Wilder.

I clasped my hands in front of me to hide their trembling, and kept my head bowed as if I was praying. I might have been. Praying. Throwing a general shout out to whatever gods might be listening. I couldn't hear the words though, because tsunamis of nausea pounded on the rocks of my courage.

"Lady Elizabeth. Despite the efforts of the criminals you call friends, I have with me a warrant for your execution. You will come with me now and meet your fate."

He held his hand out to help me up but I ignored it, afraid that if he touched any part of me he'd know the truth. I said nothing, and Elizabeth's ladies parted around me. But when I passed Wilder he leaned in and whispered into my ear, "And when your body lies dead, I shall make my own fate by stealing yours from your blood."

I shuddered violently and nearly vomited. He must have sensed it because he stepped back from me and took up the forward position as our little group left the queen's apartment.

The visions I'd seen through Elizabeth's and Archer's eyes and the reality of the moment had blended in a way to make the edges too sharp and the colors too bright. It was like looking at a 3D screen without the glasses, and the shaking in my hands was getting worse. Wilder stepped away to the side before we got out to the green, and I sensed that his whole focus was now on the wait for my headless body. Well, too bad. He couldn't have it.

The people lining the walk to the scaffold were all Tower folk – men and women I'd seen working and living in the Tower complex. It wasn't a public execution; that would have been done on Tower Hill, but it was public enough. The people were mostly quiet, with some murmurings as William and Lurch escorted "the princess," which I heard muttered, to the scaffold. This wasn't a popular execution, and I knew Mary wasn't a popular queen.

My face was hidden in the hood of my cloak, but the waves of long gold hair just visible down the front, and the fine cloak and dress were enough to show the people what they expected to see: Elizabeth Tudor walking to her death. It was dusk, but the overcast sky that had made Wilder's rise possible would hopefully also give Archer a head start on the night. I wondered though, since everything seemed earlier than it had happened the first time. We finally reached the scaffold after what felt like a thousand steps. The executioner was a small man, and I didn't recognize the eyes glittering at me from beneath his hood. I hoped Ringo was here, because this man looked like a professional who wouldn't hesitate to complete the downward swing once his sword had been raised above my neck.

I climbed the steps to the scaffold on shaky legs, and Lurch pushed me to my knees in front of the block. I resisted the urge to punch him, but only because malice rolled off him in waves. It was a relief when he stepped back from me.

The executioner readied his stance and I bowed my head. A priest in a long robe stepped onto the scaffold with a prayer book in his hands. He began reciting something in Latin and I smiled for the first time. My Shakespeare-reading, bible-knowing, video-gaming friend had learned some Latin, too.

Ringo finished his recitation and stepped back to the edge of the scaffold. From the corner of my eye I saw him kick something off the side and suddenly there was a flash of light.

BOOM!

People screamed. Yeoman Warders poured out of the Lord Lieutenant's Lodgings, and five of them went down on the rabbit-snare trip wire. The executioner ripped back the hood of my cloak just as Ringo pushed him off the scaffold and dove after him.

BOOM!

Another explosion ripped through the courtyard, and the crowd swarmed like cockroaches scurrying away from the light and noise. More Yeoman Warders emerged, stepping over their struggling comrades. I pulled my candle end from under the cloak and began drawing on the scaffold floor.

A spiral. My exit plan.

BOOM!

The third and final explosion filled the green, and the executioner climbed back up onto the scaffold, his giant, deadly sword in hand. He raised the sword with both hands, and for a moment I thought Ringo was dead and the executioner was going to finish his job.

"Stop! Stop! There will be no killing today!"

The voice came from far away, and I thought, idly, that Lord Brydges had finally grown a pair.

Too late. The sword was poised over my body. The hooded executioner stood ready to swing.

The hum and glow of the spiral I'd nearly finished wouldn't save me this time.

"Saira. Go!"

Ringo. It was Ringo under the executioner's hood, holding a sword over me. Protecting me.

So I went.

I'd barely even finished the spiral before I felt a pull *between* that forced me out of the moment. And until I was in the nothingness, I realized I hadn't chosen when to land.

My brain screamed. My lungs burned for air and my body stretched and pulled like a rubber band with no substance beyond the sound that felt like the end of sanity.

I hadn't locked onto a time.

I had nothing to guide my Clocking.

Nothing to help me land.

And then I slammed into the ground so hard whatever breath was left in my lungs was crushed out of me. I'd been hurtled out of *between*, thrown out like something distasteful or wrong.

I cracked my eyes open. Looked out into the first darkness of night.

Okay. I was outside. The smell of the grass under my cheek confirmed it.

I rolled over and looked up a tower like I was looking up its nose. The White Tower. But when?

I held onto the white stone wall as I dragged myself to my feet. I looked down to see Elizabeth's clothes on my body. Had I slipped in time? Had I skipped the part when I was there, to return the moment after I'd gone forward to change things? Was that why I'd been thrown out of *between* so hard?

I gulped at the night air, thick with mist, and steadied my legs under me. Breathe, Saira. And think.

It was dark. Archer would be up and looking for me. I knew that with the certainty that I knew my name. Saira Emily Elian. Descendant of Time.

The ring of steel clanged in the mist. It sounded far away, but the ringing in my own ears took up all the space there. I stepped around the side of the tower toward the sound, where the scaffold stood like a monument to death.

Two men fought on the green. With swords. They used the scaffold like a set piece to parry and block and trap and evade each other. It was the sound of their swords clashing that cut through the night, but I couldn't see their faces in the heavy mist that had settled over Tower Green.

I could feel them as I edged closer. The malice gave Lurch away. If it had a color it would be slimy and green and he would slip in it so the other guy could cut his throat.

The guy Lurch was fighting was smaller, and tired. And clearly the thing that had kept him alive this long was his agility. He bounded around the scaffold like it was a jungle gym. And

371

when he swung his sword at Lurch with two hands I recognized Ringo.

No! Lurch would kill him.

I looked around for something to use as a weapon. Something I could join the fight with to buy Ringo the space to breathe and maybe rest.

I pulled my little Sanda knife out of my boot and prepared to throw it. I didn't think I could hit Lurch, but at least I was armed with something. Just then, two people came running out of the mist, past the few who still milled about on the edges of the green watching the battle.

"Saira!"

Archer's voice reached into me and wrapped me in his fear. Ringo faltered for a second, but it was long enough for Lurch to send him backwards off the scaffold with a slice to … something. Something that bled, judging by the line of dark red on the blade of Lurch's sword.

"No!" Archer leapt to the scaffold just as Lurch was preparing to jump down and finish the job. He knocked the sword away and clocked Lurch in the jaw with his fist. I started for Ringo, still down behind the scaffold, when Tom grabbed my arm.

"Saira, wait!"

Tom spun me around to face Beauchamp tower just as Pancho stumbled out of the door, half-running, half-carrying his brother Thomas onto the green. I almost yelled to him, but Tom clenched my arm even tighter. Behind him, Wilder stepped into view, crazy and wild with fury.

 TOM

What was happening? My legs were locked and my feet frozen to the ground. Even my voice seemed to have deserted me as Wilder grabbed Pancho and spun him away. He caught Thomas Wyatt and held a knife to his throat.

No. There was no sound attached to the word in my head, but every molecule in my body was screaming it. Just no!

Pancho begged something I couldn't hear. Wilder screamed at him. "Tell me!" Pancho sobbed. And then told ... something. Wilder smiled demonically.

And then he cut Thomas Wyatt's throat.

Nearly decapitated him.

The blood spurted in an arc and Pancho screamed. Or maybe I did.

Wilder threw Wyatt's body down in disgust and stormed past the prostrate boy on the ground. Then threw one glance in my direction as he stalked toward the Royal Apartments.

"Oh my God. He's going for Elizabeth!" I turned and ran.

I couldn't look behind me. I couldn't think about Ringo, lying on the ground in a pool of blood. Or Archer, fighting a demon-ish creature with his fists. Or my poor, brotherless Pancho. Or even Tom, struggling to keep up with me at a full sprint. I just ran.

Wilder had a head start and I couldn't fight him one-on-one. All I could do was beat him to her and get her away. I veered toward the north kitchen, panic hitching the breath in my lungs.

No one stopped me. No one challenged me. It was as if the time stream itself held its breath.

The north kitchen was empty, so I bolted through the tunnel and burst into the sub-crypt. I felt the cold of the ward evaporate around me as I found Elizabeth and Courtney, huddled against a wall, staring in speechless horror.

I dropped to my knees and started scratching out a spiral in the hard-packed dirt floor. The edges glowed and I drew like lives depended on it.

"Saira." Elizabeth's voice couldn't cut through the panic in my head as I finished the spiral portal. I had to get Elizabeth out of here. I had to take her away and hide her someplace safe. Someplace no one could find her. Where no one could betray her.

"Saira!" Her panic finally found its way in and I stood to find her face in the near darkness of the crypt. Her eyes were staring into an alcove hidden in the wall.

A voice crawled up my spine and I choked on puke. "Thank you for that. I'd been waiting for you to come. Your ward could stand against anything but its maker."

Wilder's voice told me I'd just killed Elizabeth. I'd smashed through the one thing that kept her from the pure evil that hid in the shadows at my back.

I still had Sanda's knife in my hand and I spun to face Wilder. "You can't have her," I panted desperately. I was trying to split my brain, frantically re-setting the ward behind me while standing my ground against a pure predator. I felt a ward come up around myself and tried to shift it to Elizabeth, but I couldn't make it understand somehow.

"Courtney!" I yelled for her to help me. She could feel wards, maybe she could hold one.

Tom arrived behind Wilder and he shrank away in instinctive terror. I could hear his footsteps racing back down the tunnel. I couldn't blame him really. Maybe I could, but I wouldn't. Wilder was pure evil and if I had any sense I'd be running too.

I backed up, still protected by the ward, but trying desperately to get it around Elizabeth too. "Courtney, take it!"

I pictured it like a bubble that could be moved from one person to another without popping, and I silently begged her to understand what I meant.

"That's it, protect yourself from me, little mixed-blood." Wilder's voice was the source of nightmares and I was nearly hyperventilating. I kept swishing Sanda's knife in front of me like it was a light saber and I was Luke. Because Leia always used blasters, and Han Solo only used a light saber once, when he cut open the Ton Ton's belly to save Luke. That's how I knew I was losing my mind, which wouldn't matter anyway, because Wilder would split time when he killed Elizabeth Tudor. And then nothing would matter.

The sound of running feet came back. Was it Archer? Or Lurch coming to aid his master? I could feel Courtney at my back, feel her inside the ward letting it close over her. Wilder swung his fist at me. A closed fist that would have knocked the teeth out of my head. But it connected with the ward that barely covered me. I shivered from terror. From cold. From the certainty that I couldn't survive against this Vampire with preternatural skills, who fed on rage and fear and killed for pleasure.

It was Tom who appeared in the crypt. Holding a sword. Limping and out of breath. This time Wilder spared him a glance, more for the sword than for Tom. Wilder was unarmed. Tom was not. It still wasn't even close to a fair fight because Wilder couldn't die.

Tom swung the sword up and faced Wilder.

"You are not of this time." Wilder spoke to Tom, but threw an annoyed glance at me. Like *I* was the one breaking the rules.

"Neither are you," snapped Tom.

I liked Tom's snarkiness in the face of pure evil. Who knew he had it in him? While Wilder's attention was on the sword, Courtney and I slowly backed up. I needed to get to Elizabeth so I could set her inside a ward.

I eyed Tom's sword jealously. My knife seemed seriously wimpy in comparison, and if I lived I thought I'd take up sword-fighting. Wilder lunged and grabbed at Tom's arm. He would have gotten him. Should have gotten him. Except Tom wasn't there anymore.

He lunged again. And came up empty.

Tom wasn't swinging the sword, he was using it to block Wilder's hands as he darted out of the way. Leapt out of the way, actually. Every move Tom made seemed to happen a millisecond before Wilder's, like he anticipated them. Like he Saw them. Like he *knew*.

Wilder growled. An animal growl that made every hair on my body stand on end. And lunged.

And missed.

Wilder's eyes narrowed. Calculated the boy in front of him. Took in his strange clothes, his strange skills.

And then he knew too.

Courtney and I backed to the wall, to the place where Elizabeth watched the scene in front of us in horror. "He'll kill him," she whispered in my ear.

"He has to catch him first."

I wrapped the ward around them and somehow *gave* it to Courtney to hold. I didn't look back at them, I just knew they were inside the bubble when I stepped out to help Tom.

Because as good as Tom was at dodging Wilder, he couldn't finish this. He was getting tired, the sword was dropping a little further with each lunge and parry. I could hear other footsteps coming down the tunnel. Someone else to help, or protect, or defend against.

I looked for a weapon. Something bigger and more dangerous than the knife I held. And then I found it. My shaking hands pulled the cloth roll from my dress. My shaking hands untied it.

Lunge.

Parry.

The scalpel dropped to the dirt. Not that.

The brown bottle. And the Zippo. Those.

Wilder lunged again. At me.

Tom yelled and threw the sword to Elizabeth. It skidded across the stone floor, and she picked it up, holding it like a warrior, ready to fight.

Archer appeared in the room, his eyes everywhere at once. He saw me. Saw what I was about to do. And then he lunged at Wilder and knocked him off his feet. Wilder landed on the spiral, right in line with my aim.

I hurled the ether at Wilder. It broke on his robes. He grabbed for me, violently.

Tom hurled himself at me.

I lit the Zippo and threw it.

Tom knocked me backwards out of Wilder's grasp.

Wilder's robe burst into flame.

His hand closed on Tom.

My friend looked horrified. And resigned. And then Tom ... smiled.

And they disappeared.

"Tom!"

I reached for the spiral, reached for anything that could save him. Archer dragged me back, off the still glowing portal and I fought him.

"I can follow them. I'll get him back!"

"Where? Where will you go?"

"There must be a trace of them *between*. I'll find them!"

I struggled against him but Archer held me. "They could be anywhere, Saira. Forward, back, in England or Spain or China. You don't know!" He was yelling, trying to shake me out of the single-minded focus that gripped me. I couldn't let Tom go. I couldn't let Wilder win this.

"He knows Tom can See. He'll kill him, Archer. He'll drain him of his blood and Tom will die." A sob caught my voice. "I brought him here. He wasn't the target. Wilder was going for *me*." I was in danger of dissolving into agonized tears until Elizabeth stepped forward and spoke in her calm, officious way and broke through the hysteria.

"Courtney, go check the Bell Tower room. There is a spiral in it. He could have gone there. Insist that Lord Brydges go with you."

Courtney nodded and left immediately without question. Then Elizabeth turned to Archer.

"Is it safe for me to show my face, or should I be looking for my own escape routes?"

Archer had stopped shaking me and had pulled me into his chest, effectively trapping me inside his embrace. "Alvin and Wyatt are dead …"

I suddenly gasped. "Ringo?"

"Alive, but in need of stitches." I sagged a little in relief even as my brain spun furiously on ways to find Tom.

Archer continued speaking to Elizabeth. "Lord Brydges stayed your execution at the eleventh hour, so in the eyes of history you are still alive."

His words cut through the pain in my head.

Elizabeth Tudor was alive.

And maybe, just maybe, time still flowed in the direction it should.

The thing that strangled me released, and I could feel the blood trickle through my veins. The air gasp through my lungs. The heartbeat in my chest.

A muscle twitched in my face. In a different time it could have been the beginnings of a smile. I didn't feel capable of joy or humor, but maybe I could allow myself a measure of relief.

Elizabeth looked at me for a long time and when she finally spoke her voice cracked with emotion. "I shall see to young Master Ringo's sutures. And I shall expect you in my chambers before you leave."

She swept out of the underground room. "Bossy." I said it under my breath, but Archer's grip tightened on me.

"It's a wonder you two can be friends."

"We are that, aren't we."

Archer kissed my hair, then pulled back in surprise. "You showered?"

I looked up at his bruise-free face. "You healed."

There were pools of fear and sadness in his eyes. "I left you alone."

I touched his face gently. "No, you didn't. You slept. There's a difference."

GOODBYE

The gash across Ringo's arm was deep. Elizabeth insisted on stitching it herself, but he made her wait until I could pack it with green medicine before she used her perfect embroidery skills to close his skin. He was pale and his eyes looked too big for his face. I held his hand while Archer assisted Elizabeth in her surgery.

"Milady told me about Tom." Ringo searched my face, but the anguish was already turning into something fierce and determined.

Archer's concentration didn't waver as he tied a knot in the thread of the needle Elizabeth handed him. "We know Wilder's plan now. And he'll try it again."

Elizabeth's head shot up, her eyes wide with worry, but I shook my head.

"He won't come back here. You know too much, and now he has his Seer. The only thing left is a Shifter."

There was a knock on Elizabeth's door and we froze. Archer signaled that we should retreat into the shadows of Ringo's chamber. Elizabeth left the room to answer her door, wiping Ringo's blood off her hands with a strip of linen bandage.

We listened in silence.

Courtney swept into the room. "There was naught in the Tower, Milady. But Lord Brydges would speak with you." There were two people with her. I couldn't see them, but I recognized Lord Brydges' voice.

"My Lady Elizabeth, it is my sincerest wish that you accept my apology for the lateness of the hour, especially as this has no doubt been a most trying day." He sounded uncertain. He should. His indecision could have cost Elizabeth her life.

Her voice was clear and confident. "You are forgiven, Milord."

He hesitated a moment, and I knew he got the double meaning of her words. His voice caught, he cleared it, and I could tell her forgiveness mattered to him. "Thank you, Milady." He cleared his throat again. "First, a small matter. My Warders found a Wyatt pup on the green. He was huddled over his brother and wouldn't leave him. I won't clap him in irons, even I have my limits. I thought perhaps …?"

My heart stopped. Pancho.

"I find myself in need of a new taster, Lord Brydges. Please see that he is cleaned up and brought to Courtney."

The air surged back into my lungs. Elizabeth would see that he was safe. I could feel Archer and Ringo breathe again behind me and realized Pancho had found a place in all our hearts.

"Very well, Milady." Lord Brydges paused before he continued speaking. He was more nervous than before. "Her majesty the queen has sent her Mistress of the Robes to you with a message. Lady Elizabeth, may I present Lady Valerie Grayson."

Grayson. Henry Grayson's mother?

"Thank you, Lord Brydges. Please wait outside."

If he was surprised at being dismissed he gave no indication. I could practically hear the bow. "Ladies." The door to the chamber opened and then closed softly behind him.

A few seconds later, Courtney opened the door to Ringo's rooms and whispered quietly to us, "Lady Grayson would like a word with Saira."

Ringo was still sitting on the table as Archer finished bandaging his arm. I wasn't going to leave either of them for another minute. "Invite her in. I'll talk to her here."

Courtney's eyes widened fractionally and I'd probably just said something very rude, but I truly did not care. A moment later, Lady Grayson and Elizabeth swept into the room.

Valerie Grayson was an interesting woman. She had a quiet regality to her that made the air around her seem very calm. Her voice was strong, but gentle, and her eyes took in the whole room at a glance.

It was a gesture I recognized because I did it too. A glance to get bearings, to assess danger, to find the exits. Lady Grayson was a Clocker.

"I believe you know my son, Henry."

Archer stiffened almost imperceptibly, but I caught it, and so did Lady Grayson.

"I don't know your son, but I did meet him for about a minute."

Her eyes searched my face. "You made quite an impression then, as he sent a message to me immediately."

My eyes narrowed. "And you're only just coming now? It would have been nice to have had some royal help before Lady Elizabeth's head was almost removed from her shoulders."

Lady Grayson didn't flinch, though everyone else in the room did. Even Elizabeth, and I remembered that she was still very much at her sister's mercy.

"I am not here on the queen's business, though I am sorry for the horror of your experience, Milady." She said the last part to Elizabeth, who bowed her head slightly in response. Lady Grayson returned her gaze to me. "I am able to feel … disturbances … in the time stream." She waited a moment for that to sink in. She knew the effect her words would have, and they most definitely did. "The threat began before you met my son, and it grew to something immense and dangerous."

My voice was somewhere between a whisper and a squeak. "You can feel the changes?"

She nodded. "The threat is less now, much less, but it is not extinguished. The danger is further away in time and distance, so the ripples feel smaller. But they will still come." Her composure cracked for just a moment as she took her next breath. "What you did here must be repeated. I know not where or when, but I believe you know why. And when you need it, you shall have whatever aid I can give."

The fire crackled on the hearth and it was the only sound I heard besides the pounding of my own heart. "Thank you, Lady Grayson. I may take you up on that offer."

She looked at me another long moment, then nodded. She turned to Elizabeth and dropped into a proper curtsy. "Lady Elizabeth, again, I am sorry."

She swept from the room, and left the queen's apartment with just one backward glance … at me. Elizabeth and Courtney followed her out to make sure the door closed behind her.

Archer moved up behind me and wrapped his arms around me in a protective cloak. I leaned back into his embrace and sighed, "I guess we're not done."

Ringo smiled a small, crooked smile. "Good that ye know it's 'we' who'll be doin' what needs to be done."

It was the first thing that made me smile since night fell. "You say that like I have a choice in the matter."

HOME

The black sheath dress my mom left out for me was lovely, and totally appropriate, but it didn't go with my new combat boots. My concessions to today were black jeans and a black silk shirt from Archer's wardrobe. A black teardrop pearl Elizabeth had given me was tucked down inside my shirt on a long chain. I never took it off.

I knew I'd be running tonight. The dress wouldn't work for running.

Ava was already downstairs with her parents. I'd been home a month and I still couldn't shake the feeling of dread every time they came to school. They found my avoidance of them puzzling and probably rude. Because in their world, everything was exactly the way it had always been.

Nothing had happened.

Aislin's cuff had never been stolen, so they'd never accused me of stealing it, or locked me in the Seer Tower, and no one but me and Tom had heard what Philip Landers really thought of being Tom's father.

Time had repaired itself in a way that only Archer and I remembered. I'd told Mr. Shaw and my mom what happened. And Ava and Adam knew, because I had to explain why Tom had gone with me back in time. Some people just thought Tom had run off with the Mongers like he did before. But there were people who knew he was gone. And those people were at St. Brigid's today to remember Tom.

Even the regular kids were back at St. Brigid's with no memory of having been banished for their safety. My mom explained it as a product of temporal inertia. The ripples had fixed themselves way back on the time stream, so by the time it got to us, everything had returned to the way it would have been if Elizabeth's life had never been threatened. Everything except Tom. And the Mongers. They were still busy being jerks, though Domenic Morgan was just a bookkeeper, and Seth Walters was just as charming as he'd always been.

We came back to a world that made sense again, and my friends believed my crazy stories because they trusted me. Mr. Shaw made a point of talking to Archer and Ringo separately though. I think it took three retellings of the events for them to sound real.

Then Mr. Shaw took out Ringo's stitches, gave him a smallpox booster shot, and I took him home.

Ringo wouldn't let me go to his flat with him. He just hugged me fiercely, told me to take care of his brother, and sauntered away. If he had run I would have run with him, because when he turned away from me there were tears in his eyes. But his walk was a man's walk. Even at sixteen, Ringo had seen and done more than most men ever did. And as a man, he had my respect.

My heart still hurt with how much I missed him. When Archer and I ran in the woods around St. Brigid's we both imagined him with us, laughing, taunting us for being slow or clumsy or loud. We didn't talk about him, or wonder about his relationship with Charlie. We knew we'd see him again.

I slid down the bannister just for the practice, then took the long way around at top speed. I avoided the Seer Tower, the empty third floor wing where I had taught Tom the key trick, and the east attics where we escaped. Guilt is a useless emotion, but I wasn't done indulging it where Tom was concerned. Not yet.

I knocked on Mr. Shaw's door and his gruff voice invited me in.

"Mom said you wanted to see me?"

"Close the door."

I did as he said and then took a seat in front of his desk, touching my father's microscope as I went by the bookshelf. As usual.

"Philip Landers wants an investigation into Tom's disappearance."

"Why is there a memorial tonight if he doesn't believe he's dead?"

"He believes it. We all believe it. But Tom's mother doesn't and he's humoring her."

I snorted in disgust. "What, he's looking for a body now?"

He leveled his gaze on me. "Why, are you going to find them one?"

I looked back, unblinking. "Sure. Are you fine with me going back to search for him?"

He sighed. I'd been extra prickly since we got back, and to his credit, he hadn't told me to grow the hell up and quit brooding. I knew I deserved it though, and I softened the edges.

"Archer and I are researching with Mom and Miss Rogers. If there's another mention of Wilder anywhere in history, we intend to find it."

"And if you find him again, what then?"

I looked at Mr. Shaw and knew that the conversations Archer and I had been going around and around on were something he should hear too.

"We know he's taking skills from Descendants through their blood. And he seems to be tracking down powerful ones, because the queen of England would not have been a low-profile kill. So we're using the genealogy to piece together a historical map of the more famous Shifters. We figure Wilder's ego will send him to the ones he's read about in history books, so we've also borrowed whatever we can find on Shifter family trees from Miss Simpson. But we don't know how far Wilder can Clock, for example, or how restricted he is. He took Mom's blood, but he doesn't seem limited to focusing his travel with our family's necklace like she is. I'm not limited by that either, which makes me wonder if there's

386

something in my mixed blood that opened up different skills for me."

Mr. Shaw absorbed it all with intense concentration. "Technically, Wilder is a mixed-blood now too."

My eyes widened, and then narrowed again thoughtfully. "This summer, when my internship with Professor Singh is done, Archer and I will be working out of Elian Manor. Mostly because of Millicent's library and the keep, but also just to piss her off." That got a startled laugh from Mr. Shaw. "Any chance you'll be dating Mom enough to be around and help us?"

The look he shot me was an odd mix of grateful and happy. "Perhaps I can dust off my powers of persuasion enough to convince her, but why don't you tell me if the offer still stands after I say what I called you in to say."

Hammer time. I raised an eyebrow. "The offer stands. Say whatever you need to."

I could tell he didn't believe me. "I don't want you to go to the memorial this evening." He watched me carefully, but my expression didn't change, so he continued. "As I said, Phillip Landers will be there, and as you know, probably better than any of us, he's a mess of unpredictable anger. It's starting to find a focus on you, and that concerns me." He went on quickly before I could interrupt, probably because he could see on my face I was going to. "Also, the Monger kids will be back today. Miss Simpson could only justify a suspension for their first offense, and even that almost got shot down by the Council. There's a chance their uncle could be the one bringing them back."

Awesome. Seth Walters was one of my very favorite people on the planet. It always gave me the warm fuzzies when he was around, and based on Mr. Shaw's expression, I wasn't the only one who thought he was only slightly less nasty than a port-a-potty at a Burning Man festival.

The only reason I didn't protest was that Mr. Shaw seemed genuinely worried. "The hunt for mixed-bloods hasn't gone away, Saira. Your escapade with the genealogy didn't help matters with the Mongers, and even though it didn't technically happen, the incident you described with the Armans and their heirloom indicates a serious fracture of the Descendant Families is in the works. You are starting to look like the eye of the storm, my dear, and it worries me. I'd like you to please consider not putting yourself in their sights unnecessarily."

I got up from the chair and Mr. Shaw rose at the same time. I went around his desk and kissed him on the cheek. "If you get a chance, could you tell Ava and Adam what you said so they don't yell at me?"

The Bear looked startled, and then grateful, and I loved him for it.

"Also, I'm looking for sword-fighting lessons. Know anyone who can teach me?"

"I'm sure Devereux knows swords." Mr. Shaw's voice was gruff and I knew I'd made him happy.

"Yeah, but he doesn't want to accidentally cut me." Mr. Shaw's expression turned serious and I couldn't resist the tease. "Not because he can't control his bloodlust; a century's a long time to practice. No, he's afraid I'd take his head off, and apparently he can't come back from that."

The sun had just set, and the torches they'd lit for Tom's memorial were like giant candles in the conservatory. Archer silently joined me on the roof where we could see down into the glass room. I leaned back against him comfortably.

"Shaw told me not to go."

"He's probably right."

We looked down at the solemn gathering below. Ava and Adam stood with their parents. A beautiful, dark-haired, bronze-skinned woman I thought must be Tom's mother was next to Camille Arman, and Phillip Landers stood a little apart from all of them. My mom was there with Mr. Shaw, and Millicent Elian, wearing a bad-smell-sneer, held herself stiffly next to Miss Simpson. The rest of the staff of St. Brigid's and most of the students were also there, and I thought Tom might have been surprised to see so many people come out to remember him.

388

"Is that Aislin's cuff on Camille's arm?"

I nodded. "Kind of appropriate that she wore it, considering Tom's the one who stole it."

Below us, Adam was speaking, but his voice was muffled so I couldn't hear what he talked about.

Archer's voice was soft in my ear, and it made shivers run down my skin. The good kind. The kind that made him mine.

"What would you have said if you'd been there?"

He wrapped his arms around me and I melted into them. I thought about the words I'd choose. "The first time I saw Tom he tried to kill me. The last time I saw him, he saved my life. And in-between we were friends."

"Perfect."

We sat in silence while Adam finished. Then Mr. Landers got up to speak and I tensed at the sight of him. I would probably always be bitter.

"Even though time fixed itself and no one else remembers what he said, I will. And so will Tom."

Archer turned me around to look at him. "You believe he's still alive?"

I shook my head. "No, but I think you can't un-ring a bell like that. Maybe it was the reason Tom had that weird smile on his face when Wilder took him. He looked kind of, I don't know, satisfied."

Below us, it was Miss Simpson's turn to speak, and I thought I caught the slightest glance up just before she did. Of course she knew we were there. She knew everything.

"I don't think I ever told you the prophesy Miss Simpson told me."

He shook his head and nuzzled my ear. His touch made my toes curl and did very funny things to my stomach. "What was it?"

I replayed her words in my head, then spoke them out loud.

"The Dream remains for none to see,
And time of War is what shall be.
Unless the child, Death by her side,
Can choose the path to turn the tide."

Archer had stilled while I spoke, and then it seemed like he finally breathed again. "I guess you're stuck with me then."

"Huh? I mean besides the fact that I'm crazy in love with you, and you're probably more stuck with me than the other way around, how do you figure?"

His eyes were beautiful in the moonlight, and the way he looked at me made me feel like I was the loveliest thing he'd ever seen.

"You're the child, right?"

"If you believe their prophecies, yeah, probably."

"Then you need death by your side. That's me, minus the cape and the scythe, and, you know, the skull face." He grinned and I kissed him.

With all my heart.

Because I knew I'd chosen my fate.

And it was Archer Devereux.

The End

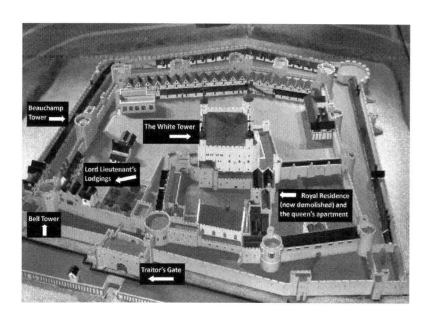

The Tower of London as it appeared in 1554
Adapted from a photo of a scale model of the Tower.
Photo courtesy of Onofre_Bouvila

A word about Elizabethan history...

The best explanation I've heard about authors is that we're people who make sh*& up. And I do. All the time. Just ask my kids. But it's much more fun to weave my imaginary people in and around actual historical facts. In *Tempting Fate,* the fact upon which Elizabeth Tudor's story was originally built is that Lord John Brydges, Lord Lieutenant of the Tower at the time Elizabeth was imprisoned there, did, in fact, refuse to execute Elizabeth despite an unsigned order from the Queen to do so. This, in my opinion, makes him a smart man with a strong self-preservation instinct and an interesting moral code, especially given his personal politics.

The Wyatt Rebellion did happen, and it finally gave Elizabeth's political enemies the ammunition to have her imprisoned. Thomas Wyatt was beheaded on April 11, 1554, while Elizabeth was held in the Tower. Apparently, before they led him to the scaffold, he dropped to his knees, and declared her innocent of any participation or knowledge of his plans.

Historical mysteries are the temptation I can't resist, and draw me in the way tunnels, castles and secret places do. When researching Elizabeth Tudor's imprisonment in the Tower of London, I stumbled across a couple of intriguing little mysteries which I've woven into the story.

For example, nearly all available online documents, websites, and blogs state that Elizabeth Tudor was held in the Bell Tower. Unfortunately, the chambers of Bell Tower, one up and one down, are inaccessible to the public because the only way in is through the Lord Lieutenant's Lodgings, otherwise known as the Queen's House in honor of the current queen (it was the King's House when her father was on the throne). As I wasn't able to see the Bell Tower rooms in person, a very kind historian at the Tower Archives sent me a drawing of both rooms.

Based on that drawing, the rooms in the Bell Tower seemed much too small to have held someone of Elizabeth's status, so I did a little digging and found a more obscure theory that Elizabeth was likely held in the queen's apartments in the now demolished Royal Residence (Queen's House vs. queen's apartments – one can see the potential for confusion). In Tudor times, the apartments had been renovated for Anne Boleyn's coronation as Henry VIII's queen, and three years later she stayed in them before her execution. Lady Jane Grey lived in the queen's apartments for the eleven days she was England's queen, before she was imprisoned, and ultimately executed. It is also known that despite Mary Tudor's hatred of Elizabeth's mother, Anne Boleyn, Mary always treated her sister as the royal daughter of their father. I believe Mary would have had Elizabeth imprisoned with several of her attendants in the queen's apartments, a large enough space to house them all, as befitting her rank of king's daughter.

Another mystery is what happened to Mary Stuart's (Mary Queen of Scots) black pearls. Mary Stuart and Elizabeth Tudor were first cousins and despite their political differences, they shared a love of all things bright and shiny. There are six stunning strands of black pearls draped around Elizabeth's neck in the Armada Portrait, which she apparently bought for 12,000 crowns from Mary Stuart, via Scottish agents, while her cousin was a prisoner of grudge-holding Scottish lords. The pearls were likely inherited by James I after Elizabeth I's death, and his daughter was said to have been a collector of jewels. But the pearls have since disappeared from records, and even the Jewel House guards at the Tower of London had never heard of them. It's possible they could be in Queen Elizabeth II's private jewel collection, but there have been no sightings of the pearls since the mid-seventeenth century.

The Armada Portrait c. 1588
Reproduced by kind permission of His Grace the Duke of Bedford and the Trustees of the Bedford Estates.

I discovered some fascinating tidbits as I wandered around historical research sites. It's true that the Tudor crown, which sits on the table behind Elizabeth in the Armada Portrait, was picked apart and melted down by Cromwell's government in 1649 – along with almost the entire collection of crown jewels. And at one time the crown jewels actually were hidden in the sub-crypt of St. John's Chapel in the White Tower. Historical record also shows the future queen's childhood friend, John Dudley, was held in Beauchamp Tower when Elizabeth Tudor was a prisoner. And there's a story that a child, whose parents worked at the Tower, brought Elizabeth a posy of flowers which may or may not have come from Dudley. There is speculation that something about Elizabeth and John Dudley's relationship changed after that time. Maybe it was the shared experience of fear, or maybe it was something more …

And finally…

Thank you so much for reading *Tempting Fate*. If you enjoyed this book, your review on Amazon or Goodreads would be very appreciated. You can find more information and my blog on www.aprilwhitebooks.blogspot.com.

I sincerely appreciate hearing from readers, and thank you, again, for joining Saira, Archer and Ringo on their adventures in time.

~April White

The Accolades

The people without whom sanity would be optional as I wrote this book deserve trips to Tahiti. But barring that, VERY SPECIAL THANKS (in shouty caps) are in order.

Mom and Valerie, you leave no room for self-doubt, and you are the standard-bearers for the unconditional support of moms. Angela Houle, you are an extraordinary editor and an even better friend. That the two are not mutually exclusive is as awesome as it is shocking.

Alexandra, Tania, Linda, Jess, Maria, Dawn, Patty, Jill, Heather and Silvia; there is a special place reserved in heaven for readers who slog through beta drafts. May yours be filled with good books and great wine. My Hopeless Romantics Book Club; There. Are. No. Words.

My amazing boys, you are my reason for breathing. And Ed, my heart and soul, you *inspire* me. And if there are sexier words in the English language than those, I don't know them.

Printed in Great Britain
by Amazon